In Name Only

a Novel

Ellen Gable

This book is a work of fiction. The setting for this novel takes place in 19th century Philadelphia, but the names and characters are products of the author's imagination. Any similarity to actual persons living or dead is entirely coincidental. Events and settings are used fictitiously.

IN NAME ONLY

copyright by Ellen Gable/Full Quiver Publishing
PO Box 244
Pakenham, Ontario
K0A 2X0

ISBN Number: 978-0-9736736-3-0
Printed and bound in Canada

Cover design by
James and Ellen Hrkach

Scripture texts are taken from the 1820 edition of the King James Bible and the Douay Version of the Holy Bible

NATIONAL LIBRARY OF CANADA CATALOGUING IN PUBLICATION

Gable, Ellen 1959 -
In Name Only/ Ellen Gable
ALL RIGHTS RESERVED

Copyright 2009 by Full Quiver Publishing
a division of Innate Productions

For James

"To every thing there is a season, and a time to every purpose under heaven: a time to be born and a time to die...a time to weep and a time to laugh; a time to mourn and a time to dance...a time to love and a time to hate."

Ecclesiastes 3: 1-2, 4,8

"A gentleman...submits to pain, because it is inevitable, to bereavement, because it is irreparable, and to death, because it is his destiny."

John Cardinal Newman 1852

1

Death, Caroline's father had once told her, was a natural part of life, one that she did not like, not in the least bit. This aversion was not based on the eventuality that she would have to yield to it someday, but because losing someone so precious took its emotional toll on one's heart and often at a most inappropriate time.

Presently, she was surrounded by more people than she had seen in five months, and it unnerved her. In fact, Caroline expected the other passengers to point their fingers and urgently declare, "That woman ought to be traveling in the front cars with the rest of the third-class passengers!"

It was a cloudy, threatening-to-rain day, the 21st of April in the year of our Lord, 1876. Caroline stared blankly out the window of the train. She attempted to take a deep breath, then concluded that in the dictionary, there ought to be a new definition beside the word corset: vexatious. The horrid garment made her sit so straight, she felt like one of those wax figures at the museum.

On the seat beside her sat Mrs. Shepherd, who had been employed by her uncle to serve as Caroline's chaperone for the journey. The elderly Mrs. Shepherd seemed like a kind lady who had skin that was almost translucent, and gray hair that seemed a shade of light blue under her indigo-colored hat. She sat rather straight and unmoving which led Caroline to believe that the elderly woman's own corset was most likely the cause of her severe posture.

Caroline smoothed out her black dress then folded her hands on her lap. Papa had often told her that she was beautiful, but Caroline knew that her physical traits, namely, her copper hair and pale, freckled skin, were not as sophisticated as the upper class women she had seen in Boston, the ones with the finely-made dresses, fashionable hairstyles and face paint.

With her father now gone and her mother having already passed years before, Caroline had few choices. One was to take a job as a kitchen servant at an upscale home in Boston. The other was to move in with her Uncle Edward and her cousin, Elizabeth, in Philadelphia. She knew that they lived in a grand mansion but couldn't remember when, if ever, she had met them. Uncle had generously sent her money to remain in her small row house in Boston, as it was her desire to spend the bulk of her initial grief in private. In the past few weeks, however, Uncle Edward had been sending constant telegrams urging her to come to Philadelphia. Since he had been so kind, the least Caroline could do now was to yield to his request.

The train had not yet begun to move as passengers were still boarding. Glancing around the interior, Caroline was in awe of the plush seats, freshly painted walls and sparkling fixtures. The pungent odor of smoke suggested that a man behind her had lit his pipe.

"There aren't very many people on the train," offered Mrs. Shepherd, in a faint British accent. "In a month, the Centennial Exhibition will open and there shall be many more people traveling to Philadelphia. Perhaps you and your uncle and cousin might attend, my dear."

Caroline nodded and smiled in the most polite fashion she could muster, but in actuality, she wanted the woman to be quiet. Right now, she only wished that life could return to the way it had been, a simple life with her father.

When Papa was well they were not penniless, by any means, and the two of them always had enough to eat. However, once he became ill, Caroline worked hard trying to make ends meet mending for neighbors, although her father's care occupied most of her day.

"All aboard." The conductor stood on the platform of the train just below her closed window. Behind him, Caroline noticed a young man holding onto his hat and running toward the train.

She glanced at the man who had struggled to make it to the train on time. He was sitting across the aisle and one seat ahead. His hat now off, he was endeavoring to catch his breath. The train whistle blew and it began to move.

The elderly Mrs. Shepherd leaned close to Caroline. "Isn't this exciting, dear? What a fine way to travel to Philadelphia. I remember years ago as a young girl traveling from London to. . ."

The woman's nostalgic memories became background noise as Caroline loosened the tie on her black bonnet. She smiled at Mrs. Shepherd, then stared at the young man, now seated calmly and reading a newspaper. His shoulder length blond hair was pulled back neatly and he had a short, well-kept beard. As she studied him, she concluded that, despite the facial hair, he couldn't be much older than her own 19 years. He wore a dark blue coat and lighter blue breeches. He reminded Caroline of the Union officers who had played cards with her father back in the latter days of the Civil War.

She again peered out the window of the now fast-moving train, which was making its way through the city of Boston with row houses, markets and other businesses still the common sight. Caroline had never traveled to the southern section of the city and she found herself staring at the quaint shops and houses.

When Papa had first spoken to her about the option of moving in with her relatives in Philadelphia, it had seemed like it would be many years before it happened.

"Dear Carrie, listen to reason. You have been taking care of an old man since you were 14. You've been taking part in activities a son ought to be doing. You deserve to have someone take care of you. Please reconsider."

"You're not an old man."

"I am. And you're a young lady in need of companionship. Elizabeth is now, what? 17 years old?"

"I suppose so."

"I won't be around for much longer."

"You mustn't say that."

"It is true and you must come to accept it when it happens."

Caroline used her handkerchief to wipe her eyes.

"Are you unwell, dear?" the woman asked.

"No, I. . ." she began.

"You must be missing your father."

"Yes, I am."

"The first year is most difficult when you've lost someone close."

Caroline forced a smile and stared out the window. A few

moments later, she turned to find the elderly woman asleep.

Caroline nonchalantly glanced at the young blond man across the aisle as he was reading the newspaper. She studied him more closely and observed that he was impeccably dressed, from his coat and breeches to his shiny shoes. Definitely upper class.

She turned her attention to the countryside moving quickly beyond her window. Caroline was happy to see the green grass and spring flowers dotting the landscape, despite the dullness of the day. Lulled by the movement of the train, she began to close her eyes.

"Excuse me, Miss?"

Caroline opened her eyes to see a young man with dark hair and a mustache bending down close to her. She glared at him and, with her elbow, nudged her chaperone to wake up. The woman continued to breathe heavily beside her. *Mrs. Shepherd sleeps so soundly.*

"Miss, haven't we met before?" the man whispered as he leaned ever closer to her ear.

Caroline's eyes narrowed and she sank back against the seat.

"Excuse me, sir, may I help you?" she heard someone say. As Caroline allowed herself to look up, she could see that the blond man from across the aisle was standing next to the stranger, almost leaning on him.

"I was just. . ."

"Leave off, sir. Are you a fool? This young lady is in mourning." His sharp tone demonstrated that he meant what he said.

The dark-haired man stroked his mustache. "I. . .thought that I. . .was acquainted with her. I must be mistaken. My apologies, Miss." Caroline exhaled as he retreated to the back of the train, then she made eye contact with the blond gentleman.

"Thank you, sir."

The man smiled. "It was my pleasure."

"I have no idea what has come over my chaperone. She sleeps so soundly. May I know your name?"

"Liam O'Donovan."

"I'm Caroline Martin."

"I am most pleased to make your acquaintance, Miss Martin.

"You're Mr. Martin's niece, are you not?"

"Do you know my uncle?"

He lives next door. And I am very sorry for the loss of your father."

"Thank you."

"Your uncle is quite delighted about your impending arrival. It is the only topic he's been talking about for weeks."

Has Uncle told them that I'm lower class? Caroline glanced at her hands and was grateful that Mrs. Shepherd insisted she wear gloves.

"So," he continued, "I suppose that we shall be neighbors. Again, I am very pleased to make your acquaintance."

Caroline allowed herself to smile. "Thank you, Mr. O'Donovan. You have been so kind."

"It was my pleasure, Miss Martin." He nodded towards her, then moved across the aisle.

The train was not fully occupied, perhaps a quarter full. If Mr. O'Donovan had not stepped up to her rescue, who would have helped her in that most troublesome situation? Certainly, her chaperone was in no position to assist her. She cringed when she thought of the alternative.

Caroline made an effort to relax against the hardness of the train seat, but her heart was still pounding. Despite the rigid corset, she managed to take a few deep breaths.

"Carrie, I want you to start reading the Bible to me every day."

"The Bible is dull," 14-year-old Caroline responded.

"It is on my dresser."

Caroline lifted up the small black book and brought it next to the bed.

"What do you want me to read, Papa?"

"Start at the beginning."

Caroline's eyes narrowed. "There are a lot of pages in here. It will take a long time."

"It will, but now that I'm confined to my bed, it will give me peace to hear you recite it to me."

Caroline studied her father. Lying in bed, his now lean body and thinning gray hair made him appear much older than

50 years. His eyes were always bright and interested despite his gaunt face.

His expression was so loving and tender that she crawled into his bed beside him, embracing his already thin body. Although he was ill, she still felt safe in his arms.

Caroline sat up and reached for the Bible.

"First Book of Moses, called Genesis, Chapter 1. In the beginning, God created the heavens and the earth. And the earth was without form and void and a darkness was upon the face of the deep. And the Spirit of God moved upon the face of the waters."

The halting and whistle blowing of the train forced Caroline to sit upright. She turned to her chaperone. "Mrs. Shepherd, we have arrived in Philadelphia." Seeing no obvious response, Caroline shook her shoulders. "Mrs. Shepherd, please wake up." Caroline's hands now began to tremble. She leaned in close and whispered urgently into the woman's face,   "Mrs. Shepherd, please!"

When there was still no response, she inspected the elderly woman's pale face. It was frightfully still. "Oh, no!" As her eyes darted around the train, Liam O'Donovan jumped up.

"She's not breathing! Please help her." Caroline, her heart pounding, stared at the woman's unmoving face. She forced herself to exhale.   Mr. O'Donovan bent down close to Mrs. Shepherd's face and studied her motionless body. He straightened.

"Miss Martin, I do not wish to be the bearer of bad news, but I think that your chaperone has. . .uh. . .passed away."

"Good gracious! How could this happen? She was fine a short while ago." She again shook the elderly woman's still shoulder. Caroline was finding it hard to catch her breath and her hands were shaking. "What shall we do?"

"I'm not sure," he said, stroking his beard. "I suppose I ought to alert the conductor. You remain seated beside your chaperone."

Oh, no, he's not going to leave me here alone, is he?

Her panicked expression caused him to stop. "I shall only be a moment," he said reassuringly.

She nodded.   He walked away and Caroline attempted the simple task of taking a breath, then letting it out.

"Miss, are you having some trouble with your chaperone?" she heard a man say.

"I . . ." She tentatively looked up and saw the dark-haired man walking towards her. A small group of passengers had gathered behind him, a faceless crowd that surrounded Caroline like a claustrophobic wall.

"Is your chaperone ill?" the man said.

"She's. . .passed away."

"She what?" Avoiding eye contact, Caroline now kept her gaze directed toward the front of the train for Mr. O'Donovan. When she saw him rushing back, she breathed a sigh of relief.

Her eyes shot him a pleading expression, then she glanced at the man beside her and the crowd beyond him.

Mr. O'Donovan spoke up. "Sir, I would thank you to leave this young lady alone. She's just endured a terrible ordeal."

"And who are you, sir? Her protector? Her chaperone?"

"You could say that I'm protecting her from the likes of you, sir. Now, move along, all of you, or shall I call the conductor or a police officer to assist me?"

"I thought perhaps I might be of some assistance," the dark-haired man said. "If that is not necessary, I intend to leave. Good day, Miss."

As the man walked away, Caroline whispered, "Thank you."

"My pleasure. The conductor will be along shortly to stay with her body until the doctor arrives. I would be glad to accompany you to meet your uncle."   He checked his pocket watch. "We're already twenty minutes late."

"Perhaps I ought to stay with her, Mr. O'Donovan."

"Then I shall remain with you until the conductor arrives."

"Yes, that would be most welcomed." As she stood up, she felt light-headed and her body fell awkwardly against Mr. O'Donovan.

"Excuse me."

"It's fine. Please do be seated," he said, as he nudged her into his own seat across the aisle.

"She. . .was breathing just a few moments ago. How could that happen?" she asked, wiping her eyes with her handkerchief.

"I don't know, Miss Martin." He paused. "Is she a relative?"

Caroline shook her head. "I only met her yesterday."

"I see."

"We must notify her relatives."

"Yes, of course."

A short while later, the conductor, a portly middle-aged man arrived. "I will take care of this, sir," he said to Liam. "If you and your sister would like to leave, then it would be. . ."

"We're neighbors," Liam offered, smiling.

"Yes, yes, we're neighbors," Caroline responded, and once again grateful that Mr. O'Donovan had been present.

"What about the funeral arrangements?" Caroline asked. "What about her family? They will need to be notified."

"Yes, Miss Martin," Mr. O'Donovan offered. "It would be helpful to have her address and other information."

Caroline attempted to lift up Mrs. Shepherd's purse from her lap. As she tugged on it, she found that something was keeping her from lifting it up. She looked more carefully and noticed that Mrs. Shepherd's hand was still clutching the bag. Caroline shuddered, then took a deep breath. "Allow me," she heard then watched as Mr. O'Donovan pried the woman's fingers from the purse. He handed it to Caroline.

"Thank you." She opened the bag and lifted out some papers. "I believe this is what will be necessary."

Liam checked his watch again. "Come, Miss Martin." He offered his arm and as Caroline held on to it, she noticed that he was quite a bit taller than her five foot three frame, perhaps just under six foot or so, and in spite of his short beard and deep voice, his facial features were almost delicate.

As they stepped off the train, Liam commented, "My brother is supposed to be here. " He assisted her off the train and into the station. "But it would be prudent to search for your uncle first." His voice sounded reassuring and kind.

"Of course."

The weather was partly sunny and warm. The Germantown station area was small in comparison to the downtown Boston train terminal and was swarming with people. They walked by a wooden building with a covered porch where people were waiting to board the train.

Liam walked to a pile of bags next to the train.

"Ah, our luggage."

"There's my trunk, Mr. O'Donovan," she offered. "And I believe that is Mrs. Shepherd's suitcase as well," she said, pointing to the bag beside her own.

"Yes, and," he said, as he dragged the trunk closer to them, "this is my bag on top." Caroline waited as he lifted the suitcase off of the stack. She pulled her bonnet down to shade her eyes from the sun.

"I don't see your uncle, Miss Martin." He looked about fifty feet away at a man and a woman standing at the side building of the train station. The man, who had dark curly hair, wore no hat or coat, only a shirt and breeches and appeared to be leaning against the woman in a most inappropriate manner.

All of a sudden, the man looked up, then waved at Liam.

Liam cleared his throat, then sighed.

The man kissed the girl quickly, almost roughly, then picked up his coat and hat from the ground. He tossed his coat over his shoulder, threw his hat on his head, then ran toward them.

"This is my brother, David O'Donovan. David, this is Mr. Martin's niece, Miss Caroline Martin."

Caroline put her hand forward as David's eyes became fixed on her. He had a smirk on his face which made her feel uneasy and his stare seemed too familiar, as if he had some intimate connection with her. As she studied him, however, she found it difficult to believe that these two young men were brothers. Liam was taller and slight in build with a longish facial structure. The dark-haired brother, David, was several inches shorter, swarthy, with a day's growth of hair on his face.

David ignored Liam and directed his comments to Caroline as he took hold of her outstretched gloved hand and kissed the back of it. "Well, Miss Martin, if I had known you were this pretty, I would have gone all the way to Boston to fetch you myself." Though the brothers looked dissimilar, their voices sounded identical.

Up until now, Caroline had had little interaction with any young men and she was unsure how to respond. "Thank you, Mr. O'Donovan." She pulled her hand away from him.

David paused, then turned his attention to Liam.

"Lee, Mr. Martin had an emergency meeting and was unable to be here so he asked us to bring his niece and her chaperone home."

"Well. . ." Liam shifted from side to side. "Miss Martin's chaperone passed away on the train ride."

David's mouth opened. For a moment, it appeared as if he were going to smile, then he pulled his lips together and lowered his head.

Caroline was now having a hard time catching her breath. Her father's passing, Mrs. Shepherd's untimely death, the fact that Uncle Edward was not present, the vexatious corset, it all overwhelmed her. She blinked back the tears. "Would it be possible to sit down?"

"Yes, yes, of course, Miss Martin," Liam said. As he put his hands on his hips and scanned the area, Caroline plopped down on her trunk and wiped her eyes.

David's eyes lowered as Liam spoke. "Miss Martin, it would not be appropriate for us to be escorting you to Mr. Martin's without someone to chaperone."

"I'm not sure what to do."

The brothers stepped back and Liam spoke privately, whispering, but Caroline could hear them. "I don't see any other alternative than to drive her to her uncle's. Besides, we can't leave her here with men such as him," he said, pointing to the dark-haired man who was now walking away from the train platform. David glanced at her and winked. Caroline looked away awkwardly. Liam stepped forward.

"Would we have your permission to take you to your uncle's house, unchaperoned?"

"I suppose so." In all honesty, Caroline wanted nothing more than to get back on the train and return to Boston.

As the group approached the carriage, David smiled. "We'll be taking Miss Martin to the Martin house, Kip," he said to the driver, a mixed race man who was probably about ten years older than herself. He was dressed in a brown overcoat and beige breeches. The man tipped his hat as Caroline approached.

The brothers attempted to lift the trunk. As they struggled, she could hear David whispering. "What in the world has she got in here, bricks?"

Ignoring his brother, Liam said, "Kip, would you come down and help us hoist this onto the back of the carriage?"

"Yes, 'course, Mr. Liam," he said in a deep, low-toned voice.

The three men now easily lifted the trunk onto the back of the buggy. However, as they were laying it down, David released it too soon and the edge of it scratched the back section of the carriage.

"Now you've scuffed the surface."

"It's a three-inch mark, Lee. No one will be able to see it."

Liam shook his head, then assisted Caroline into the carriage, with David following close behind. Smiling, he sat beside Caroline. She moved away from him on the seat. Liam frowned. "David."

"What, dear brother?" he said, feigning concern.

"Over here." Liam pointed to the opposite seat in the carriage.

"Perhaps another time," he said, then he gave her a wink. Caroline let out as deep a breath as she could in her corset. Liam slipped in beside David, then called out the window, "We're ready, Kip." The driver flicked a whip and the carriage began moving.

Liam whispered something into his brother's ear. Caroline couldn't hear what he said, but when David turned and again smiled at her, she was certain that the comment had been about her.

She studied the O'Donovan brothers as they spoke comfortably with one another. David poked the side of Liam's arm.

"Did you remember to bring the Mulligan contract this time?"

"Yes, yes. You won't allow me to live that down, will you, David?"

"No," he laughed. "You never make a mistake, right? So what about the contract for the Grahams? Did you get them to sign?"

"Of course. You are the one more likely to forget. Remember the time you. . ." Liam stopped, then glanced at Caroline. "We'll be arriving at your uncle's house in about ten minutes, Miss Martin."

Caroline nodded, then peered out the carriage window.

A short while later, they were driving up a lane with a mansion in the distance. Young maples lined the road leading to her uncle's house and the lawn was green and lush.

"This is a pretty time of year in Philadelphia, Miss Martin."

As they rode closer to the residence, Caroline observed the beautifully kept lawn and garden with several older maples to the right front and a group of blue spruces lined up like sentinels along the left side of the house. The grass extended 50 feet on either side of the mansion, but thick forests framed the house on both sides.

Caroline stared wide-eyed at the majestic building itself, a gray stone mansion with two white marble pillars plastered against the middle of the house. The style reminded her of the Greek temples she had studied in school. Dark green shutters swung open on the many windows. Wrought iron railings and ten or so stone steps led up to a polished white covered porch leading to the more-than-adequate front entranceway of the house. A small gable extended the roof and the trimmed bushes and spring flowers in front gave the house a domestic atmosphere.

The driver halted the carriage and within seconds, Liam jumped down, then held his hand out to assist Caroline onto the stepping block in front. She took his hand, then heard, "My dear niece!" Caroline's attention was drawn to the booming voice of her uncle approaching the carriage. He was a broad-shouldered man, his white hair and beard framing his face. As she stepped down, his rotund body embraced her and he practically lifted her up off the ground. "You're as light as a feather, my dear. Patsie's cooking will fatten you up in no time."

Uncle Edward faced the O'Donovan brothers. "Thank you, Liam, David, for bringing my niece home from the train station."

"It was our pleasure, Mr. Martin," said Liam.

"My dear, I do apologize most sincerely for not being at the station when you. . .where is Mrs. Shepherd?" Uncle Edward inquired, glancing past her.

"I'm afraid we have some sad news about Mrs. Shepherd, sir," Liam offered.

"She passed away during the train trip, Uncle. I feel dreadful."

"That must have been frightful for you," he said as he stood beside her and rubbed her shoulder.

"I want to contact her family as I should like to go to her funeral. She was very kind to me, Uncle."

He glanced at Liam. "How did she die, Liam?"

"I'm not sure, sir. It appears as if she passed away in her sleep."

"I see."

David stepped forward. "Why didn't you tell me how pretty your niece was? I would've gone to Boston to pick her up myself," he said.

Liam rolled his eyes.

"I think you know why," Uncle Edward responded.

He leaned down and whispered, "There will be no courting my niece, David."

"I am crestfallen," David replied, in mock disappointment, putting the back of his hand to his mouth.

"It's getting late, David. We need to return home." Liam turned toward Caroline. "It was a pleasure meeting you, Miss Martin."

"Mr. O'Donovan?" Both brothers turned around.

"I mean that Mr. O'Donovan." She pointed at Liam.

"Yes, Miss Martin?"

"Thank you especially for your kindness today."

"As I said, it was my pleasure. Good day," he said, tipping his hat again.

2

In the carriage, David slapped his brother's shoulder. "So?"

"So what?"

"When will you ask Mr. Martin if you can court his niece?"

"She's in mourning. Could you not see how upset she was?"

"Waiting for the right time?"

"I am certainly not in the habit of asking to court a girl on the first day we meet. Do you not have any manners?"

"No, I don't. Lee, you're not in the habit of courting any girl."

"I am waiting for the right girl."

"You could have any girl you want. Besides, I saw the way you were looking at Miss Martin. You like her. Admit it."

"Of course I like her. She's a very attractive young lady."

"Personally, I got the feeling she wanted to shoo me away, like an annoying mosquito."

"Well, you *were* speaking in an inappropriate manner."

"I don't think my charm impressed her at all."

"Her father just passed away a few months ago and her chaperone died on the trip. Why must you conduct yourself in such a fashion?"

"What are you talking about?"

"The way you behave around women. It's downright crass and...well, ungentlemanly. I've told you that before."

"Now, when have I ever wanted to be 'gentlemanly,' Lee?"

"Probably never."

"Besides, I treat women well, that is, those who. . ."

"Yes, yes, I know what you mean. Really, David. Sometimes you're just like Father."

David scowled. "I'm nothing like him."

Liam O'Donovan fell silent and sat back against the carriage seat. Deliberately, his thoughts turned to Miss Martin. David could obviously tell that he was attracted to her.

Liam was relieved that he had made it to the train on time. His last business meeting of the day had stretched on for an hour longer than he had anticipated. Although he had considered staying the extra night in Boston, that would have meant an extra expenditure of three dollars. He despised being late and would rather be two hours early than one minute late for any event, most especially for the train, which was unforgiving with regard to punctuality.

When Liam first noticed Miss Martin, his initial impression was how pretty she was. The color of her hair was unusual, like honey mixed with copper. He found the sprinkling of freckles on her nose and cheeks particularly appealing. And her eyes were the most alluring shade of green he had ever seen, like the color of Christmas holly.

Thankfully, she didn't wear face paint like most upper class women and her hands had piano fingers, long and thin within her black gloves.

A few weeks ago, Mr. Martin had told Liam that it had been five months since his brother had died, and that his niece would be coming to live with him. Five months meant that there would likely be at least one more month of official mourning and he would be free to ask Mr. Martin's permission to court her. Until then, it was his hope to see her as much as possible and to get to know her in a cordial and polite way.

"David, did you remember to bring Mr. Martin's box of china from home?"

"No, I didn't. I just woke up a few hours ago. I overslept because I stayed up most of the night at Paddy's Pub. I took part in a poker game and won nearly $300."

"I thought you told me you were going to stop gambling."

"You misunderstood. I told you that I would only take part in poker games once a week."

"I suppose that is an improvement."

"I guess it will be necessary to make an extra trip tomorrow to drop that off."

Liam nodded. In actuality, he was glad that David hadn't brought the box. An excuse to visit the Martin house was just what he needed.

* * *

Before the carriage reached the end of the driveway, Caroline heard a squeal, then saw a young woman run towards her on the Martin veranda. The girl enveloped Caroline in a tight hug.

"You're so small, so skinny, Carrie!"

Caroline groaned inwardly. The only person who ever called her Carrie was her father and she felt ill at ease to hear anyone else call her that. She never really cared for the name Carrie, and yet it seemed natural when her father used it as a term of endearment.

"My dear, this is your cousin, Elizabeth."

Elizabeth remained close to Caroline, their shoulders touching. Caroline studied her cousin, who was a year younger, big-boned like Uncle Edward with a pretty round face and green eyes. Her long blonde hair was pulled up fashionably behind her head.

"I'm so happy you are finally here, Carrie. I have never had a sister and you shall be my sister."

Caroline responded politely. "Elizabeth, I would be very pleased to be your sister."

"Then it's settled. No longer my cousin, but my dear sister. We shall share secrets and all sorts of sisterly activities. And sisters need to have special names so do call me Lizzie. Carrie and Lizzie. Those will be our special names for one another."

Before Caroline could respond, Uncle Edward spoke up. "Elizabeth, give your cousin. . ."

"Sister, Papa, sister."

"Very well, your sister. . .some breathing room."

Elizabeth stepped back and looked into the distance.

"I missed the O'Donovans?"

"Yes, you did."

"Are they not the most handsome men you've ever laid your eyes on, Carrie?"

"Well. . ."

Elizabeth continued. "That David is. . .well, he's quite the 'Casanova.'" She was raising her eyebrows and smiling.

"Casanova?" Caroline asked. "He seemed rather capricious."

"Most certainly. Do you know that he. . ."

"Elizabeth, that's quite enough," Uncle Edward interrupted.

"Anyway," Elizabeth said, "Liam O'Donovan is one of the nicest people you shall ever meet. I've been told that he was a sickly child, but now he is as robust and healthy as anyone."

"My dear, you must be tired after your trip from Boston. And having to endure Mrs. Shepherd's passing must have upset you greatly."

"Yes, Uncle."

"Your chaperone passed away on the train ride, dear Sister?"

"It was most distressing."

"Of course it was." Elizabeth reached out and tenderly touched her shoulder.

"Escort Caroline up to her new room."

"Yes, Papa." Elizabeth whispered to Caroline, "I hope you will enjoy your bedroom. It's been freshly papered and painted, just for your arrival."

Caroline forced a smile, but inside she felt a twinge of sadness again and she fought back the urge to cry. She liked Elizabeth and Uncle Edward, but they seemed like strangers and this house was so unlike home. However, they were both trying so hard to make her feel welcomed and for that she was grateful.

"Come, Carrie." Elizabeth took Caroline by the hand and led her into the foyer. The Martin household smelled pleasantly of lemon and beeswax, the tile floor so white that Caroline almost squinted. The walls were a beige and green Heraldic design which made the high ceilings seem more so.

Elizabeth motioned for Caroline to follow her up the right curve of the long staircase in the center of the front hallway. At the top, they turned right and passed the lavatory. They walked through the long corridor of the east wing. Elizabeth stopped at the last room on the left, then opened the door.

They stepped inside and Caroline stifled a gasp. It was spacious and bright, the freshly-papered walls a yellow background with rose-colored flowers. The far wall held a tall window with a simple white shade. The right side served as the backdrop for the carved maple bed and a small brick fireplace lined the left side. Her trunk had been placed at the foot of her bed.

Caroline took off her gloves and laid them on the dresser. She walked to the window, opened it wide and breathed in the fresh air.

"We've ordered some curtains for your room, Carrie, but they haven't as yet arrived. They are being custom made to match the wallpaper."

"Drapes aren't necessary. This simple shade will do just fine." She paused, then commented, "There is no dressing screen in here."

"Yes. It ought to be here by the end of the week. Do you think you can manage without one until then?"

Caroline grimaced, although she quickly tried to change it to a smile. "Yes, I suppose so."

Elizabeth took Caroline's hand and pulled her toward the walk-in closet next to the door. First, she stopped and pointed out the two ropes which were attached to the ceiling and hanging beside the closet entrance. "These are the servants' bells. If you need Patsie or one of the other servants, pull on this one on the left to reach one of the servants in the kitchen. The rope on the right rings a bell in the servants' quarters. They will know from the tone of it that you are calling for them."

Elizabeth walked into the closet and lifted out one of the silk gowns. "Father had these made especially for you, Carrie."

Caroline nodded. "It's beautiful, Lizzie. I've never really owned such a finely-made dress." She paused. "Well, I should like to rest a while before supper, if that's acceptable to you."

Elizabeth stepped back and lowered her head, then forced a smile. "Yes, of course. If you need anything, just let me know. Perhaps we might have a lengthy and heartfelt conversation when you wake."

"That would be fine."

Elizabeth let herself out of the room and closed the door.

The first task that Caroline wanted to accomplish was to remove her corset. In the first stages of her father's illness, she was only 14 years old, scarcely at an age to wear one. Since she seldom ventured outside the house, there was no reason to make use of such a garment. When Mrs. Shepherd insisted that she put one on for this trip, Caroline was sure that she would die of embarrassment as the elderly woman assisted her into the tight-fitting garment. Once it was firmly in place, Caroline figured that it would be necessary for her to stop breathing or hold her breath for the entire trip. Now, her first opportunity alone, she wanted nothing more than to take it off.

She undressed down to her corset and shift and stood before the mirror. *What a ridiculous piece of clothing this is.* As she turned and studied herself, she remembered that the string to undo the corset was behind her and that she had no way of reaching it to take it off.

Caroline sighed. Now, she was either going to have to sleep

with it on or call someone to assist her. She pondered about it for a few moments, then decided to leave her corset on. It would be too humiliating to ask one of the servants for assistance as they would most likely question why she didn't realize she needed help.

Caroline opened up her trunk and lifted out the smaller box containing her books and placed it on the floor. She took off the lid; the first book on top was her mother's Bible. She picked it up and tenderly ran her fingers along the cover. She next lifted out the novel "Jane Eyre," and read the first page's inscription, "Caroline, may words always soothe and comfort you, Your Loving Father."

"Novels are not real life, Carrie."

"But the characters are real to me. And the stories are. . ."

"Remember that stories are just that, stories, a way to escape. Life rarely presents itself in such a way. Difficult and challenging situations will happen that will not always have tidy conclusions to them."

"Papa, don't be so maudlin."

She dropped onto the massive bed and sank into its comfort. Despite the rigid corset and the anxiety of being in an unfamiliar place, Caroline felt herself drifting off to sleep.

"Carrie, are you awake? 'Tis time for supper."

Caroline blinked her eyes and cleared her throat. "I shall be down in a few moments."

She tried to sit up, but the hard unmoving corset prevented her. She rolled onto her side and slid off the bed. Caroline pulled her dress on, buttoned up the front, then walked to the vanity next to the closet and brushed her long hair into place. She stared at the mirror and the ornate design framing it. She had no interest in seeing her reflection. Instead she studied the flawless glass, devoid of any imperfections unlike her spotted and ancient one at home. When she did finally focus on herself, she was rather taken aback by how pale her skin was, how dark her freckles seemed and the true shade of her copper hair.

She made her way down the long corridor to the grand staircase and slowly descended the steps. The foyer area was bright with the late afternoon light. There were numerous artworks adorning the wall. One that drew her attention was a large painting of a woman at a piano and a child, who was drawing, laying on the floor. The red and black colors seemed almost ominous, and yet something about the painting exuded hope, perhaps the child's innocent expression.

"There you are, Carrie. That was painted by the local artist, Thomas Eakins. Come, come," she motioned toward her, "we're waiting for you in the dining room."

At the bottom of the steps, Caroline followed her cousin as she turned and passed through a parlor, then entered the massive room. Caroline surveyed her surroundings and concluded that this room was entirely too large for the one long table and chairs which were situated in the center.

Elizabeth guided her to the head of the table where Uncle Edward stood.

"My dear, you are looking well-rested."

It's a miracle I slept at all with this ridiculous garment. "Yes, thank you, Uncle."

"Caroline, you sit here to my left and, Elizabeth, you may sit in your usual position to my right."

They bowed their heads so Caroline followed their example. Uncle recited a prayer.

"This is such a spacious room, Uncle."

"We use it for receptions. It is capable of holding 100 people comfortably. Slightly less with an orchestra."

Caroline stared at the shiny linen tablecloth which covered the long table. There was an intricate design of flowers running down the center and Caroline ran her hand along the soft material.

"Elizabeth can show you the rest of the house tomorrow, if you'd like."

"That would be fine, Uncle."

A young, pretty servant entered the room through the side door. She carried a large bowl and proceeded to serve each person some beef broth. Caroline studied the young slender girl, who moved about confidently. Her long brown hair was pulled back under a servant's mobcap. Her huge dark eyes were intent on performing the task efficiently.

Caroline leaned close to Uncle and whispered. "That servant seems young, Uncle. How old is she?"

"Selly is young, just turned 15, but quite a remarkable servant. She has been employed here since she was 12. Both her parents were dead at that point and she needed a place to live so we gave her work and she lives and eats here without cost, of course. And she takes direction splendidly, a bright girl."

"Yes, she does." *That poor girl.*

"As an added advantage, she can read and write."

Caroline cringed and glanced away. She could be that girl right now, working as a kitchen servant in Boston.

Another servant, a stout middle-aged woman, came into the dining room to retrieve the emptied soup bowls. A minute or so passed and Selly returned, this time with a fruit cup.

"Thank you, Selly," Caroline said, as the girl placed a cup in front of her.

The young girl's eyes widened, then she smiled.

"Caroline," Uncle Edward whispered, "Elizabeth and I must teach you about the finer methods of socializing."

"Socializing, Uncle?"

"Of course. We don't speak with the servants unless we are asking them to do a chore."

"We don't?"

"No, my dear."

"Oh." Caroline now fidgeted in her seat and began to nervously tap her foot. Social skills were not at the top of what she believed life's priorities to be, especially when it came to interacting with servants, to whom she was more closely connected.

"After supper, I want to show you a painting in my study."

"Yes, of course, Uncle."

After the main course of roast chicken and dessert of chocolate cake, Uncle Edward and Elizabeth escorted Caroline across the hall to the study. He turned on the gas sconces which flanked the mantelpiece, then lit a cigar. Bookcases lined the walls and the darker, masculine cherry wood paneling hinted that this was a room that he had designed himself.

Uncle stood before a painting of two young men at the seashore. "Come and see this picture, Caroline," he said.

Caroline squinted to look at the young men more closely.

The smaller one had an expression which seemed vaguely familiar. "Oh, my, that's Papa, isn't it?"

"Yes, my dear, and Yours Truly. We were handsome young
men, weren't we?"

"Oh, yes, yes!"

"This was painted while we stayed at Margate beach one
year."

Caroline examined the painting and she observed that her
father, the younger of the two at fourteen, wore a broad grin with
his arm reaching up and firmly around his brother's shoulder.
Uncle, around 18, kept a cautious smile. Caroline's eyes began to
tear.

"This is wonderful. I don't have any pictures of my father. It
is such a gift that you have this painting."

"My dear, if you should like, I could hire the local artist to
paint a smaller reproduction for your bedroom."

"Yes, yes, thank you very much, Uncle."   Staring at her
father's portrait and seeing the vitality of his youth, Caroline felt
herself overcome with emotion. "Uncle?"

"Yes, my dear?"

"Why is it that you and Father did not see each other?"

Uncle glanced away, then stared at the painting again.
"Well, your father, he was very headstrong."

"Yes, I know that well."

"He met your mother and she was lower class. Our father
was very particular about whom his sons married, so he threatened Andrew, told him that he would be written out of the will if
he married her. Your father did not waste a moment and married
your mother. I often tried to send him money, even after your
mother had died, but he always refused.

"I had not heard from him in many years, Caroline. When I
received his telegram saying how ill he was, I wrote to him and
insisted that he take some money for you and I also offered to take
you in like you were my own."

"You've been most generous, Uncle."

"It has been a pleasure. Now, come and see this portrait of
your aunt."   Uncle and Elizabeth led Caroline across the room to
a large painting of a heavyset woman with blonde hair, a warm
smile and a dark blue gown.

"My Ruth was the kindest woman I have ever known. When she died suddenly last year, I thought my world had ended." Uncle Edward and Elizabeth were both blinking back tears.

"I regret that I didn't have the opportunity to meet her, Uncle."

He nodded and continued staring at the painting. Caroline cleared her throat. "Well, if you don't mind, Uncle, I'm exhausted from my trip. Might I be excused to my bedroom?"

"Yes, of course," he leaned down to kiss her cheek. Elizabeth followed behind and walked beside Caroline through the hallway. "So what is your impression of the O'Donovan brothers?"

"I only met them today, although I must say that Mr. Liam O'Donovan seems a very kind man."

"And handsome, do you not think so?"

Caroline hesitated before replying. Yes, she found him to be a very handsome man, but was unsure whether she ought to share that with Elizabeth, who seemed eager to forge a close sisterly friendship.

"Yes, I do agree with you, Lizzie."

"Oh, how wonderful! You are so beautiful, Carrie. I'm certain he feels the same way about you."

"Don't forget that I am still in mourning and it will be some months before I should even consider courting someone."

"But five months have passed since your father's death."

Caroline lowered her head.

"I'm so sorry. I didn't mean to upset you. I will agree with whatever you wish to do."

"Do not worry yourself over it, Lizzie. I shall be fine. I do need to rest, however."

"Good night, dearest sister." Elizabeth leaned in to kiss Caroline on the cheek, then she whispered, "You cannot know how delighted I am that you are here."

"Thank you. Good night."

Elizabeth turned and returned to her father's study.

Caroline began to climb the stairs and held onto the banister, its polished surface smooth under her hand. She stopped halfway up and turned around to survey the high ceilings and elaborate furnishings of the foyer area. This morning, she left a humble row home in Boston, one which had dull and peeling walls, flattened out carpets and a broken banister. Now, she was surrounded by fine art, plush carpet and crystal gasoliers.

Caroline returned to her room, closed the door and crouched down in front of her trunk. One by one, she lifted out her dresses and laid them neatly on the bed. Caroline squinted as orange and pink light streamed in. She crossed the room and peered out the window at the back yard area of the Martin property. The sun was just setting. A stable, barn and small, older henhouse occupied the area to the right. A larger, modern-looking henhouse and a small field were to the left. Just under her window were a coal shed and a clothesline with a few shirts flapping in the wind.

"Miss Caroline?" said a loud voice in the hallway.

"Yes, yes, I'm coming." She crossed the room and opened the door. In front of her stood the older, heavyset servant. Her salt and pepper hair was pulled back under her mobcap.

"Will ye be needin' some help to dressin', Miss?"

"My dressing?"

"I can help ye, if ye like," she said, offering a gap-toothed smile.

"Oh, yes, thank you. What's your name?"

"Me name'll be Patsie, Miss."

"Patsie, I appreciate the. . ."

"Well, now then, the master himself, Himself being Mr. Edward, he says to me, Patsie, he says, ye go and ye help Miss Caroline now and that's an order."

"I do appreciate it."

"Will ye be after havin' me ta help ye choose a nightgown fer yerself, Miss?"

"That would be fine." Caroline paused. "Are you from Ireland?"

"I'm from Dublin, Miss. Came over with some relations durin' the Potato Famine. A shame, that."

"Well, I am very pleased to meet you, Patsie."

"The pleasure's all mine, Miss. Ye seem to be a sweet young colleen."

Caroline smiled as the servant lifted the dress over her head. The woman smelled of roast chicken, sage and some other herbs.

"Here, Miss, let me be undoin' this corset fer ye now."

"Thank heavens this awful contraption is finally coming off."

Caroline held it in place while the servant unlaced it.

"Ye can be takin' that off now."

"Well, yes, I. . ." Caroline wished that she had the privacy of a dressing screen.

"Come now, Miss Caroline. I'll take yer corset."

She dropped the corset on the floor. The only garment left was her shift. Caroline's face was flushed. "Would you mind turning your head, Patsie?"

Patsie's eyes widened. "Well now, yer a sweet young thing. Certainly, I'll turn me head while ye be takin' that off and slippin' inta yer nightgown."

Caroline removed her slip then pulled on her nightgown. She breathed deeply. "Oh, Patsie, I hate that wretched garment. I wish never to wear it again!"

"Miss Caroline, sure an' all young ladies'll be after wearin' a corset."

"I think I shall start a new trend. No corsets. That is pure torture!"

When Caroline glanced at Patsie, she was frowning.

The servant walked to the window and lifted it up higher. "Well now, Miss, sure ye'll be after needin' lots of fresh air too."

Passing the bedside table, she picked up one of the books. "What's this here, Miss Caroline?"

"That's a novel that I've read called 'Little Women.'"

"So what'll that be 'bout, Miss, some wee ladies or some'n'?"

"No. It's about four sisters. Would you like to borrow it?"

"I'll not be knowin' how to read or write, Miss."

"That's too bad, Patsie."

"Ah, well, never ye be mindin' that. I'll not be havin' time for that anyhow."

Caroline felt sorry for Patsie. Everyone in the world should be taught to read. Books, especially novels by Jane Austen with their engaging stories and rich language, allowed Caroline valuable escape time, especially when she was caring for her father. Now, it afforded her an opportunity to be someone else, to forget that her father was gone and that she was in an unfamiliar home.

3

The sound of horses whinnying woke Caroline from a deep sleep. She sat up in her bed and stretched her arms over her head in mid yawn. She pulled her night-cap off and ran her fingers through her hair. A soft breeze blew in through the open window. Caroline inhaled, relishing the sweet spring air. Hearing voices, she walked to the window and stared at the scene below. Liam O'Donovan was speaking to one of the servants at the stable below her window.

"Is Mr. Martin in his office, Ben?"

"He's been up since eight, Mr. Liam."

As if on cue, Liam glanced up toward Caroline's window. Seeing her, he smiled. Awkwardly, she stepped away.

After a few seconds had passed, she again peeked at the scene below. Liam's eyes remained fixed on her window and when he saw that she had returned, he gave her a wide grin. This time, she offered a shy, coy smile.

"Miss Caroline, y'awake?"

"Yes, Patsie, what is it?" she said, turning toward the door.

"I'm here to help ye with yer dressing."

"Thank you. But I shall not be needing any assistance." Caroline opened the door. Patsie's eyes narrowed and she was shaking her head.

"You need not give me that look."

"How'll ye be goin' to get yer corset on by yerself?"

"I'm not putting it on, Patsie."

"Now then, ye can't be goin' about with just yer slip on, t'aint fittin' fer a young lady."

"I'm not going anywhere, am I?"

"But Mr. Liam's here and sure an' he might be seein' ye."

"Oh."

"Sure an' ye need to be wearin' yer corset. How will ye hold yer. . .well, yer. . ." She leaned close to Caroline's ear and whispered, "Bosom up?"

Caroline's face reddened. She hadn't thought about that.

"Well, it's not as if I am all that heavily endowed anyway, Patsie. This shift will do just fine."

Patsie regarded her with raised eyebrows. "Yes, Miss." The exasperated servant walked away, shaking her head and mumbling to herself.

Caroline finished buttoning the front of her dress as she walked to the window. She looked out to find that Mr. O'Donovan was no longer in the back yard area. Her thoughts turned deliberately to her new neighbor.

Mr. O'Donovan was certainly a handsome, if not intriguing, young man. She wondered what kinds of foods he ate and what he liked to do with his spare time. She found herself daydreaming about what it would be like if he asked to court her. However, she brushed the thought aside. A girl in mourning ought not to be thinking of those sorts of frivolities.

She picked up a novel from her bedside table and quickly made her way to the hallway, then to the top of the grand staircase. She hoped that Mr. O'Donovan was still in her uncle's study.

At the bottom of the steps, she nearly ran into the younger, pretty servant girl, Selly, her dark eyes lowered in apology.

"Excuse me, Miss." She watched as Selly ran along the grand staircase. Curiously, Caroline's eyes followed the young girl as she bolted through the doorway to the downstairs kitchen area.

The door to Uncle's office opened and Liam O'Donovan moved into the hallway, Uncle following behind.

"Well, my dear, I see that you are awake."

Caroline nodded, then quickly glanced at Mr. O'Donovan's face. He was grinning at her. She returned the smile.

He placed his bowler hat on his head, tipped it and said, "It is good to see you again, Miss Martin."

"As it is to see you, Mr. O'Donovan."

He shook Uncle's hand and tipped his hat again.

"I hope you have a good day, Miss Martin."

"And you as well, Mr. O'Donovan." He turned and walked through the door with a stride so confident that Caroline felt a small pang of regret that he was leaving, not only because she enjoyed his company and felt grateful to him, but because she was feeling particularly lonely in this huge, unfamiliar house.

"So how are you this morning, my dear?"

"I'm fine." Had Uncle said anything to Mr. O'Donovan about her being lower class? She lowered her head.

"Are you all right, my dear?"

"I. . ."

"Now, see here, if you have a problem, I want to hear about it, Caroline. If you're not happy. . ."

"No, no, Uncle. Does anyone know that I'm not from wealth?"

"Only Elizabeth and myself know of your humble beginnings, and it is of no concern that anyone else possess that information. Besides, you are no longer 'not from wealth,' as you call it, but now a part of my immediate family." He pulled her to a warm embrace. "Well, my dear, what does Elizabeth have planned for you today?"

"I'm not sure. I haven't yet seen her this morning. She may still be asleep."

"She is a night person. I have seen her walking the halls at two o'clock in the morning. Trying to wake her is like rousing the dead!"

"Well, I'm normally the opposite."

"As Ben Franklin said, 'Early to bed, early to rise, makes a man healthy, wealthy and wise.' Of course, you're now already wealthy. If we can just get you eating some of Patsie's fine cooking, you'll look healthy as well. As for wise, it's really not all that important for a woman to be so wise, right, dear? After all, for a young girl like yourself, meeting a fine gentleman and getting married to someone who can take care of you is what's important in life, now, isn't it?"

Caroline forced a smile, inwardly, cringing. She disliked Uncle's patronizing tone, as if all women were dolts and possessed no intelligence whatsoever. However, Uncle meant no harm. She admitted that part of his comment was true, it was her desire to meet a nice young man, someone with whom she could fall in love and get married. Besides, Uncle was overly generous and appeared to be trying to treat Caroline with great respect and charity, despite the fact that she did not truly belong in the upper class.

"Uncle, would it be permissible for me to explore the grounds? I do so relish the early morning and it is a beautiful spring day. I should like to find a spot where I can read my book."

"Of course, my dear, but don't stray too far. Our property extends to and includes the wooded area just beyond the stable. Much of the forest on the other side belongs to the O'Donovans. And although I'm certain they would not mind your exploring there, it would be prudent for you to remain on our property."

"Yes, Uncle, of course."

She walked outside and lingered in the front yard. The sweet fragrance of spring flowers and the sounds of a few birds singing high up in the trees caused her lonely heart to rejoice. Despite her grief, she felt an overwhelming gratitude that she was alive and enjoying this day. A group of maple trees seemed inviting and she settled herself against one of the trunks and began to read.

* * *

For the past several days, Caroline's routine had remained the same. She rose early, explored some of the grounds and returned to her room to read. Days seemed dreadfully long, although she had already read three novels since arriving last week. Caroline stood at the top of the staircase and stared downward. The sun had just risen and the house was devoid of the usual hum of daytime activities.

Yesterday, her 19th birthday came and went without any fanfare. She didn't blame Uncle or Elizabeth as she decided not to say anything to them. She was in no mood for celebrating anyway. Elizabeth had invited her to the sewing club. Knowing that she would be required to remove her gloves for that activity, and that others might judge her on the state of her callused hands, it seemed best to refuse. She remained in her room, reading, for most of the day.

She quietly made her way down the staircase and out the front door, carefully closing it. The day greeted her with sunshine and a warm breeze. She sauntered around the side of the house, then heard peculiar sounds coming from the back yard area. She followed the noises and discovered the young servant girl, Selly, retching into the waste barrel.

"Selly, are you unwell?"

The girl spun around and gasped. "Miss Caroline!"

"I am sure Uncle will permit you to take the day off."

Patsie stepped through the back door. "Now then, Miss

Caroline, Selly be foin. She's havin' a bit of a rough mornin',' she is."

"But if she's sick. . ."

"Sure an' she's doin' foin." Patsie stepped inside the kitchen.

Selly stuck her head over the waste barrel again and retched. Caroline reached out and caressed her back. "Selly, you are ill." The girl straightened and wiped her mouth with the back of her hand.

"Come," Caroline said, "sit down."

She led Selly into the kitchen and onto a chair near the door.

Caroline glanced at Patsie, who chopped vegetables at a table in the center of the kitchen, her eyes focused in front of her. Beside her, another dark-haired servant kneaded dough.

"This here be Missy. She be comin' a couple days a week to help out with the chores."

The girl glanced up, offered a perfunctory smile, then became engrossed in kneading the dough in front of her. Missy looked similar to Selly, except she was slightly taller and older, perhaps Caroline's age. "Are you a relation of Selly's?" Caroline asked.

"No, Miss, I'm not," she said, her eyes momentarily leaving the dough to glance at Caroline.

"Do you feel better, Selly?"

"Miss Caroline," she heard Patsie say, "don't be after worryin' yer head 'bout Selly. She'll be foin." Patsie's tone was authoritarian, despite the two teeth missing from the front of her mouth.

Caroline studied the young girl, whose eyes were red and puffy.

"No, really. I'm certain that Uncle will allow you time to rest."

"Look here, Miss," Patsie said, wiping her hands on her apron and approaching Caroline, "meanin' no disrespect. I know ye be meanin' well, but. . ."

"Please, I want to help." Caroline glanced at the other servant, who appeared to show no interest in the conversation.

"You can't help me, Miss Caroline," Selly whispered. Caroline was struck by how young this girl sounded.

"If you're ill, then I wish to help you."

"The colleen's not sick. She's. . ."

Caroline looked down at Selly, her small hands folded like a knot on her lap, her eyes on the verge of tears. This younger girl, so beautiful, so efficient, so undemanding, was deeply troubled.

"Please. I must. . ." Selly jumped up, pushed past Caroline and rushed out the door. The gagging sounds ceased and were replaced with quiet sobbing.

Caroline walked into the back yard area. Patsie followed her.

"Miss, I'm after tellin' ye already, tain't nothin' ye can do for the girl. Just be leavin' her be now."

Ignoring her, Caroline gently touched Selly's back. "Please allow me to help you."

Selly turned around and Caroline gently cradled her as she sobbed. "There, there. You're going to be fine."

"No, I'm not going to be fine." She leaned close to Caroline and whispered, "I'm. . .carrying."

"Carrying?"

Now, Patsie leaned towards her and whispered, "With child, ye may be sayin', Miss Caroline."

Caroline caught her breath and lowered her head. "Oh."

"So you see? You cannot help me.   Patsie was telling me about the midwife bringing on my monthly."

"Your monthly?" Caroline stepped back. "What do you mean, bringing on your monthly?"

"I'd be after telling ye, Miss Caroline, tain't no reason fer ye to be helpin'."

"But doing that would make her no longer with child, wouldn't it, Patsie?"

"Sure an' all, Miss. That'd be the whole point of it. . ."

Caroline faced Selly and placed her hands gently on her shoulders. "You mustn't do that, Selly. What about your child? A child is a great gift from God."

"Miss, I'm not married. And it's not a child yet."

"No, Selly, that's not true. How long has it been since your last monthly?"

"Three months, Miss."

"What about the father of this baby? Where is he in all this?"

"He told me he doesn't know that it's his child."

"Oh, what a horrid thing to say. What sort of man says. . ."

"It's Mr. David, Miss."

Caroline gasped.

"Miss Caroline, I had never been with any other, just him. I was a. . .I had never. . .before him."

"Look here, Miss Caroline, ye be needin' ta leave Selly be. I told ye we'll be knowin' how to fix the problem."

Caroline stepped forward and placed her hand on Selly's shoulder. Months ago, Caroline had been given the option of coming to Uncle's instead of working as a kitchen scullery maid in Boston. This girl had few choices now. That licentious David O'Donovan had abandoned Selly when she needed him the most.

"Patsie, I cannot and I shall not allow her to go through this alone. She has no one to take care of her. This is not totally her fault and she should not have to bear the entire responsibility on her shoulders alone."

"Well then, Miss Caroline, sure an' that's not true. Selly has us. The midwife will take care of it."

"No, Patsie. You mustn't take her to the midwife. I intend to help her."

Later that afternoon, Caroline sat under the maple tree in front of the house. She tried to read, but her thoughts instead turned to the servant girl. Selly was three years younger than Caroline and yet was in a most dire predicament. How would she find suitable accommodations for the young servant? She had told her uncle that she wished to visit the minister's wife later this week and was hopeful that the kind woman would be able to offer some information as to where Selly could stay for the duration of her confinement.

"Carrie!" she heard Elizabeth calling to her.

Caroline straightened and walked to meet her cousin halfway to the house.

"Carrie, I must speak with you," she whispered. Her cousin was frowning.

"What ever is the matter?"

"Is it true that you plan to find some sort of home for Selly?"

"Lizzie, the poor girl is with child and in need of. . ."

"Yes, I realize that, dear sister, but servants tend to their own. You need not worry about such a matter."

"Lizzie, you are my new sister, are you not?"

Her cousin's face brightened. "Why, yes, certainly I am."

"Then you need to support me in assisting this poor girl. I could be her right now if it weren't for you and Uncle."

Elizabeth stepped back, and at first her mouth turned into a thin worried line, then a smile formed. "Very well. I shall be a humanitarian. Whatever you need, Papa and I shall provide."

Caroline leaned in to embrace her. "You are too kind."

4

Two days later, Caroline descended the back staircase to the kitchen. Although she hadn't taken note of the room before, she found it to be spacious with two cast iron cooking stoves which lined the far wall and a large wooden table with a grinding apparatus attached to it in the center of the room. Servant bells lined the wall above the door. Patsie was chopping a yellow squash at the center table and Selly was washing dishes at a long table which lined the outside wall. The smell of baking bread caused Caroline's mouth to water and, for a moment, she forgot why she had come down to the kitchen.

"Well now, top o' the mornin', Miss Caroline," said Patsie. Selly turned around and nodded her greeting.

"Selly?"

"What is it, Miss?"

"I intend to speak with a woman at the church to find you a place where you can stay for the duration of your confinement."

"You've been so kind. Thank you."

"You should not be going through this alone."

Just outside the kitchen, a loud voice bellowed. "Get the damn horse or I'll be telling Mr. Martin to fire your black ass."

One of the bells above the door began to ring.

"I must go. I do not wish for *him* to see me," Selly was wiping her hands on her apron and walking toward the stairs to the main floor.

"Him?"

"Mr. David," she whispered, and pointed toward the back door.

"Yes, well, I want to see him. I should like to tell him what's on my mind."

"But, Miss," Patsie called out. "Sure an' ye can't be talkin' ta a man by yer lonesome, tain't proper. I'm just after tellin' ye that."

"I'm not alone. You'll be in the kitchen. Besides, it's improper for a man to not take responsibility for his child."

Patsie shook her head as Caroline rushed out the doorway.

David O'Donovan was speaking to the black servant. She had no idea what they were discussing, but Mr. O'Donovan had a distinct frown on his face. She approached him, her chin raised. The moment that he noticed her, his expression softened and he became charming, almost inviting.

"Miss Martin, to what do I owe the pleasure of your company?" As he spoke, she could smell alcohol on his breath. She stepped back, kept silent and glared at him.

"Pray tell, have I done something to displease you?" he asked, his mouth curved in slight amusement.

"Displease may be an understatement, sir." She regarded him with the angriest scowl she could muster.

"Well, you certainly have gotten my attention, young lady. And may I just say that you are looking lovely today, despite the frown on your beautiful flawless face. If every girl looked as you do in black, she would want only to wear that color."

She walked closer to David and whispered, "Why do you refuse to help the girl who carries your child within her?"

His face darkened. "Oh, so that's what's troubling you. Well, you know, Miss Martin, with girls of her sort, one has to. . ."

Caroline cut him off with a slap to his face. Surprised, he rubbed his cheek, his frown quickly turning to a smile. "Oh, dear. Would you like to slap the other side," he asked, then turned his other cheek toward her.

Caroline remained silent, her eyes narrowed with contempt.

He leaned close to her face, his voice quiet but firm. "Did Selly tell you I was the only one? Well, my dear Miss Martin, I'm certain I was not."

"And you know this how?"

"Miss Caroline?" Patsie's high-pitched voice stopped Caroline from continuing.

She quickly leaned her head through the kitchen doorway.

"Patsie, what is it?"

"I'm havin' ta tell ye, Miss," she whispered, "a colleen shoun't be a talkin' 'bout such things."

"I don't care." Turning back toward David, she walked close to him, the top of her head an inch or so away from his chin. "Mr. O'Donovan, Selly told me there was no other."

"And you believe a common lower class servant?"

Caroline cringed. *Common, lower class?*

"Of course. Why would she lie?"

"Well, no one forced her."

"Today if ye shall hear his voice, harden not your heart."

David raised his eyebrows. "I never took you for a Bible thumper, Miss Martin."

"I'm a Christian, Mr. O'Donovan."

"Your naivete is endearing and I don't want to destroy your obvious innocence, but the servants freely do this."

"Your behavior makes me ill."

"Ah, you are even more beautiful when you're angry. Do you realize your freckles darken? It's very becoming."

Caroline again glared at him.

"Aren't you going to slap me again? I was hoping you would."

"You are. . ."

"What? I'm what?" He stepped back and eyed her up and down.   "Well, Miss Martin, I'll tell you what I am. I am. . .shocked!" he said, a huge smirk on his face.

"Whatever do you mean you are shocked?"

"Most certainly I am, Miss Martin." He leaned in close to her and whispered. "You're. . .not wearing a corset, are you?" His eyebrows were raised and now he was smiling broadly.

All of a sudden, Caroline's face became flushed, her eyes widened. Now she was embarrassed that she had left her corset off. David O'Donovan, of all people, *had* noticed.

"Miss Caroline?" she heard Patsie call her again.

Caroline sighed and hurried into the kitchen.

5

Caroline brushed her hair as she watched the softly falling rain outside her window. A timid knock almost went unnoticed. She opened the door to discover Selly standing in the hallway. The young girl cleared her throat. "Pardon me, Miss Caroline. Patsie told me to come and assist you with your dressing this morning."

Yesterday, after David O'Donovan had commented about her lack of proper lady's attire, Caroline had admitted to the older servant that it would be necessary for her to begin wearing a corset. Knowing that Caroline would need assistance, Patsie had sent Selly, and for that, she was grateful as she felt more comfortable around the younger girl.

"Thank you, Selly. Come in," she replied, stepping back to allow Selly inside, then closing the door. "It would be fine for you to call for me anytime using the ropes over there, Miss Caroline."

"I feel as if I'm calling a dog when I use those. I'd much rather just go and search for you." The young servant stood before her.

"May I begin, Miss?"

"Yes, of course." Caroline went behind the dressing screen, which thankfully had arrived late last week. "I can manage to remove my own nightgown."

"Certainly."

While Caroline was putting on her slip, Selly spoke. "I cannot tell you how grateful I am to you, Miss Caroline, for assisting me."

"I am happy to help, Selly. Besides, you didn't place yourself in that condition alone, did you?"

Selly replied quietly, "No."

Caroline came from around the screen, now dressed in her shift. "I am now prepared for that wretched piece of clothing," Caroline said as she motioned for the corset.

Caroline held the garment in place as Selly began to tie the back and pull on the strings.

"It's just," the servant whispered.

"What, Selly?"

"I'm frightened. I've never. . .given birth before. I remember watching my mother when my sister was born."

"How old were you?"

"About nine years old." Selly pulled hard on one of the strings and Caroline gasped.

"I apologize, Miss. Is this too tight?"

"Yes, Selly, although I suppose that it is necessary. So you have a sister?"

She slowly shook her head. "She died a few weeks after birth. My mother passed away shortly after that. It was just my father and me until. . ."

"Until what, Selly?"

"Until he passed. I was 12."

"How awful."

"Then I came here and met Mr. David."

Caroline cringed.

"I thought he was the most wonderful, charming, humorous man I had ever had the pleasure to know. And now I'm. . ." She remained silent for a moment. "My mother screamed when she was giving birth. Do you suppose I shall do the same?"

"I don't know, Selly. But I promise you this, I shall be there for you when you have the baby."

"You've already done so much for me."

"I want to be there."

"That would be so kind of you. Again, I am so grateful," Selly said, as she tied the last string on Caroline's corset.

* * *

Liam O'Donovan entered St. Mary's Episcopal Church and couldn't seem to stop his hands from trembling. He had just observed the Martins emerge from their carriage and Miss Caroline Martin was not wearing black. He had been waiting for almost a month now.

He walked down the center aisle and passed the Martin family pew to his own seat across from them. He suddenly felt nervous and awkward.

He knelt to say a few prayers, but again found himself distracted. Miss Martin was just behind him and to the right. *Stop it,*

Liam. This is an inappropriate place to be infatuated with a girl.

He smiled inwardly when he remembered asking the servant Ben which room Miss Martin would be occupying. He had hoped that she would be watching for him. Despite her mourning, seeing her at the bedroom window was a sign that she was interested. Liam had to be absolutely sure that she would say yes before he asked her uncle for permission to court her. The shame and the uncertainty of being refused would be too much for him to bear.

* * *

Caroline sat upright in the church pew, trying hard to breathe with the stiff corset plastered to her body. Since it had been over six months since her father had died, she was now able to wear lighter colored dresses. Today, she wore a gray dress with a light gray blue fitted bodice and matching gloves.

A few moments ago, Liam O'Donovan walked by and entered a pew on the left side of the congregation. Her heart began to pound at the thought of speaking to him after service.

The organist began to play, the loud chords jolting Caroline into attentiveness. Elizabeth lifted up the hymnal.

Rock of Ages, cleft for me,
Let me hide myself in Thee,
Let the water and the blood,
From Thy wounded side which flowed
Be of sin the double cure
Save from wrath and make me pure

As they sang, Liam's voice was on key and pleasant sounding and Caroline was happy that he was singing so loudly.

When I draw this fleeing breath,
When my eye-strings break in death
When I soar to worlds unknown
See thee on Thy judgment throne
Rock of ages, cleft for me
Let me hide myself in Thee.

At the end of service Liam passed several groups of people milling about. He approached and walked alongside the Martins.

"Good morning, Mr. Martin, Miss Martin, Miss Martin."

Caroline offered a warm smile. She attempted to act as if she wasn't nervous, but in reality, her heart was pounding and her hands were shaking.

They reached the outside courtyard and Liam stood beside Caroline.

"You are looking lovely today, Miss Martin."

Caroline felt a warm flush coming to her face. "Thank you, Mr. O'Donovan."

"Sir, I wonder if I might have a word with you," Liam said to Uncle.

"Certainly."

Liam tipped his hat to Caroline and Elizabeth and walked alongside Uncle Edward a short distance away. Caroline watched as Liam shifted from one foot to the next.

"I wonder what he's talking to Father about, Carrie! He is so handsome."

"Yes, he is. I was a bit surprised at how beautifully he sings."

"He most certainly does. Both O'Donovan brothers have wonderful voices, Carrie. Of course, you shall never hear David sing in a church." Keeping her gaze on her father and on Liam in the distance, Elizabeth continued, "The way Liam looks at you, I wouldn't be surprised if he is asking Father to court you. I'll wager that he was just waiting until you stopped wearing black. And wouldn't that be the most wonderful event for you, Carrie, to have Liam O'Donovan courting you?"

Inwardly, Caroline hoped that Elizabeth was correct. Of course, she wondered whether she ought to be considering courting a man as it had only been six months since her father died. And what would Liam think if he knew that she had come from such humble beginnings?

"I don't know, Lizzie. After all, I slapped his brother."

"Yes, well, Carrie, you must learn that there are certain activities that a proper young lady does not partake in."

"Like slapping a man who says vile and inappropriate, if not callous, comments?"

"Well, what did he say?"

"I'd rather not repeat it. I know that I should have controlled my temper. It usually only surfaces when I see an injustice taking place. Selly had no idea of the consequences. David is a very charming and handsome man, even I could see that. But Selly is only 15 years of age."

"Yes, well, girls her age are married."

"Selly was most definitely not married."

"Anyway, I am so pleased you started wearing your corset again. I know it's rigid and uncomfortable, but it is essential."

"Essential?" *Vexatious. That's what it is.*

Liam and Uncle Edward approached the girls. Liam was smiling at Caroline.

"Caroline, Liam has asked my permission to court you, if you would be agreeable?"

A soft flush came to Caroline's cheeks. "I. . ." She glanced at Liam's face. His eyebrows were raised in anticipation of her answer. He then cleared his throat. "Miss Martin, I would be honored if you would allow me to court you."

Caroline remained silent, her eyes sweeping from Liam's expectant expression to Uncle's grin to Elizabeth's wide eyes.

"Perhaps my niece needs more time to think about it."

She then blurted out, "No, no, it is not necessary to think about it, Uncle. I should like it very much if Mr. O'Donovan courted me."

Liam stared at Caroline with his mouth partly open. He exhaled and said, "Miss Martin, you have made me the happiest man in all of Philadelphia."

His wide smile and bright eyes softened her heart. How could this man be any relation to David?

"Now, Liam, I'm sure that since you'll be courting my niece, it would be appropriate to call her Caroline."

"Yes, that would be fine, Mr. O'Donovan," Caroline offered.

"Then I insist that you call me Liam." He tipped his hat, then proceeded to his carriage.

When he was out of ear range, Elizabeth squealed. "Oh, dear, Carrie, that's wonderful! Liam O'Donovan has asked to court you!"

"Yes, Lizzie."

"Do you realize how many young ladies would like Liam O'Donovan to court them? He's not anything like his brother. Won't sleep with any of the servant girls."

"Elizabeth!" Uncle Edward interrupted.

"Yes, Father?"

"That is inappropriate talk, especially standing in front of church."

"Yes, Father."

"My dear, Caroline," Uncle began. "You are a beautiful young lady. I have noticed how Liam looks at you, so I was not surprised at his request."

Uncle continued. "Perhaps you underestimate your own beauty, my dear. 'Tis a rare commodity to be in the presence of such a beautiful woman with no pretentiousness."

Caroline blushed. Uncle Edward paused.

"I should perhaps take some of that back, Caroline. I have been meaning to discuss with you the manner in which you spoke to Liam's brother." He hesitated and looked directly at her.

"You cannot speak to him in such a manner," he hesitated, then whispered, "and slapping him on the face. I recognize that he can be a very callous and self-centered young man, but we do a lot of business with the O'Donovans and we need to keep our relationship civil."

"That may be impossible, Uncle. How can one be civil to someone like that?"

"You must give me your promise, Caroline, that you shall never again show discourteousness to David."

"Very well." Caroline glanced at the steeple of the church. She was going to need God's help to keep that promise to her uncle.

6

Caroline waited at her window and watched for Liam, who was scheduled to leave his horse at their stable and travel with Uncle, Elizabeth, Patsie and herself to the Centennial Exhibition.

The previous week, with the assistance of several women from the church, she had found a group of nuns in a convent in Cheltenham who agreed to take care of Selly for the rest of her confinement.

"Miss Caroline, sure an' will ye be a comin' down?" Patsie said through the closed door.

"Yes, Patsie. I'm watching for Liam to ride up. I shall be down momentarily."

Always punctual, Liam rode up and tied his horse to the back hitching post. On cue, he glanced at Caroline's window and waved. Her mouth curved into a smile, then she backed away from the window.

As she walked by her vanity, she studied herself in the mirror. Her complexion looked healthier since she moved here. Patsie's cooking was delicious and Caroline loved the fresh air of her uncle's estate. She found it difficult to believe that it had been two months and that her beloved father had been dead for nearly seven months.

Looking at herself in the mirror, she studied her gown, a light blue-gray patterned cotton dress. She fixed her hat in position with some pins, her trembling hands causing one pin to poke her in the head. "Caroline Martin, if you don't calm down, Liam is going to think you're a dolt."

She stepped back and studied herself from different angles. She had to admit that she was becoming accustomed to wearing a corset and, despite its rigidity, agreed that it made her figure look more feminine. "Yes, Mr. O'Donovan, I do believe that you shall find me agreeable today," she said, "if I can stop the dreaded shaking of my hands." She pulled on her gloves and, hurrying down the large staircase, she could see across the front hallway that Uncle, her cousin, Patsie and Liam were standing on the porch beyond the door.

She stopped at the bottom of the steps and walked slowly toward the group. When Liam glanced at her, his face brightened, then he tipped his hat. She returned a smile.

"There you are, my dear. We are ready to leave. Ben will take us in the large open carriage to the Exhibition." Uncle Edward hesitated as he walked to the buggy.

"Liam, if you don't mind, you and I will sit on this side and, Caroline and Elizabeth, you can occupy the other seat."

Uncle Edward helped Elizabeth into the carriage while Ben assisted Patsie into the front driving seat beside him.

"May I assist you, Miss Martin?" Liam offered his hand.

Caroline nodded. He took her hand and gently guided her into the forward section beside Elizabeth, then pulled himself into the carriage in the facing seat with Uncle.

"A pleasant day," commented Uncle Edward.

Caroline nodded politely.

"I remember going to. . ." Uncle Edward's words now became a monotone background noise. Liam glanced at her and smiled.

Why did her stomach feel queasy? Caroline wasn't sure whether it was his handsome looks or the kindness in his eyes, a sweetness that displayed a genuine care for others.

Within a half hour, they had arrived at Fairmount Park. They stopped for fifteen minutes as other carriages allowed passengers to step down. They finally reached the area near the entrance gate and Ben stopped to allow everyone to get out.

Uncle Edward helped Elizabeth and Patsie down as Liam assisted Caroline off the carriage.

"Thank you, Mr. O'Donovan."

He leaned closer to her and whispered, "You're supposed to call me Liam, Caroline." She blushed and stepped back beside her cousin while Liam approached her uncle.

"Isn't this exciting, Carrie?"

Caroline nodded, then glanced at Liam and Uncle, standing only a few feet from them. Uncle was talking in financial jargon, and Liam seemed to be listening intently.

All around her, the conversations centered on the Philadelphia Exhibition. "I've already been to the main building many times and one can get lost for hours it is so large," one woman said.

"Every person in Philadelphia must be attending this Exhibition," Elizabeth said. "Don't you agree, Carrie?"

"I suppose so."

They walked onto the grounds of Fairmount Park and stopped. The ticket booth had four orderly lines of people and Uncle Edward motioned for them to stand in the far left line. She was thankful that it was a breezy summer day, not too warm and not too cool. In the distance, a band was playing a lively marching song. More exhibition goers filed in behind them and Caroline clutched onto Liam's arm more tightly. He leaned down and whispered, "Is there something wrong?"

She nodded. "I am not accustomed to crowds."

"Not to worry. This should not take too long."

As they came away from the ticket booth, Elizabeth squealed. "Papa, I've never seen so many large buildings in one place!"

"Guides, get your guides here!" yelled a boy in knickers and a cap.

"Excuse me, Caroline. I'm going to purchase one of those books," Liam said.

Liam returned with a small booklet, "Authorized Visitors Guide to the Centennial Exhibition." "I imagine this will be useful and can help us decide where we want to go today."

They walked straight ahead and stopped. Uncle Edward read the inscription. "Bartholdi Fountain. It says here that this is the man who designed that big hand and torch over there." As the wind blew, minute bits of water sprayed the group.

Besides the enormity of the buildings, the landscaping and flowers were breathtaking. The air smelled of mouth-watering roasting peanuts, popcorn and foil-wrapped bananas. A band continued to play festive music in the distance.

"Let's visit Memorial Hall," offered Elizabeth. "I want to see that painting by Eakins everyone's talking about."

"Which painting is that?" Liam asked.

"The one where the doctors are operating. I think it's called 'The Gross Clinic.' It's rather bloody, I've been told."

"Oh," replied Liam, with a slight smirk.

"I think Liam and I would probably much prefer to visit Machinery Hall, don't you agree? After all, we all want to see that talking machine and the Corliss Steam Engine, do we not?"

"To be quite honest, Mr. Martin, I would be happy to go wherever Caroline wishes to go."

All eyes on Caroline, she replied, "I should like to visit the Main Building first," she pointed to the right, "if that is agreeable."

"My dear, that's a fine choice," said Uncle Edward "There will be interesting exhibits from many different manufacturers."

Liam held out his arm for Caroline.

In front of the building's west entrance, the group stopped by a cannon. "I imagine this was used in the Civil War," Uncle Edward commented, looking for a plaque to read. "Liam," Uncle continued, "have you informed Caroline that your father was a Civil War hero?"

"No, I haven't, not yet, sir."

"How exciting, Liam. Your father was a hero?"

"That's what it says on his medal. He fought in the Civil War, 48th Infantry, and was awarded a Medal of Honor for carrying three of his wounded comrades across a battlefield in Virginia."

"He must have been very brave to do that."

"I suppose." He shrugged his shoulders.

"Was he wounded?"

"He was shot in the thigh, just a flesh wound."

"And," Uncle Edward said, "it was after he was wounded that he carried two of the three soldiers."

Liam lowered his head, then straightened and walked briskly to the doors of the main building. Caroline had to quicken her pace to keep up with him.

Inside the building, Caroline stared in awe at the ceilings which seemed to reach up to the sky. The tall windows on either side of the building shone generous light into the exhibition area. Uncle Edward offered, "Well, I intend to peruse the exhibits on this side," he said, pointing to the far left side. "Liam, perhaps you and Caroline can cover the exhibits in the middle?"

"Yes, sir, if you think that would be fine."

"I'd best be goin' with Miss Caroline, if ye take me meanin'."

"No, Patsie, that won't be necessary. You and Elizabeth may accompany me."

Elizabeth's eyebrows were raised and Patsie had a frown on her face. "If ye think so."

Caroline held onto Liam's arm as they strolled alongside the long row of exhibits. They walked without speaking for several moments. Farther down, there appeared to be an exhibition from Paris, a display entirely of. . . Caroline immediately slowed her pace, almost stopping. She was certain her face was flushed.

"Are you unwell?" Liam asked.

She lowered her head. "I. . .I'm fine," she said, pulling him towards the right side of the exhibition area. He stepped back and looked at her with raised eyebrows. Directly behind him was the offending display.

"This is all so exciting," she said, somewhat unconvincingly.

"Yes, it is," he replied.

"And, well. . ."

"I know. You're wondering whether you ought to be so happy with your father gone."

Caroline's eyes widened. "Yes, with my father gone, it is difficult to be happy."

"He would want you to be enjoying yourself, would he not?"

"Yes, of course, he would."

Liam cleared his throat. "My father died four years ago. He had a few too many drinks and fell asleep in the stable and it caught fire."

"How awful."

"It was more difficult for David. I wasn't very close to my father."

"That's dreadful."

Liam shrugged his shoulders.

"What about your mother, Caroline? When did she pass away?"

"I was only about two months old."

"So you don't remember her. That's a shame."

"Yes, it is. But my father has told me many stories about her. He says I look just like her except for the color of my hair."

"Your mother must have been beautiful."

Caroline blushed and, distracted, she began to walk again, still holding onto Liam's arm. He turned to continue in their original direction and before she could stop him, his eyes fell upon the display she had been hoping to avoid. He glanced casually at the forms, seemingly undisturbed by the large exhibition of corsets by Lenoir and Farcy & Oppenheim. When he looked at Caroline, she could feel her face turning crimson. She lowered her head and avoided eye contact. Liam, thankfully, mentioned nothing.

Coming upon an instrument display, Liam said, "Pardon me, Caroline," as he let go of Caroline's arm. "Do you mind?" he said to the man behind the table.

The vendor, a well-dressed older man with a full beard replied, "Certainly not." Liam picked up a violin and held it out to study it. "Looks like a fine instrument."

"Do you play, Liam?"

"Since I was a child."

"I should like to hear you play."

"It would be my pleasure to do so."

"Could you play now?"

He shook his head. "Perhaps another time. . . with my own violin." He paused. "Do you play an instrument, Caroline?"

"No, I don't. I should have liked to learn but I never did." She paused. "Liam, did you do well in school?"

"Yes, I suppose I did. And you?"

"My teacher voted me the most proficient reader in the class the last year that I attended school."

"Was that secondary school?"

Caroline shook her head. "I didn't attend secondary school because my father was ill and I wanted to care for him."

"Didn't your father have enough servants to care for him?"

"I. . .well, I. . ." *Should I tell him that we had no servants?*

"I know, you wanted to care for him yourself?"

"Yes." Caroline recognized that was close to the truth.

He nodded, then cleared his throat. "Who is your favorite author?"

"I like Jane Austen."

"I've heard of her. She's British, is she not?"

"Yes. Do you read much, Liam?"

"Hardly anymore. When I was a teenager, I read most of Charles Dickens' books, although I don't have time for reading these days with our business. David and I work as much as four men."

They walked for a short distance, then arrived at a "Hires Root Beer" display. The sign at the top of the display touted, "The Greatest Health-Giving Beverage in the World."

"Would you like to taste a new drink?" the vendor, a young man around Caroline's age, offered Liam.

"Well, I will sample just about any sort of beverage – or food – at least once," Liam said. The vendor gave him a small paper cup filled with a dark fizzling liquid. He sipped at first, then downed it.

"Tasty. Different. Sweet. Caroline, try some."

Caroline glanced from Liam to the vendor, then said, "Very well." She took a cup from the man and sipped it. "That's quite good. It's sweet and very tingly."

A short while later, the group met at the entrance.

"Papa, please, may we visit the Art Gallery in Memorial Hall," Elizabeth asked, pointing. "It's right across the street."

"Liam, Caroline, would that be agreeable to you?"

"Sounds fine to me, sir."

They walked across the street, over the railroad tracks and approached Memorial Hall, a round neoclassical building. Caroline's head tilted upwards to study the fine architecture. The five of them entered the massive structure. Uncle Edward stopped several feet from the entrance.

"I cannot wait to see 'The Gross Clinic!'" Elizabeth exclaimed.

Upon hearing her, one of the guards commented, "Miss, that painting is not in Memorial Hall. It's in the Army Post Hospital near the US government building."

Elizabeth lowered her head. "I see."

"Since we're here, let's visit this building, then we'll take a stroll over to the hospital before we go to lunch," Uncle suggested.

Elizabeth's eyes widened. "Thank you, Papa."

"Liam and Caroline, would you meet us back here in one hour?"

Liam took out his pocket watch. "It's quarter past eleven. So quarter past twelve, Mr. Martin?"

"Fine. Then we'll see what sort of culinary fare they have here."

Uncle, Patsie and Elizabeth walked ahead into the museum.

Inside the main entrance, Caroline's eyes followed the wide columns up the grand archways to the high ceilings. Above them swung an enormous crystal gaslight chandelier. The walls and ceilings were a bright white. Caroline found herself squinting and pulling her hat down. The floors were smooth checkered tiles. Liam held his arm up and she grasped onto it.

They strolled about, gazing at paintings and sculptures in the central dome area, keeping silent as they walked. Caroline studied Liam as he scrutinized the art works. When he was really concentrating, Liam absentmindedly stroked his beard with his thumb.

Ahead of them a small crowd gathered in front of an art work. Caroline couldn't see whether it was a painting or a sculpture but as they inched nearer, Caroline's pulse quickened. This was a statue of a. . . Caroline drew her breath in and instinctively glanced away. Liam appeared to be studying the sculpture of an unclothed woman intently. The crowds surrounding this piece made it impossible to get too close and for that, Caroline was grateful. She could feel Liam's gaze on her and again, knew that her face was flushed. Behind her, she heard a woman say, "Vile statue!"

Liam cleared his throat. "Perhaps we ought to make our way to the front to meet your uncle and cousin."

"Yes, of course," she replied, thankful that they would be moving on. "What time is it?"

Checking his pocket watch he replied, "Ten past noon."

"I wonder which restaurant we will go to," Caroline asked.

Liam pulled out the guide. "There are several listed here. The Great American Restaurant, Trois Freres Provencaux...pardon my poor French...Restaurant of the South, Lauber's German Restaurant. Do any of these appeal to you, Caroline?"

"I'm not sure. And you?"

"Well, all these seem like good dining establishments."

"What kinds of foods do you like, Liam?"

"That's a difficult one to answer, because I eat just about anything put in front of me. I'm not a fussy sort, at least about food."

"But you must like some foods more than others?"

"Well, I like baked ham, roast beef and Jane makes a delicious Irish stew. And you? What foods do you prefer?"

"I like sweet potatoes, carrots. And fruit, I enjoy apples, pears, strawberries, oranges. And sweet cakes."

"Well, I know you like sweet food if you like root beer, but you obviously don't eat a lot of cakes. You're awfully small."

"Do you think I'm too small?"

"No, not at all. I think you are perfect." His warm smile and gentle tone made him seem more handsome and for a moment, she felt breathless.

As she held onto his arm, her heart was beating rapidly. Would he know how he was affecting her?

"There you are," called Uncle. "Let's make our way over to the US government building to see that painting."

"I'm thrilled that we're going to finally see the Eakins' painting, Carrie. I've heard and read so much about it. It's caused quite a controversy."

"Why, Lizzie?"

"It's supposed to be quite realistic."

Caroline cringed and wondered whether she ought to suggest that she and Liam go elsewhere. Instead, she remained silent.

At the US government building, Uncle led them toward the smaller hospital building. Inside, he followed a group of people into a ward room with beds lining each side of the room. Numerous people stood in front of a tall painting at the far end of the room. From her vantage point, Caroline observed that it was a rather dark painting.

She and Liam followed Uncle, Elizabeth and Patsie to join the crowd in front of the painting.

"Is this it, Liam?"

"I'm not sure," he replied. As they moved closer, Caroline saw the top half; it was a dark painting of men in the upper left-hand corner and the top of a balding man's head in the center.

Several people in the small crowd began to shove and Liam protectively pulled her against him, putting his arm around her shoulder.

"I must get closer," complained Elizabeth.

Together, she and Liam followed Elizabeth as she maneuvered through the crowd. "Excuse me," she said apologetically. People parted as they inched forward. When they reached the front, Liam let go of Caroline's shoulder and straightened. She grasped onto his arm. He looked down and smiled.

When she lifted her head and stood before the painting, she

gasped. The painting depicted a group of men surrounding an open and gaping cut on a naked leg. The crimson blood depicted in the painting made her nauseous.

From behind her, Caroline heard a man say, "Shocking."

Elizabeth's eyes were widened and she stared, silent.

"Interesting," said Liam. "What do you think, Caroline?"

"It's. . .very dark." Caroline's stomach felt queasy and she wanted nothing more than to leave.

"Come, let's go," Liam said. He guided Elizabeth and Caroline to where Uncle and Patsie were standing and together, the group made their way out of the room.

"Rather bloody, wasn't it, Liam?" asked Uncle.

"Yes, sir, but I found it most interesting."

Caroline did not agree. She had lost her appetite. She looked at her cousin, who had not said a word since they had seen the painting.

"Lizzie, are you unwell?"

Her cousin shook her head. "I suppose, despite all that's been written about it, I didn't expect it to be that realistic." She leaned close to Caroline and whispered. "I didn't mind the blood so much as the naked leg and. . ."

"Time for lunch," Uncle said.

Elizabeth groaned.

* * *

David O'Donovan welcomed a leisurely rest beside Missy in the basement bedroom off the Martin kitchen. Most of the household were spending a day at the Centennial Exhibition. It was refreshing to have his pleasure outside of the henhouse or stable. And today, he'd be free to have Missy as often as she allowed him.

When Liam had asked him if he would like to go along, he had declined. David knew that his presence would ruin Miss Martin's day. Her distaste for him was most amusing.

Missy roused and kissed David. He had missed her the last three weeks or so. Each time he visited the Martin house on the days she was scheduled to work, she was "indisposed" according to Patsie.

"It's good to be with you again, Mr. David. I've missed you."

"Well, I wasn't the one indisposed. Were you ill?"

"No. Just taking care of a problem, that's all."

She kissed his lips again. "I told you that there's no need to worry. I'm all fixed now." Missy snuggled up close to David and soon she was drifting off to sleep.

He hoped that Liam was enjoying the day with Miss Martin and that it was going well for both of them. David was thankful that Miss Martin liked his brother because Liam was smitten with her.

He laughed to himself when he thought of how dissimilar he and his brother were. Liam, the neat one, who followed all the rules, his mother's favorite, his father's disappointment. They were not only different in appearance with Liam favoring his mother's fair looks and David his father's "black Irish looks," they were also opposite personalities, with David outgoing and Liam reserved.

Despite the differences, the brothers shared a deep bond. Both boys grew up under the heavy hand of their father and they often ran off to the woods together to escape his foul temper. Sometimes they would spend hours playing war or hide and seek. They often visited a secret spot in the forest amongst the ruins of an old stone house.

* * *

Liam placed the ticket inside the box on his dresser. The worst aspect about the day was that it had ended. The best was spending time with Caroline. It would not be premature for him to state that she enjoyed the day as well.

Liam thought back to his favorite moments; it would be impossible to choose only one. He enjoyed their conversations and learned much about her. He held back a smile when he recalled her reaction to the corset display. Her embarrassment at the nude sculpture was also endearing. Despite her age and maturity, Caroline O'Donovan was very much an innocent. No, Liam told himself, a young lady could not get any more gently born and bred than that.

He needed to control his desire to see her every waking moment. Last night, he could not drop off to sleep anticipating the day ahead. Now that it was over, he longed for more time with her. On his way home from the Martin household, he decided that the O'Donovan House would host a cook out and invite the Martins, and all the surrounding neighbors. It would be the ideal way to spend another day with the girl he hoped that he would marry.

There was a quick knock at his door then it swung open. David strolled into the room. "How was your day at Fairmount Park?"

"Very well."

"That's good, Lee."

"I think she likes me."

"What girl wouldn't be enamored with your charm?"

"I hope so. I enjoy being with her. I want her to like me."

"At least she doesn't cringe every time you walk into a room."

Liam laughed. "That's your own doing."

David shrugged. "Care to join me in a game of chess?"

"I don't think so. You always win."

"Besides, we never finished our last game. The pieces are in the same position as when we last played."

"That's because I was about to lose, David."

"Indeed."

"Well, good night."

"Night, Lee."

7

In the parlor, Caroline sat in the reading chair beside the hearth; her book lay open on her lap. She could not seem to concentrate on the words this morning. Liam O'Donovan was kind and good-hearted, of that she was certain. She found herself thinking about him constantly and wishing that he would have some reason to call on her today.

"There you are," Elizabeth called from across the room.

Her cousin sat in the nearest chair. "I wanted to speak with you privately. May we have a sisterly chat?"

Caroline closed the book and set it on the table beside the chair. "Of course."

"Well?"

"Well what?"

"I simply must know the details of your conversations with Liam. I couldn't inquire of you last night with Father sitting across from us."

"There's not much to tell."

"What sort of conversationalist is he, Carrie? I would venture to guess that he is intelligent."

"He most certainly is."

"Do tell. What did you and he discuss?"

"Just the normal polite conversation."

"Well, I must say, you looked enamored with him and he seems to be quite taken with you."

"I hope so."

"So you have feelings for him, already, dear Sister?"

Caroline felt heat rise to her cheeks. "I know this is early, but yes, I do."

"That is the most wonderful news. I do hope we shall have a wedding this year!" she exclaimed.

"I suppose we ought not to be planning any nuptials yet."

"Miss Caroline, Miss, 'Lizabeth, sure an' there be an invite which has come fer ye," Patsie said excitedly.

"An invite?" Caroline asked, as she and Elizabeth joined Patsie outside on the veranda of the Martin house.

Elizabeth leaned close to her cousin's ear. "An invitation."

"Sure, 'tis to the O'Donovan House. Himself just told me to give this to ye, Miss Elizabeth. Himself said Mr. Liam and Mr. David be after havin' a cookout this Saturday in t'aft'noon, and Himself is gettin' an invite fer all o'ye."

At the mention of Liam's name, Caroline's heart fluttered.

"Carrie, we're going to the O'Donovan house for a cook out!"

"Yes, that is indeed wonderful news." Excitement welled up in her at the notion of seeing Liam again. Liam had been her last thought before falling asleep and her first thought upon waking. And in less than a week, she would be seeing him again.

That Saturday afternoon, as they rode up to the O'Donovan residence, Caroline observed that the O'Donovan mansion's architecture appeared similar to that of their own house. The building was built with darker stone and the shutters were brown instead of green, with the structure being three stories, instead of two. Ivy was plastered across the left front of the house and climbing onto the roof.

"Did you know Liam's father well, Uncle?"

"I probably knew him better than most, but he never said much until he had a few glasses of whiskey," he laughed.

"Oh my, Carrie, the dress you're wearing looks to be almost the exact color of Liam's coat and breeches!"

"You're right." Caroline smoothed out her blue patterned dress and adjusted her hat. Her heart began beating more rapidly as she saw Liam on the front veranda welcoming guests. For a moment, she stared at him, trying to determine what was different.

"Carrie, look at Liam, he's shaved his beard! Oh, he looks so much better without that hair on his face."

Caroline could think of little else but how handsome Liam looked. Beside him stood David and Caroline turned away.

"My mother used to say that even a homely man looks better clean shaven."

Caroline laughed. "You do say the most amusing things. And Liam is definitely not a homely man!"

The carriage pulled up to the front veranda and Liam moved forward to assist first Elizabeth, then Caroline onto the stepping block next to the carriage.

"I have missed you," Liam whispered in her ear.

"Miss Martin, you are looking more lovely every time I see you," David said. He put his hand forward and waited for her to extend hers. She gave him her hand begrudgingly. "Mr. O'Donovan."

"Good day, Mr. Martin," said Liam.

"Good day, Liam. Caroline, would it be acceptable if I left you with Liam?"

"I shall take good care of her, sir."

"That would be fine, Uncle," Caroline said.

"Come, Elizabeth, I want to talk to Pastor Selkirk." The two walked off.

"Caroline, I want to show you something," Liam said.

"Will you be playing violin? I should like to hear you play."

"That comes later." He pulled her inside the foyer and stepped back. "So what do you think?" He offered her a wide grin and rubbed his face on both sides.

"You mean shaving your beard?"

He nodded. "Which do you prefer?"

"Well, it doesn't matter whether you have a beard or not." She paused and studied him for a moment. "Although it is rather nice to be able to see your whole face."

He took hold of her hand and led her into the house. Caroline immediately felt at home. The design was similar to that of their home, except for the wallpaper and floors. From the flowered wall coverings and soft pastel colors of the carpeting, Caroline guessed that Liam's mother had been the one who had made most of the decorating decisions.

Caroline surveyed the front hall area and her eyes grew wide at the white marble staircase. "This is lovely," she said, as she ran her hands over the polished surface of the banister.

"My father's idea. I cannot begin to guess how much that staircase cost, but it wasn't inexpensive. It's all Italian marble. I am glad my mother insisted on the carpeting. I can just imagine how many times David and I would have injured ourselves on those stairs without it."

Liam walked her toward a room to the side, where Uncle's study would be at their house. They passed a grandfather clock which stood against the wall near the entrance. Caroline's eyes were drawn to the painted words above the front doorway, "*Cead Mille Failte, Ma Achora.*" As she stared at the words, Liam said, "It's Gaelic. It means 'A hundred thousand welcomes, my friend.' Again, my father's idea. He was very proud of his Irish heritage, but I'm not sure he really meant those words."

Liam led her to the study off the foyer. Although the blinds were open, the dark paneling, walnut desk and bookcases made the room seem dark and foreboding. Model ships of every size and variety lined the top of the bookcases.

"Did your father build those?"

"A few. David actually built most of them when he was 12 or 13. He has quite a talent for that sort of activity." Caroline shrugged her shoulders.

He stopped before a painting on the far side of the room near the window.

Caroline looked up and observed the painting of a beautiful blonde woman, a ruggedly handsome dark-haired man and two boys, one a smaller golden-haired boy and the other, a dark curly haired boy.

"Is this your family?"

He nodded. "My mother was beautiful, wasn't she?"

"Yes. Now that I see you without your beard, you resemble her."

"I know."

"And David looks like your father."

"And acts like him, I'm afraid." He paused. "I have always liked this picture, although I remember being annoyed that we had to stand still for so long."

"How old were you when this was painted?"

"I think I was around six and David was eight."

"You were such a beautiful little boy."

He laughed. "I hope they burned that silly outfit."

Liam proceeded to explain that his mother had given birth to two stillborn boys before David was born. "Then I was born too soon and was quite sickly until I was about eight years old. Mother always said that God must have had a special plan for me."

"That's beautiful." She searched the room with her eyes, then said, "I notice that there are no servant ropes in here."

"I had them removed after my father died. David wanted to keep them all over the house, but I insisted that we take them down. Certainly, I can go and find any one of the servants easily enough without calling them like they're animals."

"My sentiment exactly. I despise those at Uncle's house."

Liam held his arm out and Caroline took hold of it. They walked around as he showed her various paintings in the front hallway. "This one here," he said, pointing to a picture of his mother, "was commissioned by my father. This was six years ago." He paused, then stopped in front of a tintype of the same woman. "This was taken shortly before she died."

"She was lovely. I wish I could have met her."

"She was very special. She would have had to be to tolerate my father." He guided her back into the study and picked up a small package from his desk.

"And this, Caroline, is for you."

"A present? For me? But it isn't even my birthday."

"When is your birthday? I should like to know."

"April 26th."

"I must remember that for next year. Accept this as a belated birthday gift. I hope you like it."

"I am certain I will," she responded, then tore off the brown wrapping paper. She squealed in delight. "It's the book 'Emma!' How did you know I don't own this one?"

"I asked your uncle. Do you remember a few weeks ago he asked you which book you would like to add to your collection?"

Caroline laughed. "Yes, I do. I thought he was going to buy me another book! Thank you so much for this, Liam. I shall treasure it."

A servant, perhaps a decade older than Caroline, a pretty woman of mixed race with green eyes and long light brown hair pulled back under a mobcap, approached them.

"Would you care for a glass of strawberry punch, Mr. Liam?"

"Yes, Hallie."

To Caroline, she said, "Would you like some punch, Miss?" Liam lifted up one of the glasses and handed it to Caroline.

"Yes, that would be fine."

Caroline glanced up to see David walking toward them.

"Lee, what the. . ." he looked at Caroline and his eyes narrowed, "What happened to you? Am I supposed to host alone while you take Miss Martin on a grand tour?" Caroline shuddered at David's cutting tone.

"You've never had a problem hosting alone before, David."

David turned away, muttering something under his breath. He passed a mirror, studied himself for a moment, brushed a piece of hair in place and walked away.

"I'm sorry, Liam. You really ought to be acting as host. I'll attempt to find Elizabeth and Uncle."

"Very well. Most of the guests have arrived and it should only take a few moments."

Caroline nodded. She had just begun looking for her uncle when she nearly bumped into a servant carrying a tray. "Excuse me," she said to the young woman, who wore a pleasant expression and was rather thick around the middle. Her brown hair was pulled neatly back under a white mobcap. But what Caroline noticed most about her was that her eyes displayed unmistakable kindness.

"No, that's fine, Miss Caroline."

"How do you know my name?"

"Jane, Miss. My name is Jane."

"Oh?" Caroline knew that she had never met this particular servant before, yet she seemed familiar all the same.

"Yes. My ma told me about you, Miss."

"Your ma?"

"Patsie."

"Yes, your mother told me you worked here. Well, it's nice to make your acquaintance, Jane."

"As it is to make yours, Miss Caroline. Good day."

"Good day, Jane."

There was a tap on Caroline's shoulder. "There you are."

"Yes, Lizzie. I'm just waiting for Liam to finish greeting guests. He said there's going to be a performance. I do hope he will play the violin. He's quite good."

"It looks like there is a group of musicians setting up in the reception room over there." Elizabeth pointed to the larger room to the left of the staircase.

At that moment, Liam was coming down the stairs with his violin in his hand. "Miss Martin, how are you today?" Liam asked Elizabeth. Her response was to giggle and say, "Very well, Mr. O'Donovan."

"Caroline, if you would be so kind as to accompany me into the parlor, a few of the men are going to play some songs. I've just learned a new amusing song called "Grandfather's Clock.""

Elizabeth and Caroline followed Liam to the reception room where four rows of seats were arranged.

"Carrie, let's sit up front."

"Yes, Caroline, I prefer you to be closer to the front," Liam said.

"Of course."

Within minutes, an announcement was made and soon, most of the chairs were occupied. Caroline made a quick visual search but could not see Uncle. "Where is your father?"

"He is most probably still speaking with Pastor Selkirk. When I left them, they were talking about the new fishing laws. It was enough to put me to sleep."

The man at the piano began playing a lively tune. After the short introduction, Liam put the violin to his chin and started playing. Although it was an amusing song, Liam played as if it were the most important melody in the world. People began clapping and singing along. Caroline couldn't take her eyes off Liam.

"Liam is quite proficient on the violin, isn't he, Carrie?"

Caroline nodded. "Yes, Lizzie, he most certainly is."

8

Caroline drummed her fingers on the sill as she waited at her bedroom window. Liam would be arriving any minute and she was anxious to see him again.

"Miss Caroline," Patsie said through the closed door.

"Yes, Patsie, what is it?" Caroline asked, opening the door.

"Sure an' ye've got a message from the convent in Chelten'm."

Patsie handed the envelope to Caroline, who immediately tore it open and read it. She gasped.

"Selly's gone into labor. It's too soon, Patsie, and she must be scared to death. I must get there immediately. This letter says that she began having pains in the middle of last night. Do you think Uncle will take me?"

"Himself is bein' out and about the whole day, Miss."

"That's right."

"Well now, I don't have a mind as ta who could be takin' ye ta be with Selly," she said as she left the bedroom.

"But she needs me," Caroline pleaded, as she followed Patsie down to the basement kitchen.

Caroline glanced out the doorway and saw that Liam had arrived and was walking his horse to the back hitching post.

"Liam can take me."

"No, Miss Caroline. T'wouldn't be proper, what with him courtin' ye n'all."

"Well, what about Ben?"

"He's bein' in town for a bit. But I'm fair certain he'll bring ye along ta the convent later on, with Miss 'lizabeth, if ye still a mind ta go."

"I must leave as soon as possible. I am certain that Liam will do this for me."

"But a colleen's got to be thinkin' 'bout her reputation."

"I shall worry about that later. I promised Selly."

Caroline leaned her head out the doorway. "Liam."

"I didn't see you up at your window."

"No." She took hold of his arm and pulled him into the warm kitchen.

"Selly's having her baby and it is imperative for you to take me to the convent in Cheltenham. Do you know where that is?"

He glanced away then looked directly at her. "Of course I do, but Selly has people assisting her, does she not? The nuns will care for her adequately."

"I promised her, Liam. Please."

He regarded her with raised eyebrows. "Caroline, we're a courting couple, not a married couple. I can't very well take you across town without a chaperone."

"Where's Elizabeth, Patsie?"

"I'm thinkin' she went to the city with Himself."

"Patsie, can you come with us?" With raised eyebrows, Caroline regarded the servant.

"Miss Caroline, sure an' I got a chicken roastin', pies half made and I'll not be able to leave."

"Well, then we'll just have to go alone."

"I told you, we can't be traveling alone, especially for the reason you want."

"What I want isn't important, Liam. I promised Selly that I would be there for her. She doesn't have anyone in the world to care for her."

"You told me that the nuns agreed to take care of her."

"Yes, but it's not the same as. . ." Caroline stepped back and studied Liam. His face was without its usual pleasant expression.

"Besides, I have an important business meeting that I must attend to. Be a good girl. The sisters will take good care of her."

Caroline began to grind her teeth and clench her fists. She turned away from him.

"Please do not act like a child. I really cannot go, nor will I take you. There are certain rules one must follow when one is courting and if I broke one of those now, well, it would do nothing for either of our reputations."

Caroline couldn't believe that he wouldn't take her. Of all people, she was under the impression that he would do whatever she asked. There was no use attempting to convince him. For the moment, Caroline decided to pretend as if she were brushing it off. She forced a smile.

"Well, I suppose I should never have promised her something I wouldn't be able to follow through on."

"That's right," he said. "Well, I hate to leave so quickly but I have an emergency meeting with a customer from out of town. Patsie, I dropped off two boxes for Mr. Martin. Make sure that Ben puts them away when he returns."

"Yes, Mr. Liam, sir."

"See you tomorrow, Caroline." He tipped his hat and left.

Caroline forced another smile as he left, although she was angry with him. She hated how rigid he was with regard to rules. As Liam was riding away, Patsie's loud voice bellowed behind her. "Now, that Mr. Liam'll be havin' a good head on his shoulders. I'm glad he won't be fallin' for no feminine wiles. Ye know, Miss Caroline, sure an' it ain't safe or seemly, and t'would've been causin' scandal. . ." Patsie's lecturing became background noise as Caroline's eyes welled up and finally, she allowed herself to cry. Patsie pulled her to a motherly embrace. For several long moments, Caroline sobbed.

"Now, now, don't be takin' on so, Miss."

"Patsie, I promised that I'd be there when her time came."

"Sure an' ye jest can't be there fer her, not jest right now. Ye best be waitin' till Ben or Himself comes home. Besides, Selly'll understand," Patsie said soothingly. "The colleen knows already how much ye've done fer her."

Caroline stiffened and broke away from Patsie. "If Liam won't take me there by horse, then I shall go by foot." Caroline immediately began to walk briskly down the laneway.

Patsie's high-pitched voice screeched. "Miss Caroline, sure an what in the world do ya think ye'll be doin'? Ye can't be walkin' 'cross Philly ta the convent. It'll be after takin ye days ta get there."

"I don't care how long it takes me," she yelled, without turning around. "I must make an effort. I promised her."

"Now then, sure an' ye can't be after doin'. . . oh, me breath . . . Miss Caroline, ye can't be. . ." Her dress swishing back and forth, Patsie was trying hard to keep up with her mistress, who rushed down the laneway like a runaway horse with its first taste of freedom. Caroline had almost reached the road when a small carriage pulled in. The two women stopped as the carriage came to a halt beside them. David had that ridiculous "happy go lucky" expression on his face, a smirk that was completely inappropriate for the occasion.

"Well, Miss Martin, good afternoon. Seems an odd place to find you. Taking an afternoon jaunt?"

Caroline avoided eye contact, then shot the servant an expression which said, "Don't speak to him."

"Mr. David, Miss Caroline's walkin' to the convent in Chelt'nham where Selly be stayin' and she went into labor. . .Selly I be meanin', and she wants to go. . .Miss Caroline, I be meanin'. . .but no one'll take 'er an. . ."

"Whoa, hold on. Miss Martin wants to be with. . .Selly?" He looked at Caroline, who now glared at him.

"Yes. You remember Selly, don't you? The girl you took advantage of and who carries your child?" As she finished saying it, even Caroline was surprised at how cutting her tone was.

David let out an audible sigh.

"Excuse me, I have a very long walk ahead of me and I. . ." As Caroline began to walk away, David grabbed her arm. "Just a minute."

"Remove your hand from me, Mr. O'Donovan," she said, without glancing up at him.

"I will take you there." He said it so softly that she wasn't sure she heard him correctly.

"What?" she asked, convinced that he would be smiling or teasing her. But when she studied his face, she found it to be without the normal hint of playfulness.

"I will take you there," he said more distinctly.

"Now, Mr. David, sir, ye can't be takin' Miss Caroline anywheres. There'll be a scandal and ye can't. . ."

"Quiet, Patsie. Besides, I certainly don't intend to tell anyone and I know Miss Martin won't say anything. That just leaves you."

"Well, ye can't be doing this, Mr. David. Yer not thinkin' 'bout Miss Caroline's reputation."

"She has two options, to walk or to allow me to take her there."

"Ye be forgettin' the third one, Mr. David, sir, to stay home."

"Indeed, that is an option. So, Miss Martin, which shall it

be? Allow me to take you, walk or. . ." Before he could finish, Caroline stood alongside his carriage, her head held high.

David raised his eyebrows. "Well, I suppose we can figure out which option Miss Martin has chosen."

"Have a mind o' me words, Miss Caroline. Ye be in trouble if someone finds out."

Caroline turned around. "Patsie, I know you won't say anything. It's up to you to keep my reputation sound."

"And what'll I be after tellin' Himself, when he comes home, Miss?"

"Tell him that I. . .that I took a leisurely walk on the grounds. I'm always doing that anyway, right?"

Patsie snorted her disapproval. "I'm not in the habit of lying to Himself, Miss Caroline."

"It's just a white lie, Patsie."

"Sure an' a lie is a lie and dressin' it in white won't be makin' it any better."

"Well, then you're not lying," she said, "I did go for a walk. It just so happens that Mr. O'Donovan came by."

Patsie snorted again.

David assisted Caroline into the carriage. For the next half hour, it was a quiet, awkward ride. Caroline wasn't sure whether to feel gratitude or disgust. After all, he owed her this ride to the convent.

David finally spoke up. "Ben Franklin once said, 'Three may keep a secret if two of them are dead.'" He was chuckling under his breath. Caroline scowled at him.

After that, both remained silent and Caroline wondered whether she had made the right decision to allow Liam's brother to drive her to the convent.

"You must turn left at the top of the hill. We're going to Cheltenham," Caroline eventually said.

"Well, I'm taking the back roads. It's best that we're not seen together and I know several roads that are less used. The chances of us running into anybody will be more remote."

"But how shall we find the convent?"

"I know where Selly is, Miss Martin. I've been there."

"You've visited Selly?"

"No. . .but I. . .had to be in that part of the city to do some business and I wanted to check out the place and. . ."

"All of a sudden you have a conscience?"

"I suppose I deserved that."

"You most certainly did." Caroline paused. "What shall we tell someone if they see us together?"

"That there's been an emergency and that I'm. . .your. . . brother."

Caroline gasped then lowered her head.

"Well, you know, it's not that far from the truth, is it?"

She ignored him and remained silent.

They continued with only the clopping of the horse, and the occasional chirping of birds filling in the silence.

9

In the downstairs study after meeting with his client, Señor Mendez, Liam organized the receipts and contract and filed them away in his desk drawer. It was only through his shrewd handling of his Cuban customer that their company would continue to import the high quality cigars.

Unfortunately, David had consumed too much whiskey before the last meeting. When Señor Mendez had suggested an increase in price for his company's cigars and tobacco, David had told him to shove his cigars in an inappropriate place. Yes, the O'Donovan Trade and Merchant Company could possibly have gone out of business over that one incident since more than 20 percent of their imports came from their one Cuban client. Instead, Liam cajoled Señor Mendez, apologized in the most polite manner possible and even offered to waive the import fee. Thankfully, Señor Mendez not only agreed to allow the O'Donovan company to continue to import his tobacco plantation's goods, he graciously accepted a reduced increase.

Over the last hour or so, he could not seem to erase Caroline's disappointed expression from his mind. Liam could imagine what sort of discussion he would have to endure with Mr. Martin to convince him that it would be acceptable to marry Caroline if he had spent the whole afternoon driving her to and from the convent. Liam didn't want to say no to Caroline's request, but Caroline seemed to deal well with his refusal. That in itself illustrated what kind of obedient wife she would make. With a feeling of complacency, he shut the desk drawer and made his way upstairs.

* * *

"I'm letting you off here," said David. "The convent is down the street, last building on the right."

"I know where the convent is."

"I won't move from this spot." He assisted Caroline down onto the street and she rushed off without further words.

A gust of wind caused her hat to slip and her hand flew up to keep it on her head.

She reached the last house on the right, a brownstone with a horse tethered to the front hitching post and a young nun dressed in a brown habit standing next to it. Caroline could faintly hear dogs barking from behind the house and high-pitched moaning from the open upstairs window.

"Where is the girl who's laboring?" she asked the nun.

"Are you a relation?"

"She doesn't have any family. I am Selly's friend. She asked me to be present when her time came."

"In the bedroom upstairs, first door to the left, Miss."

She picked up her skirts and climbed the stairs quickly, taking two at a time. She heard a scream, then followed the guttural sounds.

Caroline knocked on the door. It was quickly opened by the Mother Superior, also in brown habit. She was a tall, imposing woman who seemed to take up the entire doorway.

"Miss Martin, please do come in."

Caroline took off her hat and lay it on the nearby desk. The middle-aged Mother Superior and an even older midwife were the only people in the room with Selly.

The nun leaned in close to Caroline. "Selly's having a dreadful time."

"This is too early," Caroline whispered to Mother Superior.

"I know, dear. Here, sit by her head." Caroline sat at a chair beside Selly's bed.

Selly's long black hair was wet and her face was drenched with sweat. "Selly, it's me, Caroline. I'm here."

The young servant's eyes were sunken but in a minute were wide as the next pain gripped her small body. Caroline quickly removed her gloves and spoke quietly into Selly's ear. "Hold on to my hand and squeeze as hard as you need to." Obeying the order, Selly squeezed Caroline's hand so hard, her nails dug into Caroline's palms. "Yes, that's good, Selly. You're doing a fine job. Your baby will be born soon."

Caroline glanced at the midwife who was whispering something to the nun. The midwife was a large woman, not so much tall but round, her salt and pepper hair pulled up. Sister then quietly said in Caroline's ear, "She thinks the baby is likely dead."

Caroline held Selly's hand as the girl endured another agonizing contraction. In between pains, Caroline wiped Selly's brow with a cool cloth. As each pain subsided, Selly gradually softened her grip.

After an hour or so, Caroline watched as the midwife again spoke with Mother Superior, and she studied both women to decipher what was being said. The midwife was shaking her head and the nun blessed herself.

Selly clung onto Caroline's hand and within minutes, pushed the child free of her body. Caroline watched the midwife smack the lifeless infant, which she could see was a girl, in an attempt to revive her.

Selly looked up, her eyelids heavy, and tried to smile. "Miss Caroline, I'm so glad you came," her voice just above a whisper.

"I told you I would."

Seconds turned into minutes as the midwife rubbed the baby, but after two or three moments, she looked up at Mother Superior and shook her head. "Born too soon," the midwife said.

"I don't feel so good." An ever increasing puddle of blood was seeping out from under Selly's bottom.

"Selly's bleeding!" the midwife yelled.

The midwife's round fists began to frantically knead Selly's abdomen, pushing. punching the servant's nearly flat stomach. "Come on, dearie," she urged. Selly's hand became limp in Caroline's grasp. Thinking that the girl had fainted, Caroline reached for a cloth and began wiping Selly's forehead. As she sponged her face, Caroline noticed that Selly seemed frightfully still. Moving closer to her head, she exclaimed, "She's not breathing. Please, please, help her!"

The midwife stepped back, then felt Selly's head and listened for her heartbeat. "Nothing can be done for her. I'm sorry, dear."

"No!" Caroline's head lowered. She began to sob quietly.

"There, there, dear. I am sorry for your loss," said Mother, her hand gently patting Caroline's shoulder. "She was so brave."

"Yes, she was."

"May I remain in here with her?" Caroline whispered as she wiped her cheeks and straightened.

"Certainly," said the midwife as she departed the room.

"Take all the time you need," Mother Superior offered. "I shall be sending someone for the priest, to give the poor girl Extreme Unction." Sister quietly closed the door.

Caroline dabbed her eyes with her handkerchief, then reached for the young girl's limp hand and held onto it, still wet with perspiration. She tenderly brushed back a lock of hair on the girl's forehead and caressed her damp head. Caroline released a long, mournful sigh. Ironically, a burst of sunlight lit the room in glorious color.

She hadn't noticed the surroundings before now, but as she glanced about at the white walls, it gave her comfort to see Selly in such a clean and bright room. The plain white linen sheet was devoid of lace or any sort of monogram. She glanced up at the wall above Selly's bed to find a simple wooden crucifix.

Caroline gently placed Selly's hand under the sheet and moved to the small desk. A piece of parchment was on top. The ink well was positioned to the top right of the paper and the quill pen, hastily cast aside, lay on top of the letter. Small droplets of ink like blood had dripped onto the page. Caroline picked up the paper.

"Mother Superior has asked me if I would like to stay here after the baby is born. She said that perhaps I can work in the kitchen."

Caroline lifted the first page from underneath.

Dear Miss Caroline,

She closed her eyes and sighed.

"I want to thank you so much for the kindness which you have shown me these past few months. When I received your letter, I was especially happy. You have treated me with the utmost respect as if I was someone special. I never before felt special. Thank you for that, Miss Caroline.

"And please don't go on about Mr. David. I don't know why he said the things he did to me, accusing me of being with some-one else, but despite that, my heart still aches for him. I can't help

it, but after everything that's happened, I still love him with all my heart. And isn't that the way love ought to be? Loving someone even when he is unkind to you is what it means to truly love him.

Caroline shook her head, then repeated the girl's last words, "Loving someone even when he's unkind to you is what it means to truly love him." She felt herself cringe as she thought of the reason Selly was in this predicament and why she was now dead. She folded the letter and placed it in the pocket of her skirt. Then, walking to the foot of the bed, she studied Selly once again. In death, she remained lovely, her eyelashes long. Her hair, though damp, was a vibrant shade of brown.

The young servant looked as if she were sleeping, the cover pulled up to her chin, yet traces of blood had seeped through the top sheet. For a moment, Caroline thought she might retch, but the feeling passed as her eyes caught sight of the bundle beside Selly's covered, motionless feet. Out of curiosity, she lifted the sheet and gasped when she noticed how small the baby was. The miniature girl's skin was gray and covered with a whitish coating. She lay on her side, curled up, like a tiny porcelain doll long ago discarded. Caroline caressed the baby's moist arm and was surprised to find it was warm. *Sleep well, little one.*

She glanced again at Selly's face, peaceful, yet beautiful in death. Had she not been so pretty, David would never have paid her any attention and she would never have found herself in this situation.

There was a knock, then Mother Superior opened the door. "Excuse me, Miss Martin."

"Yes?" Caroline responded.

"Do you need more time? The priest is here."

"No. I should be going." She straightened and turned toward the door. She nodded to the priest, who was dressed in a black cassock and carrying a small book and a crucifix.

She paused. "How much do I owe you, Mother?"

"Nothing, dear. We received a sizeable amount of money last week to cover her expenses. It may have been from the father of the baby."

"I see."

Mother Superior nodded. "Good day."

Caroline reached for her hat. She turned and stared, one last time, at the dead servant girl, the image now etched in her mind. This girl, who was younger than Caroline, was now gone.

*   *   *

Caroline stumbled onto the street and began to walk without making a conscious effort to put one foot in front of the other. She passed the area where David's carriage had been parked but did not stop.

"Miss Martin," she heard from behind her.

She stopped and turned around. She could see him motioning for her to come to the carriage. He was parked on the side of the street, the horse tethered to a small tree.

Caroline pressed her back against a lamp post, allowing it to bear the weight of her body and her heavy heart. Within minutes, David stood before her.

"What happened?"

Caroline stared straight ahead, her eyes unfocused.

He leaned close to her face. "Miss Martin, is everything all right?"

She shook her head, then looked into his eyes and said, "She's dead."

He gasped.

"Along with your baby daughter." She began to walk away, then felt his arm on her shoulder. She jerked away. "Don't touch me," she said through her teeth, her back facing him.

"I'll take you home."

"I am not going home with you."

"Miss Martin?"

"Leave me alone."

"Miss Martin, please. . ."

She spun around so quickly that David stepped back. "This...this is your fault. You killed her as sure as you put a gun to her head. She died delivering your child!" Impulsively, she began to beat his chest as he stood motionless. "No, no, no," she yelled, then she began to sob. He took hold of her gloveless hands and, studying them, his eyes widened. Soon, she could feel his arms begin to embrace her, but she pushed away from him.

"Leave me alone."

"Caroline," he whispered. "Come," he pulled her to the buggy.

Neither spoke for the duration of the ride. David pulled up to the end of the Martin house driveway.   "I know it will be dark soon, but it's best for you to walk the rest of the way, in case Ben or your uncle are home," he said, his voice a soft monotone.

He stepped out of the carriage to assist her. He took hold of her middle and lifted her out. She cringed as he touched her.

She started toward the house, then stopped as she heard the rustling of the parchment in her skirt pocket. Selly's last words. He ought to have the letter, to know what a kind girl Selly was, to know that he was responsible for her death.

"Wait," she called. David turned and walked toward her. Caroline lifted out the letter from her pocket.

"You should have this." She handed it to him, then turned and ran down the laneway.

Closer to the house, she heard Patsie's loud piercing voice, "Miss Caroline, ye be home! I jest can't be believin' ye be home so soon. Why, Himself isn't back yet."

Caroline avoided eye contact, her eyes filling with tears.

"Miss Caroline, what in all that's holy happened? Did ye get to the convent then?   Why sure an' that Mr. David didn't do naught to ye, did he? I was scared he might be after tryin' some'n."

Caroline finally brought her gaze up and shook her head.

"Ah, Miss, what is it that's ailin' ye, then? Ye can tell ole Patsie 'bout it now."

"She's dead. Selly is dead, and so is her baby."

"Oh, no, Miss Caroline, the poor colleen and the wee baby," she said, and pulled her to a close embrace. Caroline laid her head on Patsie's shoulder, and they both began to weep in earnest.

10

David, dressed in his night shirt, leaned on the window sill and watched the sun turn the bottom half of the sky into a deep array of red, orange and pink. It was a breathtaking summer sunset, the kind that he yearned for this time of year. Taking in the intense colors provided almost as much pleasure as bedding women. However, tonight he couldn't fully enjoy the beauty of the vibrant colors.

His dark paneled bedroom, the maple bed, dresser and corner gun cabinet contributed to the sullen mood.

David downed his glass of brandy, then opened Selly's letter and began reading. When he saw his name, he exhaled slowly.

"And please don't go on about Mr. David. I don't know why he said what he did to me, accusing me of being with someone else, but despite that, my heart still aches for him. I can't help it, but after everything that's happened, I still love him with all my heart. And isn't that the way love ought to be? Loving someone when he is unkind to you is what it means to truly love him.

He could almost hear her young voice as he read the words. Nostalgically, he remembered the first time he met Selly at the Martin house. At first, he had been overwhelmed with her natural beauty and obvious innocence. It didn't take long to charm his way into her heart and bed. After a while, however, she wasn't all that enticing anymore. For David, bedding a girl for the first few months, the awkwardness, his own expertise in allowing her to feel pleasure for the first time, made for the most entertaining and indulgent experiences.

"Mr. David, I must speak with you about an urgent matter."
"What is it, Selly? I'm leaving."
"I'm missing my monthly and I think I may be. . .with child."
"With child? Certainly not mine."
"Mr. David, I haven't been with anyone but you."

"How am I supposed to be sure that it was me who. . ."
"I love you, Mr. David."

He was certain that he was the only one, yet he began to think perhaps Selly had strayed from him and that's why she was pregnant. It was a ludicrous thought, to be sure, but he was careful, oftentimes withdrawing at the last moment. That was not very satisfying; in fact, it was frustrating. It was natural to think that she had perhaps been with someone else, wasn't it?

Why did he feel responsible? He did what he could to protect her, didn't he? He dismissed the guilt and immediately, he felt an overwhelming need for sexual release again. As usual, the most convenient choice would be Hallie. A longtime servant of the O'Donovan house, Hallie knew that she was never his first choice since she was older, but at this point David had no other alternative. There was a chance that she might refuse tonight, at least at first, since Jane, the household's servant in charge, had begun sharing an attic bedroom with her.

* * *

Afterwards, Hallie slept beside him, her caramel-colored arm draped across his chest. Strangely enough, he felt neither content nor drowsy. His need for pleasure, although it had just been fed, hungered for more. It never seemed to be satisfied.

"David, get up. Today, you're 16. Time to become a man."
"Where are we going?"
"You'll see. Just get dressed and come with me."
In the carriage, David's father said little of their destination, just that this was Jack's surprise gift and that now David would be a "man."
They arrived in the center of Philadelphia on a street in which few, if any, people strolled about.
"Who are we visiting?" David asked, still unsure of what would happen.
"Pretty girls, son, pretty girls."
When they got out of the buggy, David's mouth opened at the wonder of the City late at night. The moonlight was bright and the lampposts trembled with the gas lights. He could see the

majestic Cathedral's dome off to the left and the moon illuminating the church's gold cross at the top. A few carriages and a wagon were hurrying in the night, the horses' clopping sound seeming out of place with the otherwise quiet evening.

"Come with me." David followed his father as they walked down a long alleyway and up several marble steps. David, now nearly as tall, noticed that his father wore a wide grin and had his eyes focused on the grand entrance of the house just ahead.

"Ring the door bell," his father said.

David turned the bell just below the draped window. The door swung open immediately. In front of him stood a young woman, probably five years or so older, with a red satin gown, her breasts pushed up and spilling over the top of it. She had blonde hair and a face of red cheeks and lips. Although she was somewhat shorter than David, she seemed larger than life. David stepped back.

"Well, hello, Sweetie. Your Father told us you were coming. I'm the lucky one who gets you tonight."

"Gets me?" David asked, then he glanced at Jack. His father winked at him.

She pulled him inside the lavishly decorated foyer. Just behind the girl was a grand staircase similar to the one at home.

"Come with me." He glanced at his father whose smirk seemed permanently fixed to his face. Jack handed some coins to another garishly dressed woman and, although he couldn't hear much of what was said, David got the impression that his father knew her and was bantering with her.

Once inside the girl's room, David stared in awe at the mirrors on the ceiling, then his eyes became fixed on the ornately designed four poster bed. He could sense the girl behind him but was almost afraid to turn around. Within seconds, he could hear her clothes rustling. He felt her hands on his shoulders lifting his coat off. Now, he was trembling so much that when he tried to help her remove his coat, he accidentally scratched her arm. He fumbled his way through the rest of the experience which seemed over before it had really begun. The physical pleasure had been so intense that he knew, hoped, that he would return. As he was lying beside the girl, he wondered whether they might be able to do it again or did his father only pay for one time?

Where was Jack? David imagined that he was indulging in the same pleasures.

Those women taught David many lessons. For one, he learned that he's more likely to pick up maladies from them. So he began to coax local servant girls to fill his needs on a weekly, if not daily, basis. Not only was it safer, it was cheaper.

Despite that experience, those "ladies of pleasure" had taught him what a girl likes. Knowledge of that sort came in handy when you wanted to bed her more than once.

Liam often said, "You're just like Father." As much as David had denied it, he was living his father's life.

He thought again of Selly, her stomach just beginning to swell with his child, and who was now dead. She was a sweet girl who loved him. He didn't protect her at all. Miss Martin was right. He killed her, and her innocence, as sure as he put a gun to her head.

David could feel Hallie's even breathing and her soft hair as she lay her head against his chest. Was this the sort of life he wanted to lead? Did he want to end up like his father with prostitutes who stood in line to have him as a customer? Did he want to end his life in a drunken stupor?

He kissed the top of Hallie's head and inhaled her sweet scented hair. She roused. "Mr. David, you know how to make a girl tired." She stroked his face, then his chest. He immediately felt his attraction rise again. He shouldn't give in to the urge and yet he had to possess her, one more time tonight, to make him forget that Selly was dead and that he couldn't stop himself or the life he seemed destined to lead.

11

The next morning, Caroline cried softly into her pillow. She couldn't fall asleep last night thinking of Selly and her baby. *She was so frightened. And there was so much blood. All of that because she gave herself to David. It's so unfair.*

"Miss Caroline, y'in there?"

Caroline opened the door. "Yes, Patsie, what is it?"

"Ye be all right, Miss?"

"I suppose I will be. I still can't believe Selly is dead."

"Sure an' that be sad," the servant said, lowering her head.

"What did you want, Patsie?"

"Mr. Liam's here fer ye then."

"He is?"

"Yes, he's in the office with Himself. Sure an' I think. . ."

"What, Patsie?"

". . .he'll be askin' fer yer hand in marriage."

Caroline gasped. "My hand in marriage?"

"Well, Miss Caroline. Sure an' the way he looks at ye, I'm thinkin' them eyes o'his, surely they be in love."

"Really, Patsie? If he's so in love, why didn't he take me to be with Selly?"

"Why sure, 'cause he's a proper, respectin' gent, Miss Caroline. I was just hearin' him say some'n about marriage. Come ahead downstairs and be hearin' fer yerself."

"I don't know about that."

"Sure now. Come along then." Patsie took Caroline by the arm and they started down the hallway. The servant continued speaking.

"Ye know, Miss, every one of us, we be knowin' that look. Why sure, Mr. David now, he don't ever have that look, not like Mr. Liam does fer ye. Sure an' Mr. Liam's the good one o' that family and he be after wearin' his heart on his sleeve, that one does." Patsie leaned in close to Caroline's ear and whispered. "Sure ye know then, that a proper respectin' man would niver have taken ye ta Chelten'm 'lone."

If Caroline were to be honest with herself, she was in no mood for marriage talk. However, she followed Patsie to the door to Uncle's study. Caroline could hear muffled voices inside.

"What're ye be tellin' 'im, Miss?"

"I don't know, Patsie."

"Now, now, Miss Caroline, ye be deservin' some happiness fer yerself then, after losing yer Da and all. Sure an' he's a foin young man, an who'll be after makin' ye very, very happy." Patsie hesitated. "If ye be puttin' yer ear close to the door, ye be hearin' everythin' jest foin."

"I don't know, Patsie."

"Go on, Miss Caroline. Sure an' ye jest lean in a wee bit and rest yer ear ta the door."

Caroline hesitated and the door suddenly opened and Caroline gasped, then stepped back, an obvious flush coming to her face.

"My dear, have you been listening to our discussion?"

Her mouth open, Caroline glanced at Liam and he was chuckling under his breath. As she searched his face for some help, he winked at her and replied, "I'm certain that Caroline would not be listening in on our conversation, Mr. Martin." He was grinning.

"Liam would like to discuss something with you, my dear."

"Caroline, would you be so kind as to accompany me on a stroll outside? It is, after all, a beautiful day." He offered her his arm.

"Of course."

Caroline took hold of Liam's arm. His pace was brisk . "Just one moment, Liam. You're walking too fast."

"I am?"

"Yes, you are."

He slowed down as they strolled to the group of maples in front of the Martin mansion. Liam studied Caroline's face. "Caroline, have you been crying?"

Caroline nodded and her tone became somber. "You know that servant girl, Selly, the one who was at the convent in Cheltenham?"

"Yes."

"Well, we received word that she passed away."

Liam's eyes widened and his head lowered. "I'm sorry."

"That's why I was crying."

"Well, I'm sorry I couldn't take you to be with her. But you do understand why, don't you?"

"I suppose," she said flatly. "So what did you wish to speak with me about?"

"Well, perhaps it could wait until you're feeling better."

"No, no, it's fine."

He paused a moment, then asked, "Did you know what I wanted to ask you?"

"Well, Patsie listened in and told me what you had said."

"Ah." He raised his eyebrows, then his face took on a serious expression. He pulled a ring from his pocket, knelt on one knee and said, "I love you, Caroline, and it would be a great honor if you would agree to be my wife."

"Liam, I don't know what to say."

"Say you'll marry me and that you would be my wife."

"Well, I. . ."

Liam stepped back and raised his eyebrows. When he finally made eye contact, she swallowed once but said nothing.

"What, Caroline?" Liam's face took on a worried expression.

"Yes, of course, I would be most happy to marry you."

He exhaled and closed his eyes. "I had the fleeting notion that you were going to say no because I wouldn't take you to be with that servant girl."

He took hold of her hand and led her around to the far side of one of the trees to allow the trunk to block their view from Patsie, who was standing on the porch. He placed a soft, gentle kiss on her forehead and pulled her to an embrace.

"Your uncle was reminding me that a young lady should never be alone with a young man before they're married."

Caroline pulled away. "What about a young girl who promised to help a servant since the man who made her with child wouldn't?"

"Look, you don't have to tell *me* about David. When it comes to women, he treats them very badly." He paused. "But I don't regret not taking you to be with that servant girl, Caroline. I'm saddened that she died, but it was the right decision."

"The right decision for whom, Liam? For you? Do you think

it was the right decision for that poor girl?"

"Whether you were there or not, she would have died. You couldn't have saved her life."

"But I should have been there for her, like I promised."

He let out an exasperated sigh. "Caroline," he said softly, "do you think that your uncle would have given his permission for your hand in marriage if we had spent the entire afternoon alone?"

"I trust you and I know that nothing would have happened."

"Of course nothing would have happened, but just the idea that we spent the afternoon alone. Well, it's scandalous."

He pulled her again to his chest. "I'm sorry. I know that you wanted to be with her, but we can't change what has happened."

"No," she answered, "I suppose we can't."

12

A month later, Uncle Edward assisted Caroline as she stepped out of the carriage in front of their mansion. She noticed the small O'Donovan buggy and a horse tethered to the front hitching post.

"Mr. Edward," the black servant called.

"Yes, Ben?"

"Mr. O'Donovan's in your office."

"Is Liam here, Ben?" Caroline asked.

"No, Miss. It's Mr. David."

Caroline stepped back. She hadn't seen David in over a month, and for that she was grateful. In a few months, she would be his sister-in-law and, of necessity, have to live under the same roof. Caroline was dreading that particular aspect of her marriage with Liam.

"Ben, would you take the buggy to the stable?"

"Yes, sir."

"Excuse me, Caroline."

Uncle Edward went inside while Caroline remained at the front of the house. She had no desire to see David today, or any day, for that matter. She decided to take a stroll in the woods. By the time she returned, she hoped that David would be gone.

Fifteen minutes later, she emerged from the forest, refreshed. She groaned when she saw David's carriage was still there. She sighed, then went toward the front of the house. Perhaps if she quickly made her way to her room, she might avoid him.

In the foyer, Patsie was on her hands and knees, scrubbing the floor by the staircase.

"Good afternoon ta ye, Miss Caroline. Were ye after enjoyin' t'exhibition t'day? Were there a lot of folks 'bout?"

"It wasn't as crowded as the first day we went, which made it all the more enjoyable."

She started up the steps, then heard voices behind her. She thought about rushing up the stairs, then she reconsidered.

"It's quite a good deal, sir, and one that I think you should feel comfortable investing in." David's tone sounded uncharacteristically serious.

"I'm not sure, David. The last time I invested in a project you recommended, I lost a pile of money."

"This is almost a sure thing."

"What does your brother think?"

"He's cautious. Then again, you know my brother."

"Allow me to think about it."

"Of course, Mr. Martin. Good day," she heard David say.

Caroline cringed as she heard the door shut, then he said, "Miss Martin?"

She slowly turned and glared at him as she stood above him on the stairs.

"To what do I owe this great pleasure, my dear future sister-in-law Caroline? May I call you Caroline? After all, we will be related in but a few months." She stared at him with no hint of a smile on her face.

"Did my brother tell you that it is essential for a happy marriage that you at least act civilly to your brother-in-law?"

"Future brother-in-law. We're not related yet."

He leaned close to her and whispered, "Besides, I did you a huge favor just a month ago, if you'll recall."

"A favor for me?" she almost yelled.

Patsie shouted from across the room, "Miss Caroline?" She was putting her finger to her mouth and pointing toward Uncle's study.

"And," he whispered, "we have not yet spoken of the reason your hands are so callused, have we?"

Caroline's eyes widened as she remembered him looking at her bare hands when he brought her home the night Selly died. "I have nothing to say to you."

"Could it be that perhaps you were not born in wealth? Or maybe despite your wealth, you're an equestrian who forgets her riding gloves?"

She regarded him bitterly.

"Ah." He leaned close and again whispered, "My guess is that you were not born in wealth. Well, not to worry." He winked. "Your secret is safe with me. I have not as yet told my brother of your, shall we say, humble beginnings."

"You. . ." Caroline tried to think of some distasteful name she could call him, but in her anger no name seemed insulting enough.

"Now, Miss Martin, why do I get the distinct feeling that you don't like me?"

"Because I don't.   Now, if you will excuse me, Mr. O'Donovan."

"Come now. Can't we be less formal? Please do call me David."

"Good day, Mr. O'Donovan," she   said, drawing out the 'O'Donovan.'

Caroline brushed past him. She followed Patsie along the right side of the staircase and through the doorway down to the kitchen.

"Sure an' ye don't be likin' Mr. David, do ye, Miss Caroline?"

"I certainly don't hide my emotions, do I, Patsie?" Caroline laughed.

"Sure an' ye be tellin' the truth there, now," Patsie let out a loud belly laugh and moved beside Caroline. "Tch. Where has that Missy got ta now? She's bein' gone ten minutes ta fetch me eggs. Where'd she go for 'em? New Jersey?"

"I would be happy to go to the chicken coop and get her."

"I'll be thankin' ye, but no, Miss Caroline. I'll be goin' out ta get her," Patsie said, then gasped when she saw smoke coming from the oven. She rushed across the kitchen. She swung open the oven and removed the muffin tins.

"Oh, the divil take 'em. Beg pardon, Miss Caroline. They be charred now and no good fer naught but the dust bin. I'll be havin' ta make 'nother batch." Patsie put her hands to her ample hips and stared at the tins.

"I'm certain they will be fine, Patsie. They don't look burnt."

"Sure an' now Himself don't be likin' cornbread muffins overcooked. I'll jest be havin' ta make a new batch, but I'll be needin' them eggs now."

"Allow me to get Missy, Patsie."

"Sure an' I'd 'ppreciate that, Miss Caroline. She'd be in the newer coop, Miss, not the one that be near the stable. That one's not after bein' used no more."

"Yes, of course, Patsie."

Walking outside, Caroline passed by the newer henhouse to the left and heard some chickens clucking but when she peered inside, no one was there. Noises to the right beyond the stable caused her to glance in the direction of the smaller, older henhouse. Didn't Patsie tell her that one was no longer used?

As she walked closer, she heard an unfamiliar noise. It sounded like someone was moaning, perhaps stifling a cry for help. *Who is hurt?*

She hurried to the small open window of the henhouse. Leaning down, she stared at the spectacle before her, then quietly gasped. She stood still, paralyzed for the moment. Inside, David stopped moving, and lifted his head to listen. Caroline stepped back and around to the side of the small house. She held the palm of her hand to her chest to quiet the pounding of her heart.

"Mr. David," she heard Missy say, "I heard someone out there."

"It's fine," David whispered.

Caroline returned in haste to the kitchen, breathing heavily, hands trembling. When Patsie noticed her crimson face, she asked, "Whatever's happen'd? What's the matter with ye? Ye be lookin' like ye seen a. . ."

Caroline remained still, her eyes downcast. "In the older henhouse. . ." she whispered.

"What 'bout then, Miss Caroline?"

"Missy, David. . ."

"Oh, heaven preserve me! Was that there Mr. David with Missy? Oh, no, and Patsie sent ye out back to. . ."

"He was. . .they were. . ."

"He's jest after doin' what comes naturally t'im, me lamb."

"What are you talking about?"

"Sure an' ye know. . .well that there's jest. . .they was after doin'. . .that's, ye know, what married people do."

"Oh." She began wringing her hands. "I feel stupid, Patsie."

"Now then, Miss Caroline, don't ye be thinkin' ye are 'cause y'ain't. Ye be innocent like. That's a much different thing."

"How can he be doing that again after what happened to Selly?"

"Some men, Miss Caroline, they jest be after havin' no thought t'all that it's wrong. Ta them, it be jest 'nother itch ta scratch. Most o' these colleens'll be after knowin' that. Selly was diff'rent. She was young and believin' Mr. David loved her. I was tellin' her all the time he didn't, but she wouldn't be listenin'."

"Patsie?" Missy rushed into the kitchen. "I'm so sorry I took so long with the eggs. Here they are." Missy, her olive skin flushed and sweating, her long dark hair pulled back with a few strands hanging down, placed the basket of eggs on the table and was buttoning up the top of her dress. "Miss Caroline, good afternoon."

Caroline awkwardly kept her eyes focused on the floor. "Good afternoon, Missy." She avoided eye contact and awkwardly remained in the kitchen for a few moments as Patsie and Missy began to prepare the evening meal.

She walked upstairs to the front hall. She heard muffled voices out front and wondered if Uncle had come out of his office.

Stepping onto the porch, Caroline could see David unhitching his horse. She glanced at him and he winked at her. She immediately turned away.

"My dear future sister-in-law, wait. I must speak with you."

"I have nothing to say to you," she said, lowering her head.

He quickly came onto the front veranda, then whispered, "I've been told that if one applies butter to callused hands, it will soften the rough spots."

"Leave me alone."

He stopped and leaned close to her ear. "So what did you think of my. . .what shall we call it? Exhibition in the henhouse?" Caroline gasped and her face reddened. She tried to walk away, but David grabbed her arm. She yanked it away, but he reached for her again and held on firmly. "Now, now, please."

"Let go of me or. . ." she looked him right in the eye. "Or I swear I will kick you so hard down there, you shall be limping for days," she spat at him.

His eyes widened, he dropped her arm, then he bellowed a hearty laugh. "Now, I didn't just hear that out of the mouth of a proper young lady. Oh, right, you're not really a proper young lady, are you, Miss Martin?" He winked.

She glared at him. "And if you don't think I'll do it. . ."

"Oh, no, no, no. I think you'll do it." He stepped back.

Caroline faced him squarely and shot him a scorching look.

His expression was one of amusement. "Miss Martin, you

certainly are a spirited young lady," he laughed.

Caroline gritted her teeth, then lowered her head.

"Excuse me, David, Caroline, I heard loud voices. Is anything wrong?" Uncle Edward asked from the doorway. Both glanced in the older man's direction, with Caroline lifting her head and David attempting to take on a serious expression.

"No, sir, there's. . .there's nothing wrong. Your niece and I were having a disagreement about. . .animal behavior."

"Caroline?" Uncle Edward asked.

"It's fine, Uncle." She turned around and glared at David, then released a long and audible sigh.   "Good day, Mr. O'Donovan," she said, then she hurried into the safety of the Martin household.

*   *   *

David fixed a smile on his face as he rode away from the Martin residence. His insatiable appetite had been fed by the servant's luscious body. And he, and Missy, had been right. They had heard footsteps outside the henhouse. Knowing that someone might be watching, and he was hoping that it had been Miss Martin, made the experience all the more exciting.

Of course, when he noticed her trying to avoid him, he knew without a doubt she had seen them. Ben or Patsie would have recognized their moans and avoided the area. Of course, Mr. Martin almost never poked his head outside his office during the day. That would have been a disaster, as Missy would likely lose her job and he and Liam could possibly lose his business.

A grinding, gnawing feeling in his stomach rose up and wiped the happy expression off his face. She had just seen part of him unclothed and she hadn't yet seen Liam in that way. David counted on her not saying a word to Liam. Of course, for modesty's sake, she would be too embarrassed, he was sure of that. However, if Liam ever did find out, he would be furious.

So why was there a gnawing feeling at the pit of his stomach? Caroline Martin was a beautiful girl, and of course, his brother's betrothed, but she had a lot of spirit in her, liveliness which at times seemed to contradict her innocence. No, he couldn't think of any other young lady, upper or lower class, who allowed herself to speak so freely. It was obvious that Miss Martin had scant experience in the finer points of polite society. And, for that, he was grateful.

He dismissed the feeling and smiled again. David found himself thinking of ways that he could interact with her. And, contrary to what Miss Martin was feeling at this moment, he greatly looked forward to her upcoming marriage to his brother. Bantering with her was more entertaining than watching saloon girls dance. He laughed out loud at her comment about kicking him. *Oh, Miss Martin, any time, any time.*

13

The late October afternoon air was warm. Caroline decided to take advantage of the weather and read outside. She settled beneath the maple tree, using the trunk to steady her back. She had been reading, for the second time, the book "Emma" which Liam had given her some months before. However, she was too distracted and closed the book. She began to make a mental list of what needed to be accomplished before her wedding to Liam next week. *Final gown fitting, Friday at two p.m.*

She and Liam would begin their new life together, welcome children and, similar to the stories in most of the books she had read, they would live happily ever after.

The clopping sounds of a horse and carriage drew her attention to the laneway. She recognized the smaller O'Donovan carriage and Liam in the driver's seat.

Liam wasn't scheduled to come for a visit until tomorrow. He had told her that he had business to attend to in Cheltenham.

She picked up her skirts and hurried toward the carriage which had stopped in front of the house. She slowed her pace when she noticed that Liam had not yet emerged. From her vantage point, it appeared as if he was waiting. Without seeing his face, Caroline sensed that something was wrong. Liam almost always drove the buggy or his horse around to the stable. Coming closer, Caroline could see that Liam's head was lowered.

As he heard her footsteps, he finally looked up. Liam said nothing, but his expression seemed sad, disappointed. The way his eyes peered at her, she knew that whatever was bothering him had to do with her.

"Liam, what's wrong? Did someone die?"

He silently shook his head. He stepped down from the carriage and wound the horses' reins around the front hitching post. His movements were measured and it took a long time to accomplish a task which should have taken a few seconds.

He finally stood tall and silent before her.

Still holding onto her book, she blurted out, "Look, I'm reading the book you gave me. It's quite good, a wonderful story. It's . . ."

He nodded, his expression somber, his eyes avoiding hers.

She took him by the hand and led him to the porch and sat down on the steps, pulling him down to sit next to her. He resisted and withdrew his hand.

"I should rather stand," he said flatly.

Caroline immediately stood up as well, leaving her book on the top porch step.

"What's wrong? We are to be married next week."

"Well, that may well be under discussion." His tone seemed uncharacteristically sardonic.

"Under discussion? Whatever do you mean?"

"I just returned from Cheltenham where I met with a client of mine, Mr. Olson, who does chores at the convent there."

Caroline imagined the color must have drained from her face. *He knows about the trip to the convent.*

"You were there with the servant girl after I told you I would not take you."

She gasped; her throat closed like a rosebud. What could she say? Her husband-to-be just caught her in a lie and now he was about to break off his commitment to marry her.

"You have nothing to say?"

"I made a promise, Liam, and I. . ."

"What about me? There were prudent reasons for not taking you, reasons that were sound and for your safety."

"I realized that no one would take me and so I began to walk. Patsie was trying to convince me not to walk, and that it would be dangerous. But I'm rather stubborn."

She stopped and studied his face. He was not smiling. In fact, there was a hint of a frown. "Go on," he said.

"I kept walking and. . . someone stopped and asked where I was going and agreed to take me."

"Someone? Did you know this person?"

"I cannot tell you that because he did me a favor and I was able to be with Selly when she died."

"He? A man took you?"

"Nothing happened. Can you not trust me?"

"How can I trust you after I've found out you've lied to me?"

"I'm not lying now. And I don't want this person to. . ."

"Caroline, he could have. . . I don't even want to think about it."

"I told you. Nothing happened."

"Nothing happened? You're out cavorting with some other man and. . ." Liam was now raising his voice.

"We weren't cavorting. He was just driving me to. . ."

"Stop." Liam exhaled as if he had been holding his breath the entire time. He turned his back on her and walked ten feet away, close to the horse. He remained quiet for several long moments.

Caroline wanted to cry, but she knew that she couldn't do that right now. She wished that he would say what he had come to say, break the commitment, cancel the wedding, and leave so that she could go to her bedroom and release her tears.

She had never regretted being with Selly. She knew that David wouldn't tell anyone and she was sure that Patsie wouldn't reveal their secret. It never occurred to her that perhaps someone might have seen her there and mention it to Liam.

He continued to stand beside the horse, in silence, his shoulders squared. Although he was only ten feet away, he seemed unreachable.

"Miss Caroline, I. . ." Patsie stopped as she stepped onto the porch and saw Caroline's face and Liam, his back to them, standing near the horse. She tiptoed down the steps and whispered into Caroline's ear, "Mr. Liam, is he bein' upset 'bout some'n?"

Caroline waved her hand to indicate to Patsie to go back into the house, but the servant remained beside her. Caroline mouthed, "Go on." Patsie shook her head, but the older woman eventually did what she was told.

Caroline studied Liam's back, his shoulders slumped. *What is he thinking?* She anxiously rubbed her hands and shifted from one foot to the other. She wanted to shout at him, "Just tell me that you're calling off the wedding, just be done with it."

He finally turned around and walked up close to her. Despite his disappointment and pain, his eyes regarded her with affection.

"I don't want to break off our engagement."

Caroline closed her eyes and exhaled.

He placed his hands on her shoulders and pulled her to a close embrace. She responded by hugging him tightly. "Liam, thank God. I love you and I don't want to break off our engagement because of. . ." Now she couldn't even say it.

"But you need to promise me right now that you'll never, ever lie to me again."

For a few seconds, Caroline was silent, her head lowered.

"Caroline?"

"Before I promise that, I ought to tell you that I'm not the person you think I am."

"What?"

"I. . .was not. . .born wealthy."

Liam closed his eyes, then he regarded her with a slight smile. "Your uncle has already told me about that. You are from wealth presently, are you not? And even if you weren't, I would not care about that. What is important to me now is that you will never, ever lie to me again. Will you promise me that?"

"Yes, Liam, I promise that I shall never lie to you again, ever."

"No matter what the consequences?"

"Of course. I shall never, ever lie to you, Liam, never. Please believe me."

"I do, Caroline. And will you promise. . ."

"What?"

"That you will herein always obey me."

She blurted out, "Yes, yes, of course."

"If you cannot trust that I know what is best for you, then you ought not to be marrying me."

With that, he kissed her forehead and broke away from her. He untied the reins and got into the carriage. He paused before tipping his hat and forcing a smile. She waved until he was out of sight.

"Sure an' ye know, I told ye there'd be trouble, Miss Caroline," she could hear Patsie say as she stepped onto the porch.

"I told you to go inside, Patsie."

"Ye'd better be after thankin' the good Lord fer that one, Miss."

14

One week later, Liam lifted out the cigar box from the top drawer of his desk. It was the only possession he owned of his father's that did not have negative memories attached to it. Jack offered him the container years ago after he had finished using the box. As a boy, Liam used it to store his marbles. Now, he kept items in here that served to remind him of the important events in his life.

On top, and probably the best memory in the box, was the admission ticket to the Centennial Exhibition.

He carefully unwrapped the brown paper covering his father's gold pocket watch. Despite a thorough cleaning, the piece still reeked of smoke. His father had worn it on the night he died in the fire.

Liam held onto the watch, the metal casing cold in his hand. It really was an exquisite looking timepiece. He found himself wincing as he studied the thick gold chain. Liam still carried scars on his legs from the marks the chain made when Jack had used it to reprimand him. He exhaled, and with one swift motion, ripped it from the timepiece, then wrapped up the watch and placed it inside the box. He dropped the chain in the trash can next to his desk.

He picked up the envelope. The coins inside were a cruel reminder that saying no to Jack was the worst offense.

"Get up, son. It's your 16th birthday. Time to get dressed. Time to become a man." His father lit the oil lamp next to the bed. *"Wake up, I've got a present for you."*

Liam had gone to bed a few hours earlier, but roused enough to say, "Father? A present? It's not my birthday until tomorrow." Liam sat up in bed and ran his fingers through his hair. He had dreaded his 16th birthday since David shared his experience two years ago. Thinking that he would have one more night before having to confront Jack, he was caught off guard and unprepared.

"It's tomorrow, Liam. After midnight. Get up. Get dressed. I've got a surprise for you in town." Although his father was several feet away, his whiskey breath burned Liam's face and he turned away.

Liam remained in his bed and made no attempt to remove the covers or get up. He kept his gaze downward.

"Liam, I don't have all night."

"I'm. . .I'm not getting dressed."

"Yes, you are, now get up, before we wake the entire house."

"I'm not going with you, Father." He said it quickly before his courage faded.

"You have no idea what you're talking about. I'm giving you something which will make you a real man."

"I'm not going. . .to the. . .whorehouse. . .with you, Father." Liam's voice was trembling.

Jack O'Donovan stepped back. "And who told you I was taking you there?" he roared.

Liam remained silent. There was no need to get David in trouble too.

His father reached out and slapped the side of his head. Liam winced.

"What? Are you a pansy?"

"No. I. . ."

Jack O'Donovan began to yell at the top of his lungs. "You ingrate! You damned pansy! I offer to give you a gift and you refuse? Do you think you're better than your father?" He stopped. Liam wouldn't look at him, but he could hear the heavy breathing then a deep sigh. "I only have one son from now on. You're nothing to me anymore. Do you hear me? Nothing!"

His father stomped out of the room, his feet dropping like anvils on the floor.

Liam's heart was thundering in his chest. He had had two long years to think about how he would tell his father that he would not be accepting his gift and that he would refuse to go. How could he share with his father that the idea of being naked with an unknown made-up woman repulsed him, that he didn't want to pick up diseases from these women? How could he tell him that he only wished to do that with his wife someday?

His bedroom door swung open again and Liam gasped. His father stood quietly in the doorway, his shadowy figure black and foreboding. Liam said nothing, but his heart continued to pound.

All of a sudden, Jack threw something in the room, then slammed the door again. The small white envelope landed with a quiet smack on the floor beside his bed.

He slipped out of bed and picked it up. Inside was a note, scrawled in his father's handwriting, bold and heavy on the paper, "When you decide to become a MAN, here are the coins I was going to give you to do so. Happy Birthday".

His hands were shaking as he put the note and coins back inside the envelope.

Liam placed the envelope back into the cigar box and exhaled with relief. A man? His father had no idea what it meant to be a real man. Caroline would never need to worry about her husband's drinking too much or his unfaithfulness. And although he was more than disappointed that Caroline had lied to him, he believed her when she said that she would never be dishonest or disobey him again.

In the carriage on the way to the church, David shoved his brother's arm.

"You nervous, Lee?"

"Yes, I'm nervous. Who wouldn't be on their wedding day?"

"I don't think I would be, if it were Caroline Martin I was about to wed. A fine young lady you've found."

David leaned across the seat and straightened his brother's collar and tie. "There, that looks better."

"Since when do you care about appearance?"

"Since my brother is getting married and he does." David paused, then spoke again. "Mother would have loved Caroline."

"I know." He stared at his brother, then asked, "You do have the ring, right?"

"Yes, Lee, I've got the. . ." David stopped, then opened his jacket and checked his inside breast pocket. "Lee. . ."

"Please don't tell me that you forgot the ring."

"Oh, here it is," he said as he pulled it out.

At the church, they stepped out of the carriage. Liam and David walked quickly around to the side, then rear of the church. As they approached the back door, David whispered, "I'll be right there, Lee." Liam frowned, then watched his brother walk across the street toward the general store.

Liam knocked on the church's back door. The preacher opened it and greeted Liam.

"Right this way, Mr. O'Donovan. Miss Martin and her family have not arrived as yet."

He nodded and followed the man to a small room. "You can wait here until I call you for the ceremony."

"Thank you."

Liam peered out the open window at the back yard area of the Episcopalian Church. Autumn was a beautiful season to be married. In the distance, the crisp orange and red maples dotted the landscape like blossoming flowers.

Liam began to wring his hands, then started to pace back and forth. He wondered if Caroline was just as nervous or whether she was handling the stress of their wedding day with ease. Liam thought ahead to this evening's intimacy and immediately he was concerned for Caroline. Had anyone told her what to expect tonight? Being raised by only a father would suggest that this could possibly be an awkward situation. Despite that, Liam looked forward to the night ahead and resolved to get the whole ordeal over as quickly as possible for his new wife.

David came through the door and checked his pocket watch. "The Martins aren't here yet. I'll let you know when they ride up."

* * *

"Carrie, you look lovely. Are you nervous?" Elizabeth asked as Caroline surveyed herself in the vanity mirror in her bedroom.

"Yes, I am. Uncle has invited so many people."

She stole a glance in the mirror and stepped back. Generally speaking, she didn't like wearing her hair up, but today, it looked graceful and it made her look mature. She was especially pleased with her gown, an all lace-tapered bodice, a silk skirt and ten foot train. *Yes, Liam, I think you will be quite satisfied with your bride today.*

"Ye better be speedin' things up, me girl, sure an' the buggy be ready to take ye ta church an' all. It's good that it be yer own weddin' 'cause ye could be missin' the whole affair. . .ye be late 'nuff already. Sure an' Himself be ready and waitin'."

"Yes, Patsie, I'm almost finished."

"Miss 'Lizabeth, would ye be lettin' yer father know about the buggy, now?"

Although Elizabeth remained silent, her expression said, 'Isn't that what servants are for?'

"That would be so helpful, Lizzie, thank you."

Her cousin sighed loudly and left the room.

Patsie finished buttoning up the back of Caroline's dress. "I was wantin' to talk to ye, me girl, 'bout bein' married an all."

"Yes, Patsie, what is it?"

"Well, I be knowin' that ye were after seein' what it is that married folk'll be doin'." She hesitated.

"To be honest, I'm trying to remove that image from my mind. It was a most unpleasant sight." Caroline had decided not to ever share with Liam that she had seen his brother and a servant girl in the henhouse that day.

"Well, ye have a mind then what I be sayin' 'bout that bein' what married folk do?"

Caroline nodded.

"Sure then, ye bein' a poor orphan, and no Ma ta be talkin' ta ye 'bout these. . . ah, matters."

"Yes, Patsie?"

"Well, sure an' ye know, ye bein' pure an all and niver bein' touched by no man. . ."

Caroline leaned closer towards Patsie's pudgy face. The older servant was biting on her bottom lip.

"Well, ye know, then, the first time it be happenin' to a young colleen. . .well now. . .it's bein' a bit. . .well then. . . what I'm after sayin' is. . .'tis awkward, that is, for a young colleen."

"Awkward?"

"Sure an' it is that, me lamb. But 'tis a wife's duty, that is, the marriage bed. It's after bein' some'n that us women must endure."

"I see." *Why did Selly and Missy keep going back to David?*

Patsie continued. "But I'm right sure, that I am, that Mr. Liam'll be gentle with ye."

Caroline regarded Patsie with an affectionate glance. "Thank you, Patsie."

"Ye be lookin' so beautiful, Miss Caroline." Patsie caressed the side of her face. "I'm thinkin' I'll not be likin' the thought of ye livin' next door. Sure an' ye've made this place a joy to be workin' in. Ye be havin' a good heart, what's filled with much kindness. And ye be right spirited too. Been lookin' forward to ev'ry day."

"I shall only be next door, Patsie."

Patsie's eyes were moist. "Sure an' ye mights well be 'cross town. I'm after bein' glad my Jane'll be with ye. She's a good worker, my daughter."

"Now, now, I'll visit soon."

Patsie left the room. The older servant's comments had been kind. However, it was seeing what supposedly happened between a husband and wife that frightened her the most. She was decidedly nervous thinking ahead to what this evening would bring. The only conversation she had about the subject was with her father when she was 14.

"And Onan knew that the seed should not be his; and it came to pass, when he went in unto his brother's wife, that he spilled it on the ground, lest that he should give seed to his brother. And the thing that he did displeased the Lord; wherefore he slew him also."

"Papa, what did he spill?"

Andrew Martin paused before answering, then shifted awkwardly in his bed. "Well, Carrie, I. . ."

"Did he spill his seed?"

"Well, dear. . .you see. . ."

"Where does a man keep his seed. . .and does this have to do with a man and woman getting married?"

"Well. . ."

"All I know, Papa, is that whatever it means, it greatly displeased the Lord and the Lord killed him for it. It sounds pretty serious."

"Well, yes, dear, it is."

Andrew Martin began coughing and Caroline, distracted, began pounding his back.

Caroline wiped her eyes. Although this was supposed to be the happiest day of her life, it was bittersweet, for her beloved father would not be walking her down the aisle. She loved Uncle Edward, but wished that her father had lived long enough to give her away.

*   *   *

Caroline and her uncle waited at the rear of the church. The organist began to play "Jesu, Joy of Man's Desiring."

"Well, my dear, are you ready?" he whispered.

"Yes, Uncle, I am." Caroline took hold of her uncle's arm and began walking down the center aisle of St. Mary's Episcopal Church. In the distance, Liam stood at the front of the church with David. Liam was the most handsome man she had ever met, but his kindness made him so much more attractive. Caroline carefully avoided David's eyes as she didn't want anything to spoil the moment.

Moving closer, Uncle gave her arm to Liam and the young couple stood in front of the parson as the ceremony began.

Later that day, at the reception at the Martin mansion, Caroline held Liam's arm as they spoke to a group of people at the side of the spacious dining room. Caroline nonchalantly glanced past Liam and watched David and an invited guest, a beautiful young girl, interact as they stood together near the band. She shook her head.

"Caroline?" Liam asked.

"Yes?"

"You know that David is. . ."

Caroline turned away.

"I know that you and David have. . .well. . ."

"Why must you ruin the moment and mention him?"

"He's my brother, and he is now your brother-in-law and a relative. You must try harder to get along with him."

She controlled her urge to retort. She was going to have to make an effort to tolerate David, despite his obnoxious personality.

A tall bearded man approached them. "Mr. O'Donovan, I was surprised to learn that you and your brother have expanded your mercantile business and opened another store in Boston."

"Yes. Opening a store there allows us to do business with more Canadian exporters."

Caroline again studied David as he interacted with the beautiful young girl. He was smiling and staring like he was eyeing her up for dinner.

"Excuse me, Liam. I shall return shortly." This seemed like an opportune moment to attempt to 'get along with David.'

She walked up to David and his companion, then waited a few seconds until David acknowledged her. When he noticed her, his eyes widened and he practically laughed out loud.

"My dearest sister-in-law, you make a most stunning bride."

Caroline blushed. "You haven't yet asked me to dance."

David looked at the girl, who appeared to be waiting on his next word, then, glancing back at Caroline, said, "No, I have not. But I would be honored to dance with you, Mrs. O'Donovan."

He whispered something in the girl's ear, she nodded, then he held out his arm to Caroline. "Shall we?"

The small orchestra was playing a slow waltz and they began to dance.

"You must pardon me, David, as I am not a skilled dancer. I just learned a few months ago."

"Allow me to lead and you shall have no problem." As he spoke, Caroline could smell liquor of some sort on his breath.

As they danced, Caroline found herself admiring David's grace and competence as a dancer. He began humming along with the band's song, "Oft in the Stilly Night." At the refrain, he sang along, "Thus, in the stilly night, 'ere slumbers' chain hath bound me, sad memory brings the light, of other days around me." He sounded very much like Liam with a singing voice as good, if not better, than her husband's. When he finished, she said, "That was beautiful."

"Our mother used to sing that song to us when Liam and I were small boys. That's how she would put us to sleep," he said, his voice louder than usual amidst the sounds of the musicians as they began a lively waltz.

"Your mother sounds like she was a wonderful woman."

"She was." David nodded. He then eyed her up and down. "I must say, Caroline, you look especially beautiful today."

"Thank you."

I suppose getting along with David won't be as difficult as I. . .

"Almost as lovely as the day you spied on me in the hen-house."

Caroline gasped, stopped dancing and pulled her hands away from him. "That was almost nice. Why did you have to ruin it?"

"I couldn't help it." His tone was playful. "The sight of you, flushed and embarrassed was. . ."

"Stop. I will not allow you to talk to me in that manner. I will get along with you despite your crass behavior." Caroline held up her hands to begin dancing again, then made eye contact with him.

"Miss Caroline, you are certainly made of fine stock," he said in a mock southern accent.

They continued dancing, this time with no dialogue. Caroline now avoided looking at David, instead following his lead. When the waltz finished, she stepped back and curtsied.

"Thank you for the somewhat pleasant dance," she said. His head was lowered. She remained in front of him until he glanced up at her.

"Listen, Caroline, I apologize for the comment about. . ."

"Your apology is accepted." When he leaned in to kiss the side of her face, she pulled away, then reconsidered and offered her cheek to him. He kissed it so lightly that she could barely feel his lips.

She began to walk away, so he stepped beside her and the two continued across the room.

"I really am incorrigible. Mother, God rest her soul, said so."

"Mothers are wise, aren't they?"

"And your mother, Caroline?"

"She died a few months after I was born. I never knew her."

"A shame. Our mother died two years ago. Our father died a few years before that. It's been more difficult for Liam. He hasn't been indulging in the, shall we say, pleasurable distractions that I have been."

"And I'm very thankful for that. It's a pity the manner with which you treat women."

"I treat women better than most men treat them. I have

never harmed a woman. And I don't hear any of them complaining and there's always someone who is willing. . ."

Caroline stopped walking and faced him. "Selly is dead so she cannot complain."

He stepped back, his smile fading. "Touché. You do seem to be able to respond to my, say, incorrigibility."

"Thank you again for the *somewhat* pleasant dance. I must be returning to my husband."

When Caroline looked back at him, he was gazing at her, smiling, but with a peculiar look on his face, one that seemed to be studying her. She couldn't quite explain why, but his expression made her feel awkward and anxious.

* * *

When they returned from the Martin house, David quickly excused himself and retired to his bedroom. Liam watched as Jane and Hallie urged Caroline upstairs. With a flush on her face, she glanced at Liam, then avoided eye contact with him. Liam guessed that Caroline might be attempting to postpone their intimate time together. If so, he hoped that putting it off would calm her somewhat, if she were at all nervous. He had wished that she had consumed some wine during the wedding festivities, but each time he placed a glass in her hand, she refused it. He was feeling a bit tipsy now, mainly because he downed each glass he tried to coax her to drink. Liam's own inhibitions were dissolving and his excitement was increasing.

He hoped that she wasn't too disappointed that they wouldn't be embarking on a formal honeymoon but, as he explained to her several weeks ago, it would not be prudent to take any sort of holiday during one of the busiest times of the year for the business.

Caroline remained beside the servants, conversing with them and recalling moments from the day. Liam wondered if she had any idea how much he loved her. She laughed out loud at a comment from Jane and his heart began to pound. Caroline was a naturally beautiful woman, yet she had a sweet innocence and a non-worldly way about her, not to mention a somewhat rebellious spirit, which he hoped he would be able to tame.

"Miss Caroline, your bath is ready in your room. . .whenever you're ready." Jane proceeded up the staircase, Hallie following.

Liam studied his young wife's face. It was flushed and she was clearly embarrassed. "Caroline, would you like some wine?"

She glanced at Liam. "I don't drink alcohol."

"I know you don't, but. . ."

"I'll be fine."   She was nervously rubbing her lace-covered arms.

"Are you cold?"

"Somewhat."

"Well, then, a nice hot bath is just what you need."

Although she nodded, she remained standing beside Liam. When she glanced at him, he regarded her with an expression of tenderness and understanding.

"Caroline?"

"Yes."

"When you're finished your bath, come to my room."

"Very well."

He kissed her forehead. "See you soon."

15

Caroline listened to her husband's quiet breathing. Liam was deep in slumber and she wished that she could fall asleep as easily. The soft glow of the hearth gave faint light to the room.

She wasn't sure whether she ought to be disappointed or relieved. Patsie was right when she said that wives had to endure the marriage bed and that the pleasures were for the husband alone.

She had hoped that it would be a warmer evening. As it was last night, the fireplace lit the room as bright as early morning; the full moon added to her embarrassment. Of course, all she could do was to be as still as possible. The floor and bed creaked with every movement. Liam murmured tender words and kissed her in peculiar places. When it came time for the actual. . .moment, her body tensed, her fists clenched and her eyes squeezed shut. During the whole experience, which thankfully lasted but a few minutes, she was nervous and embarrassed.

Immediately afterwards, Liam had gotten up and proceeded to relieve himself in the chamber pot. Caroline had shuddered and turned away. Could he not have done that in the necessary room down the hall? She had heard him slide it back under the bed then slip beside her. She remained facing away from him. "Are you all right, Caroline?"

When she had hesitated, he whispered, "I'm sorry, Caroline. I shouldn't have done that here. I wasn't thinking. I'm not accustomed to drinking so much."

"No, Liam." She had turned to face him. "You ought to be able to do what you wish in your bedroom." In actuality, she had wanted to grab her robe and leave his room as soon as possible.

When he had laid down, he had pulled the coverlet over them then had cradled her to his chest. He had whispered his love for her, then soon fell asleep. She concluded that laying intimately beside her new husband was her favorite moment of the whole evening.

Caroline was of the opinion that what needed to be accomplished in the marriage bed seemed ridiculous and she became fully convinced why this was an activity done in private. As one who had watched another couple engage in this act, albeit mistakenly, Caroline found herself wondering what in the world was in God's almighty mind when He created male and female and why this was all so necessary in marriage? Couldn't He have simply had the husband shake the wife's hand or some other sort of polite gesture and accomplished the deed in that manner?

Her hand now lay on Liam's smooth chest and she could feel the slight vibration of his beating heart. Caressing his chest, she found a series of small thin scars that ran from his rib cage downward and she purposefully traced the tiny lines. She made a mental note to ask her husband what had caused such strange markings. There was so much more to discover and Caroline wanted to know everything she could about him, his deepest feelings, his childhood memories. As she continued to touch him, he stirred, but did not waken. Despite the awkwardness, she had no doubt that Liam loved her and that she loved him. With those thoughts, she began to drift off.

Caroline woke with a start. *What a horrible nightmare.* She slowly sat up, not wanting to wake her husband, then gazed down at his sleeping face. *Thank heavens that was just a dream.* Her heart was pounding and she took a few deep breaths. She turned and faced the fireplace, which now consisted of smoldering coals.

"What's wrong?" Liam sat up and she felt his hand gently rubbing her back.

"Nothing. Only a nightmare."

"Well, you're safe here with me. " He laid down and pulled her close to him.

* * *

The next morning Liam, having risen and breakfasted early, met his brother at the top of the staircase. David was smiling from ear to ear, his eyebrows raised. "So, Lee. . ."

"David." Liam was certain his entire body was blushing.

"How are we feeling this morning?"

"We?"

"You know," David whispered, "The two of you weren't quiet."

"What?" Liam bellowed.

"Be quiet. I'm jesting. Didn't hear a sound."

"David, really, you have no couth."

"Brothers don't need to have couth, now, do they?"   He poked the side of Liam's arm.

*   *   *

Caroline sat in her robe at the vanity and brushed her hair.

There was a knock at the door. "Miss Caroline?"

"Come in, Jane."

The servant closed the door behind her. "How are you feeling this morning?"

"I suppose I'm well."

"You look rested and none the worse for wear."

"I slept fine, except for the nightmare I had."

"A nightmare, Miss?"

"I dreamt that I was married to David! Honestly, Jane, it was horrible. My heart was thundering in my chest when I woke up. It's difficult enough to tolerate him and try to get along. I wouldn't want to imagine what it would be like to be married to someone like him."

"Now, now, Mr. David's a good man." Jane tied the back of Caroline's corset.

"I wonder whether you harbor some deep romantic notion for David."

"It's not like that. I think Mr. David is particular about who he. . .let's just say that with my unpleasant face and round body, I'm not the most likely candidate to be the object of his affections."

"What is this nonsense, Jane? Unpleasant face?"

"You only need to look at me to see that I am not beautiful."

"That's absurd. You have a very friendly face. I think you are really too hard on yourself. That constant smile you wear makes you a most pleasant-looking girl."

"You are too kind, Ma'am. Anyway, what I was saying about Mr. David, he's done some very thoughtful things. Last year, there was a family in the city whose house burnt down. Mr. David personally brought them clothes and gave them money and found them a place to stay."

"Well, I suppose that even he has some positive attributes.

Jane, perhaps your standards are just too low."

Caroline pulled her dress on and the servant buttoned it up.

"Thank you. Are Liam and his brother still in the hallway?"

Jane opened the door and peeked out. "Yes, they are."

"Would you mind standing there and letting me know when David leaves."

"Certainly. I'd be happy to do that for you."

Caroline stood before the vanity and studied herself. After having it up all day yesterday, she decided to leave her hair down today.

"It doesn't look like Mr. David is making haste to leave."

"Very well. I suppose I shall go ahead."

"May I leave now?"

"Yes, of course."

Caroline entered the hallway. Liam and David were deep in conversation at the top of the O'Donovan grand staircase. Caroline felt embarrassed, especially around David, as he would know exactly what transpired and he would likely offer a snide comment to her. She was definitely not at ease with having her brother-in-law so near after her wedding night.

"The packing company from Boston has increased their prices for all of their goods. Perhaps we should use another proprietor."

"I don't think so, David. They've been quite reliable. You ought to be happy to pay the extra price to depend on them."

Despite David's continued presence and her trembling hands, she impatiently decided to approach the two men. Caroline kept her eyes focused on her husband. Liam smiled as soon as he noticed her coming toward them. "Good morning, Caroline."

"Good morning."

"Excuse me, Liam, may I speak with you?" Caroline asked, avoiding eye contact with David.

"Yes, of course."

"Well, goodbye, Lee, Caroline. See you in a week." She looked up and watched as David began walking down the staircase. Then he turned and winked at her. Caroline cringed.

16

Later that evening Caroline sat at her vanity and began to systematically rearrange the perfumes, combs and brushes. It was already late and Liam had not yet returned upstairs. When he did, he would want her to join him in his bedroom or perhaps he would come to her room. She wasn't yet certain of the protocol of intimate marital activity and if she must be honest with herself, she would much rather remain in her bedroom, alone, this evening. However, her husband was a married man and deserved to have his wife every night if he so desired.

Caroline picked up her Bible and sat in the chair near the fireplace. The old book practically opened itself to the Songs of Solomon, the direct middle of the Bible. She was uncomfortable with the erotic imagery of this book, but her eyes were drawn to a passage at chapter 3, verses 1 and 2.

"By night on my bed, I sought him whom my soul loveth: I sought him but I found him not. I will rise now and go about the city and the streets and in the broad ways, I shall seek him whom my soul loveth: I sought him but I found him not."

Continuing, she read verse 7:10:

"I am my beloved's and his desire is toward me."

Desire. She knew that Liam desired her. She wanted to do her duty but the whole marriage bed experience had been embarrassing and awkward.

"I sought him but I found him not." Perhaps she ought to find Liam and bring him upstairs.

The warmth and crackling of the fire lulled her and with the book open on her lap, Caroline began to drift off to sleep.

* * *

In the downstairs study, Liam checked his pocket watch and sighed at the lateness of the hour. He returned the ledger to the shelf and turned off the gas lamp. He hesitated at the doorway, then he peered into the dimly lit foyer and stared upward. Before last night, Liam had reasoned that once their initial encounter was out of the way, it would be smooth sailing.   Now, he was feeling more awkward. Despite the disdain he felt for David's cavalier attitude toward women and intimacy, he found himself disappointed that his brother was away. Or should he even be speaking of such delicate matters to his brother?

Lord, what can I do to assist her during our intimate time together?

"Mr. Liam, you're still awake?" Jane asked as she stood at the top of the steps.

"Yes, Jane. I'll turn off the lamps."

"Very well. Will you be needing anything else this evening?"

"Is my wife awake?"

"I don't know. Shall I knock on her door for you?"

"No, no. That's fine. Good night."

"Good night, Mr. Liam."

Liam extinguished the lights one by one. As he reached the top of the staircase, he remained still for a moment, then began to methodically turn off the lights in the hallway until he reached his room. He waited outside of Caroline's room and listened for a few moments but heard nothing. He lifted his hand, then drew away from the door without knocking. He turned toward his own room and changed into his night clothes.

Liam was almost home. He had trudged up the laneway before he realized that he would have to tell his parents that he had lost David or that David had lost him. Besides, he was nearly twelve and certainly not in need of David chaperoning him at the church youth cookout. Of course, his father would blame him and not David, because that's the way it was. Perhaps he could just slip in the back door and up the rear staircase so that no one would notice that he had returned without David. However, as he passed by the open parlor window, he could hear his father's raised voice and he stopped to listen.

"That's because you spend all your time coddling him, Emma. He's a young man and he ought to act that way. The way he sniffles and cries, you'd think he was two years old."

"He's sensitive, Jack. He's. . ."

"Boys should not cry."

Liam was unable to hear any response from his mother. The room was quiet for a moment. He began to walk away, then he heard his father speak up, this time, his tone soft.

"He's never been right. . .since he was born."

"Right? He almost died, Jack. He was sick for many months. I should think you'd be happy that he survived."

"Emma, nature has the right idea. When an animal is born weak and sickly, they're left to die."

"What are you saying, Jack? He's our son."

"Yes, well, I've had my doubts about that."

Again, Liam couldn't hear his mother's response, but soon heard his father shouting again. "He doesn't look like me, he doesn't act like me, he's a sniveling baby most of the time. What am I supposed to think?"

Liam dropped to the ground outside the parlor window and began to cry. Perhaps his father was correct. He was a baby who cried all the time. Maybe he ought to have been left to die when he was born. He quickly got up and ran toward the back of the house and inside the door.

He climbed the staircase to his room. He picked up his violin, locked himself in his closet and began to play as quietly as he could.

Liam took a deep breath and let it out slowly. Evenings tended to be more difficult for him, and the loneliness seemed to consume him, especially when David was away. He longed to share some of this with his wife, yet he didn't want to burden her with his memories. She had her own painful history and she was certainly not in need of the horrid stories of his father beating and berating him. He picked up his violin, sat down in his closet and began to play.

*   *   *

She peered out the window of her small bedroom. It felt good, familiar to be back home in Boston. Distant high-pitched music caused Caroline to turn toward the open door. She moved across the room and entered the narrow hallway in search of the source. Next, she found herself in an unfamiliar forest still following the music as she glided, unconnected, to the next venue: the kitchen at the Martin house where the haunting melody continued to sound faraway. She reached the back door, stepped out and found herself falling in darkness.

Caroline gasped, sat straight up and listened. The fireplace held only red coals and the oil lamp was still aglow. Soft music echoed throughout the upstairs and the lulling quiet melody urged her to return to sleep. Stubbornly, she got up and opened the door.

Liam was playing the violin, slow and crisp, beautiful. Yet, something in the music, perhaps the melancholy tone, caused her to feel as if she was intruding on a private moment. Abruptly, the music stopped. Caroline crept across the hall and knocked. He opened the door dressed in his nightshirt.

"Caroline."

"That was beautiful, Liam."

"I didn't mean to wake you."

"It doesn't matter. I tried waiting up for you, but I fell asleep."

"Then you must be tired."

"Not at all. I've had a rest now." She paused. "Just a moment." Caroline quickly returned to her room. She turned off her lamp, then joined her husband outside of his room. "Liam?"

"Yes?"

"The music you played sounded. . .sad."

"Well, I. . ." Liam lowered his head and, at first, avoided eye contact. He finally brought his gaze to meet hers. "If you're tired . . ."

When she looked deeply into his eyes, Caroline saw a void which needed to be filled. Despite the awkwardness, she found herself desiring him in a way which seemed foreign to her. At that moment, she wanted the one-flesh experience again to some-how fill the emptiness in his eyes.

"No, I'm fine, really. I wish to be with you tonight."

"You do?"

"Yes."

Liam moved aside for her to enter his room, then he closed the door.

17

Kip leaned his head into the doorway of the study. "Mr. Liam, I'll be leaving in a half hour's time to pick up Mr. David at the train station. Will you be coming with me?"

"Yes, Kip."

Liam took the ledger off the shelf and sat at the desk. He opened the book, made a few notations, then set the quill down. He couldn't seem to concentrate and he was making too many mistakes. It had now been a week since he and Caroline had married. During the day, he found it enjoyable to spend time with his wife. Yet, as each night came and went, he became more and more uneasy. He couldn't figure out exactly what was bothering him. Eventually, he hoped that she would become with child. He greatly looked forward to being a father and for the opportunity to be a better father than his own had been.

They hadn't spoken of their intimate experiences at all, but he had decided to insist that Caroline remain in her bedroom for the last two nights. Although she seemed to want to please him, he could tell she was still feeling awkward and unsure in his bed.

Perhaps David would have some words of wisdom for him. Liam laughed out loud at the absurdity of it. Generally speaking, the two brothers spoke openly regarding every conceivable issue. Years ago, when David first visited the brothel, he shared the intimate details of each visit until Liam insisted that he keep those sordid experiences to himself.

Now, Liam tried to remember what, if anything, David had said in those early days. The only comment by his brother that he could recall was that it was possible for women to have as much pleasure as men. Perhaps he should have paid more attention.

* * *

"David, over here," Liam called at the train station.

"I thought that Kip was picking me up."

"I wanted to come and greet my only brother."

"Ah, correction: your older, wiser and more handsome brother."

Liam rolled his eyes.

"So what's the matter with you, Lee?"

"Nothing."

"You can talk to me about it."

"Well, since you asked. . ."

"That's more like it. Speak, Lee, your advisor waits to give you the outpouring of his wise and. . ."

"It's private. I'd rather wait until we're inside the carriage."

"Private?" his voice bellowed.

"David, be quiet, please."

They approached the carriage. Kip nodded to David. "Hello, Mr. David. I hope you had a good trip."

"Yes, Kip, I did."

Inside the carriage David asked, "So what is this private matter you wish to discuss?"

Liam pushed his back against the seat and tried to settle himself as the carriage began to move. Somehow, this felt wrong, like he ought not to be asking for his brother's advice. After all, what sort of wisdom would David have anyway? He had carnal knowledge of just about every servant girl in Germantown. It wasn't the sort of experience which would grant him expert status on marriage, that's for certain.

"Speaking of private matters, how is married life? Is it the wedded bliss you thought it would be?"

"Well, I. . ."

"That sounds like trouble in paradise."

"There's no trouble, David. Just forget I mentioned anything."

*   *   *

Caroline sat on the chair by the fire in her bedroom. The book lay open on her lap; she hadn't turned a page in over an hour. Liam had kissed her goodbye before he left for the train station. Her husband had insisted that she remain in her own bedroom and, in the interests of obeying him, she said nothing. Part of her felt relieved but at the same time, she was disappointed that she would not be laying beside Liam all night. And why did he insist that she stay in her bedroom? Was she neglecting to do something during their intimate time together? When Jane had helped her dress this morning, she almost asked the servant for advice, although what information could Jane, an unmarried woman, give?

Caroline straightened as she heard faint noises from outside. She placed her book on the bedside table. She walked to the window and watched the carriage ride up to the front of the house. She wasn't sure how she ought to react. Certainly, David could have stayed away until the end of the year, or next year, if she had her preference.

At the top of the staircase, Caroline waited for her husband and his brother to come in, and she found herself beginning to tremble. She slowly descended the stairs, keeping her eyes focused on her feet rather than her husband and his brother. She heard Jane's voice, "Good afternoon, Mr. David, Mr. Liam," then Liam's voice, "Caroline, David is home." She looked up and attempted to smile, but it came off as a grimace.

Jane took the men's coats and hats and left the foyer.

David stepped forward. "Caroline, it's good to see you again. Married life obviously suits you. You look beautiful."

She made another attempt at a smile. "Thank you."

"If you two will excuse me, I have a lot of work to do." David quickly went to the study and closed the door behind him.

Liam's eyes followed his brother, but he remained beside his wife. For a moment, they were quiet, listening to the tick tock rhythm of the grandfather clock.

"Liam?"

"Yes?"

"Do you wish for me to come to your room later?"

"Oh. . .well. . ."

"I would very much like to come to your room."

"You would?"

Caroline nodded. "'Tis my duty, Liam."

Her husband sighed, then quietly said, "Yes, very well."

18

"Miss Caroline, ye can't be knowin' how glad I am ta see ye again." Patsie yanked Caroline into her ample bosom on the front porch of the Martin house.

"I've missed you as well, Patsie. But it has only been four weeks since the wedding!"

"Sure an' I know that. And me Jane's been tellin' me ye and she been gettin' on so well."

"We have. She's a wonderful young woman."

"I'll be thankin' ye for sayin' so. Now then, how is it ye be gettin' home this afternoon? Will Mr. Liam be after comin' ta fetch ye later on?"

"Yes. I do hope that Uncle and Elizabeth come home soon."

"Well now, sure they said they be only an hour. That be puttin' 'em home in a wee minute or so." With that, the Martin carriage pulled up the laneway. It reached the front of the house where her uncle and cousin got out.

"There you are, Caroline," bellowed Uncle Edward as he embraced his niece. "Married life must agree with you, my dear. You are looking more beautiful than ever."

"Thank you, Uncle."

Elizabeth leaned in to embrace her cousin and kissed her cheek. "Carrie, I must agree with Father."

"Well, I hope you two young ladies have a wonderful visit. I must work in my office until this evening. Are you staying for dinner, my dear?"

"No, Uncle. Liam will be here in a few hours to take me home."

"Perhaps another time."

"Yes."

He gathered her into a tight hug and kissed her forehead.

Elizabeth pulled Caroline into the parlor.

"So?" asked Elizabeth.

"So what?"

"So what does it feel like to be a married woman?" she whispered. "We haven't had an opportunity for some sisterly dialogue since you were married. Of course, church would be a most inappropriate place to discuss that subject." Elizabeth was on the verge of giggling.

"Well, Lizzie, Liam is a wonderful man but. . ."

"But?"

"He works dreadfully long hours, which doesn't leave very much time for us to be together, and he's already traveled twice since we were married four weeks ago."

"Well, all men are like that. Papa works all the time."

"Yes, I guess so."

"So how is the cooking over there?"

"It's rather good. To be honest, I prefer Patsie's cooking. Jane prepares a lot of Irish dishes and there's soda bread at every meal."

"I've never personally liked soda bread, Carrie. It's far too bland for my tastes."

They spent the next few hours, conversing and playing parlor games. Towards the end of their stay together, Caroline looked up to find Missy standing at the doorway.

"Mr. David's here to take you home, Miss."

"Oh." Caroline kept her gaze down and dropped her shoulders. "I thought that Liam was going to pick me up."

"Mr. David was wondering how long you might be. He said he had some business to attend to with his. . .horse."

"At least another half hour or so would be fine."

"Yes, of course, Miss," she said, then quickly left.

In the parlor, a short while later, Carrie looked at the mantel clock as it struck the half hour. "It's already been over an hour, Lizzie. Perhaps I ought to see what David's doing in the stable."

"Really, Carrie, that's a job for a servant."

Caroline remembered the last time she looked for Missy in the henhouse. She didn't need nor want to know what David was doing in the stable. "On second thought, you're right. Perhaps Patsie can ask David when he'll be ready to leave." She got up and walked toward the doorway.

"Why don't you pull on the rope over there? The one on the left is for the kitchen."

"I abhor those contraptions. It's no trouble for me to go down to the kitchen and find her myself. Besides, I need to walk after sitting for so long."

"Very well. I shall wait for you here."

Caroline quickly made her way down to the Martin kitchen. As she descended the staircase, warmth drifted upward and she could smell a turkey roasting in the oven. "Patsie?" she called out. She stood at the bottom of the steps. No one was in the kitchen. She turned to go back up the steps, but paused when she heard voices coming from behind the closed door of the servant kitchen bedroom.

"What's wrong, David?"

"I don't know. I. . ."

"Come now. Don't you...want me anymore?"

"Of course I do. It's just that. . ."

"What's wrong?"

"I don't know. I can't. . .do this anymore."

Their sounds of intimacy became louder and more intense. Caroline gasped and rushed up the steps, bumping into Patsie at the top of the staircase.

"Ye be leaving soon then?"

"I. . .I'm not certain, Patsie."

She did not want Patsie to see her flushed condition so she responded, "I think I shall wait with Elizabeth in the parlor." Caroline leaned in to hug the round woman. Patsie held her so tightly and Caroline wanted to remain in her safe embrace.

Patsie whispered, "I sure do be missin' ye here." As Caroline stepped back, Patsie seemed to be studying her face.

"Miss Caroline, sure an' are ye bein' all right, me lamb?"

"Yes, yes, I'm fine, just. . ." Patsie lifted Caroline's chin and studied her face. Patsie's eyes narrowed. Leaning in close to her ear, Patsie asked, "Are ye missin' yer monthlies already?"

Caroline stared at her. "My monthlies?"

"Sure an' I was hopin' ye'd be with child soon."

"With child? I haven't really been keeping track. I suppose I have missed one. But it's only a month since the wedding."

"Sure an' that's all it takes. I'm after thinkin' it'd be foin if ye were." The servant paused. "Well, sure an' I hope ye be visitin' us again soon."

Caroline nodded and pondered what Patsie had said. For a few seconds she became distracted.

"There you are, Carrie." Her cousin walked toward her in the foyer. "Patsie, did Carrie instruct you to find David?"

"No, Miss 'Lizabeth."

"No, I didn't. I. . ."

"I'd be glad to find Mr. David for ye, Miss Caroline."

"Thank you. Please let him know I'll be waiting out front."

"Yes, 'course," she said.

"Good bye, Patsie."

"Good bye. Ye be takin' good care of yerself now."

"I will."

"Carrie, are you feeling well? You look a bit flushed."

"Well, now that you mention it, I don't feel so well."

"Truly?"

"Yes."

"Well, I just bet anything that you're carrying," her cousin whispered into her ear.

"It's far too soon to know for sure."

"But you're not feeling well. That's one of the signs, I'm told."

"I'm going to wait outside for a moment and get some fresh air."

"Then I shall come and stay with you, Carrie."

The two girls chatted on the veranda for several moments. Soon, David came to the porch area. Caroline kept her head down and facing away from him.

"Good day, Elizabeth."

"Good day, David."

"Are you ready, Caroline?"

"I. . ."

"Make certain that you ride slowly. Dear Carrie is not feeling well."

"Do you need some assistance?" she heard him say.

Caroline shook her head. "No, no, I'm fine," she said, her voice shaking, her eyes continuing to avoid contact with him.

David spoke up. "I'm waiting for Ben to hitch the horses."

The buggy pulled up to the front of the house. Ben got out and handed the reins to David.

Elizabeth hugged Caroline. She whispered, "Let me know how you are feeling."

Caroline nodded, but kept her gaze focused on the horse and carriage.

David stepped forward and assisted her on to the seat, then pulled himself in and took the reins.

As they rode off, Caroline looked up and waved to Elizabeth, then kept silent.

"Did you have a pleasant visit?" His deep voice was just above a whisper.

"Fine," she said curtly.

"Lee asked me to apologize. He had to meet with a client regarding an emergency situation."

She nodded but kept silent.

"You're not feeling well?"

She did not respond.

"Do you want me to pull over?"

Caroline shook her head.

A moment or so of silence passed before David spoke up. "Did something happen at your uncle's house?"

She shot him a fleeting glance to see if he was teasing her, looking at him square in the eyes, but his expression was full of concern.

"Please, just. . ."

She looked away and if it had been possible to do so, she would have turned her back to him. She refused to discuss this any further, most especially with him.

For the next minute or so, he was silent, respecting her wish. Then he spoke up.

"This is about me, isn't it?"

"I don't know what. . .you mean," she said, keeping her face away from him.

She could hear him sigh as he pulled over to the side of the road. A few unpleasant moments dragged by, with only the sounds of their breathing and the occasional chirping bird filling the air.

"Caroline, you were never a good liar."

"David, please."

"Look at me."

"Take us home."

"I'm not taking us home until you look at me."

Caroline slowly turned her body so that her face was now visible to him, although she avoided eye contact and said nothing.

"Did something happen at the Martin house?"

She remained silent.

"Then what's wrong?"

"Nothing."

He shook his head. "I told you. You're a poor liar, Caroline. Something is wrong. Just tell me."

"I. . .heard. . .you and Missy in the basement bedroom."

"Damn," he muttered under his breath.

"Please take us home."

*   *   *

David awkwardly assisted his sister-in-law out of the carriage. She avoided eye contact and all but cringed when he touched her hand and helped her down. He was thankful that he was wearing riding gloves.

He handed the carriage and horse off to Kip. "Is the shooting range set up?"

"Yes, it is, Mr. David. I haven't changed it since last week."

Inside the house, he climbed the staircase to his bedroom and closed the door. He stood before the gun cabinet in the far corner of his room. "Guns and girls," his father used to say, "are the most important things in life." David chose the Winchester '73, the last gift from his father, then rummaged through the top drawer of his desk for ammunition. He didn't know why, but he needed to engage in some target practice.

Behind the stable at the shooting range, he pointed at the markers in the distance. Holding the Winchester securely as his father had taught him, he slipped three fingers into the lever action but left his index finger alongside the chamber. Slowly, he drew the gun to his shoulder and lined the target up in his sight. He could almost hear his father's voice, reminding him to draw steady breaths as he moved his index finger to the trigger and gently squeezed it.

The shot hit the mark. It felt good to be doing something right.   He held the rifle under his arm and studied the marks. *A damned good shot,* his father used to call him.

Caroline, his sister-in-law, now a married woman, had once again been privy to some intimacy between Missy and him. Why was it not so amusing now? Why did it bother him so much? Perhaps because he had tried to stop and he couldn't. He was just like an animal, incapable of saying no.

He took aim, then shot. His father taught him well.

19

David stuck his hand in his pocket, then sank back against the plush carriage seat. Liam was going to be furious with him, and rightfully so. He didn't think that there was a chance he could lose that much money with three jacks and two eights. Winning was a certainty. Of course, everything seems like a sure thing when you have multiple glasses of whiskey blurring your brain. Five thousand dollars was a lot of money, and David was thankful that a lien had been accepted on their house. Now David would have to reveal to Liam that Captain Armstrong held a lien on their mansion.

All of a sudden, David wondered whether all that whiskey he had consumed was about to come back out and all over the fresh smelling carriage. He took a deep breath in, then slowly exhaled. Soon, the nausea faded.

He heard Kip utter, "Whoa," as the carriage came to an abrupt halt. With it came a renewed and more overwhelming need to retch. He was glad that the late hour meant that he wouldn't have to face Liam yet. He slipped out of the buggy and quietly made his way up the stairs.

He opened the door to his room then heard, "David, wait."

David turned to see his brother standing in the hallway. He was wearing a nightshirt and he was frowning.

"Is there something you wish to tell me?"

"Not tonight, Lee. I'm tired."

"No doubt."

David turned towards his brother. "Who told you?"

"How could you do this? How could you gamble away our home?"

"I didn't gamble it away. We simply owe Captain Armstrong some money for it."

"We? You 'simply owe.'"

"Yes, he said we could make payments every month."

"Are you daft? We don't make payments for anything. We pay in cash. I sure as hell won't pay that man any interest."

"I thought I could bring in double that."

"You said you were going to stop gambling. Two weeks ago, you lost two thousand dollars and you promised me that you were going to stop."

"But I was going to win, Lee. I could taste it."

"Enough. I don't want to hear it." Liam was now raising his voice and David could hear his name every few seconds but the other words were muffled. Then again, David didn't care what his brother was saying. He just wanted to sleep and rid himself of his throbbing, pounding headache.

"Are you listening to me, David?"

"Yeah, yeah. Can we talk about this in the morning?"

David heard his brother stomp off down the hallway. He shrugged his shoulders, then went into his room. David dropped onto his bed and promptly fell asleep.

*   *   *

"David, wake up." David roused, but turned over to escape his brother's voice. Why was Lee bothering him now?

"I said wake up."

"Leave me alone," he said, keeping his eyes closed.

"I've come up with a plan to make back the five thousand and release the lien on our home."

"Good. Tell me later on. I'm sleeping all day."

"Get up before I pour water on you."

David slowly opened his eyes and squinted. His brother was holding a ceramic pitcher over his head.

"Whoa, what the hell are you doing, Lee?"

"I'm about to pour this on you. Unless, of course, you wake yourself enough to get up."

David slowly sat up, scratched his head and scowled at Liam.

"You have no right to look at me that way. You just gambled away our home and I have devised a plan to fix it."

David stared at his brother with an annoyed expression. "You've been up all night figuring this out?"

"Yes, in fact, I have. I couldn't sleep. Here's what I came up with. We take the bulk of our liquid assets and invest it. Over a year, we'll have the money to pay the Captain with minimal interest."

"Sounds good. Now permit me to go back to sleep."

"The only problem is that we won't have access to much capital or cash over the next year or so."

"Sure, sure. Just let me go back to sleep."

* * *

Liam closed his brother's door. Daylight would arrive in an hour or so. He lingered in the hallway and stared down the black corridor to the west wing, not seeing but knowing that his mother's room was at the end of the hall. Despite the darkness, he moved with the ease of familiarity. He paused before opening the door, wondering whether he ought to enter. It had been, after all, several months since he had visited here. He opened the door, allowed his eyes to adjust to the darkness, then lit an oil lamp on the bureau near the door. The room hadn't changed; blue silk canopied bed to the right, her embroidery table lined the wall near the tall window and the unused fireplace at the left wall. The room smelled musty with a hint of lavender. He sat down in the chair next to the bed.

* * *

Caroline stirred in her sleep and leaned closer to her husband. She patted the bed beside her and found it unoccupied, the sheets cold. "Liam?" Hearing no response, she lit the oil lamp. She pulled on her robe, picked up the lamp and peered into the hallway. Caroline could see faint light coming from a room in the west wing of the house. Liam had once told her that that section was used mostly for storage but that he had hoped those rooms would eventually be filled with their children.

Slowly, quietly, she crept along the hallway until she reached the end. The door was partially opened and she heard someone in the room – her husband perhaps – then heard him sniffle. Standing at the doorway, Caroline peeked in and could see that Liam was sitting in a chair beside a canopied bed. She opened the door wider and it creaked. Liam immediately stood up and turned around.

"Caroline."

"Liam?"

"Yes?" He wiped his eyes and cleared his throat.

"I was. . .just returning to my room." He crossed the room and stood beside her.

She placed the oil lamp on the bureau, then took hold of his hand and kissed it. "I missed you, Liam. I should like for you to return to bed."

He nodded, then turned and pointed at the huge portrait on the wall above the bed. "My mother and father."

"What a beautiful couple they were."

"This was around the time of their wedding."

Caroline studied the portrait. Liam's mother offered a subtle but nonetheless happy countenance. His father wore a smirk, the same sort of expression that she had seen in other portraits around the house.

"My mother looks so happy in that painting, but I'm sure that was before she realized what sort of person my father was."

Caroline wasn't quite sure how to respond to that.

"This was her room; across the hall was my father's room."

"You don't talk about your father very much."

"It turns my stomach to do so, Caroline."

Caroline shuddered. She wanted to ask him why he felt that way but instead she kept silent.

"I wish David wasn't so much like him," Liam said.

Caroline didn't know their father but if he was anything like David, she certainly understood. "If David is so much like your father and you didn't get along with your father, how is it that you and David get along so well together?"

"David certainly doesn't have the volatile temper our father had. But tonight, I'm furious with him, although I'm sure you don't need to hear these complaints about David. Despite everything he's done, he's the only blood relative I have left, Caroline. I keep hoping, praying, that some day he'll change. Maybe when he's older, he will realize that gambling, drinking and carousing with women will not make him happy."

He turned off his mother's oil lamp and picked up the light Caroline had brought. He allowed his wife to leave, then he turned back. She watched him as he stared into the darkness, then he slowly pulled the door closed.

20

Liam placed two folded shirts in his suitcase and closed it. He opened his bedroom door and dropped the bag on the floor in the hallway. He could hear Caroline retching again. She wasn't due to deliver for two more months but continued to be ill most mornings.

All day yesterday while he prepared for his business trip, Caroline had asked him if he would reconsider going. Should he cancel the trip? That really wasn't possible. This meeting in Boston was an important one and would mean a great deal of money for the business. Perhaps his wife's nagging feeling was because of the impending birth.

He greatly looked forward to the birth of their child. But he was uncomfortable when he thought of resuming relations with his wife. He desired her very much, more than he would ever reveal to her, and the past several months had been torture for him at times. But the doctor had recommended. . .no, he ordered Liam. . .not to be intimate with his wife until after their child was born. How could he make Caroline desire him as much as he desired her?

Liam recalled the first time that he had a business meeting without David. He was just 19 and traveling alone to Boston. He could hardly contain his nervousness as he met with three much older, experienced men. As he gained more practice, he also became more confident. He mentally kept track of what sorts of dialogue led to more productive meetings and researched how his competitors gained clients. He asked many questions, expressed sympathy, then showed them he had the answer to whatever problems they had.

He began conducting business meetings over a drink and offered prospective clients cigars and other incentives. Eventually, he became very good at what he did, much better than David, which was why it was imperative that he be the one to go.

His wife's retching forced him to return to the present. He hated to hear her suffering like that. *Lord, how can I make her desire me? How do you make people become close to you?*

The good Lord had given him the gift of Caroline and he decided that for the time being, he would focus on being a better husband. Hopefully, the rest would follow in short order.

He knocked lightly on her door. Several seconds passed before he reached his hand out to bang more noisily. Immediately, Caroline, still dressed in her night clothes, opened the door. "You're not leaving so early, are you?"

"Yes, Caroline, I must catch the 9:00 train."

Her face hardened. "I wish I could ride with you to the train station, but. . ." She darted across the room, leaned over the basin and began making the familiar sounds. He walked in behind her and gently touched her back.

She straightened and wiped her face with a linen towel. Liam had already turned and started to walk toward the door when she called his name.

"Yes?"

"Could you not send David?"

"We've already spoken of this."

She sighed and pulled on her robe. "Then I should like to say goodbye to you downstairs."

"That's not necessary. You ought to return to bed."

She shook her head. "I wish to accompany you downstairs, Liam."

"Very well."

*   *   *

Caroline's shoulders were slumped and her now protruding stomach was touching the front of her husband.

"You will be fine. Jane will take good care of you."

"I suppose."   She had a strange feeling in her stomach and she was certain that it had nothing to do with her condition.   She didn't know whether she was feeling this way because she was within two months of giving birth or whether it was because she was feeling ill much of the time. Whatever it was, she did not want Liam to leave her.

"Could you not postpone it, at least for a short while?"

"I already told you that this meeting is an important one which can't be put off." She lowered her head. He lifted up her chin and kissed her forehead. "Now, now, don't pout. Besides, it's only for a week."

Caroline pushed herself away from him, turned around and crossed her arms across her chest.

"Caroline, stop. You're going to *have* a baby. You're not an infant yourself." There was a slightly caustic tone in his voice. She stiffened at his words. Remaining silent, she walked with him to the front door. A cool blast of wind almost knocked the two of them down.

"Stay inside. You're still in your night dress."

"Goodbye, Liam." Her tone was curt. She wasn't very happy with him at present. Why wouldn't he listen to her? What was so important about this trip that he couldn't postpone it or send David?

She stayed at the door and watched him ride away. Why was she worrying? What made her not want him to go this time? He had traveled several times since she had found out that she was with child, so why did it seem to bother her now?

Her unborn baby turned a slow roll within her and, distracted, she returned to her bedroom.

*   *   *

Liam stared out the window of the carriage and shook his head. Why must his wife act so immaturely sometimes?

He did not want to say the things he did to her. They just slipped out. So much for his efforts at being a better husband.

When he returned, he resolved to shower her with gifts and with his time, even if it meant not getting some of his work done.

Now satisfied, he relaxed in the seat.

21

The following week, David kicked the dirt in front of him as he waited for Liam's train to arrive from Boston. It was a cool, overcast day despite the fact that it was almost June. Although it hadn't yet rained, the dark sky threatened to do so. He felt anxious, although he wasn't sure whether it was the weather or some other reason. Of course, living in a house – albeit a large one – with someone not very fond of you could itself cause anxiety.

Although David would never admit it to anyone but himself, it bothered him that Caroline disliked him. Women, in general, seemed enamored by his charm, his good looks and his outgoing personality. Caroline, however, always seemed to have an expression of disdain when she looked at him, as if he had some sort of cancerous growth on his face. Sometimes, he could see signs that she was making an effort to be nice to him. Then he would say something that she found offensive and the expression of disgust would return.

The train's whistle grew louder and soon came to a halt. David watched a group of men getting off.

"Over here, Lee," David yelled, as he watched Liam step down off the train.

Liam glanced at David and waved.

"I trust that Caroline is well?"

Besides the fact that she avoids me like the plague? "I suppose she's fine. She always stays in her room, and the only time this past week we've had a meal together, it was spent in silence. I asked her if she would like to join me today and she declined. She's ill, as usual."

"She misses me. She didn't want me to go."

"Oh?"

"Well, this will be the last trip for a while. The baby will keep her occupied the next time I travel."

Rain began to fall as they approached their carriage.

Inside, the brothers remained quiet. Then Liam blurted, "David, do you remember years ago when you were visiting the brothel, you told me women can enjoy the. . .marriage bed too."

"I don't think I phrased it that way, Lee. And I certainly wasn't talking of the 'marriage bed.'"

"Yes, I know. But. . ."

"So you're asking me for advice about. . ."

"Forget it. I should never have said anything."

"Lee, you have to laugh at the irony here. You're supposed to be the one who does everything like a proper gentleman, correct?" David was grinning.

"How can you find this amusing?"

"Very well. I'm sorry."

"Forget it."

"You tell me something like that and now you want me to forget it?"

The two remained silent for a moment.

"Lee, Caroline would not be happy you're talking to me about such matters."

"I want to know how to. . .make it less. . .awkward for my wife."

"Less awkward?"

"How can I make it more. . .pleasant for. . .her? And I don't want her to do this merely out of duty."

"She is your wife and it is her duty, is it not?"

"Well, yes, but. . ."

"And I'm not certain what to say, Lee."

"Tell me what I can do."

David stared at his brother for several long moments.

"What?" Liam asked.

"It's a coincidence that you've brought this up."

"Why?"

"I've been thinking a lot about. . ."

"What?"

"That perhaps I ought to stop bedding so many women."

Liam gasped. "You're jesting, right?"

"No."

"You mean you're going to settle down and get married?"

"Certainly not; perhaps 'settle down' with just one mistress."

"A mistress?"

"Yes."

"Well, that's certainly a change. What brought this on?"

"Nothing."

"Doesn't feel good to use a lot of women for their bodies, does it, David?"

David shot him a stern expression.

"Then you know how I feel."

"No, I don't. If I were inclined to marry, which I'm not, I would not feel the least bit as if I were using my wife. That's what she's there for, isn't it?"

"Well, I want Caroline to come to me because she wants to, not because she feels it's her duty."

The two of them jerked forward as the carriage slowed to a halt.

David knocked on the window behind him. "Kip, why are we stopping?"

"There's an overturned carriage up ahead."

"Very well. Pull over and we'll see if we can offer assistance."

Kip stopped the carriage at the side of the road. They all got out and began walking toward the buggy in the center of the road, with Kip staying to the rear. It began to rain and Kip pulled out an umbrella and opened it, sheltering David and Liam as he followed close behind.

Beside the carriage there were two men and a woman. The woman held an umbrella over herself. One of the men was trying hard to hold onto the horse, who was pulling away from him and nickering. The man was saying, "Whoa —" The other, a tall bearded man in a suit, was leaning down and appeared to be inspecting the carriage as the rain soaked him. When he saw them, the bearded man walked toward Liam and David.

"What happened?" David asked.

The rain now began to fall in earnest. The man's head lowered and he spoke loudly, above the noise of rain. "I'm not certain. Something must have scared the horse and. . ." An ear splitting crack of thunder close by caused the man to jump.

"May we be of some assistance, perhaps help turn your carriage upright?" David yelled back.

"Yes, if you could help me do that, I would be most grateful."

"Certainly," David replied.

David and Liam followed the man and watched as he said something to the other man and he stepped aside.

The bearded man spoke loudly. "My name is Mr. John Smith and my brother's name is James. He's holding onto the horse, so he won't be able to help us."

"I'm David O'Donovan and this is my brother, Liam. Perhaps our servant can offer assistance as well?"

"That would be fine," John Smith responded.

Kip dropped the umbrella and came forward.

"If we all position ourselves on the other side, I think we'll be able to move it easily." The four men lined up along the side of the carriage. John Smith yelled, "On four. . .one, two, three, four!" It lifted easily. They steadied it, then stepped back, all four of them becoming soaked.

"Thank you very much. Sorry about your getting so wet," John Smith offered.

Kip picked up the umbrella and opened it and put it over David and Liam.

"Glad to help," David offered.

James Smith hooked the reins onto the now right side up vehicle and the woman stepped into the carriage.

"Is there anything else we can do for you?" David asked John Smith.

"Yes, there is something you could do." He abruptly pulled out a gun from inside his coat and pointed it towards their faces.

Liam and David gasped and stepped back, knocking the umbrella out of Kip's hand and onto the ground.

"Wait a minute. There's no need for anyone to get hurt,"Liam shouted.

As if in answer, the torrential rains became a drizzle.

"That's what I was thinking," John Smith said. "Give us your money and we'll allow you to leave without hurting you."

Liam reached into his breast pocket and lifted out his wallet. "Here, this is all I have." He handed it to the thief. Liam motioned for David to do the same. David glanced at Kip. He knew that Kip was waiting for some instruction. Behind his back David waved his arm in an effort to communicate to Kip to get the gun.

"And what about that nice pocket watch, Pretty Boy? Hand it over."

Liam lifted it off and handed it to the man.

"And what about you, Curly?"

David reached into his breast pocket, but pulled out nothing.

"You got a problem, Curly?" asked the bearded man.

"Yes, I have a problem, Mr. Smith, if that's even your name. We stop here to help you and you're robbing us. I have a big problem with that."

"You wanna get shot, Curly?"

"David, just give him the money."

David leaned in and whispered into his brother's ear, "I just went to the bank, Lee. I will not hand over three hundred of our hard-earned dollars."

"David, do it."

"How do we know they're not going to hurt us anyway? And don't tell me they seem like nice folks."

"We don't, but if you don't. . ."

"If you boys are done conversing, I'll take your money."

David stepped away. He took out a ten dollar bill from his breast pocket and threw it at the thief.

"Now, that wasn't nice, Curly. You better pick that up before it gets too wet."

"And if I don't?"

"I'll kill you."

David picked up the bill and handed it, now wet and soggy, to the man.

"Look," said the other man. "They are driving a pretty fancy carriage. They got to have more money."

"You're probably right. You check Curly. I'll check Pretty Boy."

John Smith searched through Liam's pockets as Liam held his arms out.

James Smith approached David and reached out his hand to open David's jacket. David swung a punch and knocked him to the ground. James Smith was rubbing his jaw and frowning.

"Is that the way you wanna play, Curly?" John Smith turned around and faced Liam. The man raised his hand and rammed the gun handle into Liam's head. Liam's eyes widened. His head jerked backwards, his arms swung open. He fell, his head hitting the ground with a loud crack.

"No!" screamed David.

"Let's get out of here," he heard John Smith say. Kip ran

after the men, but John Smith turned around. "If you don't stop right there, I'll shoot you, Darkie." Kip stopped and watched the men run to the carriage.

David's attention was now focused on his brother. "Lee, can you hear me? Lee?" Liam was lying sprawled and unresponsive on the ground. His head was bleeding and was turning the dirt under him a dark crimson.

Kip picked up the umbrella and now held it over Liam.

"Damn it!" David yelled. "I should've given those bastards my money. Lee, please wake up."

"Mr. David, I tried to go for the gun but they were watching me like hawks." He stopped and stared at Liam's unconscious form on the ground. "We got to get Mr. Liam home quick."

They carefully lifted Liam into the carriage. David grabbed his coat from the seat and began to wipe his brother dry. He laid his battered and bleeding head on his lap. Once they began moving, David peered out the window. The thieves and their buggy were a speck in the distance.

22

Caroline held her hands to her back as she stood by the window of Liam's bedroom. Sheets of rain raced down the glass, making it impossible to see anything outside. Rain usually put her in a dreary mood, but now it added to her already melancholy state of mind.

She stared at his desk, papers stacked neatly to one side, an ink well and various items to the other.

In the middle of the night, she had a horrible nightmare that she was all alone and the darkness was closing in on her. She woke up in a cold sweat and was unable to return to sleep.

Today her husband would be returning home, then she could dismiss the foolish notion which seemed to trouble her these days.

At that moment, their unborn child turned within her. "Only two more months and we'll get to hold you in our arms, Sweet," she whispered as she caressed her large abdomen. Almost instantly, the rain stopped, the remaining droplets racing down the outside of the window. All of a sudden, she shivered. Caroline felt warm, perhaps overly so. Her heart began beating rapidly. She opened her mouth but was unable to breathe.

Something's wrong with Liam. Caroline straightened. She took a few deep breaths. "Stop it, Caroline. You're becoming hysterical over nothing." She left his room and lingered in the hallway, unable to decide whether she wanted to read in her room or in the parlor. She opened the door to her room and settled in the chair by the fireplace. She began to read, but could not focus on the words. She shivered again, despite the warmth of the room. Worry now took root in her and she clapped the book shut and began to pace.

"Miss Caroline, come quickly!" The urgency in the servant's tone made her rush through the hallway. Caroline stepped down the stairs and looked out the front door. Kip and David were lifting someone out of the carriage.

"No!" She screamed when she saw Liam's dark jacket and his blond hair. For a moment, she stood paralyzed on the steps, her mouth open to speak, but unable to form any coherent words. Finally, as they were bringing him up the stairs, she screamed, "What happened?" She looked down at her husband's face, his eyes closed in unconsciousness, his skin ashen, the back of his head bleeding.

Kip, his clothes and hair dripping, recounted to Caroline the overturned carriage, the disingenuous thieves demanding money, then hurting Liam. Caroline led them down the hallway and opened Liam's door.

Kip and David laid Liam on his bed, then Kip began to remove Liam's wet clothes. Her husband smelled of rain, dirt, blood.

Caroline glanced towards David. Like Kip, his clothes were soaked. He wore no hat and his wet hair hung in dark strips around his head. Drops slid down his cheeks like tears. He stood still, his eyes focused on Liam's unconscious form, his white shirt splattered with blood. He remained silent throughout Kip's speech.

Kip continued. "He's not responding. His head likely got a bad pounding, but I think it's where he fell afterwards."

"Kip, you need to get the doctor immediately, please."

"Yes, Ma'am. I'll bring him back straight away."

Caroline whispered into her husband's ear, "Liam, can you hear me?"

He was lying unresponsive on the bed, his eyes closed, his breathing steady.

"God, please allow him to be fine. Please let him wake." She glanced at David.

"This is my fault that Liam's hurt."

"Your fault?"

"I wouldn't give that – I wouldn't give the thieves my money." His head was lowered, his shoulders were slumped as he stared blankly at Liam on the bed. "I didn't think he would hurt us. If anything, I don't understand why he hurt Liam and not me."

*   *   *

A few hours later, the doctor approached Caroline and David by Liam's bedside. "Mrs. O'Donovan, Mr. O'Donovan." He turned towards David. "I need some time with your brother to evaluate his injuries. It will likely be necessary to transport him to the hospital. So if you could escort your sister-in-law out to the hallway?"

"Yes, of course." He touched Caroline's elbow, but she pulled away. She kissed Liam's forehead, the top of his blond head, then she and David walked out of the room. David closed the door and stood quietly in the hallway. Caroline stared at his shirt, still stained with her husband's blood, a constant reminder. Could he not have changed?

Out of the corner of her eye, she saw someone coming toward them. "Miss Caroline?" Kip stuck his hand in his pocket and pulled out a pocket watch. "The thieves took this from Mr. Liam and dropped it as they were running away. I retrieved it for him."

Caroline held her hand out. Kip gently pressed it into her palm. It was cold and still damp from the rainfall. She carefully placed it in the pocket of her skirt. "Thank you, Kip."

Jane approached Caroline and David with a tray.

"Miss Caroline, Mr. David, would you like something to eat or some tea?"

"No, Jane. I don't think I'd be able to eat."

David shook his head.

The doctor opened the door. David stepped back.

"Mr. O'Donovan?"

"Yes?"

"Your brother has a severe head injury."

"What can you do to make him better?"

"I'm not certain there is anything we can do, other than to wait and watch him. Transporting him to the hospital could make him worse. Allow him to rest and inform me if he wakens. Good day, Mrs. O'Donovan." He tipped his hat.

"Mr. O'Donovan, don't hesitate to have your servant come and get me again if your brother's condition worsens."

"Yes, of course, Dr. Mayfield."

"I'll escort the doctor downstairs, Mr. David."

David nodded.

Caroline and David stood awkwardly in the hallway. She brushed past him and into her husband's room. Outside the doorway, she heard Jane and David speaking.

"Mr. David, a police officer is downstairs to talk to you."

"Very well, Jane."

Caroline approached her husband's bed, then tentatively sat on the chair beside it. She picked up Liam's limp hand and kissed the back of it. *Wake up, Liam. Please, wake up.*

Then she lifted her head to the ceiling. *Please, God, allow Liam to wake up. I promise to read the Bible every day. I promise to pray more. I will do anything. Just let him wake up.*

The last time she had said goodbye to her husband, it was a curt farewell. Now, she was feeling guilty. If Liam didn't wake up . . .no, Caroline refused to think of that possibility. When he wakes up, she would be able to tell him how much she loved him and how sorry she was for being so juvenile.

The darkness now burned a hole in her chest. She immediately bolted upright to retch in the basin on the night stand. After a few moments, she returned to sit on the chair next to the bed. There was a quiet knock at the door.

"I'll empty that basin for you," Jane offered.

"Thank you."

* * *

David motioned for the officer to join him in his study off the foyer. The policeman was tall, around the same age as David, with a handlebar moustache.

"Your servant here was telling me what happened, Mr. O'Donovan, and that your brother is seriously injured?"

David nodded.

"Can you tell us what happened? Which road were you on?"

"We took Wister Street. There aren't many houses along that stretch of road. We were coming from the Germantown train station."

"Those appear to be the kind of roads thieves target unsuspecting people like yourselves."

"My servant saw up ahead of us that a carriage had turned over and he slowed down to stop. There were three people, two men and a woman. They told us their names were John and James Smith." David paused. "I suppose those weren't their real names."

"Unlikely. Unless they're imbeciles."

David then proceeded to give the officer a description of the criminals, that they had asked for assistance, then had robbed them. David told him that he had knocked the thief named James

Smith down, then John Smith assaulted Liam.

"Mr. O'Donovan, this group matches the description of some thieves who have been swindling money from area residents. They turn their carriage over and appear to be in need of assistance. Then they take all their victims' money. But this is the first instance we've heard of someone getting hurt."

After a few more questions, the officer tipped his hat. "Thank you, Mr. O'Donovan. We'll keep you informed if there is any news on the continuing investigation."

David accompanied the officer to the foyer, then watched through the side window as the man got into his carriage and rode away. He remained there a while. He wanted to avoid being around Caroline. She hadn't said much, but he could see it in her eyes. She had every right to blame him.

"Mr. David?"

"Yes, Jane?"

"Would you like me to prepare a clean shirt for you to wear?"

He shrugged his shoulders.

"Come, Mr. David. I'll take you upstairs and get you a nice clean shirt."

He nodded and allowed Jane to escort him upstairs.

* * *

Over the next several hours, Caroline switched positions often, sometimes sitting beside her husband's bed, other times standing and studying him for signs of consciousness.

She finally half-reclined on his bed and laid her head on his hand. As the sun rose, light flooded the room and removed some of darkness within her and finally, Caroline drifted off to sleep. She wasn't certain how long she slept, but almost instantly, she felt Liam's hand moving. She lifted her head and studied his face. His eyes fluttered at first.

Caroline left his bed for a moment and hurried to the doorway and called for Jane. She returned to find that his eyes were open and he was smiling at her.

"Liam, I was so frightened."

"My. . .head hurts," he groaned.

She squeezed his hand. "Liam?"

"Yes?"

"I'm so sorry for acting like a child when you were leaving."

"And I'm sorry for being cross with you."

"Lee!" Immediately, David, Jane and Kip appeared at the doorway. He rushed to his brother's bedside and stood beside Caroline.

"This is my fault."

"No, it isn't, David."

"I'm so sorry. I should have given them my money too. I was just so damned angry that we had been taken in like fools."

Caroline sat on the edge of his bed and again took hold of his hand. "I'm so relieved that you're awake. I was so frightened." She placed two pillows behind his head and he relaxed against them.

"Caroline?" Liam said.

"Yes?"

"I. . ."

"What is it, Liam?"

At first, his eyes became unfocused, confused. Then his head flung back against the pillows and he began to shake uncontrollably. Caroline gasped and jumped off the bed as his body thrashed back and forth.

"Help him, David!"

Jane and Kip joined the group as they watched, helplessly.

David reached out to his brother, but Liam continued to flail violently on the bed. Involuntary sounds were escaping from his lips and the bed squeaked and rocked as his head, arms and legs jerked out of control. Finally, his body seemed frightfully still.

David touched Liam's shoulder and he roused slightly, but didn't open his eyes.

"What in the world just happened, David?"

"I don't know, Caroline. It must be related to his injury."

"That was horrible."

David turned toward Kip. "You need to get the doctor."

"Of course, Mr. David." Kip quickly left the room.

Liam began to moan. He opened his eyes. When he spoke, his words were slurred. "Don't feel. . . well."

"Lee, you just had some sort of convulsion or something."

"W. . .what?"

"You've had some sort of convulsion."

Liam opened his mouth to speak, then shook his head.

David leaned close to Liam.

"I've asked Kip to get Dr. Mayfield, Lee."

"No doctor."

"There's something wrong and we need to find out what it is."

"David's right, Liam. We need to get the doctor. He'll know what's wrong with you and how to fix it."

Liam closed his eyes and turned his face away from them.

*   *   *

Later that morning, Liam stared at his wife's worried expression. His head was pounding and his vision at times was blurred, but most troubling was that he felt utterly exhausted, as if he had gone for weeks without sleep. Caroline and David whispered constantly to one another, attempting to appear casual. He smiled inwardly. They were speaking with one another, which in itself was a miraculous accomplishment. His wife leaned down and spoke in a calm manner.

"The doctor will arrive soon, Liam. I'm certain he will give you some medicine to make you better."

"Caroline. . ."

"Lee, doctors can work wonders these days."

Liam glanced away. He wasn't going to get better. Perhaps it was his pessimistic nature, or maybe it was a premonition. However, his head throbbed constantly and the overwhelming fatigue made it impossible to even lift his head, let alone sit up. When he spoke, he couldn't seem to form his words quickly enough. Blurred vision, muffled hearing, slurred speech and uncontrollable seizures: no, this was definitely not something that he was going to come out of unscathed.   Caroline was putting forth her best effort to appear strong for him.   His eyes became fixed on her large middle. Their child. *God, how can I provide for my child? For Caroline? How will she react if I die, especially when she discovers the truth about me? But this isn't just about me anymore. I must speak with David and devise a plan for. . .when I'm gone.*

*   *   *

Doctor Mayfield examined Liam, then straightened. His expression was serious, his tone somber. "Mr. O'Donovan, from what your brother tells me, you have experienced a very bad seizure."

"And?"

"Sometimes a head injury will do that, bring on seizures."

As the doctor spoke, Liam began convulsing again. Caroline gasped as she watched her husband writhing uncontrollably. The wooden floor under his bed creaked.

"Please, please help him!" she pleaded with the doctor.

"It will end momentarily, Mrs. O'Donovan." Dr. Mayfield placed a pillow more firmly under Liam's head and a cloth in his mouth.

"Is he in pain, Doctor?"

"No, no, he won't remember this. And as you witnessed earlier, he's likely to be exhausted when this is over. I've placed a cloth in his mouth so he will not bite his tongue."

Caroline couldn't watch any longer and lowered her gaze. She followed a ray of sunlight from an intensely lit patch on the floor all the way to her husband's bedroom window. It was a beautiful spring day, the sky a brilliant blue. She could hear the bed shaking and muffled grunting sounds coming from her husband, noises which sounded so foreign to her.

Then all was silent. Slowly, she turned to face her husband who was still on the bed. "Thank God."

"I imagine your husband will be sleeping for some time. Would you be so kind as to ask your brother-in-law to come in here? We must discuss the course of treatment for your husband."

"Yes, yes, certainly." Caroline leaned her head out the doorway. Hallie was at the top of the staircase. "Hallie? Would you please tell David to join me in Liam's room?"

"Yes, Ma'am."

Within moments, David rushed into the room. "What's wrong, Caroline?"

She bit down on her lip, then lifted her gaze toward her brother-in-law. "Another one."

He gasped, then lowered his head.

"Mr. O'Donovan, the fact that your brother has endured two of these in one day, well, it's not good. It is imperative that he be transported to the hospital to be treated immediately."

"What sort of treatment?"

"Bromide is being used in patients with epilepsy, especially with severe seizures such as this."

"Epilepsy?"

"Well, it's a seizure disorder, but it can be brought about by a head injury and it seems obvious that is what is happening here, although I cannot know for certain without performing some tests at the hospital. As well, he most likely has some bleeding in the brain. If that is the case, his prognosis would not be good."

Caroline glanced at Liam. His eyes were fluttering open.

David responded to the doctor. "Liam ought to have a say in this decision, Doctor. And Mrs. O'Donovan as well." They both turned toward Caroline.

"He needs to get better."

"Mrs. O'Donovan, the next few days will give us an idea of whether he will improve. However, if we do nothing, he will continue to have seizures, perhaps several a day. He will not be able to ride a horse or carriage or even conduct business on a daily basis."

Moaning caused them to turn towards Liam's bed.

"What. . ."

Caroline leaned down close to him. "Liam."

He groaned, then slowly opened his eyes.

"Mr. O'Donovan, according to your wife and brother, you've already suffered two seizures in less than eight hours. If you remain at home, it's likely that you will continue to experience these seizures several times a day. We can treat you with bromide." He paused. "It is necessary for you to go to the hospital. I shall return in three hours in order to make arrangements for transporting you there." The doctor picked up his bag. "You don't really have much of a choice, Mr. O'Donovan." He tipped his hat and left the room.

Caroline sat on the edge of the bed and picked up Liam's hand. "You need to go to the hospital."

His speech was again slurred. "Don't want. . .don't want. . .to die in. . .hospital."

"Liam, you mustn't say such things. You're not going to die."

"Caroline."

"You're going to be fine."

"Must. . .speak with David."

"Yes, of course."

David stood behind her, his eyes downcast.

Liam glanced at her. "Alone."

"Liam, I want to stay."

"Need. . . to speak with David about. . .business."

"Very well."

*   *   *

Liam spoke, his words continued to be slow and measured. "I won't. . .get better."

"You don't know that. You're going to the hospital. They'll make it better."

"I. . .am going to die."

"Lee. . ."

"Don't. . .want to be. . .burden."

"Lee, that's enough. You're not going to be a burden to anyone. Caroline loves you. She would do anything for you."

"Any. . .thing?"

"Yes, damn it, anything. So will I."

For a moment, neither spoke. Then Liam cleared his throat. "You took Caroline to. . .convent."

David stepped back and his eyes widened. "What. . .are you talking about?"

"Don't. . . deny it."

"I don't know what to say."

"I know you did."

"Look. . ." David's head was lowered and he was avoiding eye contact. Finally, he said, "It was me." He paused a moment, then said, "Lee, I'm sorry. I will make it up to you."

23

Caroline paced the hallway for more than an hour. All of a sudden, she heard David screaming her name. She banged open the door to find David leaning over Liam. Her husband was having another convulsion.

"These – whatever they're called – are increasing. We must get him to the hospital!" David shouted.

Distracted by her husband's uncontrolled shaking on the bed, she stared at him, worry stretched across her face. "How do we keep him still in the carriage?"

"I don't know. Perhaps we'll be fortunate and he won't have one while we're transporting him."

Caroline sat beside her husband. She stroked his forehead with a cool, wet cloth. She began to sob. David touched her shoulder with his hand. "I'm. . .I'm sorry."

Liam roused. For a few moments, he was incoherent, moaning. His eyes blinked, then opened. He glanced at his wife, then his brother. He heaved a defeated sigh, closed his eyes and turned his head away.

"Lee, we must transport you to the hospital immediately."

"Not . . .yet."

"Liam, please," Caroline begged.

"Must rest."

"Certainly. I'll stay here with you. Then we need to discuss . . ."

"David?"

"Yes?" David leaned close to Liam's face. Liam mouthed something to his brother, then he said, "Please."

David picked up an envelope from the nightstand and shoved it into his pocket. "We'll talk about this later." He quickly left.

Caroline sat down on the chair next to Liam's bed; the seat now seemed to bear an imprint of her body. He reached his hand for hers. "You're. . . sad."

"I am sad."

"Sorry."

"I just want you to be. . ."

"The way I. . .was?"

"I didn't say that. I hate seeing you go through this."

Caroline lifted the wet cloth out of the basin and began to tenderly wipe Liam's face. Within a few moments, he began closing his eyes. "You need to rest, Liam."

Without opening his eyes, he nodded, then he winced.

"Liam, you're in pain."

"Head hurts." He continued to slur his words.

"I wish I could help you."

"Need to rest."

"I'll stay here with you."

He shook his head.

"You want me to leave?"

"Need to rest."

"Very well. Fifteen minutes?"

He nodded.

"I'll be across the hall. I'll check on you in 15 minutes."

"Yes."

"When you wake up, we must talk about taking you to the hospital."

He shook his head.

"Liam, please." She leaned down to kiss him on the lips. "I love you."

"Love you."

She began to walk toward the door, then turned around. "You're certain you wish for me to leave?"

Liam gave her a drowsy smile. "I. . ."

"What is it?"

"Well, I. . ."

Caroline hurried back to his bedside and studied him. He was contemplating her with an expression filled with tenderness, and yet also, sadness. "I want to be. . .a better husband to you."

"You are a wonderful husband. And I acted childish and was selfish to expect you to stay with me."

"You were. . .right."

Caroline stared at him and bit down on her lip. "Please, Liam, we can't change that now."

Liam reached out and took her hand in his. He took a deep breath and worked hard at getting the words out. "Caroline, meeting you. . .best thing. . .ever happened. . .to me."

"Oh, Liam." She leaned down to embrace him on the bed. "I love you so."

"I want. . . the best for you."

"What's best for me is for you to get well." She crawled in beside him. She placed her left hand on his chest and felt the soft beating of his heart, reminiscent of how she often lay with her father. She shuddered. *But this is different. Liam is young. He will get better.*

He patted her back and kissed the top of her head. "Better go."

"I don't care. I want to remain here with you."

"Must rest."

She nodded, then lifted herself off of him. At the door, she said, "I'll leave the door partially open."

Ten minutes later, Caroline could hear soft knocking on Liam's open door across the hall. She greeted David standing at Liam's partly opened doorway. "David?"

"Caroline, I need to talk to him about an urgent matter."

"He's exhausted. He's probably sleeping."

"This is important."

Caroline let out an audible sigh. "Very well." David opened the door. Her husband's room was dark except for the bed which was bathed in the dim light of one oil lamp at his bedside table. The mantle clock ticked in rhythm with their soft, slow footsteps. She called out his name in a whisper, "Liam? I'm sorry to wake you, but David must speak with you."

The two walked together to the side of his bed. "Liam?" Caroline reached down and touched his hand. It was warm, but still, too still. She placed her hand on his chest to feel the soft beating of his heart. She felt nothing, so Caroline pushed on his arm more forcefully, but there was no response. "Liam, no !"

24

David lingered in the doorway of Liam's room and watched Jane and Hallie prepare Liam's body for burial. The servants, ever respectful, kept a linen sheet draped over his brother's private parts as they washed other areas of his body. Liam looked calm and peaceful, like he was sleeping. Every few moments, Jane and Hallie paused to wipe their eyes with their handkerchiefs.

David quickly blinked away his tears and cleared his throat. The two women stopped and looked up.

"Mr. David, is there something you need?" Jane asked.

"I. . .well. . ."

Jane wiped her hands on her apron and approached David at the doorway of Liam's room.

Swallowing, David quietly spoke. "When. . .will my brother's body be ready? I want him moved to the parlor downstairs. The casket has just been delivered."

"It won't be long." Jane paused. "Are you certain you don't want Mr. Liam embalmed? There's a new embalmer on Walnut Street and my ma tells me he makes house calls."

"Yes, I'm sure. I don't want my brother tampered with. His body's been through enough already."

"Yes, Mr. David."

"How. . .is.. . .my sister-in-law doing?" He turned and glanced across the hall at the closed door to Caroline's room.

"Crying steady since Mr. Liam died yesterday. I'm worried she might lose the baby." Jane hesitated. "The men will be arriving in soon for the wake," Jane said.

David cringed and lowered his head. He did not look forward to standing around with their colleagues, drinking, being nostalgic.

"I don't think Miss Caroline will be coming down for the wake."

"That's fine."

"Mr. Liam will be ready in about half an hour. We just need

to dress him in his Sunday clothes."

* * *

"Miss Caroline, are you awake?" called Jane's voice.

Caroline opened her eyes slowly, tentatively. As she gradually wakened, the horrible truth set in, burning into her consciousness. Her beloved husband, the father of her unborn child, was now gone. A ray of sunlight was streaming in through a thin area of parted curtains and birds were singing a sweet tune. How could those wretched creatures produce such happy sounds when her heart was breaking?

"Mr. David said I got to help you get ready for the funeral," the servant said through the closed door.

"Go away," she said as she pulled the coverlet closer.

"No, Ma'am, I can't do that. People are starting to arrive to pay their respects to Mr. Liam. And they'll be waiting on you to say good bye to him."

Jane let herself into the room. "Good gracious, Miss Caroline, if you're gonna go in the chamber pot, you got to cover it. Besides, you ought to be getting up and using the necessary room down the hall." Jane crossed the room and opened the window.

"Please, leave me alone. " Caroline pulled the covers up over her head and remained in bed.

"I'll leave you long enough to empty your chamber pot. " She picked up the metal basin from the floor beside the bed. "But you need to be getting up now, Miss Caroline." Jane left the door open and hurried into the hall.

Moments later the servant returned and slipped the metal pot under the bed.

Caroline lifted her head. "How was I supposed to get any sleep last night? That wake lasted until well after midnight."

"Yes, the men were loud, weren't they?"

"David ought to be ashamed of himself participating in that . . . that. . ."

"Now, you know that Mr. David was required to be there. From what I saw, he didn't appear to be enjoying himself." Jane, her hands outstretched in front of her, stood before Caroline.

"Come. " She grasped her mistress' hand and pulled her up. "You got to keep going for your baby." As soon as Caroline sat up, she bolted off the bed and leaned over the basin at her bedside table. She gagged several times but with no success.

"You poor thing. You haven't eaten anything and you're still retching like that."

Overwhelmingly nauseated, Caroline opened her mouth again, wishing that something would come out. But all that remained was despair, a cold hard knot that couldn't be expelled or loosened.

Jane rubbed her mistress' back. Caroline offered no resistance as the servant guided her to the closet. "Now, which one of these black dresses would you like to wear?"

"I don't like black. I want to wear this blue one here."

"That's not proper. You got to wear black. This one here will do fine. And no jewelry or other extras."

She raised her arms up so that the servant could put on her shift. "Miss Caroline, pull your arm into the sleeve here." She grudgingly followed the command. Her arms dangled limply in the sleeves while Jane buttoned up the back of her dress. Her head yanked back as Jane brushed her hair.

The servant then led her mistress to the bed and sat her down.

"Miss Caroline?"

Caroline ignored her, staring straight ahead. The grieving woman felt Jane's hand patting her back.

"I know this is difficult."

Caroline began to sob, loud, insistent. She cried so hard that the walls echoed her grief, the floor sunk with the weight of it.

All of a sudden, she stopped crying and sat up. She wiped her eyes, then she caught a glimpse of her mother's Bible sitting on the dresser. She pushed away from Jane. She stomped over to the dresser, lifted up the small Bible and pitched it across the room. It landed in front of the unlit fireplace.

"Miss Caroline, don't!" Jane screamed, then ran to the front of the fireplace and carefully picked up the book and the few pages that had come loose from it. "This is your Ma's Bible."

"I don't ever want to see it again! Rip it up; throw it away!"

Jane, still holding the Bible, stood before her. "Now, Ma'am, I have never in my life disobeyed an order from you, but I just can't do that, destroy the good Lord's book."

Caroline reluctantly took her eyes from Jane then covered her face with her hands, and began sobbing again, collapsing on the wooden floor.

"Now, now. . ." Jane crouched down. "Look at me."

Caroline ignored her. With both hands, Jane gently cradled her mistress' face and lifted it up to meet her own. "I know you are grieving for Mr. Liam, but Mr. Liam would want you to keep going, for your baby's sake." Caroline shrugged.

"Come now," Jane pulled her up. "We got to get you downstairs so you can greet some people and say good bye to your husband."

Walking into the hallway, death greeted her like a stalking adversary, its subtle stench nauseating her. Its smell was sour, heavy and mixed with the distant aromas of flowers and baking bread.

A short while later, as she was standing in the foyer, Caroline greeted guests who were offering their condolences.

"Carrie, dear, I can't tell you how sorry I. . ."

"I know, Lizzie." Caroline stopped and began sobbing again. Elizabeth cradled her cousin. "Shhh, it's going to be fine." Caroline held on tightly. After a few moments, she pulled away.

"No, no, it's not going to be fine," she sniffled, "He's gone. I loved him and he's gone."

"I know, dear Carrie, I know."

"Miss Caroline, ye're goin' ta be foin. Ye jest wait'n see. Sure an' it's jest hard now, the pain so fresh 'n all." Patsie wiped Caroline's cheeks in a motherly fashion, then tilted her face upward. "Ye know Mr. Liam's in a far better place now, Miss Caroline."

A steady stream of relatives and friends repeated the comments.

"Our Heavenly Father called him home."

"He's in heaven."

"He's at peace."

Caroline had no desire to hear about our Heavenly Father or heaven or peace. It was obvious that her whispered promises to God had meant nothing. He hadn't answered her prayers for Liam's recovery. She glanced towards the staircase.

All the muscles in her body tensed as she watched David on the far side of the foyer. He was nodding and listening patiently to one of his clients, a man half a foot taller. Her brother-in-law's expression was serious and composed.

"Caroline." Uncle Edward embraced Caroline so tightly, she was finding it difficult to breathe. As he stepped away from her, she exhaled. "If there is anything we can do, my dear, please let us know."

An hour later, Jane kept her arm around Caroline's shoulder as she escorted her mistress to the parlor. Dark drapery kept light from the room and linens covered the mirrors. The flower arrangements couldn't mask the scent of death.

On the other side of the room, the open coffin waited. With each step, Caroline's only desire was to turn and run, but Jane's gentle insistence forced her to accomplish this final act as his wife.

They reached the coffin and Jane whispered to Caroline, "It's time to be saying goodbye to your husband."

She glanced at her husband's still body, a subtle odor now emanating from him, his arms crossed over his chest. *Oh Liam. Why did you have to leave us so soon?*

She leaned into the open coffin and pressed a kiss to his forehead, now cold. From this view, she couldn't see the deep gash in his head or what his body had to endure in the last day or so. His face looked beautiful, peaceful. "I love you, Liam," she whispered.

*   *   *

David cordially welcomed more guests in the foyer area of their home. He glanced at Caroline. Her black dress emphasized her pale complexion and her anguish. His sister-in-law wept most of the time or walked around, staring straight ahead, her eyes dark with pain. David was not one who shared his grief publicly, and he had already had one long sobbing episode the night of his brother's death. However, he had done his best to remain self-controlled since then.

This was all his fault, of that he was certain. He was responsible for Lee's death, for Caroline's heartache.

Now, she was the disconsolate widow, and he, the grieving brother. He must be strong for her. He owed her that.

He gritted his teeth as he recalled the conversation in the

carriage before Liam got hurt. Caroline would be appalled if she ever found out what they had discussed.

When would it be the right time to give her the letter? He made several attempts to speak with her and she refused to even look at him. David concluded that it would never be the right time and that the sooner he did so, that terrible job would be accomplished.

And how would he ever make all this up to Caroline? He would never be able to fix this dreadful situation. He was just going to have to do what his brother asked and live with that decision.

He took a deep breath and faced the man in front of him.

"That was some wake last night, David," a tall man said. "Your brother was well-liked."

"Yes, he was," he responded. In actuality, David despised that so many of their colleagues and friends had drunk themselves to a stupor while Liam lay cold in a box in the parlor. Of course, when he finally drank in earnest, he was able to toss his grief aside and pretend that Liam hadn't died.

25

At the cemetery, the wind howled with an oppressive force. Caroline remained still and stared, eyes unfocused, into the distance. Despite the number of people surrounding her, she felt alone, although she could feel their pity smothering her. No one loved him like she did. No one would ever know how this loss was affecting her, how it was ripping her heart in two.

The minister spoke in a dull monotone. A soft rain had started to fall and Caroline brushed aside a drop from her cheek. Above her, the rain seemed to stop. Distracted, she turned to see the ivory handle of the umbrella as David took it from Kip. David was grasping it firmly, as the wind pulled it upward.

The polished maple casket was lowered into the ground and large shovelfuls of earth were dumped onto it. Caroline winced as pile after pile of dirt landed on Liam's coffin. Liam couldn't be dead. He was alive just a few short days ago.

"Miss Martin, you have made me the happiest man in all of Philadelphia!"

"Caroline?" David's voice jolted her back to the present. *Why must he sound so much like Liam?*

She stared at him blankly.

"It's time to return to the house." His hand touched her shoulder and she winced.

* * *

Caroline pulled the drapes of her bedroom window aside and looked down at the people walking about below. She wished that everyone would leave. Soft knocking caused her to sigh. "Yes?"

"Mr. David is looking for you."

"Tell him I'm resting."

"He just saw you at your window a few moments ago. He knows you're not resting."

"Don't bother me, Jane."

"Ma'am, your uncle and cousin are about to leave. You ought to come downstairs and see them off."

Caroline's shoulders dropped and she let out an exasperated sigh. "Very well."

"I hope you had a good rest, my dear." Uncle pulled her to a close embrace.

"Yes, I did." She glanced at Elizabeth, whose head was lowered.

"Carrie," her cousin began sobbing. Caroline surprised herself by hugging Elizabeth and consoling her.

Uncle stepped forward and put his hand on Elizabeth's shoulder. "Come, Elizabeth, we must be going now. Caroline, let us know if there is anything that we can do for you."

Caroline nodded to Uncle.

A few moments later, she watched their carriage ride away. She stared off in the distance at the oak tree and small pond. The weather was beginning to clear; the sun now peeked through the thick clouds.

Someone behind her cleared his throat. Startled, she turned to find David, then immediately began to walk away.

"Caroline, we must talk. This is important." She continued to walk, ignoring him.

"Please." He grabbed her by the arm. She yanked it away. "Leave me alone. I don't wish to talk to you or anyone right now."

"But Caroline. . ."

Why can't everyone just leave me alone? Why did he have to die? Caroline dropped to the ground and wept. The cold damp earth seeped through her dress and she began to shiver.

"Caroline," she heard him softly say. He touched her shoulder, then she felt his soft touch on her back. She flinched and he drew his hand away. "I don't want to talk to you now, David. I just want to return to my room." She pushed herself up, indifferent to the mud on the bottom and front of her black dress. She started to walk.

"Wait. I need to give you something," she heard him say from behind her.

"Please, just leave me alone."

"Before he died, Lee. . .Liam. . .wrote you a letter."

Caroline abruptly came to a stop. At the chance that it might be true, she held her position but glared back at him. "A letter?"

He nodded. David held the plain white envelope in front of her. She stared at the letter, then quickly took it from him. She noticed Liam's handwriting and her eyes began to water. On the front was her name written in his hand, but less precise than usual, and his wax seal and initials on the back. She glanced at David, who was staring at the letter. She broke the seal and pulled it out. She read the first line and gasped.

"What foolery is this? This is not my husband's handwriting, but yours!"

"Lee was only able to write your name on the front of the envelope and he signed it."

She quickly scanned the bottom and his signature. It was sloppy, but was most certainly written in Liam's hand.

"Please, Caroline, read it."

My Dearest Caroline,

I have instructed David to give you this letter should I pass away. I have also asked David to write down my words as I am unable to do so at present. I love you very much and I want you to be happy. It is your right to mourn when I'm gone, but I would hope that you will eventually find a way to be happy, not just for me, but for our child.

You once told me that you were not the person I thought you were. But I am not the person you think I am. That is why we were so perfect for one another. Forgive me for not being honest with you. Before this point, it wasn't necessary to tell the whole truth. When my father died, he left me nothing, no money or assets. David generously gave me title to half the house but I own little else and only a meager amount of money to leave to you.

Therefore, I have asked David to enter immediately into a marriage of convenience, a marriage in name only, you and David, to provide not only physical protection, but also to ensure that our child has a privileged upbringing.

I ask you to obey my request that you marry David and give our
child a chance at having a loving father and for you to be able to
continue living the privileged lifestyle you deserve.
Yours always,
Liam

Caroline's eyes were now blurred. She felt her heart squeeze. For a moment, she couldn't think clearly. "You did this! Liam would have never wanted this for me, never!"

"Caroline, please. It's true, all of it."

As her mind gradually comprehended what Liam was asking of her, her whole body started to tremble. She dropped the letter and it landed in front of her in the mud. She sunk to the ground, her hands covering her face. *A marriage in name only? A marriage?* She wasn't married any longer. She was a widow and had no intentions of ever marrying again. "This. . .isn't possible."

"Caroline. . ."

"It cannot be possible that he has no assets."

"Our father left him nothing. I tried to give him money but he wouldn't accept it, only his half of the house. But he was a shrewd investor and he was able to make a lot of money for me, and I thought, for him. But he would never take it. He would never take a penny of anything which originally came from Father. He wouldn't have taken the house either but our mother insisted."

"This cannot be happening." Sitting straight up, she tried to take calm, even breaths, but her heart was pounding in her chest, and it became difficult to breathe at all. *Marry David? He wouldn't ask me to do that.* "I'm not marrying you, David. I don't care what. . ."

David leaned in and whispered, "This was not my idea, Caroline. I knew, with certainty, that you would not want this."

Caroline, her eyes glistening, turned to face him. "No, I do not want this, David," she spat at him.

"And I was not of the opinion that this would be the most prudent way to handle this at first, either. But the more I've reflected, the more it makes financial sense. After all, it's not like we are really marrying each other. It will be in name only."

"Just give me money or perhaps I can stay with Uncle and Lizzie. . .anything but. . ."

"I do not desire this any more than you do, but we need to marry to protect your interests. Lee's will provided no financial assets for you because all our assets are essentially mine and what little Lee owned is not available at the present time. Father left him nothing. I gave Lee half ownership in the house, but right now there's a lien on it. Lee managed our finances but everything, except for the house, is in my name only. And although Lee had signing authority with regard to everything in the business, the business is mine as well. He was essentially just an employee."

"What does it matter now?"

"Caroline, please, listen to me."

"Why didn't you just give them what they wanted? If it weren't for you, Liam would be alive now," she shouted, her voice cracking.

David's head lowered.

Caroline got to her feet. All she could think was that she did not want to be anywhere near him right now. This was too much to bear. She rushed toward the house and heard footsteps but did not look up.

"Miss Caroline, I'll escort you to your room."

"Leave me alone, Jane. I don't want. . ." She continued to shake her head as she ran across the foyer to the staircase. She passed a group of people but avoided eye contact. "Miss Caroline," she heard Hallie say. She ignored her and climbed the steps. Soon she reached the sanctuary of her bedroom.

She dropped onto her bed, her grief and anger weighing heavy as she sank into the bed.

How could Liam possibly believe that this would be the answer? And how could it be that she had no money to speak of? She despised the idea of being forced into marriage. The more she thought about it, the more angry she became with her now dead husband. She smacked the feather pillow hard, her hand sinking all the way through to the bed. *"That you will herein always obey me."* Liam's voice echoed in her mind.

Caroline promised that she would obey him. She closed her eyes and hoped that sleep would come quickly so that she could escape from life for a short while.

*   *   *

David leaned on the mantle in the parlor and downed a glass

of brandy. When Lee had asked him to write down his words, he had hesitated. But he owed it to Lee to do anything he asked, whether it was writing down his final thoughts or marrying his widow.

However, he cursed his sense of timing. Caroline couldn't have reacted in a worse manner. But how did he expect that she would behave? With a smile on her face and open arms? He lit his pipe and inhaled. He relished the taste of the tobacco, then he remembered Liam's words.

"You need to take care of her."

"Lee, I'll give Caroline money to. . ."

"Most of. . .the capital is tied up."

"Then she can just stay here."

"Please promise."

"You're going to be fine."

Liam shook his head. "I need to know . . .she will be taken care of."

"I am going to take care of her. It is not necessary for me to marry her to do that."

"If I die, you must. . . marry her."

"No, Lee, this isn't the answer."

"I need to know."

"What?"

"That she will be taken care of."

"I told you I will take care of her."

"And. . ."

"And what?"

"And that our child will have a. . .privileged upbringing."

"Your child will have all that."

"Marry her. . .right away."

"I don't need to marry her."

"Explain it need only be a marriage on paper."

"No, Lee."

"If I tell you what to write. . ."

"She will think I composed it."

"She will know." He paused, appearing to be weighing his words carefully. "If I tell her to do it, she will. She promised she would always. . .obey me."

"But she hates me. I'm not staying to listen to this nonsense."

"Stop," Liam said.

David put his hand on the door. He turned and stared at his brother.

"I have been taking care of your problems. It's time for you to take care of my wife and child." He was trying to talk quickly and his words were becoming difficult for David to understand.

"What are you talking about, Lee? What have you been taking care of?

"Selly."

"And how did you take care of that?"

"I sent the convent my money. . ."

"You sent. . ."

Liam nodded.

"Lee."

"And Missy."

"What about her?"

"She was. . .also carrying your child."

"What nonsense is this? You're confused."

"Gave her money." He stopped to catch his breath. "She used it to go to the midwife to end the pregnancy. If I had known, I would not have given it to her."

"You are wrong. She would have told me, not you."

Liam stopped and took a deep breath and spoke slowly, each word measured. "It's time for you to take care of my wife and baby. Please. . .write down my words. . ."

David poured himself another drink, downed it, then poured another. His best friend and only surviving relation was now dead. He missed his brother so much. He lowered his head and began to sob. Then he immediately straightened and wiped his eyes. Crying wouldn't, couldn't, bring Lee back. Right now, he needed to forget that Lee was gone and, for the moment, to disregard the promise to marry his sister-in-law, a girl who couldn't stand the sight of him. He emptied his pipe then hurried up to Hallie's bedroom.

26

Caroline, now awake, stared at the ceiling of her bedroom. A soft breeze blew in through the open window.

"Miss Caroline?" Jane said through the closed door. "We'll be leaving for the church in about two hours."

At the mention of "church," Caroline cringed.

"I don't hear any movement in there yet."

"Yes, I'm getting up." The past two weeks were a blur, with each day blending into the next, day and night happening and Caroline losing track of the time.

As she got out of bed, her eyes were drawn to the small painting over her fireplace that her uncle had given her, the reproduction of the picture of her father and uncle on the beach. Her heart ached. There was such happiness in the eyes of the young man who would later become her father. Joy is something Caroline would not likely ever feel again.

She had been dreading this day, wishing that some way, somehow, it wouldn't be necessary to marry David. She tried speaking to Uncle about it, hoping that perhaps he would invite her to live with him, but he seemed to think this whole farce of a marriage was a good idea. "It's for the best, Caroline. Liam had a good head on his shoulders. You shall be well taken care of," he had said.

But this wasn't just about her anymore. Caroline had to think of her soon-to-be born child. He or she deserved to be brought up in a privileged environment, rather than the hardworking, difficult one that she'd had to endure.

"Miss Caroline?"

"What is it?" she finally answered.

The servant swung open the door. "I'll help you get dressed. Mr. David's in the downstairs study waiting for you."

Caroline shuddered at the thought of speaking with him, let alone being married to him, even if it was a marriage in name only.

"Yes, very well. Thank you, Jane."

An hour later, Caroline descended the staircase to the first floor. The faint aroma of roasting turkey drifted up from the kitchen.

The door to the office was ajar and Caroline could hear glass tinkling and what sounded like books being slammed on the desk.

She knocked softly. Not hearing any response, she banged on the door.

"Yes, what is it," David said, a sharp edge to his tone.

"It's Caroline."

"Oh, yes, the happy bride. Come in."

She pushed open the door. David was sitting at his desk at the far end of the room. Caroline kept her eyes on the floor and inched closer to him. She finally looked up at him as he gulped down a glass of beige-colored liquid.

"Now, my dear." He was looking at her with that same provocative expression when they first met.

How dare he treat me in this manner? "You're drinking."

"That I am. You are not only beautiful, but observant. Would you like to join me, my dear?"

"I think not." Caroline paused. "We're supposed to be at the church in an hour. Perhaps we ought to postpone this."

"You would like that, wouldn't you? I've been so looking forward to this day, just like you, Caroline." His cynical smile and mocking tone made her glance away.

"Ah, and you're dressed so beautifully in the perfect color for a wedding."

"My husband just died, David. I'm being forced to. . ." She couldn't, wouldn't, say the word. "I'm being forced to go along with this farce."

"Yes, that you are." He paused. He stared at her with such intensity that Caroline couldn't figure out whether it was anger in his eyes or despair or some other emotion. He lowered his head. Several moments passed before he broke the silence.

"So I suppose you think that you're the only one who is not happy with this upcoming marriage? After all, you're being forced into marriage with someone you despise."

"You. . ." Caroline's words wouldn't form fast enough.

"And me? How do you think I feel? I'm also being forced into marriage. I've never considered myself a marrying man to begin with. So shed the self-piteous attitude, Caroline. You're not the only one who does not want this upcoming so-called marriage."

"You need to stop drinking." *How can he be drinking at a time like this?*

"Oh, do I now? Well, this is how we Irish drown our misery: we drink. " He held up the glass, then drank it. "Shall I pour you a drink too, to drown out your own misery?" He paused. "Oh, that's right, you declined."

"David, please stop this."

"Well, I suppose I ought to stop drinking before our 'wedding.' After all, we would not want anyone to say that our 'marriage' is not binding and legal now, would we, Caroline? Well, it's not as if this will be truly legal and binding anyway, right?" He winked at her.

She glared at him.

"Ah, there's the beautiful Miss Caroline look of hatred. It's one of the qualities I love most about you, dear sister-in-law, soon-to-be wife of mine." At the sound of his cutting tone, her body stiffened.

"If you wish to make this situation worse, you're doing a perfect job, David." She scowled at him across the desk.

As he looked up at her, his eyes darted past her and he caught sight of the painting of his family, from many years ago. Immediately, his face softened and he turned away. A few moments passed, then he turned toward her. "I'm sorry, Caroline. I shouldn't have said those things to you. You didn't deserve that." His voice was just above a whisper and Caroline could barely hear him. He appeared to be forcing a smile.

"David."

"Yes?"

"Is there any way we can avoid this?"

He shook his head, but paused before he spoke. "I made a promise, Caroline, and I. . .we must follow through with it."

27

Do you, David O'Donovan, take Caroline Martin O'Donovan to be your wife, to have and to hold from this day forward, for better for worse, for richer for poorer, in sickness and in health, to love and to cherish, until death do you part?

Earlier today, when he stood beside Caroline listening to what he was asked to consent to, David said the "I will" as quickly as possible, before he changed his mind. Yes, he had promised Liam and certainly he felt obligated to provide for Caroline and her child, but this whole arrangement was nothing short of a mockery. To have and to hold? Any time he touched her, she winced. Of course, with the manner he spoke to her this morning, he didn't blame her for hating him.

When it came time to give her consent, she hesitated for what seemed like an extraordinarily lengthy amount of time – a minute or so – and he wondered whether she was going to refuse. It was an awkward moment with the minister's eyes darting from David's face to Caroline's, then back to David's again. Then she quickly muttered the words and it was done.

He still couldn't believe that Liam was gone. David should have protected his younger brother.

Why did they have to hurt him? Most of the time, David was not able to protect Liam from their father's warped personality. In fact, David had become an expert at protecting his own interests.

He walked across his room to his dresser and poured a drink from the brandy decanter. He carried his glass to the window and looked out toward the barn. The oak tree stood tall, defiant, its endless branches reaching up toward the sky.

"Lee, just a few more feet. Give me your hand." David leaned down from higher up in the tree.

"No, David. I'm not coming any farther. It's too high. Mother's going to be upset. I don't want to get hurt."

"You're being a girl, Lee."

"I am not!"

"Then climb up to the top with me."

Liam nodded, reached his hand up to David, then placed his foot carefully on the next branch. As soon as he did, the branch snapped and Liam slid down the tree, screaming all twenty feet to the ground.

"Lee!" David quickly maneuvered himself down and beside his brother. "Are you hurt?"

Liam sat on the ground at the bottom of the tree, the front of his shirt covered with torn leaves and dirt. He began to sob. "It hurts, David."

"Shhh, be quiet." David lifted up his brother's shirt and gasped at the deep scrapes along Liam's chest.

"I told you I shouldn't have done it. Now, Mother's going to be angry and Father's going to be real angry. Why did you tell me to do it?"

David sighed. He tried so hard to make his brother more of the kind of person his father wanted him to be, adventuresome, fearless. Then maybe Father would treat him better. What could cause a scrape like this?

"Lee, let's tell Mother and Father that Golden Boy jumped on you and scratched you."

Liam stopped crying and sat up. Then, lifting his own shirt, he winced as he looked at the abrasions running the length of his chest. "You think they'll believe that? It doesn't look much like a dog did it."

"If we tell them that I coaxed you up, I'll be in trouble. If we tell them the dog did it, no one gets punished. I don't know about you, but Father's already given me the belt once this month."

"Three times for me. And this stings." Liam glanced past David at the house . "We'll tell Mother and Father it was the dog."

David pulled Liam up and helped to brush the leaves and dirt off his brother's shirt. "Let's just do it. Then we'll have some time to play war in the woods." He hesitated. "And whatever you do, don't cry. Father will just get madder if you cry."

Liam nodded as he wiped his eyes with the back of his hand.

In the parlor near the hearth, their mother sat on the sofa with embroidery on her lap. The two boys silently waited in the doorway.

Finally their mother looked up. "David, is something wrong?"

"Yes, Liam. . .he'll tell you."

She stood up, placed the embroidery on the sofa and walked quickly to her son. "Liam?"

"Yes?"

"Is something wrong?"

"Well, I. . ." he began to cry.

"Well, boys, what's going on with the two of you?" Jack approached them from behind, his voice loud and piercing.

"I. . ." Liam now began to shake.

"It's fine, Lee," David whispered. " Just tell it quick. How can Father get mad at you? It's the dog's fault, right?"

Liam's head lowered, then he mumbled, "The dog. . .jumped on me and hurt me."

"The dog did what?" asked Jack. "I can't hear you, son."

"He scratched me," Liam said softly.

"Where?" Jack asked.

David stepped aside to allow Jack to move closer to Liam. Liam pointed to his chest.

"Lift your shirt up, son," said Jack.

Liam pulled his shirt up and winced. His mother gasped. "Liam!"

"I'm. . .all right," Liam said.

Emma caressed his back and brushed the hair away from his face.

His father scowled. "Emma, stop coddling him. Get one of the servants to clean this up."

"I'll tend to him," Emma said. Her sympathetic expression and soft voice seemed to calm Liam and he stopped shaking. As Liam turned toward his mother, Jack touched his shoulder.

"So the dog did this, Liam?"

Liam looked at David. David nodded slightly.

"Yes, Father, he did."

"Looks bad, doesn't it, son?"

"Uh. . ." Liam nodded, but now kept his face downward.

Jack shoved past his sons to the gun cabinet near the hearth.

Immediately, both boys' eyes widened.

"Father, what are you doing?" asked David.

"I'm going to solve the problem."

"What problem?" David asked, his voice now quivering.

Jack did not respond. Instead, he checked the rifle for ammunition, then slammed it closed. He rushed through the living room and into the foyer and out the front door.

"Father, what are you doing?" David screamed, then ran after his father.

Liam was trailing close behind, but David could hear his shaking voice, "David, what's. . .he going. . .to do with the gun?"

David turned the corner, then stopped, with Liam bumping into him from behind. Their father had the rifle pointed at Golden Boy, their beautiful, playful golden retriever. His tail was wagging and, as he glanced at David and Liam, his head perked up, oblivious to the gun pointing at him. They saw the dog's head rip open before they heard the shot. David bit his lip and his body tensed. Behind him, he heard his younger brother sobbing quietly. Golden Boy now was an unmoving bloody heap on the ground. David gritted his teeth and turned around. "Shhh, Lee. Stop crying before Father sees you."

Liam wiped his eyes, then ran toward the front of the house.

Jack, the gun hanging to his side, approached David. "So, David, your brother will never have to worry about the dog hurting him again, now, will he?"

"But, Father. . ."

"Will he?"

"Why did you have to kill him?" David shouted, his voice now breaking.

Jack leaned down close to David's ear. He paused and David felt his father's breath on his neck. "Because you boys lied to me. That's why."

David wiped his eyes, then poured another drink from the brandy flask and gulped it quickly. It no longer burned his throat like it used to when he was a teenager. The liquid warmed his entire body and he greatly desired more. The decanter now empty, he observed, "This is my wedding day and there ought to be more celebrating, the proper kind."

The house was quiet as he crept up the back staircase. He

opened the servants' bedroom door and could hear Jane's snoring and Hallie's even breathing. He knelt beside Hallie's bed and began to stroke her hair. She roused enough to say, "Mr. David?"

"Shhh," he said and kissed the top of her head.

She sat upright in the bed and pulled away from him. "No, Mr. David," she whispered, "not tonight. Remember what I told you?"

"What are you talking about?" he whispered back.

"You're a married man now."

"I told you that it doesn't mean anything, Hal." She touched her finger to his lips to quiet him, then slipped on her robe and pulled him out into the narrow attic hallway. Although it was dark, a small hint of moonlight reached in through the window so that David could see her face clearly. She was neither smiling nor frowning. "It may only be on paper, Mr. David, but I can't do this to Miss Caroline."

"As if she cares, Hal. She can't stand the sight of me."

"You made vows today to be true to her, Mr. David."

"Nobody expects me to keep those vows, certainly Caroline doesn't."

"Miss Caroline doesn't know you've been with me, Mr. David, and I'd like to keep it that way."

He leaned down to kiss her forehead. "I need you, Hal. Please."

"Don't," she whispered and stepped back. "I mean it, Mr. David, I won't do this anymore."

He curtly said, "Fine." His mouth formed into a thin, angry line and he stared down at her without saying anything further. He turned around and stomped down the back staircase to the kitchen and out the basement door. With lead feet, he trudged into the barn. He pulled Big Red from the stall and hitched him to the smaller carriage, attached a lantern to the front and made his way over the dirt roads and countryside to downtown Philadelphia. There was a full moon to light his path, although his horse already knew the way.

The clopping of the horses on the cobblestone street jolted his senses and he questioned why he was even here in the first place. He shook away the feeling. He pulled his carriage to an area around the corner which led to the brothel. At first, he avoided the familiar house, instead sauntering down the street to Paddy's Pub. He ordered whiskey and downed several shots. Soon he felt dizzy and, at the same time, desired the pleasure which Hallie had denied him.

David left the tavern and made his way down the street to the brothel. He carefully put one foot in front of the other but found himself tripping and not able to walk straight. He reached the marble steps and knocked on the door.

A loud, made-up woman answered the door. "Well, I'll be damned, it's David O'Donovan! We thought you had moved to a faraway place. We used to have women lining up to. . ."

She left the door open, then she yanked him in and began to touch him in places which hadn't felt a skilled woman's hands in a long time. He wanted to fight the overwhelming desire but it was time to surrender. He was a married man and deserved to be that way with a woman, whether it was his wife or not.

The girl began to kiss the side of his neck and he breathed in her scent, a sour stench which carried a hint of perfume to it. He immediately broke away from her and thrust himself down the steps and onto the street, as if he were being vomited from the mouth of the brothel. "Where are you going, David?" He could hear her yelling as he rushed down the street.

He walked again, striving to search for his small carriage and the horse he tied to a post. His vision was now slightly blurred and he felt lightheaded. *Please God, help me to find my carriage.* He couldn't believe that he was actually asking God for something. Certainly, God knew that he had never attended church, except for Liam's wedding and then his own farce of a ceremony yesterday.

God, help me find my way. He lost his balance and tripped on the step of a large building. When he raised his head, he could see four columns and, gazing upward, a statue of some type. *St. Peter and Paul Cathedral.* David realized that this was not where his carriage was. However, as he stood at the bottom of the stairs, he felt peaceful, and it compelled him to climb the steps. It was after midnight, and yet he instinctively knew that the door would not be locked. He opened it, but could see only darkness ahead of him. He ventured farther inside until he came to a door, which he quietly opened and stepped inside. A few small candles twinkled in the distance. He wondered whether he was dreaming. The alcohol still numbed his senses somewhat, but he could smell something fragrant here, a sweet mixture of beeswax and roses that was warm and inviting. He walked slowly down the center aisle, then finally sat in one of the pews close to the front.

He glanced at the few flickering candles at the front of the church, which seemed to bathe a white statue of St. Joseph and the Christ Child held protectively in his arms. His eyes were drawn up toward the blackness of the ceiling. It was a starless sky which seemed to stretch out for an eternity. All of a sudden, he felt small and insignificant.

He relaxed his head against the pew. This was the first time he could recall savoring peace in his soul. The calm atmosphere and sweet aroma lulled him and he started to drift off to sleep.

"Excuse me? Sir?"

David drowsily opened his eyes.

"Oh, yes? Do you want me to leave?"

"No, no. But we have a room at the front if you'd like to have a better night's rest." The man sounded young and had a slight Irish brogue.

David couldn't see the face of the person speaking to him. However, there was an unmistakable kindness in his voice that caused him to relax.

"Oh, no, that's fine. I don't need a place to sleep. I just. . ." What was he supposed to say? David figured this man was a priest, a true celibate. He couldn't very well tell him that he had just come from the whorehouse.

"I, well. . ." He made an effort to speak clearly.

"It smells like you've been to the pub down the street."

"Yes, Father. . ."

"Father Flaherty. What's your name, sir?"

"David O'Donovan."

"Well, for the love of St. Patrick. You're Irish like myself, Mr. O'Donovan. Pleased to make your acquaintance." He held his hand out. David squinted, then shook it with as firm a handshake as he was able to in his present condition.

"I don't know what to say, Father."

"It's not necessary to say anything, Mr. O'Donovan. If you should like to remain here in church and sleep, that would be fine."

"Well, I really ought to be going. I can't find my horse and carriage. I parked it up the street near the. . ."

"If you'd like, I'd be glad to help you find it."

"Well. . .I. . ." David wasn't sure what he wanted. He desired the peace that this place gave him. Should he tell this priest what had almost happened? "I came from the brothel."

"Oh," he heard the priest say.

"But, I didn't. . ."

"Ah. That's good that you didn't." He paused. "Are you married, Mr. O'Donovan?"

"I suppose I am, but. . ." The priest didn't respond and instead remained silent.

"My brother died a few weeks ago and he asked me to marry his wife, because I gambled away a huge sum of money and it was necessary to invest money in an attempt to get it back and our Father disinherited him. Anyway, I had to marry her. It's a marriage in name only because my sister-in-law, who is now supposed to be my wife, can't stand the sight of me."

He heard the priest quietly respond, "That is a most difficult situation, Mr. O'Donovan."

"I. . .I can't stop bedding women."

"Mr. O'Donovan, you didn't do anything at the brothel. That's very good."

"Yes, but I wanted to."

"Our Heavenly Father doesn't expect us to follow His laws by ourselves. We can't do it without His grace." The man crouched down beside David and quietly recited:

As I knew that I could not otherwise be continent, except God gave it, I went to the Lord and besought him with my whole heart. Blessed is the man that endureth temptation.

"That's from the letter of James." The priest paused. "Do you see the statue of St. Joseph?"

David nodded.

"St. Joseph married Our Lady even though he wasn't the blood father of the child Jesus and he remained celibate throughout their marriage."

"Well, I'm certainly not a saint, Father, and I've done some bad things. A girl carried my child and they both died during delivery and it was my fault." David began to cry and he felt the young priest's hand on his shoulder.

"And it's my fault that my brother's dead and my sister-in-law had to marry me and she can't stand the sight of me and it's all the worse because I. . ." David stopped. He couldn't say any more.

"Mr. O'Donovan, God is merciful. His mercy is greater than any sin we could commit. Besides, you didn't kill your brother, did you?"

"Of course not. But I didn't give the thieves all my money and I was so angry that I punched one of them and they killed Liam."

"Your brother died as the result of the greed of those thieves, not your attempt to keep what was already yours."

"I just can't seem to forgive myself for what I did.   I am sorry, Father. But I don't know how to fix it all." He paused. "Perhaps you can help me find my carriage."

"I invite you to remain here overnight while you sober up. I'm certain our pastor, Monsignor Fitzgerald, would not mind if you stayed here. Besides, tomorrow is Sunday morning, perhaps you'd like to attend early Mass?"

"I can't. I'm not a church goer."

"You don't have to be, Mr. O'Donovan. Please, just come with me to the front room and sleep."

He nodded and followed the priest.

* * *

The sun was rising as David rode the carriage home. The pink clouds were nestled in a red and orange sky and for the first time, David began to appreciate it as the beauty of God's creation.

He felt tired and had a headache from drinking, but that didn't matter. Although Father Flaherty had invited him to remain at the church to sleep, he and the priest began to talk further. David could scarcely believe it when Father told him that it had been five hours since his arrival at the church and it would soon be time for the priest to prepare for morning Mass.

David decided not to remain for the Mass since he felt like an outsider, although he did accept the priest's gifts of a small De Harbe's Catechism and another book called "Confessions" by a man called Augustine.

David cringed when he recalled that he had shared with the

Catholic priest that he could not stop bedding women. Yet, the priest had patiently listened, apparently without judgment. Then he had opened the catechism and had recommended that whenever David felt a sexual urge or temptation, as his new catechism stated, "To earnestly resist it and implore the assistance of God, to not be discouraged, but to persevere in resistance and endeavor to occupy your mind with some good subject."

He quietly unhitched Big Red from the carriage and made his way through the front door, then up the staircase.

His bedroom seemed different. David wasn't sure how or why, but he was overwhelmed with a need to do the right thing.

He placed the two books on his desk, then reconsidered and wondered whether he ought to keep them hidden for now. He opened the bottom drawer and discovered his collection of French postcards brought back from Paris by his father as an 18th birthday gift. The urge rose in him again and, despite his fatigue, despite the peace he savored all evening, a compulsion to view the obscene images began to surface.

Please, God, help me to resist. He took a deep breath and shut the drawer. He glanced at the two books again on his desk and decided to move them to his bedside table. He picked up the book called "Confessions." The catechism had said, "Endeavor to occupy your mind with some good subject." This book seemed as good a subject as any.

28

Caroline opened Liam's bedroom door and stood in the doorway. Immediately, it occurred to her that she spent more time here than any other room in the house, save for her own.

Like the clock above his bed, which had been stopped at the time of her husband's death two months ago, it seemed like her life had ceased to exist. Outside, grass grew slowly and silently and nests filled the once empty trees.

She picked up their framed wedding photograph now displayed on his bedside table. She touched the picture, outlining his body, handsome in its wedding day finery, his eyes bright with happiness, a slight smile on his lips. Caroline was ecstatic that day, although one would never guess that from the stoic expression she wore in this photograph.

While Caroline found this new invention of capturing a person's image on paper fascinating, there were so many things which couldn't be revealed in this picture. It didn't, couldn't, describe how he expertly, passionately played the violin, or how he laughed in a high-pitched manner, how he ate his meal in the same fashion each time: meat, potatoes, then vegetables. The photograph didn't show the small mole on his stomach or the faint scars on his chest which, he said, were from a fall out of a tree as a child.

Her memories of him couldn't be contained in this photograph, although this was the only picture of them together. It couldn't describe how, when they hugged, her head fit perfectly below his chin. This picture couldn't sufficiently reveal the love they shared, nor could it describe their intimate moments. And as awkward as that aspect of their married life had been, she would never want to give up any of it because they had shared it together.

Her husband was dead. It took days, weeks to be able to even think it. With it came the realization that Caroline's love for him would never be gone and would remain nestled and protected within her, despite Liam's death, despite this farce of a marriage.

Caroline sighed and returned the frame to the small table.

She took a deep breath and let it out slowly. Some days, it was necessary to make a conscious effort to breathe. After her father died, it was difficult but she had been preparing herself for that eventuality over four years. Liam's death was so sudden; it seemed as if her body, large with child, was incapable of handling that shock. In the two months since her husband's death, life became a monotony of sleeping and eating. She hadn't picked up a book to read in all that time.

And to be married to David was her worst nightmare come true. It didn't matter that his behavior was recently more polite. He was still David. Was she supposed to be overjoyed?

Caroline now sat on Liam's bed and studied his room: every book in place, each piece of furniture precisely in the same spot as he last left it. His papers were neatly stacked on the desk. Ordered. Just the way Liam liked it. Caroline felt no urgency to rummage through his desk or to search his drawers. Anything she found would never be enough to erase the feeling of emptiness she now embraced.

Everything was tidy, except for the clothes on the floor of the closet. Immediately, she pulled one of his shirts from the pile of worn ones which, two months previous, had been ready to be laundered. She lifted it to her face and breathed in his now fading scent. For the moment, she was thoroughly engrossed in the memory of his presence, but what she truly longed for was his soft voice.

If only he had listened to her and not gone to Boston. If only he had not been robbed. If only David had. . .David. Caroline exhaled another long, slow breath.

The sounds of someone clearing his throat made her gasp. She turned around. Her brother-in-law stood in the doorway, his eyes making brief contact with her own, then he directed his gaze toward the floor.

"I'm sorry. I didn't mean to intrude. I needed to speak with you about. . ." He stopped when he noticed that she was holding Liam's wrinkled and once worn shirt. "Caroline?"

"Yes?"

"I intend to have the servants begin clearing out his room."

"No!" she shouted, her eyes wide.

"Please. It's only been two months."

"Yes, two months. And you'll be delivering soon. Jane and Kip will be making this into a nursery."

"No, there will be no nursery in here, David. I want the crib in my bedroom across the hall."

"You must. . ."

Caroline stared at Liam's open closet, his shoes on the floor, caked with mud, taking her back to that day when she first saw his unconscious form being brought into this room.

"Leave me alone, David." All of a sudden, a gush of fluid came from her, splashing to the hardwood floors below. She gasped.

"Caroline!"

"I think. . .the baby will be here soon. Please tell Kip to get Patsie next door."

He rushed to her side. "Allow me to assist you to your room." As he held on to her shoulder, she pulled away from him. "Stop. I wish to give birth to his child in his bed, not in mine."

David stepped back, then nodded. "Very well." He walked her to Liam's bed.

"I need to get prepared."

"Yes, of course. I'll send Jane up to you immediately, then I'll have Kip get Patsie next door."

When he left, Caroline pulled her dress and crinoline off, then began to wipe up the mess on the floor. Soon Jane arrived in the room. "Miss Caroline, I'll get that mess for you. You need to get in your bed."

"I'll do the birthing here in his bed."

"But. . ."

"No, Jane. This is where I am giving birth to my child."

"Yes, Ma'am."

"Make certain that David gets the midwife too. There's no rush. It will probably be some time before the baby is born."

Jane nodded and assisted her mistress into Liam's bed.

Now Caroline felt safe and prepared to give birth to their child. When Liam had first died, she couldn't think of sleeping in his bed without him, but over the past several weeks, frequently at night, Caroline had crawled into his bed to obtain much needed sleep. It provided comfort to be lying in the place that had held

Liam's body as he slept for many years. These days, it was the only way that she could slip into any kind of slumber.

Later that night, she pushed with the next contraction, intense but necessary pain which welled from deep within her and forced itself downward.

"Come along then, Miss Caroline, yer babe's jest 'bout here. Now then, can ye be givin' us 'nother push?"

Several more pushes followed, one contraction following another, no time for breathing, no time for thinking, just pushing.

"Sure an' the babe's nearly here, me lamb. I'm jest seein' the wee head."

Caroline opened her mouth to breathe in, but her body took over and she was pushing once again. A loud moan escaped from her lips. Someone patted her forehead and she instinctively turned her head away. *Must push.* Another contraction. She tried to push, but every ounce of her energy seemed to have disappeared.

"I can't. . .do this any. . ."

"Sure ye can, Miss Caroline. Ye be doin' jest foin. It's almost here. The babe's near out. Jest be givin' us one more push then."

She concentrated again, gritting her teeth and gripping the linen sheets. Caroline felt the child slide from her and she let out a deep sigh of relief.

"Tis a wee colleen, Miss Caroline. Ye've got a lovely daughter, ye do. We're jest be cleanin' 'er up then."

As the baby wailed, Caroline laid her wet head back on the pillow and took a deep breath despite her exhaustion.

"Ah, look at her light hair. Just like Mr. Liam. She's a beauty," Jane commented, as Patsie was cleaning her.

"She'll be after havin' a good set of lungs, that she do."

Soft knocking on the door almost went unnoticed.

"Patsie, how's Caroline doing?" David asked through the closed door.

"Sure an' she's foin, Mr. David, sir. We're jest after cleanin' her an' the babe up a bit, ye can be comin' in soon."

"Very well," he said.

"Here ye be, Miss Caroline." Patsie placed the baby girl in Caroline's arms.

"Jane and me, we'll be cleanin' ye all up, get ye all presentable like for visitors, though ye really should be restin' now. Ye sure'll be needin' some sleep."

Caroline nodded. Her baby had stopped crying and was quietly cooing in her arms.

"Are ye certain ye're not be wantin' a wet nurse?"

"Yes, Patsie. There's no reason I can't feed my own daughter. That's what these are for, aren't they?"

"Well, sure an' I know that's what the good Lord made 'em for."

"I don't care if most upper class women employ wet nurses. I wish to feed my child. She's all I have in the world and I'm going to give her everything of myself that I can."

"If ye be sure then."

"I wish to feed her now, Patsie."

"Well, sure an' this is a good time, before Mr. David'll be wantin' ta be comin' in, even though the wee colleen's not askin' after it."

She nodded and unbuttoned the top of her gown and offered her child the breast. The baby eagerly latched on and Caroline tenderly watched as her daughter suckled.

Since her husband had died, Caroline could feel nothing but despair. But now as she gazed down into the face of her child, for the first time in two months, she saw hope. Their love, hers and Liam's, was no longer only nestled in her heart, it was now safely in her arms.

As her daughter nursed, she picked up one of her tiny hands and marveled at the miracle of new life. These small hands would someday clap and wave, hold a doll, push down on a top, play the violin or piano.

Her baby began closing her small eyes. "You've been through quite an exhausting experience too, Sweet," she whispered out loud as the infant fell into a deep slumber. Caroline's own eyes began to close. Jane's voice whispered, "I'll take the baby and put her in the cradle beside the bed."

Caroline nodded.

"Maybe ye can be after lettin' Mr. David have a wee glimpse of the babe before ye be takin a hard-earned rest," Patsie said loudly.

"I suppose," Caroline answered.

"Yer flow's lookin' good. I'm thinkin' 'tis mighty glad I am, that we're knowin' what we're about, eh, Jane? The midwife must be tendin' t'another birth."

"Yes, Ma," Jane responded. "Miss Caroline, what will you name your daughter?"

"Kathleen Emma, after my mother and Liam's mother."

"That's beautiful. I'm sure Mr. Liam would have been proud," Jane replied.

She nodded as tears rose along the back of her throat.

Loud, insistent knocking accompanied David's voice. "Patsie, may I come in? Is Caroline well?"

"Sure ye best be after holdin' on ta yer shirt there, Mr. David, sir. Miss Caroline's not after bein' cleaned up yet. Can ye not be waitin' 'nother minute or so?"

"Of course," David responded.

"Sure an' that Mr. David's about as patient as a wood sprite on a moonbeam waitin' fer her mate."

Caroline shrugged her shoulders.

"Right then, Miss Caroline. Let's be gettin' 'nother night-gown on ye and brush up yer hair so ye can be lookin' presentable. Will ye be after stayin' in Mr. Liam's room for a while?"

Caroline nodded and began to close her eyes while Jane brushed her hair.

"Miss Caroline, you lie back on your pillow here. I'm sure Mr. David understands how tired you are."

She laid her head back against the pillow and closed her eyes.

She heard Patsie open the door. "Well, Mr. David, sir, it's a wee colleen then."

Caroline parted her eyes enough to see David walk in, tentatively at first, then more urgently as he rushed to the side of her bed.

"You must be tired, Caroline," he whispered.

She nodded.

He looked into the cradle beside the bed. "She's beautiful." He glanced at her with a warm, affectionate smile. "Liam would have been so proud."

Despite her fatigue, Caroline felt her eyes again filling with tears.   Not wanting to be discovered, she pretended to be drifting off to sleep.

"Miss Caroline's bushed and she's needing her sleep."

"Of course, Jane," she heard David say.

All of a sudden, Caroline felt gentle warmth on the top of her head. She drowsily opened her eyes to find David very close to her face.

"You did a remarkable job, Caroline."

Why must he be so close ?

She finally surrendered and allowed herself to drift off to sleep.

29

David closed the door and leaned against the wall in the hallway. For the past three or four hours, most especially for the last hour or so, he had been praying for the safe delivery of this child, who would be the only offspring of his brother. He felt a deep sense of relief that both Caroline and her baby were doing fine.

He made his way to his bedroom and closed the door. It was now well after midnight. Exhausted and still dressed in his day clothes, he lay his head on his pillow. He thought that he would rest for a few moments. He immediately fell asleep.

David's eyes opened at the crowing of the roosters heralding dawn. He sat up, realized that he had woken, as usual, in a condition which begged release and with thoughts and feelings he knew he needed to channel elsewhere. He got up and lit the gas lamp on his bureau. He longed to have a shot of brandy, just a small taste, but shook it off.

He began to think about Hallie, one floor above, in her bed, her soft hair spread against her pillow like it used to caress his chest.

He quietly stepped into the hallway, facing the back stairs. David walked, then stopped at his brother's room. All was quiet as Caroline and the baby slept soundly. He ascended the staircase, each step feeling black and wrong under his feet. He knew that he ought not to be going up to the attic, but he promised himself that he would only look in on Hallie, to ensure that she was sleeping well.

At her bedroom door, he carefully and slowly turned the knob, hoping to avoid making a sound. Despite his best efforts, it clicked and David froze. He waited a minute or two before turning it again and looking inside the room.

He couldn't see clearly, but could make out Hallie's motionless outline on the bed closest to the door. Jane was snoring, thankfully, as it most likely covered any noise he was making.

It would take a mere minute to wake Hallie and feel some relief. And certainly anyone would understand his need. After all, he had been celibate now for two months. He knew that he could convince her and if she didn't agree, well then he would. . .David's eyes widened. He quietly stepped back and closed the door. He couldn't believe that he had considered using her.

His overwhelming desire for intimacy and for a drink was making him want to scream. He hurried back to his room, his eyes darted about. It was important to have some distraction right now, anything. He eyed the gun cabinet. Target practice would do.

He rummaged through his top desk drawer for the ammunition, then stopped. It was not yet dawn and shooting his rifle near the house would likely wake not only Caroline but perhaps the new baby. He ventured outside to the stable and prepared a gas lamp.

"David, let's play war in the woods."

War in the woods was his and Lee's favorite game together. Their father used to allow each of the brothers to play with unloaded guns, although David remembered as a young boy searching for ammunition so they could make louder sounds. Thank God that his father had kept the ammunition well-hidden and locked.

He entered the forest, the gun at his side, the lamp held high. A hundred or so feet inside, he came to a clearing and set the lamp down. Behind him, a bird flapped, then flew overhead and he jumped. He picked up the lamp and continued beyond the clearing. All of this seemed familiar to him, darkness notwithstanding.

"Bang, you're dead, David!"
"I am not dead, Lee. You didn't hit me with that last shot."
"How do you know I didn't hit you? I was pointing the gun at you."
"Besides, even if you did hit me it doesn't mean that I'm dead."

Above him, the sky turned pale pink as it prepared for the sun's debut. He turned off the lamp and peered into the forest, still dark with night. He lazily walked for several minutes, paus-

ing every few feet while his eyes adjusted. Daylight was approaching quickly and with each moment, it became clearer and easier to
see. Up ahead, a short distance away, he noticed a bird of some
sort, a partridge or perhaps a small turkey. He crouched and took
aim, his eye looking through the scope. His hand on the trigger,
he stopped, then lowered the gun. He squinted, but could not see
whether it was the stump of a tree or something else the bird was
perched on.

He placed his gun on the ground and came upon another
larger clearing, now subtly lit with dawn. A large stone, perhaps
a grave marker, stood in the center, grass high around it, but not
hiding the angel perched on top of it. Beyond that area was the
blackened stone foundation of the ruins of a small building.

David had forgotten about this spot, but it was one of his
favorite places to hide when he and Liam were playing war or hide
and seek. Of course, Lee was easy to scare. All David had to do
was to lie flat amongst the ruins and wait until he heard his brother run by. David would scream and Liam would scream louder,
then be on the verge of tears. He shook his head. *What a torment
I was.*

He knelt in front of the headstone, pulling the weeds aside.
Heavy green moss covered it like thick carpet and he was unable
to make out a name or date. However, as he brought his eyes
upward, the angel on top smiled down at him. He closed his eyes.
He felt peaceful and no longer agitated.

Thinking back to the last meeting with Father Flaherty,
David had shared with the priest that he still felt awkward with
attending Mass, especially at the Catholic Church in this neighborhood. David's reputation unfortunately would precede him and
he knew that he would not be comfortable there. Perhaps he
would attend Mass at the Cathedral at some future date.

Recently, he had been questioning his recent vows to abstain
from alcohol and women. Now, as light filled the area, it became
clear to him. Kneeling before this moss-covered headstone, an
angel on top of it, he made another promise to God: that he would
come here every day to pray. This would serve as the perfect distraction.

30

"Miss Caroline?" Kip's voice through the closed door asked.

"Yes, what is it?" She opened the door.

"Mr. David told me to give you this. It's Mr. Liam's. Said you might want it." He held a small box out to her.

Caroline looked down at the cigar box. "Yes, thank you, Kip. I'll take this." Behind Kip, David was giving orders as the servants moved items from Liam's room. Her heart felt heavy as she watched them move the headboard from Liam's bed into the hallway. David appeared to be deep in concentration as he supervised the removal of Liam's belongings. *How can this be so easy for him? How can he act as if this were just another job?*

She closed the door quietly so she would not waken the baby, who was sleeping calmly in the cradle beside her bed. Holding onto the box, Caroline watched her infant daughter's face. Her tiny lips were puckered and unconsciously sucking. Caroline marveled at the wonder of new life just beginning. She thought of the sadness of Liam's life, one which had just ended all too soon.

And all for what? She remembered little of what was said by the pastor at the funeral. The one comment she heard was, "Liam is at peace now in heaven." Why didn't that comfort her? Should it? What is the point to our lives if we're all just going to die? And what did it mean for someone like Liam who had passed away at such a young age?

She sat down on the bed and stared at the cigar box. It had a beautiful design with a colorful eagle, the words "Bock y Ca" and Habana under the eagle.

She curiously opened the box and was greeted with a musty tobacco odor. There were several items placed inside, some with brown paper covering them.

She carefully unwrapped the largest item and discovered a man's gold pocket watch, no chain – it looked like it had broken off – with the name "John Patrick O'Donovan" engraved on the outside. In the inside of the engraved letters, Caroline could see minute bits of black dust. It appeared as if someone had tried to clean it, but in the most narrow sections of the engraved letters, black dust remained. The watch and paper smelled of smoke. Placing it on the bed, she picked up a small ticket to the Centennial Exhibition, their first official outing as a courting couple. She blinked back the tears, and smiled nostaglically as she remembered how nervous she had been that day.

Next, she lifted up a small envelope and found a note inside, written in what could only be described as a scrawl, *"When you decide to become a MAN, here are the coins I was going to give you to do so."* At the bottom of the letter was written, in Liam's hand, "May this always remind me of what a real Man is." Caroline tipped the envelope over and three coins dropped out.

The baby began to whimper, then startled a reflex, her small fingers flailed open then curled back into fists. Distracted, Caroline gathered her daughter into her arms and began to nurse.

Caroline was grateful that she hadn't worn a corset in many months. Being in mourning had its advantages, one being that she never ventured out of the house. The only people who saw her on a daily basis were Jane, Kip and Hallie. Thankfully, David almost never interacted with her.

She laid her daughter over her shoulder. The baby released a drowsy burp, then promptly fell asleep. Caroline placed her in the cradle, then picked up another item wrapped in brown paper. Carefully lifting it out, she uncovered it to find a beautiful light blue cameo pin. On the back were the engraved initials, *EOD, with love, JOD, September 15, 1854."*

"This must be Liam's mother's pin, given to her on the day Liam was born." Caroline held it in her hand and caressed the smooth surface. It was one of the most beautiful pieces she had ever seen. She pictured Liam's father tenderly giving it to Liam's mother, then recalled Liam's negative comments regarding his father. He obviously was thoughtful enough to buy this exquisite piece of jewelry and have it engraved. Wrapping it again, she placed it on the bed and surveyed the rest of the box's contents.

Knocking, then Jane's voice called to her from the hallway.

"Yes, Jane? What is it?"

"It's a beautiful day. Perhaps we can take the baby out for a walk? She needs fresh air."

She opened the door to discover Jane's smiling face. Beyond

her was Liam's room and the sorting process. "I know it's been cool, but your baby hasn't had any fresh air recently and she's almost two months old. It's a warm day today."

Jane continued. "You haven't even been to church since you and Mr. David got married."

Caroline cringed. "I have no need of church. Not anymore."

"You keep yourself cooped up in this room and this isn't healthy for her, or for you."

Caroline shrugged her shoulders. "Jane, I am still mourning." Jane scowled.

"Mourning doesn't mean you can't take in some fresh air."

"Well, perhaps later. She's sleeping and I don't want to disturb her."

"Very well then. Let me know when she's awake."

Caroline nodded and again her eyes were drawn to the commotion in Liam's room. Watching David, she again was struck by just how unemotional he really was. Did the man have a heart of stone?

"He acts as if he hasn't lost a brother."

"Begging your pardon, Miss Caroline, but different people grieve in different ways."

"I haven't seen him shed one tear since Liam died."

"Again, meaning no disrespect, just because you haven't seen him show his emotions doesn't mean he don't have any."

"I will not forget that I loved Liam. Why has he?"

"I don't know any brothers that loved each other more than Mr. Liam and Mr. David. Two such different men. . ."

Caroline shook her head. "Jane, I still believe that you harbor some romantic notions of David."

Jane let out a chuckle. "No, no, definitely nothing of that sort. But I do know Mr. David quite well. I've been in this household for many years. I've watched him and Mr. Liam become men. Mr. David, well, he is. . .he's not what you think."

"Well, I don't know about that."

"He has shown great strength over these past few months."

Noises from the far end of the hallway in the west wing caught her attention. "What's going on down there, Jane?"

"Mr. David's asked us to clean out his mother's room as well."

Caroline closed the door and stared at her daughter in the crib. The wonder of new life, a child who wasn't alive a year ago. "Just a thought in the mind of God," she said aloud as she recalled the phrase her father used when referring to Caroline before she came into the world.

Yet this miniature human being had transformed Caroline's life so much that she was no longer the same person. Her heart seemed connected to this child by an invisible, yet ever present umbilical cord, a connection which urged Caroline to check her frequently at night to see if she was breathing, to listen to her catching her breath, watch her suck in her sleep. She loved this child so much that it hurt to think of anything bad happening to her.

And what if Caroline died? What if David were the only parent she knew? Her daughter would never remember anything about this or about Caroline.

"Miss Caroline?"

"Yes, Jane, what is it now?"

"Mr. David said to give you something else."

"Yes, very well." She opened the door. Jane stood in the doorway with a tiny box in her hands.

"We found this in Mr. Liam's desk. It appears as if he was planning to give this to you when Miss Kathleen was born."

"What is it?"

"Open it, Miss Caroline. I think you'll be pleased."

Caroline opened up the box, then gasped quietly. Inside was a beautifully simple cameo pin with the painted word "mother" at the bottom. On the gold backing, Liam had engraved, *COD with love LOD*, a blank space, then 1877. Inside the box, a small note from Liam, "when baby is born, make arrangements for engraver to fill in date."

Caroline blinked back the tears and straightened, then began to weep. Jane pulled her mistress to a close embrace.

"Now, now, Miss Caroline. I knew it might make you cry, but you had to see that it's a most beautiful pin. Mr. Liam, he was so thoughtful, wasn't he?"

"Yes, he was," she said, as she wiped her eyes with the back of her hand.

Jane affectionately rubbed her mistress' arm. Caroline

pulled away and shut the door. She kept her hand on the knob for a few seconds. *Jane can probably assist me in identifying some of the items in Liam's box.* Immediately, she swung open the door. In the hallway, Kip was leaning against Jane. Caroline sensed that it was an intimate conversation and not the normal sort that servants engage in.

"Oh, I. . ." Caroline stepped into the hallway and glanced from Jane to Kip.

"Excuse me, Miss Caroline. Is there something you need?" Jane looked flushed.

"Yes."

Kip nodded toward Caroline, then backed away and into Liam's former room.

"So what was it that you wanted?" Jane asked, smoothing her skirts.

"I wonder if you might help me to identify some of the items in Mr. Liam's box on my bed."

"Of course, Ma'am, if I can be of help." Jane stepped inside her room and Caroline closed the door.

"So Jane," Caroline hesitated. "How long has this. . .romance with Kip been going on?"

Jane's eyes widened. "I don't know what to say."

"It's fine, Jane. How long?"

"A year past." She paused. "I hope this won't jeopardize either my or Kip's position here."

Caroline shook her head. "I'm sure we can work something out."

"Miss Caroline, you don't know how relieved I am. I wasn't sure about. . ."

"I wish you had come to me, Jane."

"I know, but Mr. Liam was strict about that kind of behavior, servants marrying other servants in the same household."

"I see."

"And I don't know if he agreed with white folks marrying colored folks. Of course, I think that people ought to be free to marry whoever they love. That's what Kip's parents believed too. Kip told me that his Pa was a white abolitionist who helped slaves escape through the Underground Railroad. He was only 19 when he took a group of runaway slaves to the Canadian border. One of the families had a pretty 16 year old and Kip's Pa fell in love with her the moment he saw her."

"That's a lovely story, Jane."

"Do you think Mr. David will be fine with this? I mean, you don't think he'll let Kip or me go, do you?"

"I don't know. I mean, I do know this sort of thing is frowned upon, but you are both hardworking servants. I, for one, don't want either of you to leave."

"Thank you for saying so, Ma'am."

Caroline pointed to the bed where the cigar box lay open. She picked up the packaged pocket watch and carefully unwrapped it.

"That's Mr. Jack's watch. I think Miss Emma gave that to Mr. Liam after the fire."

"I see." She picked up the envelope with the coins and took out the note. "Do you know anything about this, Jane?"

"No, Ma'am." Jane studied the note. "Although it looks like Mr. Jack's writing."

"Thank you, Jane. You've been helpful."

"Now, remember, Miss Caroline, when the baby wakes up, we must get some fresh air for her."

"Yes, of course."

When the servant left, Caroline sat on the bed and her eyes swept from the envelope with the coins to the smoke-laden watch. All of a sudden, it occurred to her that she really hadn't known Liam or much about his past.

31

Caroline busied herself in her room as baby Kathleen slept again that afternoon. Her eyes were drawn to the cigar box on the dresser. She picked it up and sat near the window, placing the box on the sill. A warm breeze caressed her cheek and Caroline closed her eyes and welcomed it.

Jane was correct that it was a beautiful fall day, the colorful leaves at their peak. She resolved to take her daughter outside when she woke up from her nap.

Below the window, her eyes caught sight of David walking below and toward the forest. Caroline cringed.

He never changes, does he? He's probably meeting Uncle's new servant girl. I'd like to give him a piece of my mind and I don't care if he's engaged in any sort of improper activity.

"Miss Caroline, may I come in?"

"Yes, Jane."

Opening the door, the servant reminded Caroline: "Don't forget. When the baby wakes, we ought to take her for a walk. It's warm and fresh air is necessary for little ones."

"Yes, of course. That would be fine." Caroline paused, then glanced down at the scene below her window. "Do you think you could remain here with the baby for a few moments? There is a matter I must attend to."

"Certainly. You go ahead and do whatever it is you need to do."

Caroline went in haste down the staircase and onto the porch. As she stepped down onto the stone drive, it occurred to her that this was the first time she had been outside in the two months since her daughter was born. It was indeed a warm, sunny day, the sky a deep blue, the few clouds an eggshell white. The air smelled like crisp fresh leaves.

At the forest, she followed a short pathway which first led to a small clearing. She stood in the middle of the area and listened. All she heard was silence, except for a few birds.

She proceeded to the other side where a patch of grass had

been flattened to form a trail. Up ahead, light suggested that she would soon come upon another open space.

She stepped quietly and carefully along the trail. At the edge of the clearing, she stopped. She held her hand to her mouth to silence her gasp as she stared at the scene before her.

David was kneeling in front of a gravestone, his hands clasped in front of him, his head bowed.

She turned around to leave and stepped on dried leaves. He immediately stood up. "Caroline, what. . . are you doing here?"

"I followed you because. . ."

"You followed me?"

"Yes, I. . ." Her eyes were drawn to the gravestone, situated at the center of the clearing, a stone sculpture of an angel on top of it. "What are you doing here?"

"I come here every day."

"Why ever do you come. . .here?"

"To pray, to gather my thoughts."

"You come to this spot to pray?"

He nodded.

"I. . .I'm sorry," she offered. "I didn't mean to disturb you." She turned and began to walk away.

"Caroline, wait. I'll follow you out."

Caroline cringed. She wanted to forget that she had disturbed him. All she had wished to do when she saw him entering the forest was to humiliate him and instead, she had been humiliated.

She kept silent as he followed her; every few moments he guided her by telling her to go left or right. With each step, she wanted to find a rock to crawl under.

As they emerged from the forest, she wished that she could bolt to the house, with no further words. Instead, she stopped and heard him do the same behind her. She slowly turned and faced him, but avoided eye contact. "I'm sorry. I should never. . ."

"It's fine," she heard him say.

"Miss Caroline, the baby's awake." Jane called from the window above them, the baby crying at a high pitch. "May I dress her and bring her down?"

"Just a moment, Jane. I will need to. . ." As Caroline's milk let down, she pressed her hand against her chest, then she glanced at David, his gaze upward and directed toward Jane at the bedroom window. "I shall be there in a moment. " She rushed to the porch and up to her room.

* * *

The bedroom was empty; his mother's bed and most of her belongings were now in the attic. Her room still smelled faintly of her. Lavender soap. Memories filled David's mind, of sitting on her lap, of her singing to him.

Now that Lee was gone and his room was cleared out, this was an opportune time to clean out this space. Time to move forward.

David began to walk, the soft click of his shoes echoing throughout the emptiness. Now standing in the middle of her barren room, he became filled with regret. This was the place where his mother had spent most of her days and nights. Yet in recent years, before she died, he couldn't remember saying more than a few words to her daily. Too many other activities had kept his mind and body occupied.

He opened the window a few inches and the fresh autumn air filled the room. Behind him, he heard a patting sound and turned to watch a small envelope flap around on the floor. He crossed the room, crouched down and picked it up. It was slightly yellowed with age. He raised it up close to his face; it smelled faintly of lavender. He turned it over and saw "Jack," written in his mother's hand.

Immediately, he was struck by the feeling of intrusion, like he ought to just take the envelope and whatever it contained to the attic with the rest of her possessions. If this were something she had wanted him to read before she died, she would have given it to him.

Earlier today, when he was overseeing the clean up of Lee's room, he found it necessary to control the urge to rummage through every drawer, every book, anything that Lee owned. When he opened up the cigar box on Lee's bureau, he practically gasped to find the watch. He smiled inwardly to see the ticket and cringed when he took out the coins and letter. He understood why Lee had kept the ticket, but why in the world had his brother saved the other, painful reminders?

At the time, all he could do was close the box and hand it to

Kip to give to Caroline. She wouldn't know the significance of the other items anyway, but she ought to have the box, to remember Lee.

However, when he discovered the "Mother" pin that Lee was planning to give to Caroline, he bit his lip and fought the urge to cry. Before he died, Lee had shared with him that he was greatly looking forward to being a father and the opportunity to be a better, more loving father than their own had been. And now David would have to shoulder that responsibility.

He turned the envelope over. The back did not carry his mother's wax seal on it and did not appear as if it had ever been sealed. Perhaps. . .no, most likely. . .never sent.

He carefully lifted the letter out. This was most definitely his mother's handwriting, but the strokes were bold, dark, the ink pressing deeply into the page.

September 15, 1870

Dear Jack,

You are angry now, but I am also full of rage. I entered the hallway and you ordered me back into my room, my dungeon, and you have refused to allow me to comfort my son. And so tomorrow, I will pretend that I did not hear you and your rage-filled voice. I will act as if nothing has happened. However, you will not stop me from loving my son and from giving him what you have never given him.

I have prayed that you will be more accepting of our youngest son and of his sensitive nature. I know where you wanted to take him this evening and it sickens me. I know that you and David go to that awful place once a week. I prayed that Liam would have the strength to refuse you and your detestable sordid gift.

I wish I could leave you and never see you again. It pains me to see the manner with which you treat your own flesh and blood.

However, I know that it is impossible to leave you as it would most certainly mean giving up everything and I would never, ever leave without taking Liam with me.

The letter was not finished nor signed.   His mother wished to leave his father? But where would she have gone? How would she survive with no money?

 He always thought that his mother knew nothing about his or his father's illicit adventures. He shuddered to think that a woman so gently bred would know of such aspects of life.

"I have changed, Mother. I am different." The words sounded hollow in the empty room, the cool autumn air still blowing.

David had changed but there were times in the last several months that he felt like the old David. Embracing a life of chastity had been difficult at best, especially when memories popped into his head at inopportune times. Every day was a struggle for him to look at women with respect.   Each day held temptations that he tried hard to resist.

He stuck the letter in his pants pocket and slowly lowered the window.

"Mother would have loved Caroline, Lee. . ."

Their mother surely would have embraced Caroline as the daughter she never had. She would have relished being a grandmother.

He recalled his mother's mood the first week after his father died.   While she respectfully appeared somber at the funeral, within days, she began to laugh more and smile frequently, her voice and manner gay and lively.

That was certainly a contrast to Caroline's grief-stricken countenance. David hardly saw his sister-in-law and when he did, like earlier today at the clearing in the forest, there were few, awkward words exchanged. From her manner, he was certain that she still found this whole arrangement, and him, distasteful.

He closed the door and stood in the now darkening hallway of the west wing. All of a sudden, loneliness consumed him. His immediate family had all passed on. The only blood relation left in this world was baby Kathleen. She would never know Lee and that caused him to be melancholy.

He proceeded downstairs to the study and turned on the gas lamps. At the bookshelf he lifted out his journal and stuck his mother's letter inside.

He pulled the chair out from the desk. An image came to his mind of the one time two summers ago when he brought a girl to this room.

He felt that urge for pleasure, the overwhelming desire to. . . No. He shook his head to rid himself of the image and made his way to his ship building table near the window. He turned up the gas lamps so the room was as bright as daytime. He sat down and began to sand down the carved-out section of the stern which he had made yesterday.

Last week, he had read a section of Augustine's Confessions which included his quote "Grant me chastity and continency, but not yet," a sentiment which so often rang true of his own heart. Many nights, as he struggled to fall asleep, he wondered whether the torture and self-denial were worth it. However, in his heart, he knew that this was one of the most important sacrifices he could ever make because at the very least, he was no longer using women for his own lustful passions.

During his meeting with the priest last week, he almost asked the young Father Flaherty how in the world he had remained chaste for so many years and how did he seem so happy. These days, when David was having a difficult time, he would go, in haste, to the clearing in the forest. Or he would retire to the study and build ships or read or smoke his pipe. Sometimes, he would find himself barking at Jane or Kip and then apologizing to them for his behavior.

He picked up the chisel and carved out a design below the stern. He knew exactly what he would name this boat.

32

Caroline placed two more logs in the fireplace. A spark flew out at her skirt and burned red for a second, then left a tiny hole in the fabric. She shrugged.

She remained close to the fire, warming her hands and her body. The past two months since Christmas had been bitterly cold and Caroline found herself shivering most of the time.

Thankfully, the fireplace kept the frigid cold at bay. In theory, the huge coal stove in the basement was supposed to keep the east wing of the house warm. But it did little to do so these days. Kip kindly brought a portable coal heater to her room which she kept close to her bed and Kathleen's crib. It had made a difference in keeping the room more comfortable but now she was out of coal and decided not to venture down to the coal shed at the back of the house at this time of the night. For one brief moment, she regretted that the household had no servant ropes. While the bitter cold spell continued, she trusted that either Jane or Kip would come into her room during the night and add logs to her fire.

She straightened and stared at the small clock on the mantel. It was a few minutes after midnight. She leaned down to put another blanket over Kathleen in her crib. The baby was warm and sleeping soundly.

She pulled her robe closer to her body and sat on the edge of the bed. The oil lamp was blazing brightly on the night table. She wasn't yet ready to extinguish the light.

Shadows under the door and noises in the hallway suggested that someone was walking by her room. Perhaps Jane or Kip were awake? Since the two servants were married last month, they seemed to be spending more time in their room during the evening hours, but they always tended to their duties.

She crossed the room and opened the door. She gasped. David was standing outside her room and he stepped back as the door opened.

"David!" She stared, her eyes widened. Then she whispered,

"What are you doing here?"

He spoke quietly. "I was wondering if you might need some more wood or coal. I didn't want to knock in case you were already asleep."

"As a matter of fact, I do need more coal as I used the last bit two hours ago. And six logs would probably be sufficient for the night."

"I'll get those for you."

"Thank you."

He quickly disappeared down the rear staircase.

Caroline closed the door and leaned her back against it. Ever since she discovered David in the forest on his knees praying, she had avoided him whenever possible.

A few moments later she heard footsteps in the hall and opened the door. David stood in the doorway with a metal can full of coal looped over his arm and five split logs in his hands. She motioned him inside and he quietly placed the can beside the coal stove, then crossed the room and laid the wood near the fireplace.

"I couldn't carry six. I can go back and get a few more, if you'd like."

"No, that should be fine. Thank you, David. I do appreciate it."

He nodded but remained silent, then left. She closed the door and stared at it, as though she could see through it. She could not hear him walking and wondered if he had stayed in front of her room.

Caroline crouched down in front of the small stove and added a shovelful of coal. She placed two more logs in the fireplace and slipped into bed.

33

David buttoned up his nightshirt, then studied himself in the mirror. He supposed that he did not look any different. However, Liam was now gone almost a year and his brother would have been shocked to know what he had accomplished today. His father, who commented that only weaklings adhere to religion, would have disowned him. His mother would have been pleased.

Earlier today, he was formally received into the Catholic Church at a solemn celebration at Mass. However, when he arrived home, there was no congratulatory dinner, and it was as if no one knew that the old David no longer lived here.

He not only had managed to successfully make it through one full year of celibacy, he also succeeded in being able to refrain from drinking and gambling. He had arrived at a place in his life where he could say with certainty that he had become one of the righteous. And, as each day passed, it became easier for him to remain virtuous. This way of life had become second nature.

During the past year, he felt at peace and happy, despite the loss of his brother, despite being forced into a marriage of convenience. He felt God's presence every time he heard Kat laugh, or during a rainfall or when he was taking a ride in the mountains. God's influence, God's hand, seemed so much a part of everything in life.

Earlier this week, Caroline had asked him to take her to the cemetery to visit Liam's grave tomorrow. It would be a difficult outing, for her most especially, but she seldom asked for anything so he readily agreed.

He picked up the Douay Bible which Father Flaherty had given him and turned to the letter of St. Paul to the Ephesians, 3:16, the reading which Father Flaherty read today at Mass:

"That he would grant you, according to the riches of his glory, to be strengthened by his Spirit with might into the inward man;

That Christ may dwell by faith in your hearts. . ."

David now felt certain that he could conquer anything, any

difficulty, any challenge, any temptation. He was a new person, clothed with Christ.

* * *

Caroline stirred as her baby began to whimper.

"Shhh, Sweet, I will pick up you momentarily," she told her daughter in the crib beside her.

"Miss Caroline, you want me to calm the baby down?" Jane asked through the closed door.

"No. I think she wants to nurse."

"Very well."

She lifted up her child and began to nurse. Kathleen gulped eagerly and began to drift back to sleep. Caroline was always comforted by her baby's sweet milk breath and the warm weight of her small body next to hers. She found it difficult to believe that her daughter was already ten months old. Her hair color, fair complexion and fine features made her a most breathtaking child.

As her baby nursed, Caroline could see out the window that it was going to be a cloudy and dreary day. It had now been one year since he had died, one year of heartache, grief and loneliness. Two months ago, she had tried to conjure up Liam's face in her mind and, unable to do so, immediately procured their wedding photograph. How could she forget his face? And what would she have done without the picture of him?

Two weeks ago, she had become so engrossed in baby Kathleen and in the day-to-day activities that by nighttime, it occurred to her that she had not thought of Liam, not even for a brief moment, that entire day. It seemed such a disrespectful way of remembering her husband. It hadn't even been a year since he had died. How could she forget him?

She resolved not to allow a day to pass by without remembering him in some way, so she made the commitment to carry around his gold watch in the front pocket of her black skirt, its heaviness always tugging at her. Every time she felt the pull of its weight, she remembered him.

And today, the one year anniversary of his death, she and David would be visiting Liam's grave.

In the small carriage, Caroline sat uncomfortably close beside David; the narrow seat never seemed wide enough for her liking. Caroline wished that they had taken the larger buggy with Kip driving since the small canopy did precious little to shelter her from the fine mist that hung in the air.

Seemingly to fill the silence, David began to point out the obvious.

"The gardens will do well this year with a spring full of rain."

Caroline did not respond.

"The apple blossom trees are beautiful this time of year."

This time, she answered quietly, "Yes." She wished that he would cease his chattering.

The carriage bounced along as the wheels sank into the road's holes. At times, it was necessary for her to hold onto the side rail to avoid knocking into David.

"I'm sorry, Caroline. There are numerous holes from the rain and it's impossible to avoid them."

She shrugged her shoulders.

When they arrived at the cemetery, David led her to the grave. At the funeral, the headstone had not yet been placed. Today, a marker was present. Grass was green and lush and the large stone which indicated who was buried there made Caroline let out a slight gasp. David had chosen well, a white-gray marble with the simple words, "Liam Francis O'Donovan, 1854 - 1877, beloved husband of Caroline, loving father of Kathleen."

Caroline remained motionless, her eyes focused on the gravestone. She blinked back the tears.

 "We can leave, if you'd like," she heard David say.

She shook her head.   "Not yet."

"Then I will wait for you at the carriage."

"Yes, very well, thank you." She kept her gaze down and facing the grave.

Caroline was grateful that he had allowed her a private moment. Now that she was alone, the tears began to flow in earnest. She missed her husband and would have given anything to return to a life with him. Two years ago, she would never have envisioned this fate, a lonely life filled with the awkwardness of being 'married' to the last man on earth she would have chosen for a husband. The only person who gave her any happiness at all was her daughter, and Kathleen had become Caroline's sole excuse to lift herself out of bed every day.

A steady rain began to fall, but Caroline remained still. Almost immediately, David was beside her, holding an umbrella over her. She straightened, then wiped her face with her handkerchief.

"We may leave, if you wish," she said, turning to face him. Her elbow knocked into his arm as he moved the umbrella to his other hand for the short jaunt back to the carriage.

They walked side by side with David holding the umbrella over her. She glanced at him and his hair and face were dripping. She stopped and moved closer to him and took hold of the umbrella to allow it to shelter him as well. "This is big enough for both of us, David," she said, as they continued walking. Soon, torrential downpours caused him to slip his hand over her shoulder to hold her closer under the umbrella. She shuddered awkwardly at the unwanted intimacy. They had almost reached the carriage, then she gasped as he pulled her away toward a small outbuilding with a covered porch. She released the umbrella and stepped away from him.

"It would be prudent for us to remain here until it lets up, Caroline. We'll get soaked in the open carriage."

She nodded and turned away. Now facing the road, she watched several closed carriages pass by.

"This will be good for the farmers," he said, staring up toward the sky.

She remained silent, tapping her foot and hoping the rain would soon stop.

34

After having little interaction with her brother-in-law for nearly two months, David approached Caroline before he ventured off to Mass.

"I think it's time to have Kathleen baptized."

"She's just a year old, David. There's no rush."

"I would like her to be baptized at the Cathedral."

"The Cathedral? I'm not sure I want her baptized, let alone baptized Catholic."

"She needs to be baptized."

"I beg to differ."

"And she ought to be raised Catholic."

"And what if I don't wish her to be raised Catholic? I am her mother. You are merely her. . ."

"Caroline, you know that she is my daughter for all intents and purposes."

"I have no desire to discuss this further with you."

"It is imperative that we have her christened. Her eternal soul is at stake."

"And what would you know of her eternal soul? Besides, as I stated, I haven't decided whether to have her baptized in any religion at present. Where did religion get me? Married to you."

He cringed and lowered his head. "Remember the scripture you cited to me several years ago? 'Today if ye shall hear his voice, harden not your heart?'"

Caroline gasped, then yelled, "How dare you speak of scripture to me! I know more scripture than you shall ever know!"

"I meant no offense."

"And who are you supposed to be? God's voice? Hardly."

"Caroline, please."

"Go off your Mass and leave me alone." She turned away. She heard him sigh, then the door opened and closed.

Caroline felt the heat rise to her face and her jaw clenched. *How dare he discuss religion with me! How dare he think that he is better than me because he is now able to cite scripture!*

Caroline sank to the nearest chair and laughed out loud at the absurdity of the whole conversation. David O'Donovan, formerly the man who used women as a hobby, had become David O'Donovan, self-righteous Catholic. Either way, he was obnoxious.

*   *   *

The sound of a horse and carriage drew her gaze to the window. She stood and looked down to see David arriving home from Mass. For a moment, she wished that she could dump commode waste on him. Then she reconsidered. That would just create a mess which Jane or Kip would have to clean up and it certainly wasn't any fault of theirs.

A soft knock at the door startled her. "Yes?"

"Caroline, it's David."

She shuddered. "What do you want?"

"We need to speak."

"There's nothing to speak about," she said through the closed door.

Silence followed and Caroline hoped that he had walked away. However, after a minute he spoke. "Please. Allow me to apologize."

She opened the door partway. He stood in the hallway, his head lowered.

"I am ready for your apology, David."

"To be honest, Caroline, I'm wondering why I need to apologize."

"Really? Well, I can tell you why you ought to be apologizing."

"Very well," he responded, in a whisper.

"You had no right to insist that Kathleen be baptized in that new church of yours. She is my daughter. You had no right to quote scripture to me."

"Why must I apologize for quoting scripture to you?"

"Because you were using it against me."

"And how was I doing that?"

Flustered, searching for a response, she mumbled, "Because you were."

"Then I offer my sincerest apology if you felt at all offended."

"I was offended, but I suppose I shall accept your apology."

He stood awkwardly in the hallway, making no attempt to leave her. Finally she mumbled, "Good day, David," and shut the door.

Later in the evening, David did not come to the table for dinner and Caroline considered that possibly her manner of speaking to him had been too abrasive. How could quoting scripture possibly be offensive to her? Perhaps because she found his tone self-righteous. How dare he quote that particular verse to her? Her heart was not hardened against God. Or, even if it was, she certainly had good reason. How many years had she spent serving God and this was what she received in return? God had not listened to her prayers so why ought she listen to his voice now?

In the dining room, Jane held Kathleen in front of Caroline. "Say g'night to your mama, Miss Kathleen."

"I'll put her down to sleep, Jane, as soon as I finish my supper."

"Of course you will, but Mr. David has asked to read Miss Kathleen a bedtime story."

"I see."

"When he's finished, would you like me to tell him to bring her to you?"

"No. I'd rather not see David at present. It would be preferable if you brought her to me, Jane."

Caroline finished her meal, then started up the long staircase. Her hand brushed against the marble banister and the image came to her mind of Liam dressed fine in blue breeches and coat, his blond hair and clean-shaven face so striking. She sighed and continued up the stairs.

In the hallway, she heard David's voice.

"And when the Philistine arose and was coming, and drew nigh to meet David, David made haste, and ran to the fight to meet the Philistine. And he put his hand into his scrip, and took a stone, and cast it with the sling and fetching it about struck the Philistine in the forehead."

She found herself drawn into the story, despite the fact that she knew how it would end. David read in as animated a voice as she had ever heard, although she imagined that his pitch was higher than usual as he spoke to Kathleen.

Caroline peeked around the corner and saw that David had Kathleen in his lap. David was sideways and facing away from Caroline, but her daughter's face was visible and her wide eyes were staring curiously at David's face as he was reciting the familiar story. For a moment, Caroline was jealous that David had Kathleen's rapt attention. She shifted her stance and the floorboard creaked. David immediately turned and looked in her direction.

"Caroline."

"I. . .was just going to my room."

"You may take the baby with you. I've finished the story."

"Very well." He stood and walked toward her. Caroline avoided eye contact but finally brought her gaze to his as he moved closer.

"Goodnight, Kat," he said and kissed her blonde head. As he gave her to Caroline, his hand brushed against hers and she cringed.

"Goodnight, Caroline."

She nodded and rushed off to her room.

35

Caroline placed Kathleen in her crib and turned the oil lamp down. After dressing in her night clothes, she sat in her reading chair beside the quiet fireplace and lit the oil lamp. She lifted up the lid of the trunk and sorted through her books searching for one she hadn't read in a while. Of course, she hadn't been reading very much in the last year. She picked up "Emma," the novel which Liam had given her as a gift when they were courting. She shook her head. Next, she picked up "Jane Eyre," then reconsidered. Certainly, reading about Jane Eyre's life, at least for part of the novel, would be melancholy reading. Then again, that character's life ended happily ever after, like most novels. Why couldn't her life with Liam have ended happily ever after?

She dropped the novel into the trunk and quietly closed it. Perhaps it wasn't her desire to read a book this evening.

She walked to the crib and stared at the sleeping form of her daughter and recalled her expression as she watched David read from the Bible. As much as Caroline did not want to admit it, Kathleen adored David and obviously enjoyed the manner in which he recited the story.

What harm could there be in allowing Kathleen to be baptized Catholic? Catholics attended a service, a Mass, where almost everything was spoken in Latin. The Catholics she knew, like Mother Superior at the Cheltenham convent, seemed like kind, charitable people. Then again, weren't Catholics idolaters? Didn't they worship statues?

David had seemed so sincere. If anyone else had suggested that Kathleen be baptized Catholic, she probably would not have been so contrary.

Was it possible that she really had hardened her heart towards God? It wasn't really the Almighty's fault that Liam had been injured, but it was His fault that Liam died, wasn't it? He could have saved Liam, but He did not.

Since her husband died, Caroline could focus only on the fact that Liam had been taken away from her. She was furious with

God and held fast to her anger and grief like a shield. Yet part of her husband lived on in Kathleen, who was a great gift from the Creator.

When she reflected on it, Caroline realized that she had prayed fervently while Liam was unconscious that God would allow him to wake. He did regain consciousness and she was able to tell him how much she loved him. Why couldn't she be thankful to God for the answer to that prayer?

Caroline opened the top drawer of her dresser and picked up the Bible. She opened it, randomly – perhaps because it was the center of the book – to the Song of Solomon.

A grin creeped across her face as she remembered the first time she discovered this section of the bible.

"The Song of Solomon. . ."

"No, Carrie, you need not read this part."

"Why?"

"Move on to Isaiah."

"But why, Papa?"

"Well, I. . .already. . .I know this one well enough."

Caroline shrugged her shoulders and paged through to Ecclesiastes.

Caroline recalled that as soon as she had finished reading to her father, she had rushed back to her room. "Let him kiss me with kisses of his mouth." She had blushed, but continued reading until she had finished the entire section. "Thy two breasts are like two young roes that are twins." The sensual words and imagery made her uncomfortable then and now. The imagery certainly was all symbolic as it couldn't have much to do with what a husband and wife do to create a child, could it?

She lifted her head and stared into the darkness beyond her bed. Perhaps David was right. Maybe she had hardened her heart against God's voice.

She closed the Bible and set it on her night table. Then she turned off the lamp and got into bed. She whispered, "Our Father, which art in heaven, hallowed be thy name, thy Kingdom come . . ."

36

David stared out the carriage window. Caroline had finally agreed to allow Kathleen to be baptized. And she was being civil and polite to him and for that, he ought to be doubly grateful.

He recalled their conversation from last week, when she asked him questions regarding the Catholic faith.

"Aren't Catholics idolaters, David?"
"No. Catholics worship the one true God."
"So Catholics don't worship statues?"
"Of course not. Catholics use statues as a reminder when praying."

In the heat of the carriage, he wiped his brow with a handkerchief, and longed for a tall glass of cold, sweet tea. David tugged at his cravat, loosening it. He cast a quick glance at Caroline, whose gaze was directed downward. She had also begun to perspire, her daughter's sleeping body lying against her chest. He searched the carriage with his eyes, then noticed Caroline's wood-silk fan on the seat. He stretched across the carriage, picked it up and began to fan her and Kathleen. She lifted her gaze to meet his, at first without expression, then the corner of her mouth rose in a half smile. She closed her eyes and accepted his gift.

* * *

When the carriage stopped outside the Cathedral, Caroline handed Kathleen to David, then he assisted her as she stepped out. The heat inside the carriage had been still and unforgiving. But David's kind act of fanning her made the ride more bearable. Now that Caroline was on the sidewalk in front of the Cathedral, the afternoon sun was stifling. Kip held the parasol above her, yet Caroline was finding it hard to breathe. Kathleen began to cry in David's arms.

"I'll take her, David."

Handing her to Caroline, he offered, "It will be cooler inside the church. Come."

She followed him up the steps. At the tall outer doors of the church, Kip took the parasol from above her and stepped back to allow the three of them to enter. "Mr. David, I'll be waiting at the carriage."

"Very well, Kip."

Inside the vestibule, there was another set of doors. David opened one door and began walking down the aisle. Caroline's shoes began to click on the shiny tile floor and she lifted her heels as not to disturb anyone.

She relished the cool air inside the church. Kathleen was quiet in her arms, but she held on to Caroline tightly.

Up ahead in the pews, she noticed a few people here and there.

In contrast to the rest of the darkened church, the front area was brightly lit with numerous gas lamps and candles. Caroline stared at the enormous brightly-colored   paintings behind the altar   as well as the side walls of the cathedral. She found this church an odd design, with no windows on either side wall.

Directly in front of her, countless flickering candles illuminated the two marble columns surrounding the altar area.   A breathtaking stained glass window lit up the center wall with deep blue, red and green glass.   David walked quietly until he reached the front. He made a quick kneeling movement, blessed himself then turned to glance in her direction. He waited for her to catch up to him, then directed her to a smaller room where a priest, whom Caroline supposed was Father Flaherty, was standing.

"David, it's good to see you. This must be Mrs. O'Donovan?"

"Yes, Father, allow me to introduce Mrs. Caroline O'Donovan."

"It is a pleasure to finally meet you, Mrs. O'Donovan. David has told me a great deal about you and your daughter." Caroline had to stop herself from cringing and she attempted to smile. Had David revealed to the priest the true nature of their relationship, that they were nothing more than brother-in-law and sister-in-law, despite their marital status?

"Thank you."

"We're waiting for your sponsors to arrive. Dr. and Mrs. Carver were delighted to hear that your daughter would be baptized and that they would be serving as godparents."

A tall older bearded man, accompanied by an attractive, well-dressed middle-aged woman approached the group.

"Good day, David." The man shook David's hand.

"Dr. and Mrs. Carver, this is Mrs. Caroline O'Donovan."

Caroline nodded toward them. "Pleased to make your acquaintance, Dr. Carver, Mrs. Carver. We should like to thank you for coming here today."

"It is our pleasure, Mrs. O'Donovan," Mrs. Carver replied.

In the carriage on the way home, Kathleen again fell asleep. The child's warm body against Caroline's chest made it nearly impossible to breathe. David had already picked up the fan and was attempting to cool them once again. This time, she offered him a more obvious smile.

Caroline brushed her daughter's blonde hair away from her face and wiped the sweat from her small forehead.

She wondered whether there was any way in which she could inform Elizabeth that Kathleen had been baptized. Elizabeth, her cousin/sister, had assumed that she would be godmother to Kathleen, and Caroline had never thought to contradict her. They had only spoken of it perhaps two times in the past year, but Caroline had simply dismissed the topic. She decided that no information was prudent for the time being. However, when Elizabeth eventually discovered that Kathleen's christening had taken place, she would be terribly hurt and for that, Caroline felt regretful and melancholy.

"Thank you again, Caroline." David's voice jolted her. "This was very important to me." He paused. "Do you wish me to take Kathleen?"

She shook her head. "It's fine." She paused. "Thank you for trying to cool us with the fan."

"I am happy to do it."

The rest of the carriage ride was spent in silence.

37

Jane held several linen-covered dresses across her arms. "Would you like me to bring these to the attic? You haven't worn them in nearly a year and a half."

Caroline cocked her head to look at the top of the dresses peeking through the linen. "I'm not sure."

"I'll lay them across the bed and you can have a look." Jane carefully placed each dress across Caroline's bed and lifted the linen up.

For a moment, Caroline drank in the sight of the bright blue cotton dress, the one she wore on her first outing with Liam to the Centennial Exhibition. She closed her eyes and recalled the joy and awkwardness of that day.

She watched as Jane stood over a blue-gray dress. "This is a pretty dress, Miss Caroline."

"I wore that when I stopped wearing black after my father died."

"Why don't you try it on?" Jane began to remove it from the covering and hanger and she handed it to her mistress.

"Very well, if you wish."

With Jane's assistance, she removed her black dress and slipped on the blue-gray dress but stopped as she attempted to pull it over her waist. "I believe I wore a corset with this dress, Jane, so I don't think it will fit."

"I think you are smaller than when you first wore this dress."

Caroline raised her eyebrows in disbelief. "I have birthed a child since then."

"And you've not been eating proper."

Caroline pulled the dress over her waist and bosom. It was a snug fit, to be sure, but she straightened and stared at herself in the mirror.

"You look so pretty, Miss Caroline. This shade shows off your fair complexion and red hair."

"I just imagined wearing black for the rest of my life."

"You're still a young lady. There'd be no shame in at least

wearing different shades of gray for a few years, now, would there?"

She stared at her reflection. This dress certainly was not too bright. Subtle and subdued. "Yes, I shall wear this dress today."

*   *   *

"Sure an' ye be lookin' pretty, Miss Caroline. I'm glad ye finally stopped wearin' all that black." Patsie and Jane stood in front of the O'Donovan house next to the larger carriage.

"Thank you," Caroline said.   "How long will you be able to visit, Patsie?"

"Oh, now, only a few hours I'm thinkin'. Jane, will ye be tellin' that husband of yours to fetch the last of Mr. David's bags to put them up on the carriage?" Patsie headed toward the back of the house with Jane's son, Isaac on her hip.

"Yes, Ma'am." Jane took hold of Kathleen's hand and walked her toward the house. The front door opened and David stepped onto the porch. "Papa!" Kathleen yelled as she let go of Jane's hand.

"Kat, you be a good girl." David lifted her up and kissed her cheek, then set her down. He turned toward Caroline and nodded. "Good bye, Caroline. I'll be gone a week."

"Good bye," she said, now facing him.

Kip kissed Jane's cheek and hopped into the driver's seat. David climbed into the carriage and it rode away.

"Papa come back?" Kathleen asked, in her high-pitched voice. Caroline lovingly scooped her toddler into her arms. "In a few days, Sweet."

Her daughter's mouth curved in a pout. She squirmed until her mother set her down and the child scurried away.   Caroline smoothed out the skirt of her blue-gray dress. Wearing this color and fabric made her feel light and airy.

"Miss Caroline, you want me to run after her?"

"Thank you, Jane. Your mother has Isaac?"

"Yes, Ma'am, she does. She's in the kitchen. And you know how much she likes to indulge him. I mean, he's her only grand-child."

"I know."

Jane ran after Kathleen, and the little girl was now playing a game of trying to get away from her.

The servant stopped running and glanced at Caroline. "Miss Caroline?"

"Yes?"

"You look fatigued. Perhaps you ought to be taking a rest upstairs. I'll keep an eye on Miss Kathleen."

"Very well."

"Would you like me to feed Miss Kathleen her luncheon?"

"Of course, thank you."

Jane took off after Kathleen toward the back of the house. After pondering about it for a moment, Caroline realized that the servant was right. She felt exhausted on these warm autumn days, somewhat relieved that David wasn't around. He was tolerable enough as of late, mostly ignoring her as usual, but striving to be an attentive father to Kathleen. He occasionally asked her if she wanted to join him in attending Mass at the Cathedral. Although she agreed to have Kathleen baptized, she really wasn't interested in attending any sort of church service at the present time.

When she reached the staircase, it occurred to her that she needed to remind Jane to give Kathleen a small portion of cheese as it had upset her stomach the last time she had eaten a large piece.

She began to descend the steps and she could hear faint chopping noises in the kitchen. The farther she went down, the clearer she could hear Kathleen's giggles and Isaac's babbling. Jane's voice seemed unusually loud and resonating. Caroline stopped when she heard Jane mention her name.

"Miss Caroline sure looks pretty these days, doesn't she, Ma?"

"That she does, I'm thinkin'."

"Miss Caroline is so full of grief that she can't see how much he loves her."

"Sure an' I'm thinkin' ye be right. Why, the way he's lookin' at her, it's plain as the nose on yer face how he feels. Sure an' that boy's niver looked at a colleen the way he looks at Miss Caroline."

He? Who in the world are they talking about?

"Yes, Ma. Mr. David sure does love her like a true husband."

Caroline quietly gasped at the same time her daughter let out a squeal.

"Does my heart good to see how much he loves and respects her."

Caroline stood transfixed and breathless on the steps. Quietly, she backed up the stairs and into the front hallway.

Despite the cool breeze coming in through the open foyer windows, Caroline began to sweat, her breathing became shallow and her hands started to tremble. She turned and absentmindedly followed the edge of the staircase until she was facing the front door. She pressed her hands to her chest to quiet the pounding of her heart.

"This is impossible. I would know. He can't. . .he wouldn't." She forced herself to breathe in and out several times.

"Miss Caroline?" She gasped, then turned when she heard Jane's voice, and saw her emerge from the kitchen steps.

"Yes, what is it, Jane?"

"Why, you look like you've seen a ghost. Are you unwell?"

"No, no, I'm fine. Just warm, I suppose." Caroline's voice cracked and she fanned her face with her shaking hands.

"Of course. I thought you were going to rest."

"Yes, yes, I'll be going upstairs now. What is it that you wanted, Jane?"

"Miss Kathleen wants more cheese but I know you were saying that too much cheese binds her up, doesn't it?"

"Yes, yes, that's right. Perhaps give her more apple slices or bread."

"Yes, Ma'am." Jane returned to the basement.

Caroline remained in the front hall and leaned against the marble banister. She wondered why the servants thought David loved her. It really was an absurd notion. Perhaps he loved her as a brother loves his sister, but true, romantic, spousal love? No, that was impossible.

Later that evening, unable to sleep, Caroline wandered through the house. *Could Jane and Patsie be right?* She found herself dismissing the idea as ludicrous. She passed by the downstairs study, then stopped. She turned the knob and found the door unlocked. Opening it, she peered into the dark room, allowing her eyes to adjust. The room smelled of pipe smoke, maple and old books.

Caroline lit a small lamp on the desk and carried it to the bookcase. She tilted her head to read the titles of the books on the shelf at her eye level: "Union Business Catalogue," "World Almanac 1874," "The Autobiography of Benjamin Franklin," "Treatise on Natural Philosophy," "Lombard Street, A Description of the Money Market," "Ancient Society."

Leaning down, she read the titles on the shelf below. More world almanacs, more money market books, not much of interest.

Caroline's eyes wandered about the room. David had been building a new ship and she moved closer to get a better look. She turned on the gas sconce and bent down to study the vessel. Not all of the sails were yet in place, but the ones that were present were skillfully made. . .no, sewn. Certainly, David could not have done that work. The fine wood construction, perhaps, but not the sails. She began to study the ships he had recently carved, but one in particular captured her attention immediately. It was a fine looking model, a larger boat, one that seemed almost enshrined on the center top of the bookcase near the window. There was writing on the side of the boat. With the dimness of the room, she was unable to see what was written there. She lifted the oil lamp high, but she could barely read the letters. "C-a-r-o. . ." She gasped. *"Caroline."* She stepped back, her mouth open, her eyes staring at the vessel.

She extinguished the lamps and returned to her bedroom. She tossed and turned in bed, unable to sleep.

Could it be true that her former brother-in-law loved her as a husband should love a wife? Thinking back, she tried to remember how they had interacted for the past year and a half. Seemingly insignificant actions, such as his avoiding eye contact with her or stuttering when he spoke to her, now began to make sense in light of this new information.

Her whole body trembled. If this was indeed true, it seemed a cruel irony that a person with his background was married to someone who did not share the marriage bed with him. Then again, it was his fault that Liam died, wasn't it? Perhaps it was more of a justice for him.

Caroline turned down the lamp and attempted to banish those thoughts from her mind.

38

A week later, David emerged from the carriage in front of the house. He wasn't sure whether Caroline would be watching from her upstairs window so he kept his gaze downwards. He tried not to glance at her too frequently.

If he knew that she wasn't looking at him, he would simply stare. She rarely smiled these days, but when she did – and of course, it was never a gesture directed toward him – that simple act gave fuel to his soul.

For the most part, he was content with her being oblivious to him and he did his best to keep out of her way. Living in the same household made it impossible to completely ignore her. In fact, he found himself noticing every expression she had, her sighs, her tones of voice, the way her lip curled when she was reprimanding Kathleen. Sometimes he would gaze at Caroline from the downstairs study window, behind the drapes, of course, while she was playing with Kathleen, watching how she, without restraint, offered all traces of remaining love to her daughter.

Caroline had grown up quickly in the year and a half since Lee had died. But it gave him hope when she laughed with childlike abandonment as she ran in the yard with Kat. Last week, however, Jane had mentioned Liam's name and Caroline became teary-eyed, then attempted to hide it by turning away. He had wanted to embrace her, to tell her that, despite his stoic appearance, he frequently felt the same way.

On his part, he tried not to think about his brother because he would weep and he wouldn't allow himself to cry anymore.

Despite the arm's length approach, his love for her deepened every day. And the fact that he was living a celibate life and that she could care less about him seemed the perfect penance. But what made almost no sense to him was that he wasn't sad or angry about the fact that their relationship more closely resembled that of a brother and sister.

"Miss Caroline and Miss Kathleen are probably waiting for you in the foyer, Mr. David," he heard Kip say.

"Yes, thank you, Kip. I'll be there momentarily."

*　　*　　*

Caroline paused by her bedroom window and watched David emerge from the carriage. Unlike Liam, David didn't glance up to see if she were there. Now Caroline scrutinized his every movement, the way he walked, the manner in which he conducted himself. She never studied him so closely before today.

Jane had been right. Caroline had been too wrapped up in her grief and too preoccupied with taking care of Kathleen to notice him as anything but a brother-in-law who had been forced into marrying her.

What of this new information? If David truly loved her as a husband loved a wife, why had David not told her how he felt?

Should she react with disgust or be flattered? It seemed evident that he had expected nothing in return, no love, no physical affection. And it must be an arduous task for him to be near someone he loves so much and not be able to demonstrate his affection.

Caroline wondered whether she ought to confront him and perhaps tell him about the conversation she overheard. After pondering it for the last few days, she had come to the conclusion that they ought to separate, with David in Boston, and that she should stay here and run the household and hire someone to run the mercantile business from Philadelphia. That would be the only way this whole charade would be tolerable.

She gathered her skirts and rushed down the back staircase to get Kathleen so that they could be in the foyer when David walked in. Caroline picked up her daughter, then hurried up the stairs. She stood in the foyer, somewhat out of breath from the jaunt up the stairs.

David came in amidst the happy squeals of Kathleen.

"Papa, Papa!" she yelled, in her sweet voice. She was so excited that she tried to squirm out of her mother's arms.

David's eyes brightened as Caroline set her down. Kathleen ran to him and he lifted her in his arms. He was laughing and smiling as Kathleen kissed his cheek.

"How's my Kat been? Been good for Mama?"

"Papa, Papa!"

David placed Kathleen down, then glanced at Caroline with

a guarded smile. Caroline tried to return the gesture but was sure that she appeared as if she were grimacing.

"Caroline."

"Hello, David," she said, now avoiding eye contact.

"Miss Caroline, do you want me to take Miss Kathleen upstairs for her bath?"

Caroline nodded. "Yes, thank you."

"I'll see you after your bath, Kat." David handed Kathleen to Jane, who took her up the stairs.

Caroline was left alone with David in the foyer. Caroline decided that this would not be the appropriate time to mention anything, so she stared at the different paintings on the wall. David cleared his throat and asked, "How are you, Caroline?" Caroline choked back a sob. *Why does he have to sound so much like Liam?*

"Fine, thank you. I trust your trip went well?" She kept her gaze down.

"Very well, thank you."

The loud chiming of the grandfather clock caused her to glance at his face. His head was just turning towards the chiming sound. Seven o'clock.

"Well, I must go upstairs to choose a story for Kat. I missed reading to her. Good night, Caroline."

"Good night."

Later that evening, Kathleen's whimpers woke Caroline out of a deep sleep. "Papa, want Papa."

"Now, now, Papa is resting in his room, Kathleen." Caroline leaned down to comfort her daughter. "We can't disturb him. He's had quite a long journey and I'm sure he's very tired."

"Want Papa!"

"I know you do, Kathleen, but. . ."

"Want Papa," Kathleen now screamed.

Knocking at Caroline's bedroom door, followed by David's voice. "It's David. Is Kathleen calling for me?"

Caroline swung the door open. David was dressed in sleeping attire and a robe.

"Yes, I'm afraid she is. I didn't want to disturb you."

"You wouldn't be disturbing me." David stepped into the

room, leaned into the crib and gathering Kathleen into his arms.

"Papa, papa," she said, snuggling up under his neck.

"Shhh," David comforted her, stroking her white blond hair, which looked blue in the darkness. "You missed me, Kat?"

"Papa, Papa."

"I missed you too."

David rocked back and forth with Kathleen in his arms, then began to hum a calming lullaby. *What a beautiful voice he has.* Caroline shivered, then she realized that she had forgotten to cover herself before answering the door to David's knocking. She slipped on her robe, then approached the crib a few feet away from David.

David kissed the top of Kathleen's head and gently placed her back inside the crib. He stood for several moments and watched her sleep in the darkness.

"Perhaps you ought to keep your oil lamp burning, Caroline."

"Very well."

"It must be frightening for her to wake up and have it be so dark."

Caroline lit the lamp until it produced a soft glow. When she glanced at him, he was just looking away from her. He again stared at Kathleen's small sleeping form inside the crib. Caroline looked past him and her eye caught a glimpse of her mother's Bible on the dresser.

"Carrie, stop reading. I'm not able to keep my eyes open and I don't want you to be wasting your time."

"Papa, it's not a waste of time. Besides, I've almost finished reading the entire Bible."

"I know, but I'm not feeling up to it today, Sweet."

"Very well, Papa." Caroline put the Bible down and studied her father. *He was pale and now his eyes were closed. She picked up his hand and he opened his eyes.*

"Ah, my Carrie. You've been an angel to take care of me."

"I love you, Papa."

"I love you, Carrie." Again, he closed his eyes.

Caroline let go of his hand, kissed his forehead, then picked up the Bible from the night table and placed it on the dresser.

When she returned to his bedside, his expression was so peaceful, so calm.

David cleared his throat. As she looked in his direction, he again appeared to be just looking away from her.

"I suppose I ought to return to my room. Good night, Caroline."

"Yes, good night, David." Caroline sat down on the side of the bed and sighed. As he was stepping into the hallway, she called his name.

"Yes?" He regarded her with tenderness that she hadn't noticed before. If she hadn't overheard the servants, she would have interpreted his expression as one of mere fondness.

"Thank you," she said.

"You're very welcome."

39

Over the next week, Caroline scrutinized David closely. She didn't know exactly what she was looking for, perhaps something that would explain and obviously illustrate his feelings. He was quiet but polite at dinner and interacted playfully with Kathleen but, as usual, he kept his distance with her.

Caroline noticed that on most mornings, David disappeared in the woods, most likely, to pray. At the end of the week, on a cool but beautiful sunny day after he had come out of the forest, David rode below her window and up the laneway. With David gone, she decided to visit the area in the forest where he prayed.

At the edge of the forest, she stepped upon a small pathway. She hadn't entered the forest in over a year, since she had first discovered David praying in the clearing. She followed it for a hundred or so feet, then gasped. Before her stood the headstone, now cleaned. An additional sculpture had been placed beside the gravestone: a marble statue of St. Joseph with the child Jesus clutched to his breast. In front was another, smaller representation of Christ on the cross.

Caroline crouched down and studied the face of the chiseled Jesus on the cross. The face of Jesus had a serene, peaceful expression, certainly not one that presented the agony of being hung on a cross. How could anyone be at peace in the midst of suffering?

She sat at the stone bench and again studied the sculptures and, more particularly, the small statue of Jesus on the cross. The trees rustled quietly in the wind and Caroline breathed deeply the cool air and understood why David had come here each morning to pray. *How am I going to tell him that I know how he feels about me? Should I even tell him?*

Although Caroline didn't hear any words, she sensed the answer.

* * *

Caroline, with Kathleen in her arms, passed David's door. It was open slightly. She could see David moving about in the room.

She had tossed and turned all night. In those long hours before dawn, she had made the decision to speak to him today and ask him about the boat and why he had named it for her. That would give him an opportune way of sharing his feelings for her, if he indeed had feelings of a romantic nature.

He opened the door and greeted them in the hallway. "Good morning."

"Papa!"

"Hello, Kat!" He lifted her up and held her while he spoke. "Is Kip available, Caroline?"

"I'm not sure where he is, David. Shall I look for him?"

"No, that won't be necessary."

Kip had just come up the stairs.

"Kip."

"Do you need something, Mr. David?"

"I'd like a bath, if you have a moment."

"Of course."

"David?"

"Yes?"

"I. . .need to. . .I must speak with you."

"One moment, Caroline." She watched as he gave instructions for how hot the water should be and where in his bedroom the tub should be placed. David's expression seemed overly serious for discussing bath temperatures. Kathleen, still in his arms, was looking curiously at David as he spoke. When Kip stepped away, David turned to face Caroline.

"Now, what is it that you would like to discuss with me?" His mouth was curved in a smile, an expression which reminded her of when they first met.

"Perhaps we could take a walk to the oak tree. What I need to say is. . .quite. . .private."

"I must say, you've gotten my attention. This must be important."

"Yes, it is."

"I'm not dressed for outside yet, Caroline. Can it wait?"

"Yes, I suppose so."

"Very well then."

Later that morning, Caroline waited near the tree in front of

the house. Her hands were shaking and she was nervously rubbing her arms, despite the warmth of the day.

She finally saw him on the veranda speaking with Jane. He
held his hands over his eyes to shade the sun as he looked in her
direction, then he made his way toward her.

"David."

"I'm sorry, Caroline. It took a long time to heat the water
because. . .well, it's a complicated story. I was not taking my
time."

"Of course." Caroline hesitated. "Perhaps we ought to take
a walk."

"A walk?"

She nodded. As she studied his face, she concluded that she
never before noticed that his eyes were such a deep shade of blue,
like the color that filled the sky on a bright summer day.

She walked in the direction of the forest and the path which
led to the gravestone and statues. She stopped and turned toward
him.

"Why didn't you tell me you had brought statues into the forest?"

"I don't know. You've returned to. . ."

"Yes. It's lovely. You've transformed that whole clearing
into a beautiful peaceful area."

"This time of year, it's even more pleasant because of the lack
of bugs."

Together, they strolled along the path until they came to the
statues. She sat on the bench. "I hope that my coming here has-
n't been an intrusion."

"Not at all."

"So you don't mind if I come here as well from time to time?"

"Of course not. Any time you'd like."

"Please, do be seated. I have an urgent matter to discuss
with you."

"Yes?" He sat beside her, keeping some distance from her on
the bench.

"I. . ."

For a moment, he seemed distracted by the soft warm breeze
that caressed their faces. He glanced at the statue and stared at
the face of Jesus. He was silent for a moment, then spoke. "I've

never been one to be at peace with suffering or anything that made me uncomfortable, Caroline. In fact, my whole life I've been a person who's tried to escape discomfort. But I requested this statue because it allows me to see what true joy, true peace really is. Here is Christ, who had been beaten, scourged, nailed to a cross and he's completely at peace with it to the point of saying, 'Forgive them Father, they know not what they do.' To be able to think and feel that when they're hammering the nails into his hands and feet? It's what true joy is all about." He paused. "What is it that you wanted to speak to me about?"

"Well. . ."

"Yes?"

"This is. . . difficult, David." Now, she became more aware of her trembling hands.

"What is difficult?" he asked, his eyes now focused on her. "Caroline, if something is wrong, you must tell me about it."

Caroline nodded. "Nothing is wrong. But. . ." She took a deep breath, then lowered her eyes.   "Last week, I stood at the top of the staircase to the kitchen. I had remembered that I needed to tell Jane something, then I stopped when I heard 'Miss Caroline.'"

"The servants were talking about you?"

Caroline nodded.

"Well, the servants do speak about us, more frequently than we know." He paused. "So what did they say about you?"

She tried to weigh her words carefully. She cleared her throat. "They spoke of you. . .as well." She finally looked at his face.

"Ah. I hope I won't be firing anyone." He was smiling as he said it.

"No, no. That won't be necessary." She held her hands on her lap to stop them from trembling, but her heart continued to pound.

"So what did they say about you and me?" He stopped. He seemed to be studying her, then he glanced away.

She avoided eye contact, then said, "They said that it was plainly obvious. . ."

"Yes?" she heard him say.

"How. . ." She swallowed once, then continued, ". . .much you love me but that I am still too full of grief to notice." She said the words quickly.

"Oh." There was an awkward silence. Then her eyes met his. He stared at her with an "I've been caught" expression, his lips slightly parted.

She waited for him to deny that he loved her, but the denial never came.

He was staring down at the ground, opening his mouth to speak, then closing it and remaining silent for the moment.

They sat uneasy and quiet, their silence a stark contrast to their previous conversation. He pulled at the top of his shirt. She could hear Kathleen's distant laughter and a few birds chirping. Caroline finally broke the silence.

"You've named one of your prized boats after me. It's quite beautiful."

He nodded, his deep blue eyes now focused on her, but he said nothing.

"Mr. David, there's a fire in the kitchen! Please come quick!" Jane's high-pitched voice called out. David immediately began to run in the direction of the house. Caroline grabbed her skirts and followed him as they rushed through the pathway and to the back of the house and into the kitchen.

The fire was climbing up the cookstove, its flames sliding up the pipe to the ceiling. Kip, his hand red and blistering, was throwing buckets of water on the small fire, which had extended to a basket of tablecloths a few feet away. Jane ran out the back door to the well and handed Hallie more buckets of water. David moved Kip out of the way and grabbed the buckets from Hallie, quickly dumping the water onto the now smoldering fire. Within a few moments, all that was left of the fire was smoke.

"So sorry, Mr. David."

"No, no, Kip, don't worry about that." David was studying Kip's hand. "You've got quite a burn there."

"I'll be fine, Mr. David. Jane will fix me up."

Jane had already begun to bandage his hand.

Several hours later, Caroline clutched onto her robe and stood before David's door. She knocked several times.

"Yes, who is it?"

"It's Caroline."

"Just a minute." A few moments later, he opened the door dressed in a long robe. He leaned toward her with his hands outstretched on the wooden molding around the doorway.

She shifted from side to side as the fingers of David's right hand began to drum against the molding.

"Perhaps we can finish our discussion somewhere else?" Caroline asked, in a quiet tone of voice.

"Yes, down the hall, in the upstairs study perhaps?"

"That's fine." She looked up at him, then shifted awkwardly from one foot to the next. "I must put Kathleen to bed first." Caroline returned to her bedroom where Jane was attempting to put Kathleen to sleep.

"I think you better settle her, Ma'am."

"Yes, of course, Jane. Thank you."

As Caroline lay next to Kathleen on her bed, she began telling her a story. "Once upon a time, there were three bears: a papa bear, a mama bear and a baby bear. . ." After a few minutes, she glanced at Kathleen, who was asleep. She placed her in the crib and waited for a few moments. Caroline, exhausted, lay back on her bed and found herself drifting off to sleep.

40

David tightened the tie on his robe and sighed with relief. His wife, and he almost never called her that, knew. With relief came joy, but also fear of being rejected by the only woman he had ever truly loved.

When they were together in the clearing and before she had revealed 'the urgent matter,' he had noticed that she was shaking and nervous. That made him love her more. Since when did she feel or act nervous around him?

Caroline had said that she wanted to discuss the matter further. He could not figure out what more needed to be discussed.

It was now midnight and he guessed that she had fallen asleep. If that was the case, he could now lie down and drift off.

"Mama, no," Kathleen's screams pierced the silence of the night. David woke quickly and was at their open doorway within seconds.

"Shhh, Sweet, it's fine, you're safe," Caroline whispered to Kathleen. She turned toward David.   "A nightmare, I'm afraid."

"Here, allow me." He tried to gently embrace his daughter. The toddler continued thrashing and screaming for several long minutes.

David began humming and soon, Kathleen was sleeping calmly in his arms. He carefully laid her down in her crib. He watched her sleep, the soft glow of the fire and the dimly lit oil lamp barely illuminating all three of them. Caroline made no noise, but sat on the side of the bed.

"Thank you," she whispered. "She's just started having horrible nightmares during the past week or so that you've been gone."

"I see."   He took a deep breath then he stared at the floor. "Good night, Caroline."

As he backed out of the room to leave, Caroline called, "Wait."

He stopped and glanced up. "Yes?"

"We do need to finish our conversation. I fell asleep."

"Yes."

"Perhaps we could go to the study across the hall, like you suggested earlier."

"Very well. We'll just leave the door open in both rooms and we should be able to hear her if she wakes again."

Caroline nodded, then followed him across the hall.

David walked to the oil lamp and lit it, the soft flame now subtly lighting the area. She was so close that he could smell her hair, the sweet scent of flowers. When he turned to face her, she was staring at different sections of the room. She pointed to the books and violin. "Those are Liam's."

"Yes. I wanted to make sure that Lee was a part of this room so I moved some of his books here." He glanced at the bookcase and Liam's violin placed neatly on the top shelf.

"You've done a wonderful job. But I haven't really been in this room since you've transformed it. I couldn't bring myself to do so."

David lifted the violin off the stand, picked up the bow and blew some of the dust off of it. He began playing.

"You also play the violin?"

He nodded. "I haven't picked it up in years. I learned at the same time as Lee, but never had any time for practice, so I don't play nearly as well." He paused. "Besides, it was our mother who encouraged us. Father believed that it was too feminine to play an instrument, especially classical songs, and I suppose that I agreed with him."

"Play more. . .please."

"I'm not sure what I remember, but I'll make an attempt." He walked to the door and closed it. "I don't want to wake Kat."

As he began to play a slow, quiet song, David reveled in the fact that she was watching him and he wanted to perform well for her. However, he hadn't touched a violin in a long time and his performance was mediocre, at best.

"It's a travesty that you have not played in a long time, David."

"I suppose it is."

Caroline glanced away.

David returned the instrument to its place on the shelf, then stood close to her, causing her to step back.

"What do you think needs to be further discussed?" he asked.

"I don't think it's fair for you to be married to someone who does not feel the same way you do."

"Any more than it is to be married to someone you've been forced to marry?"

Her glance lowered. "I don't know."

"Caroline, I have learned that life is not fair." He paused, then continued. "For so many years, I only saw women as things which could satisfy my. . ."

Caroline raised her eyebrows.

"When Kathleen was born, it made me realize more fully, to simply think of some man doing to her what I have done to so many young women made me want to hang myself."

"You have changed. This is evident."

"Yes, I have."

"And what of marriage? You could be married to anyone and there would be many who would be willing to marry you."

"But I am already married, and I am content to remain married to you, to follow through on my part of the bargain, unless of course, you wish to marry someone else."

"That will not happen, David. And I am content with the current situation, but it's awkward, now that I know how you feel."

Avoiding eye contact, he said, "I would never pressure you to have any relationship with me other than the one we currently have, Caroline. I love you that much." There, he said it. Actually saying it to her, sharing a part of his soul, liberated him.

They remained quiet for a moment, then her voice came as a whisper. "When. . .did this happen? This. . .love for me."

He brought his gaze upwards. "I can't say a day or an hour, Caroline, but even before you were married to Lee, I was attracted to you. By the time Lee was near death, I didn't want to admit it to myself, but I felt a love for you that was different than what a brother-in-law ought to feel. When Lee asked me to marry you, part of me wanted to say yes, I'll marry her, I love her." He hesitated. "But I knew how you felt about me. I knew that I was a nuisance to you, which is why I tried to avoid you when I could. I did not want to make your pain any greater than it was."

"You were not a nuisance. I was still resentful that I was forced to marry you."

"To be honest, I was also resentful. It's probably one of the reasons I drank so heavily the morning of our marriage. I have always despised being forced into anything." There was an awkward pause. "It's probably best that we return to our rooms." David felt such a strong desire to embrace her. Knowing that he couldn't, or shouldn't, he stepped back and turned the oil lamp off.

Caroline nodded and waited in the hallway, then stood in the doorway of her room.

As he was closing his bedroom door, he heard her call his name.

"Yes?"

"Would it be acceptable for me to join you in the evenings when you are reading to Kathleen?"

"Certainly. But I cannot promise not to quote scripture since some of the stories I tell her are from the Bible, Caroline."

"Yes, I know. And I wouldn't be asking you to promise that. I was hoping that you would read from the Bible."

"You were?"

"Yes."

"Then I would like that very much." He paused. "What about now?"

"Now? Well, yes, I suppose so."

"I'll return in a moment," he said. "Perhaps you can wait for me in the study?" He quickly picked up his Bible from his bedside table. He knew the ideal book they could read together, one which spoke to his heart. "Would you mind if we read from the Canticle of Canticles?" he asked, as he lit the gas lamp and pulled two chairs around the small desk. "Then perhaps we can read a favorite reading of yours, if you'd like."

"Yes, very well."

He opened to the center, paged to the beginning and began reading.

"Let him kiss me with the kiss of his mouth; for thy breasts are better than wine. . ."

"David?

"Yes?"

"This is the Song of Solomon," she whispered.

"Yes, I suppose that is what the protestant Bible calls it. My Douay Bible calls it the Canticle of Canticles."

Her face was noticeably flushed. She was anxiously rubbing her hands together and staring at the floor.

"Is something wrong?" he asked.

She remained silent and kept her head lowered.

David sighed. He sat back in his chair and opened his mouth to speak, then reconsidered. He supposed that he had been too enthusiastic in wanting to read this particular book out loud. Although it was one of his favorites, he should have known this would have upset her or, at the very least, make her uncomfortable. And yet with its imagery, it served as one of the most beautiful illustrations of divine love.

He wished that he could explain to her that the imagery is meant to compare God's passionate love to spousal love. He wanted to tell her that he probably understood this book of the Bible more than most people because it helped him to understand the mystery of the deep burning love God has for all of us.

However, for now, he could not share those things with her. Which other book of the Bible could he read out loud? Which book would help her to see how they could best approach their own situation?

"Perhaps we might read from Ephesians then?"

She exhaled, as if she had been holding her breath. "Yes, that would be fine."

"St. Paul to the Ephesians, 5:21-32."

"*Being subject one to the other in the fear of Christ. Let women be subject to their husbands, as to the Lord. Because the husband is the head of the wife, as Christ is the head of the church. He is the savior of his body. Therefore, as the Church is subject to Christ, so also let the wives be to their husbands in all things. Husbands, love your wives, as Christ also loved the Church and delivered himself up for it.*"

He continued reading further on.

"*So also ought men to love their wives with their own bodies. He that loveth his wife, loveth himself.*"

He looked up to see Caroline again fidgeting in her seat and avoiding eye contact.

"David?"

"Yes?"

"I'm quite tired. Might we read from the Bible again tomorrow?"

"Certainly."

"I should like you to read from one of the Gospels, if we could?"

"Yes." He paused. "I would like that very much."

He closed his Bible, turned off the gas lamp and joined her in the hallway.

"Caroline?"

"Yes?"

"Perhaps I shouldn't have read from the Canticle of Canticles. I suppose the detailed nature of the imagery was awkward for you?"

She blushed.

"I apologize. I didn't mean to offend you. This is, after all, the Bible."

"Yes, I know, but. . ."

"Next time, we shall read from the Gospels then, if you would prefer."

"Yes."

"Goodnight, Caroline." Moonlight streamed in through the hall window and landed like a square in the hallway near her room.

David stared at her as she walked across the hallway. He went to his own room and shut the door.

41

The following morning, Caroline woke to find Kathleen missing from her crib. She put on her robe and, leaning her head out in the hallway, called for Jane, who appeared momentarily.

"Yes, Ma'am, what is it?"

"Where is Kathleen?"

"Mr. David took Miss Kathleen to Vernon Park."

"Why did you not wake me?"

"You seemed to be sleeping pretty soundly. Miss Kathleen was in her crib quietly playing. Mr. David asked me to dress her so he could take her to the park and allow you some rest time."

"I intend to dress but I'll be down for breakfast."

"Will you be needing some help?"

"No, I shall be fine, Jane. My new corset ties in the front."

Later, Caroline entered the hallway. She hesitated at the closed door of the upstairs study. She opened the door, crossed the room and glanced at the desk, then recalled David reading from Bible. It was an awkward moment with him choosing to read from the only book of the Bible which made her blush. However, he did apologize; he was not purposefully trying to embarrass her.

At the bookcase, Liam's violin stood neatly on the shelf above her eye level, the bow beside it. Caroline let out a long, winded sigh. It seemed such an awful waste for his violin to sit, unused, gathering dust.

She recalled David's playing last night. He did not have Liam's polished technique, but she was certain he could play better with practice. She lifted the violin from the stand and held it for a moment. She caressed the side of it.

Caroline scanned the closest bookcase for sheet music. Not finding any, she studied the room, perusing another book case. She laid the violin and bow on top of the desk, then quickly searched the drawers. In the bottom one, stacks of sheet music were haphazardly thrown in. Carefully, she lifted out the top half of the stack and placed them on the desk beside the violin. She paged through the sheets, "The Shepherd Boy," "Northern Pearl,"

"Grandfather's Clock." Several more pages had Liam's handwritten notes of music he had composed, and more songs with which she wasn't familiar, then "Oft in the Stilly Night," the song which David had said their mother had sung to them at bedtime.

A short while later, Caroline sat on the veranda enjoying the cool autumn air. Some of the leaves were absent from the trees, yet beautiful color remained. The air smelled of crisp apples and burning maple. The carriage pulled up to the front of the house and David lifted Kathleen down. When he put her down on the ground, she held her hands up.

"Hol' me, Papa?"

"Kat, Papa's tired. I held you for almost the entire time at the park."

"Please, Papa?" David looked down at her sweet expression, then relented.

Caroline studied him and the obvious expression of love for Kathleen. When he glanced at her, she felt a strange tingling sensation in her stomach and her pulse quickened. "Did you have a good time at the park?"

"Well, she had a good time. I felt like a horse!"

"Wait till she gets older and bigger."

"Miss Caroline, I'll take Kathleen inside and wash her up, if you'd like."

"Yes, that would be fine."

"I wonder if you would do me a favor, David."

"And what would that be?"

Caroline took the violin and bow from behind her and handed them to him. "It would give me pleasure if you would practice playing the violin. You have talent, and I would very much like to hear you play."

He took the violin from her. "If you want me to play, I will. And what will I play?"

Caroline picked up a stack of papers from the small chair on the veranda. "I found these, if they are of any help. I think they were Liam's. They have his notes and markings on them."

She handed the sheet music to David and he laughed under his breath. "He certainly was the fastidious one." He paused. "I suppose that's what got us into our present predicament."

"Predicament?"

"Yes, this marriage of yours and mine."

"Yes, I suppose so. But I would hardly call it a predicament."

"Perhaps that is a strong word." David paused, then he held the door open for Caroline and followed her inside.

In the downstairs parlor after dinner, David and Caroline sat together on the couch and he began to read from the Gospel of Matthew. "The book of the generation of Jesus Christ, the son of David, the son of Abraham; Abraham begot Isaac and. . ."

"David, you could probably skip all the begetting and read the part about Mary and Joseph."

"Yes, certainly."

"Mr. David?" Jane called from the doorway, holding Kathleen.

"Yes, Jane?"

"Miss Kathleen's ready for her story."

"Bring her to me."

"Papa, story."

"Yes, Kat, I'll tell you a story."

Then David began to recite the account of Mary and Joseph and the birth of Jesus. His voice was animated and clear and full of expression, so that he could appeal to Kathleen, her rapt attention evident in her bright eyes. But Caroline was also drawn into the story. With his infectious enthusiasm for God's word, David brought the words of the Gospel to life.

Later that night, as Caroline lay Kathleen down to sleep, she could hear soft violin music coming from David's room.

She listened as he played, somewhat unpolished, hesitating every few seconds, but nonetheless pleasing. When she realized what he was playing, she almost caught her breath. *He's playing 'Oft in the Stilly Night,' the song their mother sang to them as children, the song he sang when we danced at Liam's and my wedding.*

Kathleen was now asleep, and she opened her door to hear the music more clearly. For someone who hadn't picked up a violin in many years, David played this haunting song surprisingly well.

Five minutes passed and the music continued, with David repeatedly playing 15 or so notes.

Then the music stopped abruptly. Why had he stopped in the middle of a song? She crept closer until she reached the closed door to his room. She heard sounds that she couldn't quite. . .*oh, no, he's crying*.

She stood mesmerized outside his door. After listening for a few moments, she knocked softly. "David? May I come in?"

A few seconds later, he opened the door. He was holding the violin in one hand and wiping his eyes with the other. His head was lowered.

"David, you were playing so beautifully. You stopped in the middle of. . ."

He nodded and, hesitating, stepped back to allow her to enter. The sheet music was spread out on top of the quilt. He laid the violin next to the sheet music, then sat on his bed.

"I was playing, reading Lee's notes on the sheet music. Lee played this song many times, especially at night when he was missing Mother." His shoulders were slumped and he began to cry quietly. "It's my fault that he's dead."

Caroline inched closer to David, facing him as he sat on the bed.

"David, it's not. . ."

"No, Caroline. It's my fault. I should have given those thieves all my money. I should not have fought back. That's why he died."

"It wasn't your fault."

"Yes, it was," his voice was cracking. "I should have protected him and I didn't. I never protected him as well as I should have."

"David."

"I. . .miss him so much."

Caroline leaned into him as he sat on the bed. She put her arms around him, her breath settling into the curve of his neck. "I know you do," she said, her own eyes watering. He relaxed his head against her shoulder, clinging to her and crying quietly, his tears falling onto her neck like rain drops.

Caroline had never seen David shed a tear in the months after Liam's death. However, she had been so wrapped up in her own self-pity, that it had been difficult for her to focus on anyone else's sorrow.

He pulled away from her embrace. "I never told him I loved him."

"He knew. The first time I met you, it was evident how much affection you felt for one other."

He wiped his eyes again and straightened. "I ought not to be crying."

"Why ever not? You're sad. You miss Liam."

"Father told us only babies and girls cry."

"Oh, no, David. That's not true."

Caroline again pressed against him, seeking to absorb his sadness into her own. As she held him, it occurred to her that this was the only other person who truly knew how she felt and who missed Liam as much as she did. All of a sudden, she understood that she and David had much more in common than she had ever believed.

42

David awkwardly busied himself in his room, taking special care and effort to tie his cravat. Perhaps by the time he was ready to go downstairs, Caroline would be outside. He had overslept and missed his opportunity to slip out early.

He couldn't believe that he had cried on her shoulder last night, but as she held him, it felt so good, so comforting. However, he wondered whether she was being kind to him out of pity. Tears always evoked that reaction from women and he wished that he could have controlled himself.

His eyes glanced at the crucifix on the wall above his bed. What he really wanted right now was to sit in the forest and pray. He opened the door, and stepping into the hallway, heard, "David?" He turned around but avoided eye contact. "Good morning, Caroline."

"Good morning." Her voice sounded light and carefree. As he finally brought his eyes up to hers, he found her offering him a warm, wide smile. He cleared his throat. "I'm heading to the forest to pray."

"Of course. Afterwards. . ."

"Yes?"

"I should like to speak with you."

"Very well."

When he emerged from the forest, he watched Caroline and Kathleen playing near the front of the house. Caroline was laughing and running after Kathleen. When his wife was happy, it made his heart sing. He walked toward them and when Kathleen noticed him, she yelled, "Papa, play?" She ran up to him and he gathered her into his arms. "Yes, I'll play, Kat. What's the game?"

"Run!"

"You mean we run after you, right, Kat?"

Kathleen squealed and ran in the opposite direction. But David quickly caught up with her and scooped her up and began swinging her around. When he stopped, she yelled, "More, Papa!"

"No, no, Kat. Papa's tired."

Kathleen scurried away. David kept his eyes on his daughter as she began running along the high brown grass at the edge of the mowed section of lawn.

"David?" She touched his hand and he looked at her.

"Yes?"

"I wanted to apologize."

"For what?"

"For the way I've treated you over the past year and a half. You didn't deserve that. I was just so angry that Liam had died, and I resented that I was being forced to marry you."

He nodded. "I knew you would be. I told Lee that you were not going to be happy with what he was asking you – us to do. And he knew that you would not be pleased, but in his own way, he felt that this was the best way for you to be taken care of. And I think he was right."

"Yes, I suppose he was. Kathleen is very happy, David. She loves you very much."

"And I love her very much." *And I love you, Caroline.*

"When I first found out how you felt, I thought it would be best if you moved or perhaps if I moved somewhere with Kathleen. But now I don't think that will be necessary."

"Oh?"

"There is no reason that we cannot stay under the same roof together. After all, you are my husband. And perhaps we ought to begin attending Mass together."

"You want to come to Mass?"

She nodded. "I haven't gone to church in a long while."

She offered him a warm smile and his heart skipped a beat. Caroline seemed to be making a concerted effort to get along with him and for that, he was grateful.

43

Another warm autumn day. Caroline peered out her open window at the cluster of oak trees and pond in the distance. The sun reflected off the orange-yellow leaves and created a lovely painting in the still water.

She devised a plan. She hurried down the back staircase to the kitchen. Jane was at the center table, preparing the evening meal.

"Is David in the downstairs study?"

"Yes, Ma'am, I believe he's meeting with a client. Would you like me to give him a message?"

"Yes. Tell him that his luncheon shall be served at the oak tree there by the pond."

Jane raised her eyebrows. "And who is going to be serving him lunch at the oak tree?"

Caroline hesitated. "I shall be serving him lunch, of course."

"Would you be wanting me to make up a basket of food for you and him?"

"Please, and if you wouldn't mind keeping an eye on Kathleen. She's in the back yard with Kip. He's playing horseshoes with her, but she's having an awful time lifting the shoes."

"Certainly."

"Remember to include a blanket so that we can sit on the ground."

"Don't worry. I'll fix it up nice for you to have a very pleasant luncheon."

"Thank you, Jane."

Caroline arranged the blanket and waited for David to arrive. She silently thanked God that the weather was cooperating. Autumn had been unseasonably warm. Caroline hoped that the large drooping oak tree would conceal her and the blanket from David as he walked toward her. She wore a deep turquoise patterned dress with a solid blue fitted bodice.

She peeked around the tree. When she saw that he was not

yet visible, she returned to the blanket. She sat quietly at first, then fidgeted, getting up every few moments.

She carefully looked around the tree again and she saw him speaking with Jane on the front porch. Because of the warmth of the day, he wore no overcoat with his breeches, just his shirt and cravat.

Immediately, her hands began to shake and her heart pounded uncontrollably. She nervously knelt down on the blanket, and quickly smoothed her skirt. Her hands were trembling so much that she found even that simple task difficult to accomplish.

"Caroline! What is this? Jane told me that someone would serve me lunch by the oak tree." He was grinning.

She cleared her throat. "That would be me, David."

"You? Whose idea was this? Certainly not yours."

"Well, truth be told, I feel that if we are going to be married to one another, we should be civil. Well, more than civil. I believe that we ought to be friendly, you know, like the best of friends."

"Best of friends?" His eyebrows were raised, but he was smiling.

"Yes. I mean, this whole marriage arrangement does not have to be unpleasant and if we are friendly and get along, then that will be advantageous for Kathleen, don't you agree?"

"Yes, I suppose."

"Now, you sit right here," she pointed to the front section of the blanket. She then proceeded to serve him Jane's lunch of fried chicken, freshly baked biscuits and carrot sticks. She sat across from him and watched as he ate.

"Did you have a pleasant meeting with your client, this morning?"

"Well," he said, while putting down the chicken leg, "I don't think I would call it pleasant, but I accomplished what I wanted to during the meeting."

"I see."

"Aren't you having any? It's delicious."

"No. I'm not hungry."

He finished the last piece of fried chicken. The grease from the chicken still on his hands, he used one of the cloth napkins in an attempt to clean them. Not succeeding, he walked to the pond and crouched down to wash his hands in the water.

As Caroline studied his back, a voice inside of her said, "Do it." She quietly crept up behind him and pushed him in. As his body came in contact with the cold water, he gasped, his mouth remaining open. The splashing water sprayed her and she blinked her eyes.

"Why did you do that?" he asked, now sputtering water.

"I'm. . .I'm not sure." She was holding a hand to her mouth and giggling.

"The water's quite warm for this time of year. You ought to join me perhaps?"

"No, I don't think so, I. . ." David jumped out of the water and was now chasing her. "No, David, please. . ." She screamed as he caught up to her and grabbed her with his soaking wet body.

"Oh, no, you don't. It's time for you to see how cold the water is." With that, he picked her up and threw her in. She gasped as her body reacted to the cool water.

When Caroline came up, coughing and spitting water, she began to giggle and David jumped in next to her. He was laughing out loud.

"The look on your face, David, when you came up was so amusing."

"I didn't expect to spend my luncheon hour like this," he said through his laughter. "Usually I only swim in the summer, but this has been quite a. . .distraction."

All of a sudden, they both stopped laughing and stood silent facing each other. Caroline stared at his wet face. After a few seconds of awkward silence, she spoke, her voice barely above a whisper. She was shivering. "I. . .hope this hasn't been. . .too disappointing a lunch for you. I hadn't planned on pushing you in the water. I'm not sure what came over me."

"Whatever it was, I'm glad you did."

"You're glad?"

He nodded.

She struggled to move closer to him, her water-logged gown feeling like a filled-to-capacity sponge, and droplets continued to fall from her face and hair.

"You look like a drowned rat," she said, pointing to his now wet and straight dark hair. Even his small tie was dripping.

Caroline again tried to shift closer, but the heaviness of her dress and undergarments prevented her. "I can barely move."

"I can move fine," he said. His shirt was plastered to his body and she could see the shape of his muscular arms through the shirt. Then he waded closer to her until he was standing so close, his chin was practically touching her forehead.

Caroline's heart was pounding and she was having a difficult time breathing. "This is quite a peculiar moment, David," she whispered.

"Yes, it is," he said so softly, she could barely hear him.

She leaned closer to him so that their faces were only inches apart. The two stood awkwardly, silently, with David making no attempt to kiss her, despite their closeness.

Caroline's heart was beating frantically, her breathing becoming shallow. He was no longer smiling, just staring intensely at her. At that moment, all she could think was that she wanted to kiss him. She pressed her lips to his and as she did so, he took her in his arms and kissed her softly, gently. After a few seconds, he pulled away.

"Why did you stop?" she whispered.

"We have an audience on the veranda."

When Caroline glanced back toward the house, she gasped when she saw that Jane and Hallie were watching them.

"Oh dear." She felt herself blush from the tip of her neck to her forehead.

"I think I will have to assist you out of the water. I had no idea how heavy your dress would be if it got wet. To be honest, I didn't care. I just wanted to seek revenge against you for pushing me in." He winked at her.

She watched as he lifted himself out of the water. When Caroline maneuvered herself the few feet to the edge of the grass, she was unsure as to whether David would even be able to lift her out, her dress again feeling waterlogged.

"Give me your hand," he said, then attempted to pull her out of the pond. He struggled for a moment or so, then dug his feet into the dirt and pulled her out of the pond and onto the grass.

"You're a lot stronger than I thought," she responded. "I must weigh as much as a horse." He didn't respond, but appeared to be eyeing her up and down.

"You look like a drowned rat as well, my dear," he said. "With blue lips." He smiled fondly. "And, by the way, didn't you say you wanted to kick me so hard?"

"What?" His mouth was curved and his eyebrows were raised.

"Why would I want to. . ." Caroline stopped, then remembered the comment that she made many years ago at the Martin house, before her marriage to Liam. She offered him an affectionate smile. "No, I don't think I shall be kicking you today, David."

Then he whispered, "Next time you decide to push me in, let me know so that I may take off some of my clothes. It will be easier to get out of the water."

Caroline blushed and lowered her gaze. For one brief second, she was reminded of the old David, the one who felt pleasure from embarrassing her.

"Come," he said. He picked up the blanket off the ground, shook it, then covered Caroline with it.

They walked side by side to the veranda.

A cool breeze blew against them and, despite having the blanket, Caroline shivered. "David, you must be cold." She raised the blanket partially off herself and covered him. Immediately, she was struck by a not unpleasant feeling of intimately touching him.

At the porch, Jane appeared to be controlling an urge to laugh by holding her hand to her mouth. Hallie was giggling under her breath. Kathleen curiously watched her mother and father. "Mama, wet?"

"What do you think you were doing? I thought you wanted to have a nice lunch, Miss Caroline."

"Caroline pushed me in."

"Papa wet," Kathleen remarked.

"Yes, Kat, Papa is wet. Mama pushed me in the water."

"Come in here, Miss Caroline, and we'll get you out of your wet clothes."

"Jane, I don't want to wet the carpet and floor."

"Now, now, let's get you in here," Jane said, as she accompanied her upstairs. Caroline turned around and looked at David as he followed them on the stairs.

"I'm right behind you. I have a meeting in ten minutes with

one of our clients who's in town from Boston."

"I'm sorry."

"Not to worry. I'll be dressed more quickly than you."

He was taking this awfully well. He could have been angry with her but he wasn't and for that she was thankful. What had gotten into her?

44

As David got into bed, he remembered the day's events and his heart began to pound. He was delighted to discover that Caroline had surprised him with a picnic lunch. When she leaned up to kiss him, it took every ounce of self-control he could muster not to take her into his arms, kiss her and let loose the suppressed passion he felt inside for her. Doing so would likely have frightened her.

Could it be possible that she was growing to love him the way a wife should? He knew that it was too much to hope for, but he found himself laughing at the wonder of it all. He didn't deserve her, but now that she knew how he felt, a great weight had been removed from his heart. Whether she offered anything in return, he realized that it was a gift to be with her and for her to know his heart, even if they continued to live as brother and sister.

Right now, it was difficult to think of anything but how much he loved Caroline. His longing for her was so strong and so deep that oftentimes, it felt as if his heart were going to burst. He wanted her to desire him, but this was a delicate situation and he understood that he must proceed slowly.

Everything in David's life now seemed to be coming to fruition. It seemed that he had only recently begun to breathe in the richness of life. A feeling of contentment enveloped him and he found himself drifting off to a deep sleep.

David woke with a start. *That seemed so real.* His heart was thundering and his whole body was shaking. His breathing was shallow and beads of perspiration covered his face like a veil. He should have known it was a dream or, more appropriately, a nightmare. *Why must I be so tormented?* It was the third time that he had had to endure that particular dream, but the first since he and Caroline had kissed at the pond.

He sat up and lit the oil lamp on his bedside table. He tried to breathe more slowly, to calm himself. Then, slipping into his robe, he crept into the hallway. He needed to get to the liquor cabinet in the downstairs study. *I'll only have a small amount. It will be fine. Just one drink.* He had not consumed alcohol in more than a year and a half since their 'wedding.' So what could be the harm in celebrating his accomplishments with a much needed drink to calm him and assist him in sleeping?

A voice rose up in his heart. *Don't take that drink.* He brushed it aside. After all, he reasoned, he was doing so well. He owed himself one drink. He had to calm down, to stop his heart from thundering in his chest. Yes, he needed just one.

David stood before the liquor cabinet and pulled out the brandy decanter. He poured a generous glassful, tentatively held it to his lips, sipped it, then quickly swallowed. It burned the back of his throat, but it now warmed his body and he felt compelled to have more. *Just one more. I'll stop after this one.* He downed another drink, then one more and soon felt relieved, dizzy and calm. Flask in hand, he returned to his room. He placed the bottle on his desk and opened the bottom drawer. David knew that he shouldn't even open the drawer, but he needed to take one quick look at those pictures. Just one peek, he promised himself.

His hands grasped onto them and he pulled them out. As he looked at the postcards one by one, a feeling of revulsion grew in him. But they were, after all, pictures of beautiful naked women and part of him couldn't help but be aroused. He began to see these young women as persons, with feelings, thoughts, needs. He didn't know these girls, but their bodies were being used to tempt him. With one motion, he grabbed the group of pictures and hurled them into the fire. As he watched them burn, the girls' unclothed bodies blistered in the fiery blaze.

David took a deep breath, then extinguished the oil lamp and got into his bed. As soon as he closed his eyes, his mind became saturated with images from the pictures. He tried to banish them, then the nightmare filled his mind.

After tossing and turning for almost an hour, David cursed under his breath and jumped out of bed. He threw on some clothes and made his way to the stable. He lit a gas lamp, saddled Big Red and rode into the City. He needed to escape, although he wasn't sure from what or whom. David knew that he needed to get out of the house and get himself another drink.

* * *

Kathleen's shrill cries woke Caroline instantly.

"You're safe, Sweet, shhh. It's all right." Her daughter sat up and began rubbing her eyes.

"Did you have a bad dream?"

"Bad dream, Mama. Papa yelling."

"Oh, dear, Papa was yelling at you?"

"Uh-huh."

"I don't think Papa would yell at you. In fact, he doesn't raise his voice at all anymore, Kathleen."

Caroline gently rubbed Kathleen's back, urging her to lay down. Soon she had settled and she was breathing deeply again. Caroline stared at her daughter for a few moments, her mind wandering to the previous day and of David's kissing her in the pond. The sensation of being so close to him made her feel light-headed and breathless. She smiled when she remembered him sputtering in the water and then chasing her playfully near the pond until he had caught her and thrown her in. Caroline found herself wanting to spend more time with him, talking to him, getting acquainted with this new David.

The grandfather clock downstairs began its distant chiming and Caroline listened to see what time it was. Two o'clock.

She pulled on her robe and made her way to the hallway. Passing by David's room, she found the door open. She stood quietly and listened for David's even breathing. Hearing no sound, she pushed his door open. As her eyes adjusted to the dark, she could see that he was not in his bed.

He must be working late in the downstairs study. Perhaps I should see if he wants some coffee.

She quietly crept down the staircase and was surprised that most of the gas lamps along the wall beside the staircase still flickered. It was so quiet that all Caroline could hear was the ticking of the clock nearby.

She peered into David's study and found it dark and unoccupied. *Where is David?   Why are some of the gas lights still aglow?* Jane usually extinguished these at the end of the night, although David sometimes performed the task if he was working late.

"Miss Caroline, I was wondering who was roaming around."

"I didn't mean to wake you. I was endeavoring to be quiet."

"That's fine. I hadn't gotten to sleep yet."

"Do you know where David is?"

"No, Ma'am, I don't. A few hours ago, I heard him leave down the back staircase. That's why I turned on a few of the gas lights."

Caroline's mouth tightened into a thin worried line.

"I'm sure he's fine," Jane said.

The front door opened and David stumbled in. His dark curly hair was disheveled. There was a deep cut on his forehead, his bottom lip was bruised. His linen shirt was only partially tucked in and stained with a dark liquid. His jacket looked as if it had been quickly thrown on. His eyes widened when he saw Caroline and Jane standing in the foyer.

"David! Where have you been this late at night?" Caroline blurted out, now relieved.

"I've been. . .out. I had. . .business in town." He stuttered, then shoved his way past her, roughly knocking against her. Caroline could smell alcohol on him and another unfamiliar odor.

"Were you in a fight?"

"Look," he said curtly as he turned around, but avoided eye contact with her, "I'm tired. . .and I need to get some sleep. Good night." He attempted to quickly climb the stairs but tripped as he did so. When he reached the top step, he hastily turned toward his room.

"Miss Caroline?"

She looked at Jane, who began walking back up to her own room. "May I go to bed, Ma'am?"

"Of course. Good night."

*   *   *

David attempted to rescue what remained of any self control he possessed in order to keep from throwing every piece of furniture in his room against the wall. Despite his dizziness and nausea from drinking too much, he was furious with himself. Part of him wished that he had consumed more whiskey, because then he would be unconscious. Now, he not only felt undeserving, he wanted to throw his faith back at God and the Church. It was impossible to live up to those teachings.

He had little memory of riding home and didn't become consciously aware until he saw Caroline's face in the front foyer.

Why did he believe that he could stop at one drink? He should have known that one drink – or a thousand – would never be enough.

He didn't remember much about the fight or the time after, but he should never have had that first drink. His head throbbed, his eyes hurt and he probably had a few bruised ribs. For one brief moment, he stared at the gun cabinet and wondered whether he ought to end it all.

45

Caroline slept fitfully, but managed to drift off for an hour or so. Kathleen woke early and, in her sweet high-pitched chatter, asked, "Mama, wake Papa too?"

"Well, Sweet, Papa was in late last night and I'm sure he's still sleeping."

"Oh," she said, her small mouth curved in a pout.

"Miss Caroline?" Jane asked through the door.

"Yes?"

"Do you want me to fix Miss Kathleen her breakfast?"

"That would be helpful, Jane. Thank you." Caroline opened the door. Jane picked up Kathleen and the two left the room and proceeded down the hallway. As Caroline dressed, she recalled only hours ago, when David had come in so late. He seemed like the old David. Only yesterday, they had shared a tender kiss at the pond.

This other side of David, the sarcastic side, made Caroline want to take back the kiss, the sweet, tender symbol that marked the beginning of their new relationship.

She finished brushing her hair and buttoned up the front of her dress. In the hallway, when she passed David's room, she saw that the door was ajar, open enough for her to see that he was not in bed. She knocked but there was no answer. Pushing the door fully open, she could see that David was not anywhere in the room. She turned and walked down the back stairs to the kitchen where Jane was feeding Kathleen breakfast. Isaac was settled on Jane's hip.

"David isn't in his room."

"I saw him take the carriage out about an hour ago."

"Before seven a.m.? On a Saturday morning? He only came in at two o'clock."

Through the side window, Caroline could see that David was riding past in their small carriage toward the direction of the stable. Her pulse quickened. She found herself hoping that he was in a better mood.

She glanced at Jane, who seemed preoccupied with Isaac and Kathleen. Caroline crept closer to the window. She watched as David tethered the horses to the back hitching post. When he walked past the window, Caroline shrunk back and behind the curtain so he could not see her.

"I'll return in a moment."

"Mr. David must be awful tired."

"I know, but I must speak with him."

Caroline hurried up the steps and to David's room and paused before knocking. "Who is it?" David's voice had a sharp edge to it.

"It's me, David. May I speak with you?"

He opened the door and glanced quickly at her face, but again avoided eye contact with her.

"Where did you go this morning, David?"

"I went. . .to the Cathedral."

"At seven a.m.?"

He nodded. "I needed to speak with Father Flaherty about . . . an urgent matter."

"Is anything wrong?"

"I'm fine." His shoulders were slumped, he avoided eye contact and fidgeted in the doorway. "Well, if there's nothing else, I need to get some sleep." He stepped back. He seemed so distant and Caroline got the feeling that she was like an annoying mosquito he wished to rid himself of.

"Yes, of course."

He closed the door, but Caroline remained in the hallway, her body leaning against the door. She knew that he wasn't fine, but how could she help him when he wouldn't share with her what was wrong?

*   *   *

David remained facing the closed door, his hand clutching the porcelain knob. He knew that Caroline was hurt by his continuing cold, abrupt manner. He hated himself for speaking to her like that, but now it was necessary to alienate her so that she would not want to continue a future romantic relationship. He needed her to stay away from him for her own good.

And yet a deeper, intense desire gripped his heart. He loved her and longed to take her into his arms and feel her skin on his.

He wanted to give his whole life, his whole body, to her. But that should never happen. Not now. The kiss at the pond, the affection and possible attraction that she was feeling for him, all needed to disappear. He could never live up to her expectations.

When he arrived at the church this morning, he could not bring himself to go inside. He nervously paced back and forth in front while he attempted to gain enough courage to speak with Father Flaherty. The fight was clearly his fault; he remembered throwing the first punch, but couldn't recall why. Was it a comment about his father? Either way, he had only himself to blame. He realized that he needed to go to Confession, but after a half-hour of pacing, he couldn't do it. Saying out loud what he must say to another human being would be too humiliating. He dropped himself on his bed and began to sob.

"Stop crying. You're not a baby any more. Only babies and girls cry, David. Stop it."

Echoes of his father's words crushed his wounded heart.

So why couldn't he have just one drink? Why did he have to get into that fight? And why could he not forgive himself for what he had done?

All of a sudden, he began to shiver. His bedroom now seemed cold and uninviting. He gathered a few pieces of kindling and some thin pieces of maple to construct a fire, then stopped, wondering if he should just be left to suffer.

David shook his head, then decided to light the wood. He needed to keep occupied, to forget. Once finished, he breathed in the smell of the burning logs and the warmth of the fire.

His mind was clearing, but his head was still pounding from the brandy, wine and whiskey. The more he became rational, the more he hated himself. The brandy flask on the dresser beckoned him to consume more, to escape the knowledge of what had happened several short hours ago.

He placed his hand on the smooth decanter. He caressed the side of it, then lifted up the top and inhaled the aroma of the liquid. *Just one more taste.*

"No," he shouted. He grabbed the bottle and hurled it into the small fire. With a whoosh, it caused a small explosion and for a minute or so it raged as the alcohol fed the ravenous flames.

"Mr. David, you all right?" he heard Kip say through the door.

"Yes, yes, I'm fine," he yelled. "I just. . . dropped something."

"Do you want me to clean it up for you?"

"No, no. I'll get to it, Kip."

He shuffled carelessly to the front of the fireplace and screamed as he stepped on a large piece of glass. Kip had already opened the door by the time he was finished yelling. The servant winced when he saw David's bare foot, the gash now dripping blood onto the hardwood floors. "It's fine, Kip. I'll. . .I'll be. . .fine," he said, attempting to sound calm.

"Beggin' no disrespect, Mr. David, but you don't look fine. You're white as a ghost."

David hopped on one foot and plopped himself on the trunk at the foot of his bed. From the corner of his eye, he could see that Caroline stood quietly at the doorway. David couldn't — wouldn't — look at her, but he felt her gaze burning into his skin and right through to his heart.

Kip crouched down in front of David and carefully pulled the large shard of glass from his foot. Immediately, a flow of blood spurted onto the floor.

"David!" he could hear Caroline say. "What happened?" Her voice grew closer.

"I stepped on some glass. Isn't that obvious?" He knew there was a hard edge to his tone and he hated himself for speaking that way to her.

"David," he could hear her say, "I don't mean that. How did the glass break?" Now, she stood so close to him that he could feel her breath above him.

"I. . .I dropped it," he said, avoiding not only Caroline's eye, but Kip's as well. A cursory glance soon revealed that now Jane and Hallie had come into the room.

Kip pressed a cloth onto David's wounded foot. David wanted to be left alone and ignored. His foot hurt like hell but he was glad for the pain, something to focus on besides the agony of his soul. "I'm fine." The lie burned his throat. "If everyone could just leave." His voice trembled but he hoped that Caroline wouldn't notice.

"You keep the cloth on there, Mr. David. That might need some sewing. It's wide open. And you ought to put some alcohol on there."

"It'll be fine, Kip. Now, if you all could just. . .leave."

Their footsteps faded one by one. His room was now silent.

Why couldn't he stop at one drink? Why did he have to throw the first punch? Why did he have to. . .

Father Flaherty had said that when he felt any sort of temptation, he ought to pray. Why hadn't he listened? He pulled himself off his bed and knelt beside it on the hardwood floor. His foot was still bleeding, a piercing pain that continued up to his soul. He realized that he must make an effort to pray. He made the Sign of the Cross then became silent. Finally he began, "I know you will forgive me, God, but could you please help me to forgive myself?"

46

Caroline paused reflectively at her bedroom window and watched David's carriage ride away. She was relieved that he wouldn't be around for the next several days. Caroline had become increasingly uncomfortable in his presence during the past week. Although David had hugged Kathleen when he said goodbye, it was a low key gesture. He had merely nodded to her.

It had been one week since the night he had arrived home late. Caroline had spoken to him only once and she had been the one to approach him. He had avoided eye contact and made no attempt to continue the conversation. The spark in his eyes seemed to have disappeared. Why was he ignoring her? Could she have done something wrong?

What was worse was that he was paying scant attention to Kathleen as well. Her daughter had been complaining for days that he had not told her a bedtime story. And she often cried for him at night. She was certain David could hear her and yet he never attempted to come to her room or to calm Kathleen.

Caroline passed by the closed door of David's downstairs study. She wondered whether she should go into his study while he was away. He had told her once before that she had a right to be anywhere she wanted in the house or to read anything she so desired.

Opening the door, she was struck by how dark it was, despite the fact that it was early afternoon. She waited until her eyes adjusted to the darkness, then she crossed the room and lifted the shade. The room became bathed in early afternoon light.

At the bookcase by the door, her eyes caught sight of the book he told her he had been studying, "Confessions of St. Augustine" and she lifted it off the shelf. She remembered paging through this book several months ago, but she now felt compelled to read it more thoroughly. She took it to David's desk by the window. Caroline half-smiled when she saw the haphazard condition of his desk. Papers and books were strewn about leaving no area to lay the book.

She lifted her head and studied the O'Donovan family painting. Her heart ached as she looked at Liam's youthful, sweet face. Next to him, David, two years older, seemed bored with the whole affair, though Caroline had to admit that he was a beautiful boy. Her eyes wandered to their mother's face. *What a beautiful woman she was.* Despite the smile, there seemed to be sadness in her eyes. Liam and David's father had a slight smirk and Caroline had to admit that his expression looked identical to David's.

She carefully pushed aside an area in the middle of the desk and placed the book down. She began paging through it until she came to a section of the book and some notes that David had written.

"Hear my prayer, O Lord; let not my soul faint under thy discipline. . .whereby thou hast saved me from all my most wicked ways till thou shouldst become sweet to me beyond all the allurements that I used to follow."

Further on, she came to several more circled passages, until two short quotes caught her eye. *"Grant me chastity and continence, but not yet."* And later, *"Thou breathed Thy fragrance on me; I drew in breath and now I pant for Thee. I have tasted Thee, now I hunger and thirst for more."*

Caroline found herself blushing at the words. The words sounded strangely like the Song of Solomon, or the Canticle of Canticles as David had called it.

She straightened, clapped the book shut and relaxed against the chair. She closed her eyes and exhaled. Something had happened to make David turn away from her. Could it be that, despite his love for her, he still wished to remain as brother and sister? Perhaps he was finding it difficult to admit to her what he felt. And if he wanted to remain as brother and sister, then what? Caroline found herself feeling disappointed, but returning to their previous arrangement would certainly not be the worst scenario.

She returned the book and closed the door.

47

In Boston, David parted the drapes and stared out the window of the hotel. Except for an hour here and there, he hadn't slept in nearly a week. The guilt was eating away his soul. For the last week, he knew that he ought to go to Confession, but he was unable to gather the courage to do so.

This morning, before he left, he found that his Bible was opened to Isaiah 44. As he read the passage, his eyes were drawn to the words at verse 22.

I have blotted out thy iniquities
as a cloud
and thy sins as a mist:
return to Me, for I have redeemed thee.

It seemed a peculiar coincidence that the Bible had been opened to that particular page. He hadn't used his Bible in at least a week and, as he recalled, had it opened to the Gospel of John.

He memorized the phrase, *"return to Me, for I have redeemed thee."*

If he was going to get any sleep tonight – and he had to be fresh and well-rested before he met with his clients – he knew that it was essential to find a Catholic Church and go to Confession.

He didn't care for Boston, or any large city for that matter, and missed the yard and forested area that was his view at home. One building that seemed to stand out in the panorama was the steeple of what David hoped was a Catholic Church. He put on his overcoat and proceeded downstairs to the lobby where he asked the man at the desk where the closest Catholic Church was.

"Turn right as you walk outside and continue for two more blocks," he was told.

In front of his hotel, he paused. Just last week, it had felt like summer. Today it was cold and it had begun to snow, the large flakes coating the hotel's flower pots to each side of the entrance.

Carriages rushed back and forth along the cobblestone street in front of him.

He turned right and saw the wooden steeple a few blocks away.

It occurred to him that the snow made everything look – and smell – so much cleaner, newer.   But the snow couldn't make his soul cleaner.

First, he passed a United Methodist church on his left, then an Episcopalian church to his right.   Up ahead, there was a larger building, and David hoped that it was a Catholic Church.   It was just before noon and there were men proceeding up the steps, perhaps for daily Mass.   He followed in step behind a group and saw the name of the church: "Cathedral of the Holy Cross."

David hurried along inside with the group and stopped to gaze at the subtly lit interior.   It was a beautiful church, with ornate stained glass windows and the fragrant aroma that he had grown accustomed to at the Cathedral back home.

He blessed himself with holy water, then genuflected beside the back pew and knelt down.   He observed several men standing in line at the front.   He watched them enter and exit a curtained area and concluded that it was most likely the Confessional.   His pulse quickened at the thought of confessing his most recent sins. Before he changed his mind, he stood up.   He made his way to the front of the church, moved in line behind the last man and began to pray.

An hour later, inside his hotel room, David felt the immense burden had lifted.   And, contrary to what he believed earlier, his soul did feel cleaner, brighter and newer, sacramental grace acting like snow on his soul.

His confessor had been gentle and kind.   And it was, as Father Flaherty had described it, like 'whispering into the ear of Jesus.' While still in the church, he prayed his penance, then attended Mass.   He was now filled with peace instead of agony and torture.   It was as if Christ had reached in and ripped the sin from his soul and replaced it with serenity.   *Why didn't I go right away?* David smiled inwardly.   *Because of embarrassment.*   He and Father Flaherty had spent many hours, with David learning about the   Catholic Church, reading his Catechism, studying

Scripture and reading St. Augustine's Confessions. In the last six months or so since becoming Catholic, he had made the mistake of self-righteously thinking that he didn't need Confession. Now, he understood what made the Sacrament of Penance so powerful: the assurance that his sins were forgiven. He wasn't perfect, but he knew now that he could never let his guard down and take another drink. He resolved to visit Father Flaherty once his train arrived in Philly. Only then could he face Caroline again.

48

On the day that David was expected to return home, Caroline waited outside and watched Kathleen enjoying an early winter snowfall. She reveled in the fragrance of the brisk air and the burning maple. Her daughter's mouth was open, her tongue was sticking out as she tried to catch large flakes and her high-pitched voice squealed when she succeeded.

Kip had departed for the train station several hours ago and soon, he and David would be riding up the laneway.

Would David still be ignoring her? Despite his behavior, she longed for his presence and missed him as Kathleen's father.

Horse and carriage sounds caused Caroline to glance up. Seeing Kip in the driver's seat, and knowing that David was in the enclosed section caused her pulse to quicken and her palms to become sweaty. Kip yelled, "Whoa."

Jane approached the carriage and waited for it to come to a stop. Kip handed her a suitcase, then climbed down and kissed her cheek. He opened the door.

Caroline had expected David to rush into the house without a word to her or Kathleen. However, when he emerged, he immediately walked to Kathleen.

"Papa home!" Kathleen's eyes lit up as if she was seeing him for the first time. Her daughter's breath visible in the frosty air.

"Yes, Kat, Papa's home." Kathleen jumped into David's arms and he responded by hugging her, then kissing her hat-covered head. He set her down and she began to run.

"Look, Papa, catch snow!" She was holding out her tongue.

"Yes, that's wonderful, Kat. I bet you can catch a lot more!"

"Watch!"

David turned his gaze to Caroline. He tentatively approached her.

"Hello, David."

"Caroline. You look beautiful."

Caroline could feel a warm flush rising to her face.

"I still have the touch," he said, a slight smile playing on his lips. He pulled her to a tender embrace and whispered in her ear, "I'm so sorry for my behavior the past few weeks. I've been dreadful, but I hope we can start again." He kissed the top of her head.

She nodded.

"I would certainly understand if you wished to return to the way things were."

Caroline shook her head. "No, David, I don't want that. But I believed our kiss at the pond meant something."

"Our kiss meant more than you can ever know."

"Then you changed and acted like. . ."

"I know and I'm sorry for that. Everything was happening so fast and then I had a. . .I felt like I didn't deserve you. I don't deserve you."

She leaned up to brush his lips with a gentle kiss. He returned the gesture, but did not prolong it.

"I'm not worthy of someone like you, Caroline. I don't deserve you. I've been. . ."

"You've changed."

"Not enough. I haven't changed enough."

Kathleen's squealed as she tried to catch snowflakes and actually succeeded a few times. David stepped away from her, walked to Kathleen and, together, they caught snowflakes in their mouths.

49

Caroline's eyes opened and she sat up in bed. She wasn't sure if she had just heard a loud noise or whether she had been dreaming. She remained sitting upright, listening in the darkness of her room. For several seconds, all she could hear was Kathleen's slow, even breathing. It was a comforting sound, one that not only eased her into sleep, it helped her to waken in the morning.

Caroline studied Kathleen's still body and was relieved to find that she was sleeping soundly. She opened the door and entered the hallway to try to discover the cause of the noise.

It was dark, although she could see faint light coming from beneath David's door. She crept up to his door and listened. She reached her hand out to knock, then pulled back. She heard a smacking noise, as if something had fallen to the floor, then a sigh. She waited for a moment, then knocked. "David?"

He swung open the door. "I'm sorry if I woke you, Caroline. I'm moving furniture around." His nightshirt hung loosely around his body.

"You're moving furniture at one a.m.?" she asked, entering his room.

"I couldn't sleep."

"No need to apologize. I was just concerned."

"Caroline, I. . ."

"What is it?"

He remained still for a few moments. Caroline moved closer to him, their bodies almost touching. The only noise in the room was the crackling in the fire behind them. Her hand gently brushed his cheek and she whispered, "David."

With his hands cradling both sides of her face, he kissed the top of her head. She could feel his warm breath caressing her forehead, her heart now beating rapidly.

David leaned down and kissed her lips, softly at first, and soon, the kiss deepened. She didn't stop nor break off the kiss, but her eyes now began to tear. Despite her long-held grief – or maybe because of it – she kissed him with great passion and for a moment, she was kissing Liam. It wasn't him, she knew that, but she needed to kiss him one last time. All at once, David was kissing her tears, tasting her pain, taking her grief away. She began to weep. He stopped and held her to his chest.

"I miss him," her voice was muffled.

"I know." He paused. "Caroline?"

She nodded, but kept her face pressed against his chest.

"Perhaps we ought to remain as brother and sister," he whispered.

Caroline kept silent as he continued to speak.

"I want what's best for you and Kathleen. I'm very thankful that we've developed such a close. . .friendship."

She lifted her face from his chest and gazed into his dark blue eyes. He truly was one of the most handsome men she had ever met, but his eyes now seemed to regard her with such tenderness that it made him all the more beautiful to her. This expression was so different from his original provocative look.

"I should think that it has become more than a friendship, David."

"Isn't that what you said at the pond a few weeks ago, Caroline, that you wanted us to have a good friendship?"

She wiped her eyes and smiled at his playful teasing. "Yes, I suppose I did say that."

Kathleen's whimpering caused them both to turn their heads in the direction of Caroline's room. "Allow me, Caroline."

She followed him as he rushed to her room, stood over Kathleen's small bed and lifted her up into his arms. "Shhh, Kathleen, shhh."

"Papa, the pooka, the pooka, hurt me."

"They're not going to hurt you, Kat. I'm right here."

"The pooka?" Caroline asked.

"Yes," replied David, "I told her an Irish folk tale about. . .well, perhaps I was a little too descriptive."

"Papa, it's dark."

"Oh, no," he responded.

"Couldn't see Mama."

"Look, she's right here." Caroline stepped forward and rubbed Kathleen's arm.

"I didn't light the lamp tonight because she hasn't woken up in the past week or so."

David nodded, then whispered to his daughter. "Papa's going to light this for you and we'll keep it down low so it's not too bright."

Her small blonde head leaned against his neck.

"Papa and Mama will stay here with you until you fall asleep."

David gently laid her down and she turned over onto her stomach. He covered her with the small blanket. He stood by her crib and watched her as she turned over and closed her eyes. Caroline studied him, his eyes intently focused on her daughter's small form, as he caressed her hair and face. Kathleen now started breathing deeply.

When Caroline glanced at David, she could see that a small piece of his dark wavy hair had fallen forward on his forehead, and instinctively, Caroline reached out her hand and brushed it back into place. As she was withdrawing her hand, he took hold of it and tenderly kissed her palm. His eyes now caught hers, her heart began to pound and she became breathless.

Kathleen quietly moaned and, distracted, they let out a collective sigh. Still standing, she leaned her head on his chest as he put his arm around her shoulder.

"David?"

"Yes?"

"I'm very happy that I'm your wife."

"Truly?"

Caroline nodded.

"I should return to my room now."

"Yes."

"Good night," he said, then kissed the top of her head.

He walked through the doorway, the darkness hiding his expression. Part of her had wished he had remained in her room. She banished the thought and moved to the bed.

* * *

David nervously paced back and forth. How was he supposed to sleep when Caroline's growing attraction to him was making it more and more difficult to maintain his self-control. Continency was definitely easier when she was ignoring him. But he would not, could not, ever hurt her or use her for his own pleasure. She was confused, as evidenced by her sobbing, but it would be his responsibility to keep their physical relationship from going any further.

That all seemed well and good when one was rational, but he had to admit that he was not very rational around her. The scent of her hair, her soft skin and voice were enough to make him lose control. He knelt down beside his bed and prayed.

*   *   *

An hour later, Caroline stared at the soft light from the lamp, unable to sleep, listening to her daughter's soft breathing. She added a log to the fire, then picked up a novel from her bedside table and sat on the chair by the hearth. She opened the book, but quickly closed it again.

Caroline began to nervously turn the wedding ring on her left hand. Before now, she had never considered taking it off. After Liam had died and she had married David, when it came time in the ceremony for a ring to be blessed, Caroline had simply removed her present band and handed it to the minister before David placed it back on her hand. There was no need to use another ring. Now, she wondered whether she ought to remove it.

She slowly pulled it from her finger and was surprised at how easily it slid off. She held it in the palm of her hand for a few moments. This piece of gold symbolized her union with Liam. She kept it in her hand for a few moments. Caroline lifted up the top of Liam's cigar box and gently laid the ring on top of his other items.

She could not deny her affection for David. She wanted to be closer to him. He was her husband now, wasn't he?

Caroline studied Kathleen in her crib. She was about as sound asleep as she had ever seen her. The past week or so, she slept without interruption, without even one nightmare. She had already woken up once. Perhaps, she could slip out quietly. Before Caroline knew it, she was standing in the hallway in front of David's door. She knocked quietly. He opened it and his eyes widened.

"Caroline! Is anything wrong?" He was still dressed in a knee length nightshirt.

She opened her mouth to speak, but nothing came out.

Instead, she shook her head. He looked at her with such care and tenderness that, in that moment, with no rational thought, she leaned up to kiss him. At first, he seemed to surrender to their growing passion, then he forcefully pushed himself away and held her at arm's length.

"Caroline," he whispered. "We're still in the hallway. Don't you think we should. . ."

She nodded. He pulled her inside and closed the door. He backed away. As she started to move toward him, he held up his hand. "Wait."

"You don't want to?"

"Caroline, please. I want to, yes, of course. Do you know what you're doing?"

"What would make you think I don't know what I'm doing?" Caroline stared at him for several moments, wondering whether she had make a mistake in coming to his room.

"I don't know. I just want to make sure we can make a clear decision."

"Clear?"

"Just a moment. I need to add another log." He crouched down and stoked the fire, threw in a piece of maple, then stared into the flames.

Caroline reached out to touch his back and he immediately stood up.

"Caroline. . ."

"David, I love you. This wouldn't be wrong; we are married, aren't we?"

"Yes, but don't you see that if we went through with this, there would be no turning back."

"I do not wish to turn back. It is my desire to be married to you."

David's expression, though still guarded, softened. "Caroline, you can't begin to imagine how much I want this, but it needs to be for the right. . ."

"David," she whispered, "If you don't want. . ."

"I do, but I want for us to desire it for the right reasons."

"Very well."

"And I will need to speak with Father Flaherty."

Caroline stood beside him, her nightgown-clad body touching his. She caressed his cheek, the soft stubble of his jaw.

"I'm not as good as you think I am. I. . .have made mistakes."

"I know and I am willing to accept you with them."

"You don't understand, Caroline."

"David, I want to be truly married to you."

50

Father Flaherty smiled as David came up the center aisle of the Cathedral. The priest offered his hand and David shook it. "To what do I owe this unexpected visit, David?"

"I must speak with you about an urgent matter, Father."

He led him toward a small room off the sanctuary.

"I must know whether my marriage is. . .whether it is a marriage in the eyes of the Church."

"David, if you or Mrs. O'Donovan felt in any way forced to enter into this marriage, then it is not a marriage in the eyes of the Church. From what you've told me before, this sounds like it is the case. But I would need to speak with Mrs. O'Donovan as well."

"Yes, very well."

"You've said before that while part of you felt forced, you wanted to marry your wife because you loved her, even back then?"

"Yes, Father. But I did not expect it to be anything other than a marriage in name only."

"What about your wife?"

"I can't speak for her, but I would guess that she will say that she especially felt forced and did not truly mean the words of the marriage vows."

"Also, if there was no intention to consummate the marriage, then it would not be considered a marriage."

"Again, I can't speak for Caroline, but I'm certain she had no intention of doing so."

"I must speak with her as well. If that is the case, it will be necessary to perform another ceremony, if you wish to enter into a sacramental marriage."

"Yes, I do." He paused. "When could we meet?"

"Would Thursday suit you and Mrs. O'Donovan?"

"Yes, Father, I suppose that will be fine."

"Are you living as brother and sister?"

"Yes, of course."

"Fine. We can schedule a date for the ceremony for after January 6th."

David's eyes widened and he lowered his head.

"Is something wrong, David?"

"That's three weeks from now, Father. Why couldn't we get married sooner?"

"Church law forbids any marriage to take place in Advent, until after the Feast of the Epiphany."

"I see."

"Besides, it's preferable to leave it for a month or so to allow both you and Mrs. O'Donovan to reflect on the commitment you're about to make. And it will be necessary to publicize banns."

"Banns?"

"Notification on three consecutive holy days or Sundays of your intent to marry. I expect there may be numerous people who will step forward to state that you and Mrs. O'Donovan are already married."

"Yes, Father."

"Mrs. O'Donovan isn't Catholic?"

"No, she's not."

"Then she will need to promise that the children from this marriage will be raised Catholic."

"I don't think that will be an issue since she has already agreed that our daughter could be baptized Catholic."

"Very well." The priest stepped back and allowed him to leave.

"Thank you, Father. This has been very informative."

When David returned home, Caroline met him in the foyer.

"What did Father Flaherty say, David?"

"That he needs to speak with you to determine whether there was a marriage at all."

"You mean we're not really married?"

"Most probably not. According to Father Flaherty, if we entered this marriage without full consent, meaning that we honestly meant the words we said and that we intended to. . .consummate our marriage."

"Oh."

"Then we need to take part in another ceremony in order to enter into a sacramental marriage."

"I see."

"We will be meeting with him later this week."

Caroline nodded, then leaned into him. He embraced her and kissed her forehead. He felt a powerful yearning to take her in his arms and carry her up to his bedroom, but banished the thought and held her away at arm's length. "I think it is best for us to avoid any affection other than a chaste kiss or a hug. And that means staying in your bedroom at night, Caroline, until we are truly married."

"But. . ."

David explained to her why they couldn't marry until the second week of January. She lowered her head.

"Caroline, I feel compelled to do the right thing. After all the mistakes I have made, it is important to begin our marriage, our true marriage, properly. Besides, three weeks will give us both time to make sure that we're making the right decision."

51

Caroline tossed and turned in her bed, then sat up and lit the oil lamp. Today, she and David would meet with Father Flaherty. She got out of bed and stood in front of the fireplace, drawn by its warmth and mesmerizing flames. As much as she tried to convince herself their marriage was true, she knew that it wasn't.

Do you, Caroline Martin O'Donovan, take David O'Donovan to be your lawful wedded husband?

At the time, it took every ounce of effort she possessed to say yes to what was being asked. She remembered pausing, regretting, dreading what was about to happen. Then she muttered "I will" as quickly as possible. Of course, it didn't matter what the words were, they were a meaningless jumble all the same.

And what about now? Several nights ago, Caroline would have given herself to David had Kathleen not woken up, although that aspect of marriage was not one that she greatly anticipated. She did, however, very much look forward to deepening her relationship with David. Her "duty" was something that she could give to him selflessly.

The fact that David had all but pushed her away demonstrated how resolved and committed he was to entering into a true marriage. She saw tremendous irony in his attitude, considering the man that he once was.

Later that morning, Caroline sat in front of her vanity brushing her hair.

"Do you want me to put your hair up, Miss Caroline?"

"Which do you think would be most appropriate for a meeting with a priest?"

"Definitely up," replied Jane.

"Very well."

Jane proceeded to pull Caroline's hair up into a fashionable hairstyle when Hallie appeared at the bedroom doorway.

"Miss Caroline, your uncle and cousin are here to visit with you."

"Good gracious. With everything that's going on, I forgot about their visit."

"What should I tell them, Ma'am?"

"Tell them I'll be down in a few moments, Hallie. Ask them to wait for me in the parlor."

"Very well."

A short while later, in the parlor, Caroline greeted her uncle and cousin.

"Well, my dear, you are looking beautiful as always."

"Yes. Thank you, Uncle."

"My, Carrie, I do agree with Father. You are absolutely ravishing. You have this glow about you, like you're in love. Isn't that absurd?"

Caroline controlled an urge to laugh. Elizabeth probably didn't realize how close she came to describing Caroline's present condition. She and David had initially kept their romance hidden from anyone outside of the O'Donovan house. But with their upcoming possible re-marriage ceremony, David had instructed her to inform her uncle and cousin as soon as possible.

"It's interesting that you should mention that."

"Mention what, Carrie?"

"That I'm in love."

"You're in love?"

"My dear, what are you talking about?" Uncle asked.

"Well, Uncle, Lizzie, David and I are. . .well, we have a meeting with the priest today at the Cathedral to plan for our upcoming marriage."

"Carrie, you're already married to David. And do you mean to say that you've fallen in love. . .with David?" Elizabeth's eyes were wide and her mouth was open. Uncle Edward was shaking his head.

"Yes, I have. And David has evidently loved me for quite some time."

"Well, that's been the gossip for the last year or so, Carrie. I overheard Patsie talking about it. But, of course, servant gossip isn't always reliable. Mind you, David has changed much for the better."

"Yes, he certainly has."

"Why must you get married again?"

"Our marriage is not considered a true marriage in the eyes of the Church. We will likely schedule the wedding for early January, if you would both like to come."

"Carrie, that's wonderful news. I'm so happy for you."

"We would be honored to attend your wedding to David," Uncle offered.

"Thank you, Uncle, Lizzie. Unfortunately, I'm unable to stay and chat with you because David will be arriving home at any minute to take me to the city."

"Well, my dear, we'll be on our way then. And congratulations," Uncle said, and kissed her cheek.

52

The afternoon of January 8th was cold and snowy, but full of excitement. In front of the Cathedral rectory, the group emerged from the carriages. A soft snow had begun to fall as David and Kip assisted Caroline and Jane, who carried Kathleen, with Kip following close behind. Uncle Edward and Elizabeth's carriage pulled in behind theirs.

Caroline shivered and stuck her hands firmly inside her fur muff. David brushed the snow off his coat and hat. He motioned for them to follow him into the rectory, a brownstone building beside the church.

"Well, it is certainly interesting weather for a wedding, my dear."

"Yes, Uncle it is."

"Carrie, this is so exciting!"

Father Flaherty met them at the door to the rectory. "Welcome. Please do come in."

They entered and David and Uncle took off their hats and hung them on the rack near the door. The foyer area of the rectory was dark and small.

Kathleen's sweet voice said, "Papa, dark?"

"Yes, Kat, it's dark."

"Father Flaherty, may I present Mr. Edward Martin, Caroline's uncle, and Miss Elizabeth Martin, her cousin," David said.

"I am pleased to make your acquaintance, Mr. Martin, Miss Martin," he said as he nodded toward Elizabeth and held out his hand to Mr. Martin.

"Come this way." Father Flaherty led them up several small steps through the door and into a hallway. He stopped at the first door to the right and motioned for them to enter. "This is where I will perform the ceremony."

The room was a fair size, the same as their downstairs study at home, with higher ceilings. The blinds were closed.

"Don't like dark." Her daughter's voice sounded strangely low-pitched.

"I do apologize, Kathleen, I should have opened the blinds well before you arrived," the priest responded. He walked to the windows and raised the blinds. Soon, the room was bathed in early afternoon light. The wallpaper was a rather plain dark gold design. A walnut desk and three chairs were situated along the right-hand wall of the room and several religious statues lined the left wall.

"Don't like dark."

"Why couldn't I be your maid of honor, Carrie?" whispered Elizabeth.

Father Flaherty responded. "Miss Martin, are you Catholic?"

"No."

"In a Catholic ceremony, it is mandatory that Mr. and Mrs. O'Donovan have witnesses who are Catholic. David and Caroline don't know many Catholics. Dr. and Mrs. Carver, their witnesses, were David's sponsors for confirmation, and they also acted as Kathleen's godparents a few months ago."

Caroline cringed. She had hoped to tell her cousin about Kathleen's baptism before now. Elizabeth's eyes widened and she glanced at Caroline, then lowered her head.

"Here are Dr. and Mrs. Carver," the priest said.

"Good day, David. Good day, Mrs. O'Donovan. We're delighted to see you once again, especially for an occasion such as this." Dr. Carver held his hand out to David.

"Yes, thank you, Dr. Carver, Mrs. Carver."

The housekeeper, a middle-aged woman with graying hair approached the group. "May I take your coats?" She gathered their coats and the women's bonnets and left the room. With their cloaks now removed, Elizabeth quietly offered, "Carrie, you look lovely."

"I must agree, my dear," said Uncle.

Caroline's gown was composed of a long-sleeved bodice which was intricately designed with ivory-colored French lace, the neckline adorned with embroidered blue and yellow flowers. The skirt was beige and bustled in the back.

"Thank you, both."

Caroline studied her cousin's expression and it became obvious that Elizabeth had lost her enthusiasm for the day. Caroline made a mental note to speak with Elizabeth afterwards. Her cousin was trying hard not to reveal her disappointment at being passed over for Kathleen's godmother, but Elizabeth's quiet demeanor spoke volumes.

Mrs. Carver added her own compliments. "Mrs. O'Donovan, your dress is one of the loveliest I've seen."

"Thank you, Mrs. Carver."

Caroline glanced at David and his tender expression lessened her anxiety. He reached out and held her hand. David leaned close to her and whispered, "Nervous?"

She nodded.

"If you and Mrs. O'Donovan could stand in front of the window, then the witnesses to either side of them and the rest can gather behind you. " Dr. and Mrs. Carver moved in place next to the bride and groom.

The priest now addressed the small group. "In a Catholic ceremony, we begin by making the sign of the Cross and in Latin, we say, 'In Nomine Patris, et Filii, et Spiritus Sancti.'"

Father Flaherty continued to speak in Latin and Caroline stifled a smile. Thinking back to her and David's first 'wedding,' the minister could have been speaking Greek and she would have cared less. Now, when she wanted to understand what was going on and what was being said, she was unable to do so.

"Now, turn toward one another." At first, she didn't realize he was speaking in English and didn't move. "Caroline?" David whispered.

She blinked and responded, "I'm sorry." She turned and faced David.

"David John O'Donovan, wilt thou take Caroline Martin O'Donovan to be thy lawful wedded wife, to have and to hold, for richer, for poorer, in sickness and in health, till death do thou part?"

David answered, "Yes, I will."

"Caroline Martin O'Donovan, wilt thou take David John O'Donovan to be thy lawful wedded husband, to have and to hold, for richer for poorer, in sickness and in health, till death do thou part?"

"I will."

Father sprinkled holy water on the rings and recited more Latin.

David placed the ring on her finger and repeated prayers which Father had recited, then Caroline did the same.

"Ego conjungo vos in matrimonium in Nomine Patris et Filii et Spiritus Sancti, Amen." The priest, David and the Carvers made the sign of the cross. Caroline watched and followed their example, but she felt out of place. Although she had been occasionally attending Mass with David for the past few months and understood a few phrases in Latin, she wished that she could understand what was being said.

Seemingly in response to her unspoken thought, Father Flaherty said, "It means, I unite you in wedlock in the name of the Father and of the Son and of the Holy Ghost, Amen." The priest brought his hand forward to shake David's hand. "Congratulations, David, Mrs. O'Donovan. May your union be long-lasting and fruitful."

"Thank you, Father."

"You're most welcome, David."

Soon, the housekeeper brought the group their coats.

When they left the rectory and stood outside, David whispered to Caroline, "You go ahead to the carriage. I want to spend a few moments inside the Cathedral."

Caroline turned to Jane, who carried Kathleen. Her daughter held her small gloved hand high.

"Mama, snow?"

"Yes, Sweet, there's snow."   The cobblestone streets and buildings were now coated in white.

Before Caroline got into the carriage, she stopped and addressed her relatives.

"Uncle, may I have a word with Elizabeth?"

"Of course, my dear."

Caroline took Elizabeth's hand and pulled her away from the group now standing in front of the rectory.

"Lizzie dear, I must speak with you."

"Carrie, you need not worry about me today. This is your wedding day. . ." Elizabeth bit down on her lip and looked away.

"You have been the most wonderful sister to me and I am dreadfully sorry that you heard about Kathleen's baptism that way. I wanted to tell you but I didn't want to hurt your feelings."

"I couldn't be your maid of honor this time and now I cannot be Kathleen's godmother. It is very disappointing."

"Yes, I know, but it was David's wish for her to be christened in the Catholic faith, and we couldn't choose godparents who were not Catholic. I wanted to tell you but I didn't want you to be hurt. Would you forgive me for not telling you?"

Elizabeth nodded. "Of course." They embraced and joined the group in front of the carriage.

"Lizzie? Uncle? David needs to attend to something in the church. Would you mind waiting for us back at the house?"

"We wouldn't mind at all, my dear." Uncle Edward leaned in to kiss her. "You will always be a ravishing bride."

"Thank you, Uncle." The two got into the carriage.

"Jane, I shall return momentarily."

"Mama, you comin'?"

"Yes, Sweet. Please wait with Jane in the carriage."

Caroline crossed the street, climbed the steps of the Cathedral and opened the heavy door to the church.

Close to the front, her husband was kneeling, facing the altar at the rail. When she reached the tenth row of pews, she moved into the seat.

Father Flaherty walked up the aisle to greet her. He leaned down and whispered. "Mrs. O'Donovan, is everything well?"

"Yes, of course. I just wanted to be with my husband while he prayed."

"Do you know what he's doing?" he whispered again.

"Praying?"

"He's praying before the Blessed Sacrament. That box is called the Tabernacle. Inside is Jesus in the Holy Eucharist." The priest paused. "David asked me to let him know when it is a quarter to the hour. But I think you ought to let him know."

"I don't wish to interrupt him, Father," she continued to whisper. "And it's not quarter to the hour yet, is it?"

"Not yet."

"Could I also kneel beside him or would that be improper?"

"If you feel called to do so, Mrs. O'Donovan, it would be fine."

Caroline had been meaning to ask David about what would

be required to become Catholic. Instead, she decided to ask the priest, then she could surprise David with the information later. "Father Flaherty?"

"Yes, Mrs. O'Donovan?"

"If I wanted to become Catholic, what would be required?"

"Well, it would entail instruction in the faith and studying on your part. With your attendance at Mass these past few months, I was expecting that you might be so inclined."

"I've always been a spiritual person and believed in God and, in fact, read the entire Bible to my father while he was sick."

"He must have been sick a long time."

"Yes, he was." She paused. "When Liam – David's brother – died, I thought my life was over. I was so angry with God. I suppose I blamed Him for what had happened."

"That's understandable, considering your grief."

"When could I begin taking instruction in the faith?"

"I'll speak with David about it."

"May I tell him, Father?"

"Yes, of course. And congratulations, Mrs. O'Donovan."

"Thank you."

"I hope you will join us for lunch at our house?"

"Yes. I told David that I would come after the noon Mass."

Caroline slowly began the trek up the remainder of the aisle, until she reached the area immediately behind her husband. His head was lowered, his eyes were closed and he was making small silent movements with his mouth. Caroline quietly knelt down beside him. He gasped and his eyes were wide when she brushed against him. "Caroline?"

She held her finger up to his mouth to quiet him. "Shhh. I believe there are still five more minutes to pray before the Blessed Sacrament and I should like to be here with you. Is that acceptable?"

His mouth curved into a wide grin and he nodded.

Together, they faced the tabernacle and David closed his eyes.

Caroline offered her own request. *Almighty Father, bless us as we begin our new life together.*

53

David paced the floor, now a regular routine for him. He wanted a drink desperately but was determined not to surrender. One glass of brandy or whiskey could ruin the evening.

Earlier today, when Caroline had knelt down beside him in front of the Blessed Sacrament, he had rejoiced. The fact that she wanted to become Catholic was the best possible gift he could receive today.

She had told him earlier that she would come to his room and he had been waiting for over an hour. His hands were shaking and his heart was pounding. Why was he so nervous? After all, he was a man who had carnal knowledge of most of the girls in this neighborhood. Memories from his former life began floating through his head: Hallie, Selly, Missy, faceless servants and prostitutes.

This morning, he had pledged his life and heart to Caroline. *Please Lord, give me the grace to think only of my wife. Help me not be lustful, but to love my wife as Christ loves the Church.*

* * *

Caroline stood in front of David's door. Her new gold wedding band was slightly loose on her finger and she began to nervously turn it. Weeks ago, she had asked David to choose rings for them both. Hers was rather ornate for her tastes with minute diamonds in the center and carved designs on either side. But she cherished it because he chose this to symbolize their unity.

She took a deep breath. Caroline held her hand out to knock, then quickly pulled it back.

David was on the other side of this door waiting for her. It sounded as if he was reading or praying. Caroline began to tremble. Although she deeply desired David and wanted to fulfill her duty as his wife, this was one aspect of true married life for which she felt particularly awkward. Of course, it meant that she would hopefully become with child and she greatly looked forward to that.

How could she possibly be married to a man she once

despised?   She recalled the sight of David and Missy in the hen-house and shook her head to rid herself of the image.

*   *   *

Hearing sounds outside his door, David opened it to find Caroline standing in the hallway. "How long have you been waiting there?"

"A few moments."

"Why didn't you knock?"

"I. . .don't know."

"Come in." He took her by the hand and pulled her inside the room and closed the door.

David could see that she was trembling and he tenderly gathered her into his arms. As he held her, David recalled the last conversation he had with Liam before he was hurt.

"I want to know how to. . .well. . .make the. . .marriage bed less awkward for my wife."

David pulled away. "We can postpone this, if you'd like."

She shook her head.

He gently placed his hands on her shoulders. "I want you to tell me whatever is on your mind right now, whatever you're feeling."

She remained silent for several long moments.

"I want you to talk to me about anything your heart desires." She remained quiet as he caressed the side of her face and kissed her forehead. She pulled away from him and glanced at the oil lamp, then made eye contact with him.

"Caroline?"

"Yes?"

"Do you wish for me to turn down the oil lamp?"

"Off would be preferable."

"Off? But. . ." Now, David closed his eyes. He was going to have to take this very slowly. "I can turn off the oil lamp, if you'd like."

"Thank you," she whispered.

"Your body is beautiful." Caroline's head lowered and she remained silent. He tipped her chin up to look at him. Her face was flushed. "Do you trust me, Caroline?"

"Well, I. . .yes," she replied, nodding. "But. . ."

"But?"

"I can't seem to erase from my mind the image of you and Missy in the henhouse."

"I can't do anything about that, and I'm having difficulties forgetting my own sordid memories. But this is who you married. It is impossible to change my past, only my future."

"I know." Caroline again glanced toward the lamp, then her eyes begged him to turn the light off. "It ought to be dark when we . . ."

"Why?"

"Because that's the way it's supposed to be."

"That's not been my experience. There's nothing wrong with having a lamp on."

"I don't want you to see my. . .I'm uncomfortable with. . ."

"Your body is beautiful."

"David, please."

"What if it were daylight? There would be no lamp to turn off, would there?"

"Surely, you don't intend that we do this in the daylight," she said with wide eyes.

"What if I turn it down to a flicker?"

"Yes, very well."

When he turned to face her, his wife stared at the ceiling, then at the floor. She was wringing her hands. He stepped quietly toward her. She made eye contact with him.

He pulled her to an embrace and stroked the hair off her face. His wife's heart was beating against his chest. David took a deep breath and stepped away. Caroline was avoiding eye contact, her head was lowered.

"Caroline?" he said, as he tipped her chin up to look at him.

"David, I. . ." Crackling from the fireplace distracted her and, for a moment, she stared silently into the bright flames. David placed his hands on her shoulders and waited for her to look at him. When she did, he took hold of her trembling hand and kissed it.

"What we do here, now, with our bodies, this very act is ordained by God."

"But 'tis also my duty, David."

"Yes, it is, but I will never insist on this if you are in any way uncomfortable or not feeling well. Caroline, I want you to desire this as much as I do. Come. " He walked her to his desk and picked up his Bible, already opened to the book of Tobias. He made the Sign of the Cross, then faced the crucifix and prayed the words of Scripture:

"*And now, Lord, thou knowest that not for fleshly lust do I take my sister for my wife, but only for the love of posterity in which Thy name may be blessed forever and ever. . .have mercy on us, Lord, and let us grow old both together in health.*"

Caroline responded, "Amen." She avoided eye contact, her face now flushed. She began to shiver, so he gently guided her to the bed.

54

David sighed with a deep sense of fulfilment. Caroline slept beside him, her soft arm draped across his stomach. He didn't want to fall asleep. Right now, his only desire was to watch his wife rest, listen to her breathe, feel her heart beating and thank God for this wonderful gift. She exhaled and he gazed in awe at her face. In slumber, her inhibitions had disappeared and her body completely relaxed against his.

Caroline was now truly his wife. A few moments ago, with their bodies, they repeated the vows they had recited earlier in the day. He had experienced this act with many women and yet this was the first time that it felt right, good, even sacred.

How many times had he given his body to prostitutes whose names he didn't know, to servants he didn't care about? David wished that he could erase that part of his life, but it was impossible. The best he could do now was to forget, to leave it in the past, where it belonged.

He had never before thought much about the potential that he could be creating a child, not with the prostitutes, for certain. With the servants, he knew there was a possibility but, back then it wasn't an important part of the bedding process. He sometimes offered his own feeble attempts to have the pleasure of it without the consequences of making the girl with child. Most of the time, though, conceiving a baby was the last thing on his mind.

Now, however, he was overwhelmed with the likelihood, maybe probability, that at this moment or in the weeks ahead, Caroline would be carrying their child, a baby created from their most intimate act of love. Not only did he hope it would happen soon, he now prayed for it.

And yet, deep within, he couldn't help but feel guilty that he was enjoying the fruits of marriage with Caroline. What would Liam have thought of this situation?

Caroline stirred and he kissed her forehead. "I love you," he whispered. He caressed the soft skin of her arm and shoulder. He recalled her modesty, her fear of showing herself to him, her trembling, and these all filled his heart more deeply with love for her.

How can I ever thank You for the gift of Caroline's love and for allowing us to truly be one?

The Almighty was now giving him an opportunity to start anew. David concluded that he would never be able to adequately show his gratitude to God, but he vowed that whatever the Lord asked of him in the future, he would joyfully accept.

* * *

Caroline woke from a deep sleep. Her head was on her husband's chest and she listened to the soft beating of his heart, a heart which had captured her own so completely.

Lifting her head, she watched him as he slept, deeply, contentedly. Caroline could not fathom that she was here, with her former brother-in-law, now husband, in his bed. How was it possible to love him this much?

David had been patient and tender with her, just like his brother had been. She cringed inwardly as she remembered the first time with Liam and her closed eyes, clenched fists and still body. How naive she had been and how selfish.

Oh Liam.

Caroline pulled on her robe and quietly slipped out of bed. She stifled a gasp when her foot touched the cold hardwood floor. She carefully placed another log onto the fire.

She walked to the window and gazed at the softly falling snow outside. Thick frost grew like smiles on the inside of the windows. As day was beginning to dawn, the whiteness outside bathed the room in a light blue-gray glow, a radiance which seemed to illuminate the area surrounding their marriage bed. David was sleeping soundly and breathing audibly. Her eyes were drawn to the crucifix on the wall above his bed and she recalled David's words: *"This very act is ordained by God."*

Again facing the window, she remembered Liam's concern after their first time together.

"Are you all right, Caroline?"

"Caroline?"

She let out an audible gasp. *He sounds so much like Liam.* Her back to him, she answered, "Yes," her voice trembling.

David slipped out of bed and embraced her from behind as she stared out the window, the snow continuing to accumulate on the sill outside. "I love you," he whispered, then kissed the side of her neck.

She nodded but made no sound.

"What's wrong?"

Caroline shook her head.

"Please. Tell me," he whispered.

"I couldn't help but think of. . .him. . .tonight."

He gently turned her to face him. "I've been thinking about him too." He gathered her into his arms. "Lee would want us to be happy."

"I know. But I miss him so much." She leaned against his chest.

"I wish he could have known me as I am now."

"He would have been happy, David."

"Yes." He paused. "Have I ever expressed my gratitude to you?" he whispered.

"Your gratitude?"

He nodded. "You're part of the reason I wanted to change."

"I am?"

"Yes. You always looked at me with such disdain. If for nothing else, I wanted to please you."

"I am pleased, David, very pleased. Now, what were you saying about expressing your gratitude to me?"

55

David pressed a lingering kiss to his wife's lips. He could engage in this holy, intimate act of marriage every day and it wouldn't be enough for him. It wasn't merely because of the physical pleasure, although that was a great gift. With his body, David repeated the vows he made to Caroline at their wedding and she reciprocated.

Memories from past experiences still occasionally haunted his dreams, but he and Caroline had begun to pray before bedtime, and most especially, before they became intimate.

"Caroline, I have never been so happy."

She snuggled up close to him. With her finger, she traced an invisible line from his wrist to his shoulder and down his chest. He caught her hand and brought it to his lips, kissing her palm. "So you think you may be with child?"

"I'm not certain. But I have missed my second monthly, and I can't think of any reason other than I'm carrying. I'm not sick at all, though. With Kathleen, I retched early and practically until the time I delivered."

He kissed her stomach, then began to caress it. "Perhaps it means that my son is in there and he's making it easy for you."

"Of course."

"This would be a most wonderful event for us."

"Yes, it would."

Soon, Caroline fell into a deep sleep. Beside his wife, David felt like he had just been given a most extraordinary gift. A baby, perhaps a son that he could love and nurture and go fishing with, teach how to ride. . .or another daughter he could spoil and take to the park. Yes, for David, this was a sign that God had forgiven him.

He woke to the sounds of moaning. David blinked his eyes and listened. Beside him, Caroline grabbed his arm. He sat up. "Caroline, what's the matter?"

She winced. "I don't know. My stomach, it's. . ."

David jumped up and turned on the oil lamp next to the bed.

Caroline pushed the covers aside and gasped at the now red flannel sheets.

At the sight of the blood-filled bedding, David's heart became heavy, but he couldn't allow her to be aware of his anguish. "It's fine, Caroline. I'll call for Jane."

"No, no, don't leave me, David. Please!" She moaned and squeezed his wrist.

He reached for a small towel and helped Caroline to put it between her legs, but within moments, it was soaked through. "This couldn't be my monthly; it's too heavy and it hurts." Caroline began to cry. He leaned in to embrace her.

"Mr. David?" Jane asked through the closed door.

"Jane, come in," David said.

The servant opened the door, then rushed to the side of the bed. "What's wrong?"

Caroline moaned again, while David tried to keep the towel between her legs. "Jane, I think she may be. . ."

"Yes, Mr. David. Might be a miscarriage."

Caroline screamed. "It hurts!"

"I know. I'm sorry, Caroline."

An hour or so later, his wife miscarried their baby. Caroline was crying, but David was now staring in awe at several clots of blood surrounding the smallest human being he had ever seen, tiny, red and all curled up, the size of which could easily fit into a child's palm. Caroline's eyes were wide as she noticed the small form, still and unmoving, on the bed.

"David."

"Yes, Caroline, our child."

"I'll see to this, Mr. David," whispered Jane as she gently and carefully picked up the miniature baby.

A short while later, the bleeding slowed and Jane assisted Caroline into a clean gown, while David changed the bedding. As he stood up, Caroline stared at the mid-section of his nightshirt. He was covered with blood, hers and their baby's. "David, you need to change your nightshirt." His head lowered as he studied his shirt, then he whispered, "I'll get to that later."

"Miss Caroline, perhaps I should accompany you back to your room?"

"No, Jane," answered David, "I'd prefer that Caroline remain here with me."

"Of course, Mr. David. I've put another thicker piece of flannel down there in case there's more bleeding, but it looks like it has slowed down. Let me know if you need me."

"Thank you."

Jane left the room and as they rested quietly together, Caroline began to sob. "Shhh. There will be others," David whispered.

As she cried herself to sleep, he finally felt her relax, her face wet against his chest. Only then, did he allow himself to quietly weep.

* * *

David genuflected and knelt in the front pew. Earlier, he had sent a message to Father Flaherty to meet him at two o'clock. It was now 1:45 and David decided to use the time to pray before the Blessed Sacrament until Father arrived.

He was on the verge of tears as he remembered Caroline losing their baby last night. After he had fallen asleep, he had dreamt that a large group of people were screaming at him that it was his fault that his child had died. He woke up in a sweat and couldn't fall back to sleep. Perhaps this *was* his fault. After all, they had been engaging in the marriage act frequently. Sometimes, Caroline was tired yet she never refused.

He must speak to Father and maybe go to Confession. Did God truly forgive him for the previous life that he had lived? Or was he now being punished?

"David," Father whispered.

David looked up, relieved. "Good day, Father."

"Would you like to come into the rectory or do you want to talk here?"

Only a handful of people were in church, mostly toward the back. "Here would be fine, Father. Perhaps I ought to go to Confession."

"Well, let me determine whether that shall be necessary."

"Caroline. . .well, she had been. . . "

"Had been what, David?"

"We didn't know for sure, but she was. . .with child."

"That's wonderful news."

"But she lost the baby last night."

"I'm sorry."

"It's my fault."

"Why do you believe it's your fault?"

"I insisted that we . . .well, that we engage in the. . ."

"I don't know about that, but it could hardly be your fault if you didn't know."

"I should have known."

"David, you are striving hard to be a man of faith. You do not need to be forgiven for something you may have unknowingly done."

"Could it be that perhaps God has not forgiven me?"

"No. That's the beautiful aspect of Confession. You have the assurance that God has forgiven you."

David wiped his eyes and sat quietly beside Father Flaherty. "God grieves with you, David, and so do I." He patted David on the back. "I don't think you need to go to Confession today, unless there's something else on your mind."

David shook his head, then knelt down to pray.

56

Caroline looked down into the pleading eyes of her daughter two months later in the back yard area.

"Mama, mama, please. Wanna go 'xplorin.' Jane take me."

Jane placed her son down on the ground and watched him scurry off after Kathleen. "I'll take Isaac and the two of them can have fun exploring. You know how much Miss Kathleen enjoys the wooded area between our property and your uncle's."

"I know, but last time she got poison ivy on her arms."

"That was last summer. It's still spring."

All of a sudden, Caroline felt as if her lunch was going to come back up.

"You don't look well, Ma'am."

"I feel sick to my stomach."

"Please, Mama?"

"Just a minute, Sweet." Caroline took a couple deep breaths in, then out to allow the nausea to pass. "Yes, very well. Jane, please be careful that she doesn't get her new dress dirty."

"Yes, I will."

The young children rushed off to the wooded area, Jane following close behind. Left alone, she smiled. As each day passed, she seemed to become more fatigued and sick to her stomach, though the queasiness seemed to disappear by mid-day. The fullness in her breasts made it difficult to sleep on her stomach. At least this pregnancy seemed to be making itself more known.

Yesterday, she had barely made it to the basin before she retched. As she returned to the bed, David had regarded her with a mixture of sympathy and joy.

He leaned across the bed to kiss her stomach. "I have a feeling that our child is growing in there." He caressed her just below the navel.

"I'm afraid, David."

"This one will last. I have a feeling."

Again feeling the urge to retch, Caroline began searching for an area to succumb to it. She reached the waste pail at the back of the house before spilling the contents of her stomach. Once finished, she felt better, at least for the moment.

In the kitchen, she drank a cool glass of water. She sat down and breathed in the sweet spring air that blew through the kitchen.

"Why are you sitting in here?" she heard her husband say.

"I felt a bit queasy. I made it to the waste barrel just in time."

"Have you made an appointment with the midwife yet?" He kissed the top of her head.

"Not yet, but I will."

"Papa, Papa!" Kathleen yelled as she, Jane and Isaac walked into the kitchen. Both of the little girl's hands were behind her back.

"We returned early because Miss Kathleen has a gift for you, Miss Caroline, and she wanted to give it to you right away."

Kathleen brought forward a large bouquet of dandelions. "For you, Mama. I picked 'em."

"Thank you so much, Sweet. They're beautiful."

David lifted her in his arms and squeezed her small body in an affectionate hug. "Hey, Kat, were you 'xplorin' again?" he asked, mimicking her.

"Uh-huh, Jane and Isaac took me. I picked flowers for Mama."

He smiled at Caroline.

"Mr. David, Miss Caroline don't look so well. Perhaps you should tell her to take a rest."

"Yes, Caroline. I'm free for the next two hours, so I can play with Kathleen while you rest upstairs."

Caroline nodded. As she stood up, another wave of nausea swept over her. "Maybe I should remain here until this passes," she said, sitting down again. All of a sudden, despite the rest, she felt her stomach beginning to convulse. Again she jumped up to quickly reach the waste barrel outside and expelled what was left in her stomach. She soon felt David's hands gently rubbing her back as she finished the task. She glanced at him to find him smiling sympathetically.

"I think you ought to have a rest."

She shook her head.

"Perhaps I should assist you, Miss Caroline?" asked the servant, leaning her head out the back doorway.

"No, Jane. I'll be fine as soon as it passes."

"I can take you, Caroline. I'm going upstairs to the study," said David.

"No, that won't be necessary. I'll just take a moment." Caroline returned to the seat at the table and took a few deep breaths. Jane began to chop up a whole chicken. Each time the knife slammed down onto the raw chicken and the table, another queasy feeling came upon her. "On second thought, perhaps I will go upstairs and have a short rest."

"Rest well," Jane said as Caroline quickly passed by the table. "I'll keep an eye on Miss Kathleen."

"Thank you."

Within minutes, she was in her room, lying on the large bed, neatly made. The feeling of nausea had subsided. She moved her hand to her stomach and smiled. There was no denying the usual signs that she carried their child within her. The sickness, missed monthlies, breast tenderness and extreme fatigue gave her hope that this one would last.

57

In her bed, Caroline heard the chiming of the clock downstairs announcing that it was three o'clock a.m. She had been having difficulties sleeping for the past hour, listening as it struck each quarter hour. Caroline despised sleeping in her own bed, but once her pregnancy was confirmed two months ago, David insisted on it. When she protested, he remained steadfast. "For our baby's safety, Caroline."

He told Caroline that years ago he had dismissed as barbaric the modern medical recommendation that couples abstain from the marriage act during pregnancy. Now, David had concluded that perhaps Caroline's miscarriage was caused by the frequency of their intimacy. She was not convinced that was the cause, but hesitantly agreed that it was best to sleep separately until the baby was born.

Of course, it had been a moot point for the last two months as she had been so ill that she gladly welcomed sleep every night to provide relief from retching. And Jane, to whom Caroline owed more than a great deal of gratitude, had strategically placed basins around the house so that Caroline would not have to bolt from any given room to be sick.

Her husband was most thoughtful during the day, often keeping Kathleen occupied while Caroline slept. In the evenings, he sat with Caroline in the parlor reading from scripture or discussing various issues. Most recently, she had especially enjoyed his recitation of the Canticle of Canticles and their lengthy conversations regarding the imagery and symbolism of that particular book.

As well, he shared so much of himself with her, unlike Liam who, for whatever reason, found it difficult to reveal deep feelings and thoughts to her.

She pulled on her robe and checked on Kathleen, who was sleeping soundly. She carefully opened David's door and crept inside his room. It was silent except for his deep breathing. She took off her robe and slipped into the bed beside him. He hardly roused, except, in his slumber, he embraced her. Soon, Caroline drifted off into a deep sleep.

As she awoke, David was kissing her and on top of her. Although rational, Caroline surrendered to the moment. When it was over, David – now awake and realizing what had happened – was apologetic. "Caroline, I shouldn't have. . .we shouldn't have."

She touched her fingers to his lips. "Shhh. It's fine."

"We shouldn't be doing this, Caroline."

"Why, David? We were intimate many times in the first few months when we didn't know for certain I was with child."

"Yes, I know, but I. . ."

"I miss our nights together."

"As do I," he said, then he caressed her stomach. "I just want to protect him. . .or her."

"I know. But can I remain here with you for now, please?"

He smiled, then kissed her forehead. "Just for tonight. . ."

The next morning, Caroline awoke in his embrace and studied him as he slept. She enjoyed watching her husband sleep, oblivious to the world, in total slumber.

A cool waft of air caressed her skin, the smell of an early autumn morning gave her a sense of well being. At that moment, her unborn child stretched within her.

There was a quiet knock followed by, "Miss Caroline?"

"Yes?"

"Miss Kathleen's pestering me to be with you and Mr. David."

David roused as Caroline spoke. "Just a minute, Jane." Caroline pulled on her robe over her nightgown and opened the door. "Mama, Papa!" Kathleen exclaimed, as she climbed onto the bed.

Jane was smiling as she closed the door.

"How do you like your new room, Kathleen?"

"Don't like it."

"Kathleen, I. . ."

"How's my girl doing this morning?" David asked.

" I miss Mama."

"Well, Kat. . ."

"Want to sleep with you and Mama?"

"Kat, I. . ."

He glanced at Caroline, a smile now forming on her lips.

"Are you not going to help me here, dear wife?"

"I think you're handling this fine."

"I want to sleep with Mama and Papa."

"Well, I don't know about that, Kat. We'll see if we can arrange something."

Kathleen threw herself at David. He embraced her small body as she placed wet kisses on his cheek. *They love each other so much.* For a moment, Caroline's eyes glistened as she remembered Liam. *How proud he would have been to have a daughter.*

Kathleen's squeals caused Caroline's heart to leap with joy. Her husband's loving expression and tender voice, the early morning light just peeking its way into their room, gave her a soothing, peaceful sensation. Caroline had never felt so loved, so calmed, so happy.

58

Caroline couldn't figure out which to focus on, the small snowman Kathleen was building or the laneway which should have brought her husband home hours ago.

"I told you not to worry," Jane said from the porch.

"David said that he would be home at eleven this morning. It is now three o'clock." Caroline's breath was visible in the frigid air.

"I'm sure Mr. David's fine."

"But he's coming from Quakertown. He said he would leave early and arrive home by eleven or noon, at the latest. He's four hours late. What if he's hurt?"

"You got to stop doing this to yourself. Mr. David's a strong man and he wouldn't take any chances. If he's not home, it wouldn't be through any fault of his own."

"I know, but. . ."

"Mama, help me."

"Yes, Sweet." She turned and began to pat the side of Kathleen's snowman's head.

Jane pulled her wool sweater closer to her body. "Perhaps we'd better go inside."

"I want to remain out here as long possible to wait for David."

"You'll be delivering in the next few weeks and you can't be prancing around in the snow. You might fall."

"Jane, please."

The servant shook her head and went back inside the house.

"Mama, put the head on."

Caroline lifted up the smaller snowball that they had rolled and placed it firmly on top of the two larger balls. All of a sudden, a pain in her abdomen, a familiar one, made her gasp, then hold her breath.

"Mama, here are sticks."

As the pain subsided, she exhaled. "Yes, Sweet, we can't forget the arms."

Kathleen stuck the sticks on either sides of the large middle ball of the snowman.

Soon, Caroline saw their small carriage coming up the laneway. She wished that she could run and greet him, but that would not be safe with her advanced pregnancy. David pulled the carriage to a stop, then tethered the horse to the front post. She hurried over to him and embraced him.

"I'm sorry I was so late, Caroline. I hope you didn't worry too –" He tried to back away, but her grip tightened. "I was worried, David," she said, her voice muffled with her face pressed up against his coat.

"Papa, Papa, home!" Kathleen shouted.

"Well, Kat, you're building a fine looking gentleman," he said, while his wife still held onto him. Kathleen ran back to the snowman.

"One of the wheels was cracked and I had to stop outside of Quakertown to get it repaired."

Caroline finally stepped away from him. "David, I love you so much."

"I love you too. More than I can ever express."

"You've already expressed it quite well." She took his hand and placed it on her large stomach.

He kissed her, then took hold of her hand as they walked together to the snowman.

"Ah, look at this handsome fellow. He needs a proper top hat." He took off his hat and placed it on top of the smaller ball.

"I like that, Papa."

"I'm not sure my head will like it very much." He glanced at Caroline and gave her a warm, affectionate smile. "It's awfully cold out here, Caroline. Perhaps you should return indoors."

"I'm fine."

"You'll be delivering any day. You don't want to catch cold, do you?"

"I assure you that I am dressed very warmly. And at least I've got a warm bonnet on my head, which is more than I can say for you." She reached up and brushed the accumulating snow from the top of his dark curly hair. As she was moving her hand away, he caught it and kissed her palm through the glove. His tender expression made her want to embrace him again.

"Papa, coat too?"

David shook his head, then fixed his gaze on his daughter. "No, Kat. The snowman may have my hat, but not my coat. I'm afraid I need my coat."

"Papa, Christmas tree?"

"Kat, I'm tired. I spent most of the day waiting to get the carriage wheel fixed. Perhaps tomorrow. Christmas is still a week away."

"Please, Papa, please. . ."

David glanced at Caroline, who was grinning, and Kathleen, who was looking up at him in breathless anticipation.

"Very well," he said.

Kip was standing beside the horse, untying the reins.

"Kip, would you mind getting me the ax?"

"Sure, Mr. David. You want me to come with you to chop the tree down?"

"No, that's fine, Kip. I think I can manage. As long as the women folk can make haste in deciding." He paused, then stared at Caroline's stomach. "Caroline, perhaps Kathleen and I should do this alone. You ought to be going back inside. It's starting to snow more heavily now."

"I can walk a short way, David. If I feel tired, I'll return."

The three made their way into the wooded area and only ten feet or so inside the forest, Kathleen shouted, "Papa, look at the pretty tree!" She ran toward what appeared to be a perfectly shaped pine tree about ten feet high.

"Yes, this is quite beautiful, David."

"Splendid. This took much less time than I expected," he answered. As he leaned down to cut the trunk of the tree, he discovered that there were two trunks.

"What's the matter?"

"Well, this is not one tree, Caroline. It's two. Look."

Caroline leaned down as far as her pregnant body would allow her. "Yes, yes. There are two here. But it looks so much like one tree."

"Cut it, Papa! Cut it!"

"I'm afraid I can't, Kat. It's actually two trees and when I cut one trunk, it will only be part of the tree. See?" He showed her by partially separating the two trees with his hands.

Kathleen's eyes narrowed and her lips formed a pout.

"Don't worry. We'll find something else."

Caroline crouched down and intensely studied the trees. *It looks like one tree, yet it's really two.* Caroline smiled inwardly as she thought of the marriage bed and why their child grew inside her. *The two shall become one.*

"Want to let me in on your thoughts?"

"Well, those trees look so much like one tree and yet it's two. But the way it has grown, it grows like one tree, despite the two trunks."

"I didn't think you were that interested in the way trees grow."

"I'm not, really. But that's the way it is in marriage. There are actually two people, but they become one and their oneness is a child." She pointed to her stomach, then glanced at David. His eyebrows were raised and he was smiling.

Caroline gasped as she again felt a familiar cramp deep in her abdomen. "David."

"Yes?" he said.

She was wincing and holding her breath.

"What?"

"I think that perhaps we ought to return to the house. It might be soon time for me to. . ." Caroline stopped and closed her eyes.

"Will you be able to walk back to the house?"

She nodded, tensing her body, holding on to the trunk of a large oak tree beside her. She reached out and grabbed David's shoulder and squeezed.

"Come, Kat, we must return," David said. "Your new little brother or sister will be coming soon."

"Yay, yay," Kathleen squealed, jumping up and down. Then she stopped and said, "What about the Christmas tree?"

"We'll have to cut it down later, Kat."

Kathleen began to whine. "Don't want to do it later."

They emerged from the forest, with David now close beside his wife, holding onto her shoulders as they moved closer to the house.

The snow had begun to fall in earnest now, the wind causing the miniature flakes to blow sideways. When they reached the side of the house, David dropped the ax on the ground and assist-ed Caroline up the steps to the porch.

"Caroline, allow me to accompany you upstairs. Kat, come inside."

"Don't want to." Kathleen stamped her feet on the ground.

"It's all right, David. I can manage the steps on my own. You stay with Kathleen. It will be some time before the baby comes. And I'll tell Kip to fetch the midwife."

"We're standing in the middle of a blizzard, Caroline. I'm bringing her in." He pulled his daughter inside the foyer.

"Don't want to go inside!"

"Well, Kathleen Emma O'Donovan, sometimes we must do things we don't want!" he shouted, yanking her coat off. She react-ed by letting out an ear-piercing scream. "Don't want to!"

Caroline stood at the bottom of the steps, her eyes narrowed as she listened to her daughter's tantrum. David lifted Kathleen up and rushed past Caroline into the parlor. At her worried expression, David turned back and said, "She'll be fine, Caroline."

"Is it time?" Jane said, coming from the basement staircase.

"Would you assist me in getting my coat off?"

"Certainly." Jane paused. "Miss Kathleen's not sounding too happy, is she?"

"She wanted to stay outside in the snowstorm and cut the tree down."

"I see."

"Could you send Kip to get the midwife?"

"Of course. I'll help you up the stairs first."

"No need. I'll be fine." Caroline started up the steps but she felt another a contraction. She pressed her hand to the wall as she breathed.

"You're not looking so good." The servant came up the steps beside her.

"No, I suppose I'm. . ." She slammed the wall and tried to breathe through the next contraction. When it was over, Jane held onto her mistress' elbow as they took one step at a time. Caroline turned to go into David's room.

"Don't you want to be doing the birthing in your own bed?"

Caroline shook her head. "David's bed."

"Yes, Ma'am."

"Let David know I shall be here, would you?"

"I think he'll know where you are," the servant said, as she escorted her mistress into the room and onto the bed.

A few hours later, Caroline pushed yet another time, a loud moan escaping from her lips.

"Mrs. O'Donovan, your baby is almost here. Just one more push," she heard the midwife say.

Caroline pushed and her child slid from her body. "'Tis a boy, Miss Caroline, ye've got a fine wee boyeen." She could see the crying face of her baby, then she heard David open the door. "May I come in now?"

"Mr. O'Donovan," the midwife said, "you should not be in here."

"Now then, out ye go, Mr. David, sir. We'll be lettin' ye know when. . ." Patsie yelled.

"I want to see my child." David crouched down beside Caroline's head. She looked up at David and offered him a weak smile. He held onto her hand and kissed her wet forehead.

"Ye've got yerself a fine boyeen, Mr. David, sir. We're jest cleanin' 'im up a wee bit."

"I'm tired," Caroline whispered.

"You deserve to be, Mrs. O'Donovan," he whispered.

She gave him another half attempt at a smile, then closed her eyes.

The baby continued to bawl while Patsie cleaned him up and wrapped him tightly in a blanket.

"Here's yer fine wee lad, Mr. David."

Caroline looked up at David, who was beaming.

"Mrs. O'Donovan, just one more push and the afterbirth will be delivered," the midwife said.

She pushed and felt something soft slide from inside of her. Now she tried to glance up, but she felt so fatigued.

"Well then, are ye after holdin' yer wee babe, perhaps nursin' 'im?"

Caroline shook her head. "Don't feel so. . ."

David said something to her but she could barely hear him. *I'll just close my eyes for a moment.*

"She's bleeding! Quick, get the. . ."

She managed to open her eyes partway and Caroline could see the midwife rushing to her side.

She felt the woman pressing down hard on her abdomen.

The room seemed to be spinning. Caroline opened her mouth to take a breath, but she could not accomplish that simple task. The muffled voices around her sounded faraway. She could hear the faint high-pitched wails of her baby. Her husband was speaking to her, but she couldn't hear what he was saying. She felt so weak, so tired, like every ounce of energy had drained from within her.

"Caroline, can you hear me?" David was beside her, leaning close to her ear. His voice sounded so distant. She tried to nod but no part of her body would move.

"She looks so gray. Do something. Can't you do. . ." David's eyes widened in terror. His mouth was open as if he was yelling, but she could barely hear him.

Then, all of a sudden, the voices became one and Caroline couldn't hear what they said. Her eyes felt heavy, her body weak. Yet she felt strangely at peace. There was no panic, just over-whelming fatigue. Soon darkness enveloped her. *I feel so weak. Need to rest.*

It was spring, flowers were in bloom everywhere and Caroline was running in a field behind Kathleen. David was off in the distance and another person, a slight, somewhat taller, man stood beside him. *Who's standing next to David? If I can just get a little closer.*

"Hello, Caroline. I've missed you."

"Liam! Oh, Liam, I've missed you as well." They embraced. A radiant light shone above him. Liam was bright and beautiful, even more handsome than she had remembered. It had been so long since she had seen his face or heard his tender words.

He and David were laughing and teasing one another.

A baby was crying, screeching, and she shook her head to rid herself of the noise.

"Miss Caroline, you've got to try to take some of this broth, please?" She tried to move her head to avoid the spoon.

Leave me alone. I want to sleep.

Caroline could hear weeping, the soft sounds of grief. *Who is crying?* Then she could hear the whispering words Holy Mary, Mother of God, in Latin. "Sancta Maria, Mater Dei."

Something on her forehead felt ice cold. She moved her head from side to side to stop the torture. "We're just wiping your face, Miss Caroline. Please be still."

In the distance, a baby continued to cry.

Again, the low tone of someone crying, sobbing.

*   *   *

David caressed her arm, hoping that perhaps his touch would waken her. In the four days that she had lingered between life and death, he could not rouse his wife enough to tell her how much he loved her and what she meant to him. *Almighty Father, please allow her to live. I'll do whatever you want me to. I don't ever want to put her in danger again, just let her live.*

Father Flaherty had visited early this morning and had given Caroline the Sacrament of Extreme Unction. David had waited to contact him because he mistakenly thought that he would be admitting that his wife had little hope of surviving, that he would be giving up. Father reminded him that a person need not be on his or her deathbed to receive the Sacrament.

Glancing at his bedside table, David caught a glimpse of the small box which held the gift that he had planned to give to his wife after their son was born. He lifted out the cameo pin and rubbed his thumb over the smooth pearl surface and the painted words, "*Mother.*" On the back, the engraved letters, *COD* love *DOD.* He blinked back the tears. Perhaps he might not get the chance to give her this gift. No, he couldn't think that. He placed it back into the box and set it carefully on the bedside table.

The linen sheet covering his wife darkened again at her chest. He cringed. The plentiful milk her breasts were producing had nowhere to go but out. Jane had applied warm compresses and in the beginning even attempted to coax the baby to nurse but their child seemed to know that his mother was in no condition to feed him.

David laid his head on her hand and allowed himself to drift off to sleep.

He studied his wife as she slept. She was so still and so pale, almost gray. When he picked up her hand, it was cold and stiff. "No, Caroline, please don't leave me." His heart-wrenching sobs filled the room with grief. If she was gone, then part of him was now gone.

"Mr. David, Mr. David!" Jane shook his shoulders.

David opened his eyes and lifted his head. His heart was beating wildly in his chest and he could barely breathe. He stared blankly at Jane then glanced down at Caroline sleeping on the bed. *Thank God, it was just a nightmare.*

"Are you all right, Mr. David? You were moaning."

"Yes, yes, I'm fine now." He held onto Caroline's hand and kissed it longingly. Her fingers were pale but warm and soft. Her breathing was labored but, thank God, she was still alive.

"Miss Caroline's a strong woman and she's not ready to give up yet. You wait and see. She'll wake up any time now."

He nodded, then sounds of his son's crying in the other room caused him to lift his head and listen. For such a small person, their baby could make enough noise to wake the dead. When Kathleen was an infant, she hardly cried at all or perhaps he just didn't remember properly. This little fellow sounded strong and hearty.

A few moments later, the wailing stopped. Four days ago, the moment that he knew that God had blessed them with a son, his heart was filled with joy. Right now, however, he couldn't focus on his child, their baby, because he needed to remain beside his wife.

"Mr. David, you got to eat something."

"I told you, Jane, I'm not hungry."

"Well, at least let Kip give you a shave."

He shook his head. Sounds of the baby's crying again drew his attention to the open doorway.

"Your son sure is a screamer. He nurses more than Miss Kathleen did, that's for sure. He's going to be a big strapping fellow."

"How is. . .the wet nurse. . .doing, Jane?"

"Just fine."

He cringed when he thought of telling Caroline about the woman who was now nursing their son. He hadn't yet met her, but he trusted that Jane employed someone who was honest and dependable. When it was obvious that Caroline wouldn't be able to nurse their child, he had told Jane to find someone quickly. Within minutes of the wet nurse's arrival, his son had finally become quiet.

"Papa, papa," he heard Kathleen squealing behind Jane.

"Hi, Kat. I trust you've been good for Jane?"

"I miss you, Papa."

He stood up and wiped his eyes with the back of his hand. He picked Kathleen up at the doorway, sheltering her from the sight of her unconscious mother.

"Mama wake?"

"Soon, Kat, soon."

He placed her on the floor and she began to jump up and down, her shoes making a tapping sound. "Come see baby, Papa."

"Yes, well. . ." With a heavy heart, he glanced back at Caroline. She remained still and unmoving. *Please let her wake soon.*

"Papa, the baby."

"Yes, Kat, take me to see the baby."

She held up her tiny hand and his much larger hand took hold. She led him toward the room which Jane and Hallie had quickly set up as a makeshift nursery down the hall. His daughter pushed the door and it creaked open. A woman with dark hair was sitting in a rocking chair nursing his son. When she saw David coming into the room, she inhaled a quiet gasp.

"Mr. David, I'm so sorry. I didn't know you were coming." The girl took the baby from her breast and fumbled with her dress, pulling the front of it together. She laid the baby on her shoulder and began to pat his back.

"Missy?" His mouth was open. He let go of Kathleen's hand.

"Yes, Mr. David."

"You're the wet nurse?"

"Yes. Jane said you needed someone to nurse the baby. I can't tell you how sorry I am that Miss Caroline isn't doing well."

"You're married?"

"Well, no, but I do have a baby."

"Oh."

"He's in there." She pointed to a crib at the other end of the room. "He's five months old."

"Papa, see baby."

For a moment, David remained at the doorway, his head lowered. Out of the corner of his eye, he saw Missy approach him. "Here, Mr. David, why don't you hold your baby." She held out his son and he carefully took him and placed him on his shoulder. "Yes, thank you," he said, stepping into the hallway and away from the nursery.

"Mr. David, you've finally come to see your son," Jane said, as she walked up to him.

"Missy is the wet nurse?"

"Yes. I knew she had just birthed a baby five months ago and needed a place to stay. You told me that I had to get someone quickly."

"Yes, but. . .well, I suppose that can't be helped now."

The baby gurgled and cooed on his shoulder. Smells and sounds suggested that he had filled his diaper, so he handed him to Jane and returned to keep vigil beside his wife.

59

Caroline attempted to open her eyes. It felt like her eyelids were made of lead or as if someone was holding them shut. *Please, Lord, help me to open my eyes.* Her entire body hurt and it seemed like every ounce of energy had been drained from her.

She finally managed to lift her eyelids partway and found herself staring at the ceiling of David's room. The oil lamp was turned down, but there was enough light to see her surroundings.

Where is my baby?

Something heavy was on her right hand, but her head was like an immovable rock. When finally she was able to move her head, she saw that David's head was lying there, the rest of his body in a chair beside the bed. She pulled her hand from under his head and caressed his face. It was rough with several days' worth of stubble, practically a beard. His curly hair was disheveled.

Immediately, he sat up. "Caroline," he whispered. His red, moist eyes brightened.

"Baby," she tried to mouth.

"What?" He leaned closer to her face.

Her tongue felt thick and she had to swallow twice before she could get the word out.

"Ba. . .by," she whispered, slightly more pronounced.

"The baby is fine. He's in the nursery with Jane and the. . ."

"How long have I. . ." she whispered.

"Five days."

She softly wept, as she lacked the energy to cry more loudly.

"Shhh. You're going to be fine now." He pushed the hair off her face and kissed her forehead.

"Name." Her eyes had a faraway expression.

"Name? You mean of our son?"

She nodded.

"John Liam. I hope that is acceptable."

She mouthed, "Yes." She began to shiver, her teeth chattering.

"Just a moment. I'll get you another blanket."

Within a few seconds, he was laying a woolen blanket on top of her quilt. She continued to tremble.

"I'll put a few more logs in the fireplace. It is rather cool in here."

She closed her eyes and listened to him throwing logs onto the fire, then clapping his hands of the dirt. His footsteps grew closer. He lifted up the blankets then crawled in beside her. Her breathing slowed and in a few minutes, she stopped shaking.

"Love. . .you," she whispered, her eyes still closed.

"Caroline, I love you so much." His words became soft, quiet sobs.

She opened her eyes , turned slightly toward him and leaned her head against his chest. Caroline slowly lifted her hand to his face and wiped his tears.

"I was so afraid that you would. . ." She put her finger to his mouth to stop him from continuing.

"I'm going to be fine," she whispered.

"Yes."

Caroline's stomach began to make noises. "Hungry."

"Of course. I'll wake Jane up and she'll prepare something for you." He checked his pocket watch. "It's 5:00 in the morning. Soon time for her to wake."

She shook her head. "Don't."

He ignored her and rushed out the door. Within minutes, the servant stood by her bed.

"Miss Caroline, I'm so happy to see you awake. Now, I don't mind one bit getting you something to eat. Would you like to try some consommé?"

She nodded.

Later than morning, Caroline sat up in bed as Jane spoon fed her some beef consommé.

"Just one more spoonful and you'll get to see your baby."

"I'm afraid I can't take anymore, Jane."

"You've only had about four spoonfuls."

"I'm sorry."

David stopped shaving and stood near her bed. "You've done a splendid job. That's a good start."

"I need to feed our baby."

"No, Caroline," he paused. "We've gotten someone for him."

She shook her head. "But I ought to feed him."

His eyes reached out in a tender attempt to comfort her. "You can't, Caroline. The doctor says that you're too weak."

Her eyes filled with tears at the thought of her baby who was now being suckled from another woman's breasts.

"Don't worry. He's being taken care of. You need to worry about getting better."

"I want to see him. Please bring him to me and I want to see Kathleen too."

"Allow me to finish shaving."

There was a knock followed by Jane opening the door. "Mr. David? Mr. Edward and Miss Elizabeth are here."

"Send them in."

Uncle Edward and Elizabeth approached Caroline's bed. In her cousin's hands was a large box.

"Well, my dear," Uncle said, "I suppose you don't remember, but Elizabeth and I visited a few days ago."

"Carrie, I was sick with worry for you."

"I'm sorry I gave you both such a scare."

"Your husband over there is the one who was the most worried," Uncle said, as he leaned down and kissed the top of her head.

"Carrie, I crocheted this quilt for you. I wasn't sure whether you would have a girl or boy, so I made it green and white." Elizabeth opened up the box to show Caroline.

"It's lovely and I shall treasure it."

Uncle turned to David. "You're also looking much better today."

"It could be because I am in the process of removing four days' growth of beard."

"Carrie, have you seen your new son? He is the most beautiful baby boy I have ever laid my eyes on!"

"No, not yet."

"I intend to bring the baby in a few moments," David offered.

Another knock at the door and Jane's voice called out, "Mr. David, Dr. Mayfield is here. Shall I send him in?"

"Yes, of course."

Caroline cringed. She felt awkward around Dr. Mayfield and dreaded an examination by a male physician.

"We must be leaving and allow you to rest. Come, Elizabeth."

"Of course, Papa. Carrie, I shall come back tomorrow and play a card game with you. Would that be fine with you?"

"Yes, Lizzie. I should like that very much."

Uncle and Elizabeth passed Dr. Mayfield as he entered the room. He nodded, then removed his hat. Caroline forced a smile as she looked at him.

"Mrs. O'Donovan, you're looking much better than you did just a few days ago." He stood by the bed and deposited his satchel on the chair. He removed the blanket from her and lifted her nightgown. She turned her head away from him and tensed her body as his hands kneaded her abdomen, listened to her heartbeat and felt her pulse. When he pulled her nightgown down and covered her, she exhaled and looked up. Dr. Mayfield approached David on the other side of the room. He spoke in a hushed tone.

"Remember what I said. . .you can't. . .your wife's weak. . .she can't. . ." She watched as David nodded and answered, "Yes, Doctor. I understand."

"Doctor?" Caroline called.

He turned to face her.

"What are you saying to my husband? I heard 'wife.'"

"No need to worry about what I said. I will leave that to your husband."

Caroline lowered her head.

"Well, good day, Mrs. O'Donovan. Make sure you take the eating slowly, but keep it constant. You need to regain your strength."

After he left, Caroline stared at her husband. He was toweling the shaving cream remnants off his face.

"David?"

"Yes?"

"What was the doctor whispering about?"

"I have a gift for you, Caroline."

"A gift?"

David walked to his bedside table, picked up the small box and handed it to Caroline.

"We must continue the O'Donovan tradition."

She opened the box and gasped at the pearl cameo pin. "David, it's beautiful."

"I'll have it engraved with the date this week."

"Thank you. It's lovely."

"And, of course, you want to see the baby, don't you?"

"Yes, David, please."

I must remember to ask what the doctor said to him.

Within a few minutes, David brought their son to her.   "He's a fine strapping fellow, Mama."   He laid the baby beside her on the bed and she gazed down at his sleeping form.

"He's beautiful."

"He is, isn't he?"

"I should. . .be feeding him," she whispered.

"I know, but we've already discussed why you can't."

Her gaze lowered and focused on the soft breathing sounds of their child. "I feel so useless."

"Useless? Caroline, that's far from the truth. You need to get well so that you can take care of our baby. He won't even remember this time."

"Or the woman who is nursing him now?"

"Absolutely not."

"Who is the woman you've employed as a wet nurse?"

"It's. . .well, it's. . .Missy."

"She's married now?"

"No, but she has a baby and was available and could nurse our son."

"I see."   Caroline felt awkward as she recalled David and Missy in the henhouse. She shuddered and tried to banish the thought.

"David?"

"Yes?"

"What did the doctor tell you?'

"Look, our son has dark hair like me."

"Yes, he does."

"He can cry longer and louder than any baby I've ever heard."

Caroline didn't respond. Instead, she studied him as he avoided eye contact with her. "What did the doctor say to you?"

He cleared his throat and said, "This son of ours is much bigger than Kathleen was."

Caroline did not respond, instead fixing her gaze on her husband's face.

He appeared to be studying the baby, then he quickly glanced at her face. She was frowning at him.

"This is not really the. . ."

"David, please." He paused for several awkward moments.

"Very well. He said that it was my job to ensure that you did not become. . .with. . .child for at least two years, to allow you to fully recover."

"What do you mean ensure?"

"That I was to make sure I did not. . .we did not. . .share the marriage bed."

"Oh." Her head lowered and she fixed her gaze on her child sleeping beside her.

"Does that mean that we can't actually share a bed either?"

"Most probably, Caroline. I'm not sure if I could be trusted to not. . .well, as you know, if you're lying next to me as I'm waking. . ."

"Isn't there something else we could do?"

"Like what?"

"I don't know."

"Until then, please just get well."

"I suppose you want your bed back."

His eyebrows raised and his mouth curved in a smile.

"Absolutely not. I would much rather you sleep in it for the duration of your illness. I would gladly sleep in this chair next to you as long as it takes for you to get well again."

Small cooing sounds and the beginning of a quiet cry caused her to gaze down at her baby. Caroline wanted so much to pick him up and put him to her breast, but she lacked the energy to do so.

She touched the baby's soft, warm cheeks. He instinctively turned his head and opened his mouth. Caroline's heart ached when she realized what he was trying to do.

"Miss Caroline," Jane said from the doorway. "Shall I take the baby to the wet nurse now?"

Caroline nodded, a defeated, sad gesture as Jane gently lifted the baby from the bed. She stared, unfocused, as the servant walked out of the room with her baby.

"Caroline?"

She turned toward her husband, now sitting on the side of her bed. He lifted up her hand and kissed it.

"Two years, David? Two years of sleeping apart?"

"You've lost a lot of blood. The doctor told me that you need two years to recover from this. If you became with child before that time and had a difficult birth, your body would not have the strength to fight it, like you did this time."

She remained silent.

"Caroline, listen to me." He lifted up her chin so that she could look directly at him. "I would gladly give up that entire part of our marriage just to have you healthy. Kathleen and John need you. And so do I. Do you understand what I'm saying?"

"I'm finding it difficult to believe that you're the same person as the David O'Donovan I first met."

"I'm not. And that's why you love me, isn't it?"

She nodded.

"Caroline, I love you for you, not for what we experience in the marriage bed. And I am willing to give that up for as long as is necessary."

* * *

Several hours later, Caroline heard her daughter's squeals. "Mama, Mama!" Kathleen exclaimed as she jumped on the bed.

"Now, Miss Kathleen, you can't be jumping on your Mama's bed. She's been very sick and you got to be gentle with her."

At Jane's comment, Kathleen stopped jumping and slowly crawled in beside her mother, who was sitting up in the bed. Kathleen leaned affectionately toward her mother. Her daughter gazed at her so tenderly that Caroline almost cried. "Mama, I missed you. I wanted to come in here but Jane said no."

"I know, Sweet, and I've missed you too."

"You're white, Mama," she said, then with one finger softly stroked her mother's pale cheek.

Caroline took hold of her small hand and kissed it. "What do you think of your brother?"

"Oh, I like him. He cries a lot, like Papa."

Her high-pitched chatter caused Caroline's heart to become

heavy with emotion, especially at the thought of David sobbing.

"Miss Caroline, you need to be eating again. Let me make something that you really like. What shall I make for you?"

"Do you have any more consommé, Jane?"

"Yes, I do, Miss Caroline. Jane's consommé coming up. Come, Miss Kathleen, let your Mama rest." The servant held her hand out for the child.

"No, Jane. Want to stay with Mama."

"Now, now, Miss Kathleen. . ."

"Kathleen, Mama does feel tired and I require a lot of rest."

Kathleen gave her a kiss on the cheek. "I'll be back soon, Mama."

"Yes, Sweet. I hope so." When Jane and Kathleen left the room, Caroline slid down in the bed until she was lying flat, then closed her eyes.

She roused when she heard the door quietly open, then close. Soft footsteps came toward the far side of the bed where she was lying. She smiled inside. She heard David pull the chair close to the bed and felt him pick her hand up to kiss it. Caroline drowsily opened her eyes.

"I'm sorry, Caroline. I didn't mean to wake you."

"I was just resting my eyes." She breathed in deeply. "I must be an awful sight, David. Kathleen said my skin looks very white."

"Well, love, it does. You've been very sick."

"And my hair must look dreadful."

"Actually, your hair is beautiful. You are beautiful."

David wore a wide smile. He leaned down and picked up a book from the floor.

"What do you have there, David?"

"A book. I would like to read to you."

"Really? Which book? One of mine?"

"No, no. It's actually one of Lee's."

"That's wonderful. What's it called?"

"The Life and Adventures of Nicholas Nickleby. It was in the study downstairs. You haven't read it, have you?"

"No, I haven't. How delightful!"

"Shall we begin?"

"Yes, please."

"There once lived, in a sequestered part of the county of Devonshire, one Mr. Godfrey Nickleby: a worthy gentleman, who, taking it into his head rather late in life that he must get married, and not being young enough or rich enough to aspire to the hand of a lady of fortune, had wedded an old flame out of mere attachment, who in her turn had taken him for the same reason. Thus two people who cannot afford to play cards for money, sometimes sit down to a quiet game for love."

David was speaking in a Britsh accent, an excellent imitation, and his animated recitation was amusing. In fact, he had such a beautiful voice and convincing accent, she wondered whether he had ever considered joining a theater group.

"David?"

"Yes?"

"When you retire from your mercantile business, perhaps you should consider a new occupation?"

"Oh?"

"Yes."

"And what occupation would that be?"

"An actor in the theater."

He smirked at her, then winked. He started reading again, same animated voice, same accent. For the next half hour, she was thoroughly entertained. Soon, however, she began to close her eyes.

"It's fine if you wish to rest."

"But I don't want to miss the story, David."

"I'll read to you when you wake. For now, it will be sufficient for me to simply be with you."

A knock at the door and Jane's voice called, "Mr. David?"

"Yes, Jane, come in."

"Do you want me to move Miss Caroline to her own bed now?"

"That's not necessary."

"But you haven't had sleep in over a week, what with the baby coming, then Miss Caroline being so sick."

"Jane's right, David."

"Caroline."

"It's selfish for me to want to remain here any longer."

"And besides, I'm going to give you a refreshing sponge bath,

Miss Caroline. That'll make you feel much better."

"Very well, then, Jane, you may move me to my room. David, you will visit me often, won't you?"

"Of course, I will, Caroline."

60

David stared at his wife as she studied the board and chess pieces on the small table between them in the parlor. He enjoyed watching her eyes sweep from piece to piece as she contemplated different moves. During the first few weeks after John's birth, he taught her how to play chess and she had become quite an apt student. He recalled their initial conversation.

"Caroline, it's important for you to anticipate your opponent's moves."

"My opponent?"

"Yes. Well, in this case, that would be me."

"You're my opponent?"

"Yes, that is, when we're playing chess."

"Calling you my opponent reminds me of our initial relationship."

"Indeed."

Chess became their favorite activity together during her convalescence. He found it more difficult to anticipate her moves, as she became proficient at guessing his strategies. He knew that she was intelligent, and he found it entertaining to watch her focused concentration.

Her hand hovered over one of her few remaining pawns. She seemed to realize that if she moved it one space forward, his rook would capture it so she withdrew it. She moved her hand above her bishop, then took it away when she likely figured out that doing so would expose her queen unnecessarily. She sighed and David's heart quickened. How was it that a simple game could make him want her so? He let out his own sigh and she looked up at him.

"I'm sorry I'm taking so long, David. I don't suppose I have any moves left."

"You have two."

Caroline raised her eyebrows and shrugged her shoulders.

She studied the board again, pursing her lips in concentration. After a few moments, her mouth opened in a wide yawn. "I'm too tired. Perhaps we can continue tomorrow?"

"Of course. I ought not to be keeping you up late."

Caroline gazed at him across the board. He leaned over the pieces to place a soft gentle kiss on her lips. As he pulled away, she whispered, "I love you."

"And I love you." *This is difficult, Lord.* "Come, I'll take you upstairs." David turned off the gas sconces in the parlor, then took hold of his wife's hand. They walked upstairs in silence. Despite her weakness, she squeezed his hand so hard that it seemed as if the blood in his fingers stopped flowing.

At the top of the steps, they turned and passed the closed door of the nursery. Soft whimpers caused them both to stare at the door as they heard Missy soothing baby John.

Caroline released his hand and pressed her ear to the door. Their baby was fussing and Missy was saying "Shhh." In a few seconds, their son became quiet.

"Come." David took hold of her hand and led her toward her room. She resisted and stood silent, facing the door. "Caroline?"

Her sad expression made him want to cry for her. He gathered her into his arms. He could tell that she wanted to cry, but instead she clung to him.

He knew that, despite her fatigue and weakness, she did not want to go to bed alone. Of course, he did not want to face his room alone either. For several long moments, they embraced, holding on to one another.

He kissed the top of her head.

"This is hard, David."

"I know."

"Not just going to bed alone, but. . .John is. . ."

"I know what you mean."

"My baby wants her most of the time."

"That will end in a few months. John will soon take milk."

"And he will cry when she's gone."

"But she'll be leaving soon. I promise you that." David said it to comfort her, but he knew that it would make this whole situation less awkward for him as well. Having Missy around, someone with whom he had history, was unpleasant, to say the least.

Thankfully, she rarely ventured outside the nursery or kitchen.

Especially now during this period of celibacy, Missy and Hallie tempted him like those old French postcards he used to keep in his drawer. Although he had disposed of the postcards, he couldn't tell every woman he had ever been with to stay away from him.

"Good night, Caroline. " He kissed the top of her head.

"Good night, David. I love you," she replied, as she closed the door.

61

In front of the Martin household, David bid his wife farewell as he prepared to leave.

"Thank you for driving me to my uncle's house." Caroline held her sleeping baby in her arms.

"It's my pleasure, Caroline." He lifted Kathleen down from the carriage. "I'm going to be about three hours in the city. You'll be fine here with your cousin?"

"Of course. Where is Lizzie, Patsie?"

"Ye know how she is, Miss Caroline. She'll be late fer her own wake, she will that."

David leaned forward and kissed his wife's cheek.

"'Bye, Papa."

"'Bye, Kat. You be a good girl for Mama."

"I'm always good."

"Yes, of course, you are."

He kissed the top of baby John's head, still in Caroline's arms, then climbed into the carriage. As he was riding away, Elizabeth ran onto the front porch.

"Did I miss David again?"

"Yes, Miss 'Lizabeth. Whatever were ye doin' then?"

"I only had a few stitches left on my needlepoint project. I thought I'd have enough time."

"Don't worry," Caroline offered. "You will be able to see him when he returns to pick us up, Lizzie."

"Miss Caroline, if ye don't be mindin', I'll be takin' the babe from ye. It'd be givin' an old woman like meself a great deal of pleasure ta be holdin' a foin wee lad so young."

"Of course, Patsie."

"I cannot believe how quickly Kathleen is growing," Elizabeth said as she hugged her cousin.

"Look, Auntie 'Lizabeth, I picked these for you!" Kathleen held up a bunch of dandelions.

"Oh, my, they are beautiful. We'll get Patsie to put them in some water."

"Where's Uncle Edward, Lizzie?"

"He'll be back within the hour. He said he had some business in town." She paused. "Come, let's go inside."

Patsie held on tight to little John and motioned for everyone to move into the parlor. "Miss Caroline, sure an' this babe is doin' a lot o' sleepin'. It must be feelin' good ta be gettin' out o' the house, after bein' cooped up fer so many months."

"Yes, Patsie, it is. And Missy has finally left. The baby's eating other foods and the doctor said we could give him milk now that he's nearly eight months old."

"That's a foin thing, sure, it musta been busy, what with two babes bein' in the house, yers an' Missy's?"

"Well, yes, but we hardly saw little Will at all since he's a quiet baby, never fussed." Caroline paused. "But I must say, it feels good to have John all to myself."

"Ta yerself?"

Caroline nodded. "John had really become attached to Missy. He's been crying a lot the last few days because he's not nursing any longer. It doesn't seem to matter that I'm his mother, though. I'm finding it difficult to soothe him."

"Niver ye be worryin' 'bout that, Miss Caroline. It'll pass."

"Mama, Mama, can Auntie 'Lizabeth take me for a walk? Please, please, Mama?"

Caroline looked at Elizabeth to gauge her reaction. Her eyebrows were raised waiting for Caroline to answer.

"Is that all right?"

"Of course it is. It's not often that I'm able to take you for a walk, Kathleen."

"Hooray!" Kathleen squealed, then skipped out of the parlor, Elizabeth following close behind.

"Miss Caroline, would ye be mindin' if I was ta be goin' home with ya? Himself is sayin' I could be havin the night off ta visit with me Jane."

"Of course, Patsie, that would be fine."

A short while later, Elizabeth and Kathleen returned.

"Mama, Mama, I'm back. Auntie 'Lizabeth and I went for a walk and we saw a pretty red fox, 'cept he wasn't really red, he was more brown." Smiling at her daughter, Caroline responded, "Well, that must've been quite exciting."

"Carrie, you need to find other children for Kathleen to play with. She can't grow up only playing with a servant's child."

"There's certainly nothing wrong with her playing with Isaac, Lizzie."

"No, no, I'm not saying that, but you need to make sure she has some. . .well, you know, upper class friends. Kathleen's four years old now and she needs to be around. . .well, proper young ladies."

"She's four, not 14. I think there is plenty of time for that sort of affiliation later."

Her cousin shook her head.

* * *

Later that day, on the veranda at the O'Donovan house, Caroline swayed back and forth in an attempt to calm down baby John.

"You want me to take the baby, Miss Caroline?" asked Jane.

"I need to become accustomed to this now with Missy gone."

"Of course."

Amidst the baby's screams, Caroline watched with interest as David played with Kathleen. "You can't catch me, Papa!" David pretended to be running as fast as he could, yet it seemed that Kathleen was always able to escape.

The baby eventually settled and began to drift off to sleep.

"Miss Caroline, I'll take the baby and put him in his crib, if you want to join in the game."

"Very well, Jane." She carefully placed him in Jane's arms.

Caroline stood before David who had finally caught up to Kathleen, who was now on the ground, rolling around.

"May I play this game, too?"

David looked up at her with raised eyebrows and a half smile.

"Of course, Mama."

He pulled her down to a sitting position on the ground. For a moment, his eyes were fixed on hers, regarding her with an expression of near reverence.

"Mama, play," they heard Kathleen say.

David kissed Caroline's cheek, then slowly moved to her lips.

Caroline so relished the feeling of his lips on hers, but within a few seconds, he stopped and whispered, "I miss our nights together."

"And I do as well."

"Papa, this is no fun anymore."

"I'm sorry, Kat. I was just showing Mama how much I love her."

"Well, you kiss me too, 'cause you love me."

He pulled her to a loving embrace and kissed her small cheek. "You are certainly right about that."

"I think Jane is preparing our favorite dinner, David."

"Ah, perfect, fried chicken and biscuits?"

"I believe so. I wanted to make sure she cooks your favorite vegetable."

"Potatoes and lots of them?"

She nodded then kissed him lightly on the lips. "I'll be back in a moment."

Caroline walked across the lawn and alongside the house to the back door leading into the kitchen in the basement. She stopped just outside the open door when she heard Patsie's loud voice.

"Now then, Jane, ye got to be after tellin' Kip ta be pullin' it out, or I'm tellin' ye, it's a baby ev'ry year fer ye."

"Now, Ma, I don't know about that. All the time I nursed Isaac I didn't get my monthly so I don't expect I'll be having a baby every year."

"Sure, when I was married to yer Da, God rest his soul, and after I was done havin' ye, I was so sick, I'm tellin' ye, with the sept'cemia, sure ye know, I almost met me Maker, I did. I'm tellin' ye we was so scared after that, wel. . .then yer Da always. . .well, ye know, always came out. . .well, he always, as me old ma used ta be sayin', if ye don't be wantin' butter, sure then ye best be pullin' the dasher out in time."

Caroline couldn't hear Jane's response, if any.

"Sure then it worked, I'm tellin' ye. It worked. We niver had no more babes after ye." There was silence for a moment or two. "Sure then yer Da died when ye were but six, an' ye were bein' all I had, no other little ones. When he was gone, I was after, ye know, regrettin' that ye didn't have no sisters or brothers."

The two women remained silent for a moment.

"'course, there's always. . .a riding coat."

"A riding coat?" She heard Jane ask.

"Sure. The man uses it on his. . ."

"Ma, I think I've heard enough."

Caroline waited a few moments before entering the kitchen. Jane and Patsie were peeling potatoes.

"Jane, you're making David's favorite?"

"Mashed potatoes, Miss Caroline."

"That's fine. Are you having a good visit?"

"Why, sure we are, Miss Caroline. Ye must be knowin' that we always have a good visit, Jane an' me an' me wee grandson."

"Yes, yes, I certainly know that." She returned to the front of the house. She paused and watched David and Kathleen continuing to run around on the front lawn. Speaking of such intimate matters seemed to come so naturally to Patsie. And what Patsie had said to her daughter made some sense to Caroline. She decided that she would speak to David about the conversation she overheard.

Later that evening, Caroline, dressed in a nightgown and bed robe, stood outside David's bedroom door. Kathleen and John were fast asleep and she wasn't sure when she would get another opportunity to speak with him.

She reached her hand out to knock on his door, then pulled it back. The light and moving shadows beneath the door confirmed that he was awake.

She again reached her hand out to rap on the door, this time, knocking three quiet times.

"Yes?"

"David, it's me."

Within a few seconds, he opened the door, his shirt unbuttoned to the waist and his pants loosely pulled on.

"Is something wrong?" he asked.

She slowly walked in, pulling her silk robe tight around her middle. She closed the door, then leaned up to kiss him, a long lingering kiss. He started to respond, then broke away from her.

"Caroline, please. This is difficult for me."

"And for me as well." She fixed her eyes on the floor. "But I love you. . .and we are married."

"And you almost died after John's birth. We need to wait so that you can fully recover."

A glint of metal caught Caroline's eyes and for a few seconds, she stared at the silver medal and chain around David's neck. She reached out and took hold of it and squinted to read the writing. "What is this?"

"A St. Jude medal. I've been having a particularly difficult time with. . . not being able to engage in. . . In any event, Father Flaherty gave this to me. St. Jude is the patron saint of impossible causes. Father recommended that I pray to St. Jude when I'm having difficulties."

"Like when your wife comes to your room and kisses you as only a wife should?"

"Yes, and when. . ."

He was interrupted by the distant sounds of baby John wailing.

"Just a minute, David. I must attend to John."

At the door to the nursery, Jane was rocking the baby. "I'll take him, Jane."

"Very well. I think he's cutting a tooth."

Caroline returned with the baby, rocking and swaying him back and forth. His high-pitched screams pierced the silence of the house.

"Miss Caroline, are you sure you don't want me to take him?" she could hear Jane say from behind her.

"Give him to me," David said to his wife, "you still need your rest at night." Then to Jane he said, "You may go back to bed."

"Of course, Mr. David."

Caroline carefully placed the child in David's arms. He laid the baby over one shoulder and began to hum and gently move back and forth.

John's screams soon became whimpers. In a few moments, the baby had settled.

"David?"

"Yes?"

"I. . .happened to overhear a conversation that Patsie and Jane were having."

"About what?"

"About preventing a woman from. . .being with child."

David's eyes darkened. He continued to gently sway back and forth, lulling John back to sleep.

"She said, well, that you could. . .well, come out before you
. . ."

He shook his head. "That doesn't always work, Caroline," he
said, his voice now with a hard edge to it. "And it's wrong. You
know, in the Bible, in the book of Genesis, there's a man named
Onan. . ."

"I'm familiar with Onan."

"Then you know that he was called upon, quite coincidental-
ly, to unite with his sister-in-law after his brother died, so that his
dead brother would have heirs. Well, he didn't want the children
to be considered his brother's, so, as the Bible says, he 'spilled his
seed.' And the Lord killed him.

"Caroline, if I did that, it would mean that I would be with-
holding a part of myself, and I can't do that."

All of a sudden, the whole passage in Genesis became more
clear to Caroline. And how was it that they had never discussed
this particular passage in their nighttime readings and discussions
of the Bible? It seemed ironic to her that she hadn't fully understood that story in all these years.

He was standing near her, the baby still in his arms. The
sight of him showing such tenderness and patience to their son
filled her heart with overwhelming affection and joy. She wished
that she could unite with him, to feel him close to her.

"You can't begin to know how difficult this is for me,
Caroline." He paused. "I lie in bed at night and ache for you, to
simply be beside you, to become one with you. It's not just at night
that I have. . . difficulties." Baby John began to fuss and whimper.

"Shhh." He started to hum, then stopped. "Caroline, we are
one whether or not we are sharing a bed. In fact, our union has
more integrity now than if we became intimate and I 'spilled my
seed.'" David continued rocking back and forth, the baby asleep on
his shoulder. He turned to her, his expression loving and tender,
but firm. "When we begin sharing our marriage bed again, I want
to be able to give my entire body to you, without reservation."

Caroline studied her husband, in awe of the transformation
he had experienced in a few short years.

"I don't want to return to the life I used to live, Caroline. I
was not truly free, but a slave to sin. I had no self-control. Now,

I do. I promised to keep you from being with child, no matter how difficult."

"But can we still be close?"

"Close? We are close. We talk, sometimes for hours at a time. We play chess, we go to the art museum, discuss Holy Scripture. I know how much you love me and that's worth more to me than sharing our bed.

"Caroline, this is difficult for me, more than you can ever know. But there isn't any other option right now. And you're still tired and weak most of the time."

"I'm much better. I can now make it through the day with minimal napping."

Still holding baby John, David leaned down and kissed her lightly on the forehead. "I never believed I would have — could have enough self-control. A real man loves his wife enough to protect her." His voice was measured and confident. "I would never, ever use you for a moment of pleasure."

"Good night, David." As she faced him, baby John still sleeping on his shoulder, he looked at her with such tenderness and love. Caroline knew that she couldn't ask for anything else in a spouse. And for that, she was truly thankful.

62

David pretended to be listening carefully as Edward Martin rambled on about money markets and other financial commodities. He nodded every so often to give the impression that he was being attentive and, certainly, Edward was family and David did not want to be impolite. It was a dull conversation, to be sure, and he was thankful for the boredom, although it would have been better if Edward's drab discourse actually distracted him.

It had now been a year since John was born and Caroline nearly died: over a year without sexual intimacy and no release except for the occasional night dream. The past two weeks had been especially torturous for him. It was difficult enough when Caroline was weak and convalescing. Now that she was stronger, it was becoming increasingly arduous for him.

To make matters worse, he had been having dreams, which he would not necessarily classify as nightmares but they were of a most sensual, erotic sort, filled with images from his past intimate experiences. He woke up many nights unable to breathe.

"Last year, I invested $500, and at the end of the year, I had made nearly $200 more. " Uncle Edward took the last puff of his cigar. "And with little or no risk."

David nodded, forcing a smile. "Well done, sir."

"David," he said, "I suppose I should find Elizabeth and we ought to be returning home." Uncle Edward stomped his cigar out in the ashtray beside him, then both men stood up.

"Yes, of course."

David waited at the doorway to allow Edward to proceed ahead of him into the foyer. The clock was letting out a chime for the quarter hour. Elizabeth and Caroline were standing just inside the parlor doorway.

"Papa, are we leaving already?"

"Yes, Elizabeth. It's getting late." He glanced at his pocket watch. "It's 10:15 and I have some work to do."

"But it's Sunday, Papa. It's supposed to be a day of rest."

"I know, but I need to prepare some papers for tomorrow and your cousin needs to retire."

"Thank you, Uncle. But I don't appear to need as much sleep these days. I seem to be almost back to my normal self."

"That's good, my dear. But we really do need to be leaving."

The two said their goodbyes and left.

"I'm going upstairs to bed. Good night, David." She kissed his cheek and when she stepped back, she regarded him with tender affection.

He forced himself to look away from her, at the ceiling, at the floor, anything but her. His pulse was racing. His mind thought about how they used to lie together in bed, their bodies touching, skin to skin, satisfied. "Goodnight, Caroline," he managed to whisper, now glancing up at her face. She was just looking away from him, then she turned and quickly climbed the stairs.

When she was out of sight, he let out a sigh that was as long as a sentence. "One more year. How am I going to do this? Please, please help me." Then he listened as a dark voice whispered into his consciousness. *She's your wife, you deserve to have her. Besides, you can withdraw before you've finished. She won't become with child and you will have your release. And no one needs to know.* "Yes," he answered the voice, "that's what Onan thought and I know what happened to him."

He shook his head to rid himself of the voice. *God, give me the grace to resist the temptation.* David returned to the study, extinguished the lamps and went upstairs.

* * *

Caroline placed the book on her bedside table. She had been having trouble sleeping over the last night or so, although John, now a year old, was waking less frequently at night. Perhaps now she no longer required so much rest.

She recalled her goodnight kiss to David earlier this evening, and it took most of her self-control to leave him standing in the foyer. She could tell that he was having a difficult time. She knew him well enough to know that he would have liked nothing better than to carry her up to his room. Recently, there were times when he had been snappy and short with her, no doubt stemming from the tension he was experiencing. But they had succeeded in abstaining from the marital act for more than a year now. Not only had they survived the experience, their relationship, for the most part, was flourishing. It just didn't include physical intimacy.

She tried to sleep for nearly half an hour before she finally got up and pulled on her robe and slippers. Taking the lamp from her bureau, she went into the hallway. She passed Kathleen's room, her door open slightly, and she could hear her daughter's loud breathing.

At her son's room, she listened at the closed door, but could not hear John. She turned the knob slowly. The door's quiet creaking stopped her from opening it wider. Faint moonlight streamed in through the window and landed like a square on the floor beside his crib. Holding the lamp up, she watched his small leg move and heard him sucking his thumb. Small reassurances, but now satisfied, Caroline quietly shut the door, endeavoring to minimize its creak and click. She waited for a minute or so to ensure that she hadn't woken him up.

I'll just slip down the back staircase and into the kitchen for a cup of tea. Passing by David's door, sounds of moaning stopped her from moving on. Caroline pressed her ear against the door and listened. *He's having a nightmare.* Pushing the door open, she held the light up and could see him sleeping on his back, chin facing the ceiling, mouth open.

Caroline set the lamp down on David's dresser and stood beside him. "Shhh," she softly said, reaching her hand out to caress his head. He bolted upright. Caroline gasped. "David, are you all right?"

"Yes, I. . ."

"I heard you from the hallway."

For a moment, she stood silent and unmoving. He appeared to be attempting to catch his breath but he was avoiding eye contact. When he finally brought his eyes to hers, she recognized his expression of desire. Her mind knew that she ought to return to her own room, but her heart admitted that her longing, her need, was bursting at the seams too. And it had been so long.

She cleared her throat and sat down beside him on the bed.

"Caroline," he said, his voice low and raspy.

"Yes, David, I'm your wife and I. . .love. . ."

He cut her off with a kiss that let loose a year and a half of denial. She welcomed it: his taste, his being, his entire self. Within moments, they became lost in each other's arms, beginning to surrender to all of their desires and needs. Just one night. One night to ease the waiting. One brief. . .

Abruptly, David stopped and jumped from the bed. He stood near the fireplace, the catch of his breath the only sound in the room. Caroline sat up and pulled her robe on.

He turned slowly and walked toward her. "I had every intention of. . ."

"I know. Me as well."

"I can't believe I was going to, and that you were going to. . ."

"Yes, David. It's been over a year and a half. It would only be once."

"I made a vow to protect you, Caroline. And I was about to break that vow."

She lowered her head and remained silent.

"Come here," he said as he pulled her to his chest. He lifted his head toward the crucifix on the wall above his bed and made the Sign of the Cross.

"Almighty Father," he prayed, "Give us Thy grace to be strong." Her head on his chest, she listened to the beating of his heart.

63

Caroline admired the green dress in the shop's window. She tilted her head and studied the gown with its intricately embroidered black thread pattern in the bodice and subtle design in the skirt. It was finely made and would be ideal for Christmas Mass in two and a half months. However, she already owned far too many dresses and this purchase would merely be an indulgence.

She heard a toddler squeal and turned to watch the little girl with her mother. Caroline so infrequently left her children at home and when she did, it was often with Jane, who was like a second mother to them. Today Jane had been insistent on traveling to downtown Philadelphia so Caroline had decided to accompany her.

She had arranged with Jane to meet in front of the new location of Wanamaker's Department Store at one-thirty. It was only one-twenty but Caroline had become disinterested with window shopping and decided to return to the department store earlier.

A half block or so away, she noticed Jane with another woman and, at first, was relieved that Jane was already there so that she would not have to wait. However, as Caroline moved closer to the pair, she recognized the other woman was Missy. She felt awkward, although she wasn't sure why, and stepped back.

Caroline watched the two women from across the street, behind a parked carriage, the horse snorting every few minutes. Occasionally, a horse and buggy would ride by and block her view. As Jane and Missy talked, Missy's son hugged his mother's skirts. Missy seemed much thinner than she remembered her and she looked like she was crying. Her hands were waving as she was speaking to Jane, who was nodding and had a sympathetic expression on her face.

A feeling within urged her to remain hidden for now. Her eyes wandered to young Will, still clutching his mother's skirt.

All of a sudden, the boy pulled away and glanced across the street at Caroline, still standing behind the parked buggy. She lifted up her hand to wave, then drew it back. However, his expression, the way he looked up, seemed familiar to her. He turned and clutched his mother's dress once again.

Missy embraced Jane and quickly rushed across the street. Caroline ducked out of sight, but again, little Will turned around and stared at her. The look on his face was strangely recognizable.

Caroline crossed the street and approached Jane. "Did you tell Missy that you were carrying, Jane?"

"No, Ma'am, I didn't. Missy's not doing very well."

"Yes, she was crying."

"She is. . ."

"Now, Jane, you can tell me."

Jane took a deep breath then began to rub her hands together.

"She helped me by nursing my son. I owe her so much. Is she in trouble or something?"

"No, Ma'am, she's not in trouble. . .well, yes, she is in trouble. She's sick, very sick, and she doesn't know what to do."

"Well, I will help her. It's as simple as that."

"She's got cancer and she's dying."

Caroline gasped. "Oh, no. And poor Will, what a dear little boy he is."

"Yes, Ma'am." Jane stared at Caroline, her servant's mouth formed a straight line, opened as if to speak, then closed again.

"What is it, Jane?"

"I'm just not sure if I should. . ."

"What exactly did Missy ask for? Does she need money?"

"Yes, but I think she's more concerned about what's going to happen to her Will."

"Oh, no. That poor little boy."

"She's not wanting to take him to the orphanage."

"Well, doesn't he have a father? Has she told him of her illness?"

"No, she hasn't, not yet."

"Well, he should do right by her and take his child."

"Yes, I suppose he should, but Missy hasn't. . ."

"Does he even know about Will?"

Jane's head lowered. "No, Ma'am, he doesn't. What I mean is, he doesn't know that Will is his child."

"Do you know this man, Jane?"

She hesitated, then responded,"Yes, I do."

"I suppose it will be quite a shock for him."

"Yes, but it may be a bigger shock to his wife." Jane was looking at her with a strange expression.

"He's married? That's awful. But Missy must let him know and he should do right for the child. Will's his responsibility too."

Jane remained silent and stared at Caroline for a moment, then glanced away. When the servant again looked in Caroline's direction, her expression was filled with anxiety.

"Do you not agree with me, Jane?"

"Well. . ."

"Jane, this whole conversation is making you uncomfortable." Her voice sounded concerned. "You should know that you can discuss anything with me."

"Well, I. . .Will. . .is. . .well, he is. . ."

"Yes?"

"Will is. . ."

"Yes, Jane, Will is quite a beautiful little boy with dark, curly hair. Just like David and John. . ." Caroline stopped. Jane had said that she knew the man who was the father of Will.

The vision of the family portrait in the study and of David, with dark curly hair and a mischievous expression came to her mind. Then the toddler Will's image, the similarity. . . Caroline shook her head. To even think such a preposterous thought would be disloyal to David. She looked at Jane, whose eyebrows were raised, waiting. The servant then shifted her stance and avoided eye contact.

"What is wrong, Jane? Why are you acting in such a manner?"

"I don't know what to say, Ma'am."

"Why are you. . ." Caroline bit down on her lip. Was it possible? Caroline couldn't think it. No, it couldn't be true. "Will's father, could it be. . ." Jane's eyes widened. There would only be one reason Jane could be acting so peculiar.

"Oh, no, Jane. Is. . .David . .Will's. . .father?"

"I don't know what to say."

"You need to tell me the truth." Caroline reached out to grasp Jane's shoulders. Several passers by stared at the two women.

"Please." Caroline was now raising her voice. "I need to know."

Jane nodded. "Yes, Mr. David is the father of Missy's Will."

For a few seconds, Caroline was stunned, her eyes wide and although her mouth was open, no words, nor any rational thoughts could come to her. She was finding it hard to breathe.

"He. . .told me he's been faithful to me," she said with tear-filled eyes.

"It happened while you and Mr. David were courting, before you got married at the Cathedral. That doesn't make it better, but . . ."

"I can't believe it. I can't believe he. . ."

"Mr. David's a good man. Good men make mistakes."

Caroline's eyes were now so clouded with tears, it became difficult for her to see. She stood motionless on the street.

"We need to be getting home. Kip's waiting."

Caroline nodded blankly as she allowed Jane to walk her to the carriage a few blocks away.

The half-hour trip was spent with Caroline sobbing quietly and Jane sitting close to her mistress, awkwardly rubbing her back. As they rode closer to the O'Donovan mansion, Jane whispered to Caroline, "Do you want me to tell Mr. David you don't feel well or are you going to be speaking with him?"

Caroline stared blankly at Jane.

"Missy's needing an answer. She needs to get her Will taken care of as soon as possible."

All at once, the sudden realization that not only had David been unfaithful to her, but now there was a child and they had to discuss whether they would take him in, David's own flesh and blood. She shuddered at the idea of approaching David, of saying anything to him. "I'm not ready to face him yet. I must. . .I need time. Perhaps you can tell him I'm unwell." Caroline used her handkerchief to wipe away her tears.

"Yes, of course, Ma'am."

When they arrived home, Kip assisted Caroline and Jane out of the carriage. Caroline glanced at Kip and he offered her a sympathetic smile. She supposed that Kip and the rest of the servants already knew about this horrid secret.

Caroline nervously scanned the property for any sign of David.

Off in the distance, toward the pond, David and Kathleen were running and allowing little John to chase after them. Hallie was on the veranda with Isaac.

"Tell David I'm not well and that I won't be down for supper. If you could watch the children for me, it would be most appreciated."

"I'd be happy to do that for you."

Caroline ran toward the porch and rushed past Hallie, without acknowledging the servant. "Miss Caroline, are you unwell?" she heard as she hurried up the stairs.

A short while later, Caroline sat on her bed, sobbing. She shoved her fist in her mouth to stop the noise. Her husband had done that most intimate act of marriage with other women before, but Will was just over two years old. This was after he had supposedly changed.

And now there was a child, an innocent little boy, who didn't deserve the fate that was about to befall him. And where will he go? Would David agree to take him in? Could she even take care of Will, knowing that he would be a constant reminder of her husband's unfaithfulness?

A quiet knock at the door made her jerk upright on the bed.

"Caroline, it's me. Jane said you're not feeling well. May I come in?"

"No, David, you may not." Her voice sounded muffled.

A few seconds of silence followed. "What? Did you say no?"

"Yes, I did. Leave me alone. I'm not ready to speak with you."

"What in the world is going on?" The door knob rattled. Caroline threw her handkerchief across the room and stomped to the door and flung it open. David, his eyes wide, stepped back in surprise. "You've been crying," he said, in a soft, tender tone of voice.

She glared at him, making eye contact. "I told you that I'm not ready to speak with you yet!" she yelled at him.

"Not ready?" His eyebrows were raised and he was regarding her with a confused expression.

She shook her head. "But since you insist, come in."

He pulled at his cravat and his eyes darted around the room.

She regarded him bitterly for several moments, keeping her gaze directed at his face. He didn't say anything, but he shifted from side to side, avoiding eye contact. Every few seconds he looked at her face to see her frowning back at him.

"You. . .you told me," she bit her lip to keep it from quivering. "You told me you'd been faithful to me."

All at once, he gasped, and all the color had drained from his normally swarthy face. "What are you talking about, Caroline? You know about my past."

"I'm not talking about your past. I'm talking about when we started courting. After our kiss at the pond."

"What do you mean?"

She allowed a minute of awkward silence to hang in the air. David continued to shift from side to side, sighing every few seconds.

Caroline blurted out, "Missy."

His eyes widened, then he glanced away, avoiding eye contact. "I. . .don't know what to say."

"You told me you'd been faithful."

He now brought his gaze up and stared at her. "I have been faithful since the first day we truly became husband and wife."

"And I'm supposed to believe that now?"

"It's true."

"But you told me you made a vow to God that you wouldn't do that again."

"I know, but she practically. . .you can't imagine how much I have hated myself for it." He paused. "It was a momentary weakness. I had not been with a woman in more than a year."

"Go on."

"I was at the pub and got into a fight and she was there and she helped me to her room. When I came home, I couldn't look at you."

Caroline nodded. "I thought I had done something wrong."

"Just the opposite. I have hated myself for it." He stepped forward and she shook her head. "If you could just find it in your heart to forgive me."

She turned her back on him and folded her arms over her chest.

"I eventually went to Confession and told the priest that I couldn't forgive myself for what I did and he told me that God forgives me and that I should forgive myself. I'm so sorry, Caroline. Please, please forgive me." His voice was cracking and he was stifling back a sob.

Her back facing him, she responded, "I. . .don't know if I. . ."

She could hear him sniffling.

A few silent, uncertain moments crept by. Her husband sighed a few times as if urging her to speak to him. But part of her remained hurt, angry. It took every ounce of self-control she possessed not to pounce at him. Then from the depths of her heart, she remembered. *Will.*

"You have a – Missy has a son, David, your son," she said, turning around to face him.

He gasped. "What?"

"Will, he's your. . .son."

He slumped against the door, silent.

Caroline let herself exhale, unaware that she had been holding her breath. "You told me that you had been faithful."

"Caroline, we weren't truly married yet."

"Please tell me you are not going to defend this."

"No, I'm not. But I love you, Caroline, I. . ."

"Don't. Stop. I don't want to hear that right now."

"I'm sorry, Caroline."

"I'm not ready to forgive you yet. You can't simply say I'm sorry and make everything fine again."

"Well, then I don't know what to say."

"Missy has cancer and she's dying."

"What?"

"The reason Jane wanted to go into the city was to meet with Missy. She's sick and she's dying. She needs money and somebody to take care of Will."

"Oh, no." David was shaking his head.

"David, right now, I really need to be left alone. I don't want to discuss this. I can't." She turned away from him and began to sob quietly.

"Caroline. . ."

"Get out. Leave me alone."

She heard the door open and close.

How could he have been unfaithful? How could he have allowed even a momentary weakness? If he was unfaithful that time, how can I be sure he won't do it again? God, please give me the ability to forgive him. I'm just so angry at him right now.

Caroline collapsed on the bed and pounded the pillow until her fists became red. She held her palm to her chest to quiet her thundering heart. Then, covering her face with her hands, she allowed the tears to flow.

Fatigue finally swept over her and she fell asleep, escaping to her dreams.

"Miss Caroline?" Jane said through her door.

She roused enough to say, "Yes, Jane, what is it?"

Caroline lifted herself off the bed and combed back her hair with her hands before she opened the door. Jane raised her eyebrows in anxious anticipation. "How are you feeling now?"

"My whole world, as I know it, has just fallen apart. I just want to run away."

"Did you and Mr. David talk about. . ."

"No, Jane. I just couldn't speak about it any longer. Thankfully, I fell asleep."

"Please, Miss Caroline, Missy needs an answer as soon as possible."

Caroline kept silent for a moment, then spoke quietly. "Very well. Where is David?"

"I think he's in the nursery reading a story to the children."

Caroline stepped into the hallway and listened. She could hear the distant sound of David's voice several rooms away.

"Perhaps you can allow him to finish the story, then I'll speak with him, here, in my room. That will provide me a few moments to compose myself."

"Yes, fine."

Caroline closed the door. She sat down at her vanity table and stared at her image in the mirror. Her eyes were red and swollen, her complexion pale.

How will I forgive him? She knew about the many women he had bedded before, when he was the old David, but he had supposedly changed. Up until now, she had never doubted his fidelity, never even suspected. Wasn't it enough that she had already forgiven him for past indiscretions? And what about the child? She slammed her fist on the table.

"Caroline, it's me," David said through the closed door.

She took a deep fortifying breath, then another. She bolted up and walked to the door, her hand squeezing the knob but refusing to turn it.

"Are you in there?"

She hesitated for a moment, then opened up the door. He was standing in the hallway, one hand on the door frame, the other about to knock. "Jane said you wanted to speak with me."

She simply nodded and stepped aside to allow him to enter. Once he was in her room, she closed the door. Both remained silent. Caroline tried to form her words carefully.

"I'm trying to figure out what would have caused you to do this."

"I don't know what to say, Caroline. I'm so sorry for hurting you."

"Help me to. . .understand this," she whispered, her eyes watering, her voice trembling.

"I don't understand it myself. I made a mistake. It was hard for me to even forgive myself."

Caroline couldn't think. Her heart was heavy with pain. What else could be said?

They turned their heads toward the closed door and the children's distant laughter beyond it.

"He's. . .your son, David." Caroline said, again her eyes beginning to water. She stared at him, studying his face. His expression was so regretful, so repentant, that despite her anger, her heart began to soften. Caroline's voice was cracking. "This child and our son, they look. . .so much like you."

His gaze lowered and he kept silent.

"What should we do, David? This child, your flesh and blood, needs a home. Missy needs treatment."

"I will pay for her care, whatever the cost."

"I suppose that will be a start." Caroline waited until he made eye contact with her. "He is your son," she whispered.

David looked off in the distance, his eyes unfocused.

"Caroline, I know what my responsibilities are, but what do you think we should do?"

Caroline thought for a moment before answering. David had made a mistake, and whether she liked it or not, Will was his son. As difficult as it would be, she knew there was only one answer. "We should take your child in."

"That's very generous and unselfish of you, Caroline. But do you realize it will be painful for you to have a reminder of my infidelity around day in and day out?"

She hesitated, then quietly said, "Yes."

"I don't want my child to be placed in an orphanage or raised by someone else." David inched closer to her, his expression tender. At that moment, she wanted to say "I forgive you," but the pain was too fresh, too deep and she couldn't imagine it lessening.

"If there is a way for you to forgive me. . . "

She began to weep again and he gathered her into his arms. She didn't resist him, but now clung to him. *Lord, please help me to forgive him.*

64

For David, there was a certain relief that his secret was now in the open. And a child. Deep down, he had suspected that Will might be his son, but he had managed to convince himself otherwise. He tried to forget that whole incident as it would only remind him of what he had done to Caroline. David knew that there was no forgetting, no starting over, only living with the mistakes which are made.

And the way that his wife stared at him, not with detached disdain but with intimate betrayal, remained with him like a second skin.

David was glad that they were not sharing a bed. If they hadn't already been sleeping apart, this revelation would most certainly have meant that Caroline would not share his bed. And who knows if they would ever again share the pleasures and intimacies of the marriage bed. At least now he had had nearly two years of practice at celibacy. Although he still experienced many moments of temptation, he continued to keep his vow of faithfulness.

How would he tell her that the only temptations he felt in the past two years were to share her bed and to unite physically with his wife, the only person in the world he desired?

Some nights, in the soft gray moments before sleep came, he would feel that urge welling up and growing within him, and yet he knew that he could not surrender to it, not yet anyway, for Caroline's safety.

There was a quiet knock at his door, so slight that he wondered whether he had even heard it. A few seconds later, the rapping became more pronounced. David quickly opened the door. Caroline's back was toward him as she stood in the hallway. She slowly turned to face him. She was dressed in a robe.

"I couldn't sleep."

He nodded. He wanted to embrace her, to again take her in his arms and squeeze her until she molded into him. Shaking off the thought, he stepped aside and motioned for her to come into his room.

She glanced at his bed, then lowered her head.

"How did you. . .what caused you to. . ."

"Caroline." He stepped forward and placed his hands on her shoulders. She shook her head and stepped back.

"Don't, David. I. . .I need to know how it happened."

"How it happened?" *How do I explain this to her?* He said nothing for a few moments. Then, from the silence came his voice, almost in a whisper. "My first mistake was taking a drink, becoming complacent, thinking I would only take one.

"In addition," he continued, "I realized that I had become self-righteous, thinking that I was better than everyone else. . ."

"But what made you want a drink in the first place?"

"The dream, or more appropriately, the nightmare."

"What nightmare?"

"I had dreamt twice before that, that you and I were. . .well, enjoying the fruits of a true husband and wife, if you know what I mean."

"Oh."

"In the dream, after we'd. . .finished, Liam is standing over us with a gun and it ends with him pulling the trigger."

"Oh dear."

"And shooting *you*."

Caroline let out a startled gasp.

"I woke up and I just couldn't handle it, especially since we had kissed earlier in the day. Just the possibility of you being shot . . .well, I thought one drink would do it."

"You must know that Liam would never have done anything like that."

"That's the absurd part. He despised guns. When Father died, Lee insisted that I move the gun cabinet to my room because he couldn't bear to even look at it in the downstairs parlor." He paused for a few seconds. "I'm the one who doesn't have a problem shooting, but I guess part of me believed that perhaps he was coming back to haunt me."

"Liam wouldn't. . ."

"I know. Anyway, I went to the pub near the Cathedral, and I took part in a poker game. I was losing, badly, from what I recall, then I got into a fight. I didn't know it at the time, but Missy was working there. Evidently, I lost the fight. The next

thing I remember I was in Missy's room above the tavern and. . .
well, you know the rest.

"I haven't had a single drink since. Father Flaherty advised
me not to drink because it's impossible for me to make good decisions when I'm drinking. I guess I'm just like my father."

"No, you aren't. You're different now." She paused. "But
how do I know you won't do this again?"

"Please believe me. I would never hurt you."

"You. . . already. . . have." Her voice trembled. "How can I
ever trust you again?"

"I'm different now. I don't drink. We haven't shared a bed
in almost two years and I have been faithful this entire time. I am
changed. When this first happened, I didn't want for us to continue our romance. I wished that you would return to hating me. I
wasn't sure I could ever be faithful to you and I guess that was my
way to protect you. Father Flaherty helped me to see that I could
be faithful, but that I couldn't do it without God's grace."

She took a deep breath. "My heart. . ." Caroline began to
weep again.

David stepped forward, wanting so desperately to embrace
her and rip away her pain. She shook her head, a warning, and
held her hand up.

"My heart feels like it's been torn to shreds."

David bit on his bottom lip in an effort to keep his eyes from
watering. He didn't want her to witness his agony while she was
forced to endure her own.

"I know that I must forgive you, David, but it's going to take
some time to. . .become accustomed to all this."

"I know." They stood quietly for a moment.

"Good night, David."

"Good night."

*   *   *

Caroline usually looked forward to visiting with Uncle and
Elizabeth. However, today was anything but normal and she
dreaded their arrival. She would have to recount the events of the
past few days, and she wished that she could forget rather than
repeat the horrid news. On the veranda, she watched them climb
down from the carriage. The expressions on both Elizabeth's and
Uncle's faces were somber.

"My goodness, Carrie, I couldn't believe it when I heard," Elizabeth screeched.

"Yes, my dear, such a travesty."

"I know, Uncle. This has been very hard on us."

"Although, Carrie, I must say I'm not all that surprised."

Uncle spoke up. "Now, now, Elizabeth. David has been a wonderful father to Kathleen and a good husband to Caroline. Is he not allowed some latitude here?"

"Well, Father. . ."

"Stop it, Elizabeth," Uncle bellowed.

Caroline spoke up. "Please, Lizzie. David has changed. This was a mistake. This has been so difficult." Caroline used her handkerchief to wipe her eyes for the thousandth time.

"Yes, I am certain that it has been," Uncle replied and gathered her into a fatherly embrace. When she pulled away from him, she brought her gaze upward. Elizabeth's head was lowered. Finally, Elizabeth glanced up at her cousin. "I do apologize, Carrie. That was an extremely callous and hurtful comment. This must be excruciatingly hard for you."

"Yes, Lizzie, in some ways, this is more difficult to endure than Liam's death." Caroline shook off her tears and kept her head up. It was bad enough to endure it in the privacy of their own home. Knowing that their situation was the main gossip all over town made it more unbearable. It would likely be necessary for her to practice holding her head up high over the next several months.

"So when will Missy's little boy be coming to live with you?"

"Friday. I'm just not sure I'm ready for. . ."

"Now, you let us know if we can help you in any way, my dear," Uncle said.

"Yes, thank you, Uncle, Lizzie."

65

Waiting on the veranda that warm afternoon, Caroline recalled unforgettable autumn days: her first wedding, the picnic lunch with David. This one would certainly be one of the most memorable.

David paced back and forth as Caroline sat on the lone chair. Sunlight beamed down on the trees' red, orange and yellow leaves, the brilliant colors and the cerulean blue of the sky painting a breathtaking landscape. It seemed too beautiful a day for the circumstances.

The carriage pulled in front of their house. Caroline and David approached it together.

Missy held the child out to David who lifted the small boy and placed him on the ground. Will's dark eyes suspiciously scowled at David.

David then assisted Missy out of the carriage and the four of them stood awkwardly beside it. David's gaze was directed toward the ground, and Missy's eyes seemed to be focused on the front of her dress. Caroline studied her and she was immediately struck by how thin her former servant appeared, her olive skin now a pasty beige.

Caroline broke the silence. "Hello, Missy."

"Hello, Miss Caroline. I can't tell you how grateful I am to the both of you. I didn't think there were many kind people left in this world."

"And this must be Will." Caroline crouched down to make eye contact with the small dark-haired boy. "Hello, Will."

He frowned and immediately turned away from her and grabbed onto his mother's skirt, burying his head amongst the folds.

"Now, Will, Miss Caroline's just about the nicest person you'll ever meet. And this man here is your Pa."

David kept silent, awkwardly shifting from one foot to the next.

Her former servant's eyes began to water. "You know," she

whispered, "I knew this day was going to come, but I didn't think it would be this hard. I just don't. . ." she stopped and tears began falling down her cheeks.

Missy knelt down in front of her son. "Now, Will, you remember what we talked about?"

The little boy stared at her, but made no attempt to respond.

"Remember I told you that I'd have to go away but that these kind people will be taking care of you after I'm gone."

Will looked up at Caroline, then at David and scowled. "No stay here. Go wif you." Caroline's own heart began to feel heavy with emotion as she listened to his sweet toddler voice.

"Will, I told you that Mama's very sick and she needs to go away."

"No go, Mama."

Missy straightened, then pressed out the folds of her dress with her hands. Though tears remained in her eyes, she held her chin high. "Perhaps we could take some time to allow Will to warm up to the both of you."

"That would be fine, Missy," David said. "Take all the time you need."

Missy nodded, then leaned down to speak with Will again. "Mama's going to stay a bit to make sure you're fine."

"No stay here, Mama. Go wif you."

"Yes, I know, Will, but I'm very sick. I can't take care of you anymore." The child yelled, "No!" and grabbed onto her skirt.

Caroline shifted awkwardly.

"Mr. David?" Missy's head lowered.

"Yes, Missy?"

"I just wanted to say that I really do appreciate what you and Miss Caroline are doing, not only taking care of Will, but giving me money so that the nuns can care for me." Her voice was cracking then she began to cough violently, holding a handkerchief to her mouth.

"It's the least I could do, Missy. After all, Will is my responsibility."

Missy fixed her eyes on young Will, who was still desperately clutching her skirt.

"Missy, let's all go inside and Will can get used to his new surroundings," Caroline offered.

Missy crouched down. "Will, we're going into their house."

"Yes, Will," Caroline said. "We have sweet cakes and freshly picked apples. Would you like some?"

Will shook his head.

"Well, perhaps your mama would like some."

"Oh, I would love to eat some sweet cake. We rarely get such delicious food, do we?" Missy took hold of his small hand, "Come, Will." The little boy walked slowly, constantly glancing over his shoulder at David and continuing to frown.

An hour later, Will sat quietly playing with some blocks on the floor of the parlor. Kathleen was trying hard to encourage him to talk to her, but after all this time, he simply grunted his responses.

"Oh, Will, you've built a beautiful castle. I'm already four and I can't build as big a castle."

"I'll return in a few moments," David said. He nodded to Missy. When David had left the room, she spoke up.

"Your daughter is beautiful. I can see Mr. Liam in her when she laughs."

"Yes, I know."

"Where's John?"

"He's right here, Missy." Jane held John's hand and stood in the doorway. "I think he wants to play in here."

Jane sat John next to Kathleen and Will. Missy leaned down beside John. "You've gotten so big." Missy straightened and the two servants embraced.

"Your Will is going to be in good hands here, Missy."

"I know."

While Missy and Jane spoke, Caroline stared at the two dark-haired boys, now playing with the blocks on the floor with Kathleen.

Jane left the room and Missy sat down again beside Caroline. "John has grown so much. He was such a beautiful baby, looked a lot like Will, he did."

Caroline nodded.

"Miss Caroline?"

"Yes?"

"I'm so sorry this has hurt you."

Caroline did not respond.

"Mr. David, he's a good man."

Caroline cringed. *If he's so good, why did he do this?*

As if she had read her thoughts, Missy responded, " He had been drinking, got into a fight. As I recall, someone accused him of cheating and saying that he was just like his father. I had never seen him so angry. I was just fixing him up afterwards. I never thought – what happened was wrong, even I know that. But when I found out I was going to have a baby, I was so thankful to the Lord. I just hate when people called Will a mistake, because he's the biggest and best gift I ever got."

Caroline shuddered with the enormity of it all: the knowledge of David's indiscretion, Missy's illness, little Will. And yet, Missy was right. Children are great gifts, no matter what the circumstance.

"Miss Caroline, I don't mean to make you feel. . ." She paused. "I wanted you to know how Will came about, that's all."

Caroline kept her head down and remained silent.

"Look, Will, that's a wonderful tower you've built," she heard Kathleen say.

Missy continued. "When Will was five months old, Jane came to see me, telling me you needed a wet nurse. I was afraid, because I thought Mr. David would know the child was his so Jane and I were careful to keep him from seeing too much of Will. I mean, he looked so much like him, even as an infant. But I really needed the money and a place to stay.

"I'm just so thankful that you and Mr. David have seen fit to take care of my Will. There's no way I could ever thank you enough."

"The nuns at the convent will take good care of you."

"I know they will." Missy stood up and now used her handkerchief to wipe her eyes. She stared at Will, John and Kathleen.

"Perhaps I should sneak out without him seeing."

"No, Missy. That would probably be easier on you and me, but you need to say a proper goodbye to him."

The former servant took a deep breath, then nodded. "Could you give him this when he gets older?" she asked, as she handed her some papers and a photograph.

"I've written Will a message that I'd like him to have when he's older."

"I would be glad to give these to him in a few years."

Missy held up a small cloth bag. "There are some clothes in here." She reached into the bag and pulled out a small frayed blanket. "This is Will's. He sleeps with it."

Caroline nodded and took the bag and blanket from her.

"I knew you were different the first time I met you. You're a kind sort. You don't hold a grudge."

"Yes, well. . ." *Please help me to let go of my resentment for her part in David's infidelity.*

David walked into the room and stood beside his wife. "There's no rush for you to leave," he whispered to Missy.

She avoided eye contact. "Thank you. But I ought to be going." Her eyes filled with tears and she held her hand to her lips as she tried to keep from sobbing. "This is so hard. Will?"

The boy turned around to find his mother, Caroline and David standing. "Mama, I like bwocks. She help me."

"Yes, Will, that's nice. Come here."

She leaned down and whispered, "I want you to know that I love you and I don't want you to forget me."

"Mama not go. I go too."

"No, Will, you have to stay here. I have to. . ." Missy's lip began to quiver. She began to sob and she pulled Will into a tight embrace.

"Mama hurt me."

"I'm sorry, Will. I just wanted to tell you how much I love you."

"Me go, Mama."

"You can't, Will. I've already told you that I can't take you."

"No, Mama, no!" Will screamed.

Missy attempted to pry Will away from her skirts. He clung onto her with such fierceness that he stuck to her like taffy. David stepped forward and helped pull him from his mother.

"I love you, Will," she said, then she rushed out of the room. He was screaming and kicking and David was attempting to calm him down. "Shhh, Will, you're going to be fine."

Caroline followed behind her as she ran outside. "Missy, wait." Missy stopped at the carriage and turned toward Caroline.

"We will take good care of him."

"I know. But this still hurts more than any sickness I have," she said, as she stared at the window of the house, listening to the distant screams of her son.

Caroline pulled her to a poignant embrace. "Is there some way you can let us know how you're getting along?"

"I'll send you word every now and then through Jane."

"And I should like to visit you at the convent, if that's acceptable."

"Yes, Ma'am, that would be fine."

"Very well. God bless you."

Kip assisted Missy into the carriage and they drove off.

*   *   *

"Miss Caroline, you want me to put the children to bed while you try to get Will down?" Jane asked, holding John.

Caroline quietly stood behind Will, his small back facing her, the front of his body plastered to the wall against the corner, his sobs diminishing to quiet hiccups.

"He must be exhausted. He's been crying for three hours."

"Yes, I know. I wish there were some way I could help him. Jane, get me that small blanket of Will's over there. I tried giving it to him earlier, but he refused. Let me try again."

"Certainly, Miss Caroline."

Caroline held the blanket in front of Will and he pushed it away. "No want it, no want you."

"Where's Mr. David?"

"He had some business to attend to. He promised he would be back shortly."

"Come, Miss Kathleen, I'm going to put you and your brother to bed now," Jane said, taking Kathleen's hand.

"Mama, I want you to put me to bed."

"Kathleen, Will is very upset that his mother has gone. It's important for me to spend some time with him."

Kathleen's lip began to pout. Her head lowered. "Yes, Mama. I would be sad if you had left."

Caroline smiled inwardly.

"That's very grown-up of you, Kathleen. Thank you for being so understanding."

Jane and the children left the room. A quiet calm seemed to

envelope Caroline.　She studied Will's motionless form, his back to her, his soft cries still audible.

"Will," Caroline whispered very close to his ear.　She turned his body to face her.　His small face was smudged with dried tears. He kept his eyes downward.

"I know you miss your Mama, but she's very sick and I'm going to take care of you."

"No want you.　Want Mama, want Mama. . ." he started crying loudly again.

Caroline tried to pull him into her arms, but he pushed her comfort away.　"No want you," he yelled.　He rammed himself against the wall, his back again facing her.

How am I supposed to help him and love him when he doesn't want it?　What am I supposed to do with this child?

"Allow me." She heard David over Will's loud sobs. He slowly approached the boy.　Caroline stepped aside.

"Will," he whispered.

"Go away.　No want to. . ."

"Shhh, come here," he said, then pulled his son into an embrace.

"No, don't. . ."

The youngster fought hard, screaming and pushing David away.

Despite Will's resistance, David held him close, his masculine strength forcing the exhausted toddler to finally surrender. Within a few minutes, David now gently held his son and tenderly stroked the child's hair.　"Shhh."

"Well, you certainly. . ."

David held his finger to his mouth.　She gave him a knowing glance, then sat down on the nearest chair.

After several minutes, David whispered to Caroline, "I think he's asleep.　Tired out, I'm sure, from all that crying."

"Yes."

"Where are we taking him?"

Caroline sighed.　"I figured he would probably be waking a lot during the night so I told Jane to put him in my room so that he doesn't wake the entire house."

David nodded and they walked up the staircase and down the east hallway to her room.　As they entered, Caroline could see that Jane had set up a day bed next to her own. David placed him gently down on the small bed then took off his shoes.

Caroline turned the oil lamp down, then joined David as he sat next to the bed staring at his son, now sleeping.

"He's a beautiful little boy," she observed. "He's got your hair and your eyes and your nose."

"And I wasn't even finished with them yet."

Caroline allowed herself to smile.

"You know, Caroline. . ." he whispered. "I made a big mistake, but it's remarkable how God can make something beautiful from something bad. Will wouldn't exist right now if I hadn't. . ." He stopped and made eye contact with her. "I had a hard time forgiving myself. And I thought that when I looked at him, that I would be reminded over and over again how I hurt you. And that is a small part of it. But now, all I can see is goodness, a little boy who very much needs our love."

Caroline whispered her agreement.

*   *   *

A weak scratching sound woke Caroline and immediately she sat up in bed. She squinted, then glanced at the small bed beside her. She patted it to find it vacant. "Will?" she whispered. The scraping sounds became louder, desperate. Caroline jumped out of bed despite the blackness and rushed to the door.

Her eyes became accustomed to the dark and she could now see Will lying against the door, his nails digging into the surface.

"Will?" she said softly.

 She crawled closer to him on the floor. Will was half-asleep, his small body worn, exhausted.

"Will, Sweet," she whispered. She gently picked him up, then a loud ear-splitting scream filled the room. "No, no, don't want, don't want you. . .want Mama," and with one small fist, he drove it into Caroline's right eye causing her to fall back on the floor.

"Hey!"

"Caroline?" She could barely hear David through the door amidst the loud screaming. "Is everything fine in here?"

"No!" she yelled, then picked herself up off the floor, moved past Will, who was kicking and screaming on the floor and unlocked the bedroom door. She held her hand to her eye.

David stood at the doorway with an oil lamp. "Uh-oh. Did Will do that?"

She nodded.

"Will's a fighter, isn't he?" He set the lamp on the dresser.

"Apparently." Caroline watched Will banging his head against the floor. "Calm him, please!"

David crouched down. "Will, it'll be fine, shhh." When David gently picked him up, his small, worn body gave no resistance. Instead, he cuddled close to David's chest.

David finally placed his son down on the small bed while the boy fell into a deep sleep. "I think I know why he woke up."

"Why?"

David moved close to the light and there was wetness against his night shirt from where he held Will. "He must have wet himself. Where did Jane put his bag of clothes?"

"Right here." She reached in and retrieved a pair of clean pajamas and laid them on the bed. David began to pull off the wet pants and Will cried out. "No, no."

"Shhh, Will." He fought with the boy and, with Caroline's assistance, was able to dress him in dry clothes. Several minutes of walking and rocking him and the boy was finally asleep again.

Caroline placed Will's blanket beside him.

David whispered, "I was lying in bed thinking. . ."

"Really?"

"Yes. I do a lot of thinking in my bed. Will's having a difficult time letting go of his mother. And he's never really bonded with a man. Perhaps that's why he's so open to my comfort."

Caroline remained silent, still holding her eye.

"I think we ought to move Will into my room."

"Very well," she responded.

"Don't worry. He will begin to love you as much as I love you and Kathleen and John love you." He removed her hand from her face and tenderly kissed the area below her eye. She gasped in pain. "That hurts, David."

"Come with me across the hall into the study and I'll take a look at your eye."

"Very well."

He took hold of her hand, picked up the lamp and led her across the hall. He held the light close to her eye, and gasped. "I think you're going to have a black eye. It already looks slightly purple and blue."

"I feel like I have a gaping hole here. Will sure is strong for such a young boy."

"Wait here. I'll see what there is in cold storage."

While he was gone, Caroline held her hand to her eye and studied the room which had once been Liam's bedroom.   She glanced at the area where his bed once had been and was transported back to a time when she and Liam were married. *Life certainly was simpler then.*

A few moments later, he returned with cold bottles of wine from the basement. He held one up to her eye and she winced and pushed it away. "Allow it to remain there for a moment, Caroline. It will feel better. I promise you."

With every ounce of effort she possessed, she strived to stay motionless and allow him to keep the cold bottle below her eye. Finally, she shook her head and pushed it away.

"Keep it there for a few moments."

"David, allow me go back to sleep. I shall be fine."

He let out an exasperated sigh. "If you insist."

She turned and stood in the doorway, hesitating. "David?"

"Yes?"

"Thank you."

"No, Caroline, thank *you*."

His eyebrows were raised and he was smiling. His expression was full of tenderness and affection. How could she love and hate him simultaneously? How could she want to pummel his chest and embrace him at the same time?

Despite her pain and disappointment at knowing that he had been unfaithful, at that moment, Caroline knew that she must forgive him, not only for him and for her, but for Kathleen, John and Will.

66

Early the following morning, Caroline awoke to bright sunlight streaming into her room. She shifted, then stretched lazily and noticed that Will was not in his bed. She sat up and felt a piercing pain under her right eye and the episode from the previous night came flooding back to her.

Caroline slowly lifted herself from the bed, her eye throbbing, and covered herself with her robe. In the hallway, she listened for any activity. *Where are you, Will?*

Muffled giggling drew her to the nursery several rooms away. She quietly opened the door and peered in to see Jane, Will, John, Isaac and Kathleen sitting on the floor, playing with blocks.

Only Kathleen faced the doorway and when she saw Caroline, she squealed, "Mama, you look dreadful. What happened?"

"Oh, I. . .I hurt it last night."

"Miss Caroline, that's awful. Why didn't you wake me?"

"It's fine. I don't want to bother you, since you're with child. You need your sleep. David tried to help with a bottle of wine."

"Getting you drunk isn't the answer."

"No, no, he was holding it to my eye."

Jane laughed. "Of course."

Will turned around and, wide-eyed, studied her with a new-found curiosity. Caroline hoped that he did not remember that he was the cause of her injury.

John was holding out his hands to Caroline and she leaned down and lifted him up. He stared at her black swollen eye and said, "Ouch."

"Yes, Sweet, ouch."

He puckered his lips as if he wanted to kiss her there and leaned close to her face, but Caroline stopped him. "No, John, kissing it isn't going to help." *Like father, like son.*

His lips formed a pout.

"But you can kiss me here, on the lips," she said, pointing.

His eyes lit up as he planted a moist kiss on her lips.

"I'm just going to make sure that Hallie's started breakfast," Jane said as she left the nursery. Caroline turned around to see Will taking one of the larger blocks and ramming it into Kathleen's head.

"Ouch. Mama, Will's hurting me!"

"No," Caroline firmly said, as she placed John down on the floor. She grabbed the block away from Will. "No, Will, no hitting Kathleen. That will hurt her."

His small eyes glared at her. She watched as he tried to pick up another block. She intercepted it and knocked it out of his hand. "No blocks right now, Will, not if you're going to hurt someone."

"Hurt you," he said defiantly.

Caroline let out a deep, frustrated breath.

"Hurt you!"

"You're a bad little boy, Will!" Kathleen shouted.

"Kathleen, please. He's been through an awful experience. We've got to be. . .ouch!" Caroline winced as Will banged his head into her knees.

"Will, stop it."

"No stop, want mama."

"Yes, I know you do, but she's sick and she's. . ."

Will ran to the book case and began pitching books across the room. One of them hit John and he began wailing.

Caroline grabbed Will from behind and tried to restrain him but the little boy's strength was more than she could handle.

"You need some help in here, Caroline?" David stood in the doorway. For a brief second, she wanted to begin pounding at her husband for bringing this child into the family, this boy who seemed to be doing everything in his power to hurt Caroline and her children.

"Yes!" she shouted, as she half-dragged Will over to David. "You can control your son!" As she released him, he began to step away from David, but David easily picked him up and restrained him. "Now, now, Will, I won't let you down until you've promised you won't hurt anyone."

"Lemme go, lemme go!"

"Go on, Caroline, get dressed if you'd like. I'll remain here with the children until you've finished."

Without replying, Caroline rushed back to her room and slammed the door. *This is what I get for helping someone. This is what I get for forgiving my husband. This is what I get for helping.* Caroline took a deep breath, then lowered herself to the chair by her vanity table and sat quietly for a moment, letting her hair fall over her face. She slowly raised her head and studied herself in the mirror, finding it hard to recognize the woman staring back. Her eye was swollen, misshapen and purple. She had never before looked so dreadful.

She quickly dressed, then hurried down the back stairs to the kitchen. She stopped midway down when she heard Hallie speaking.

"I hated to hear Mr. David talked about in such a manner."

"You can't be listening to gossip like that, Hallie."

"But they were going on about Mr. David's bastard and I just hated hearing that talk. They said that Mr. David hasn't changed and that men like that never change and that he'll be unfaithful again."

"I told you, that's just mean gossip. People have nothing better to do than talk about others in their time of distress."

Caroline attempted to quietly walk back up the stairs, the steps creaking as she did so.

"Miss Caroline, is that you on the stairs?"

Caroline descended the remaining steps to the kitchen. Hallie's hand was to her mouth and her eyes were wide.

"I'm so sorry, Ma'am. I didn't want you to be hearing what those people are saying about you and Mr. David."

"I appreciate that, Hallie. But if I hear about one more person talking about us, I'll. . ." She bit down on her lip. "Is our story in the Philadelphia Evening Bulletin?"

"Don't you mind that," Jane said. "You just think about the fact that you've done a good, fine deed, helping Missy out like that."

"Yes, well, I wish I could believe that David has changed."

"Ma'am, I told you before that he's a good man."

Caroline remained silent. Isaac pulled on his mother's skirt. Jane crouched down and spoke softly to him. Then she straightened and faced Caroline. "You know something, Miss Caroline?

Marriage isn't always easy, no matter how much you love your husband. This is one of those really hard times."

"Yes, well, that's an understatement." Caroline turned around and forced herself up the back stairs. She made her way to the now quiet nursery. She remained at the side of the doorway and peeked in. David was sitting in a rocking chair with both Will and John on his lap and Kathleen was sitting by his feet. He was reading a poem, almost acting it out with enthusiasm, and the three children appeared transfixed.

It was obvious from David's lively tone that he was enjoying the story as much as the children. They seemed so peaceful that she had a difficult time believing all the trouble Will had caused over the last day and a half.

She stepped back again and listened in the hallway. All of a sudden, Kathleen yelled "Ouch!" She was crying as Caroline ran into the room. Her daughter was holding her head and David was smacking Will's foot, "No, Will, no kicking Kathleen's head." Will began to cry, then John followed along. Now, all three children were sobbing in unison. David closed his eyes, sighed deeply and placed both boys on the floor. He crossed the room and stood beside his wife.

"Well, it was pleasant for about three minutes."

"I was watching from the hallway," she said over the screaming children.

Caroline knelt down beside Kathleen to survey the damage Will had caused. She pushed her daughter's hair to one side and studied, then felt, her head. There was no bump or open wound. "I think you'll be fine, Kathleen."

"He hurt me!"

"Yes, I know, Sweet, but he's had a hard time."

"I don't care, Mama, he's a bad boy!"

"Come, Kathleen, let's see if Jane has something cold that we can put on your head."

Kathleen stopped crying, wiped her eyes and took hold of Caroline's hand. As Caroline was leaving, she turned around to see David kneeling in front of the boys. He was speaking to Will in a low, calm voice.

67

David fixed his tie, then pulled on his jacket.

Will had slept fitfully again, but his son was now with the other two children eating breakfast. Today would be the first time they had attended Mass since Will arrived. He predicted that Will would likely not sit still, nor be quiet during Mass, but he kindly turned down Jane's offer to watch the boy.

Last night, he had seriously considered having them attend church separately, to protect Caroline and the children from the scandalous comments which David already had endured from some of his customers and neighbors.

However, he realized that many would be of the opinion that bringing Will, an illegitimate child, to church, a public place, would be scandalous. He shrugged. Was it any more scandalous than the first time David attended Mass at the Cathedral? True, fewer people were aware of his past behavior at that particular venue, but if he, a public sinner, could be welcomed, then the symbol of his past, this innocent child, ought to be accepted as well.

In the hallway David met Caroline. He avoided eye contact. "It seems too quiet."

"Yes."

He glanced at her face and she was staring down the hall.

"Perhaps a hearty breakfast will be good for Will. And hopefully, it will help him to behave in Church."

She didn't respond. Instead, she returned to her bedroom and closed the door.

David could see through the hall window that it was raining. Rain was good because it meant that fewer people would be gawking at them as they emerged from their carriage in front of the cathedral. The gloomy day also struck him as ominous.

In the carriage on the way to the Cathedral, David watched as Caroline attempted to make small talk with Will.

"No like you," was Will's constant response.

He wondered about warning her of the possibility of gossip,

but instead, continued to hope that their outing would be without incident and the other parishioners would refrain from judging him and his family.

At the Cathedral, Kip assisted them out of the carriage. Immediately, a group of women about twenty feet away began to stare. Caroline was distracted by the children and didn't appear to notice, but they pointed and whispered, then pointed again. Most of the ladies were older, and seemed to have nothing better to do than to prattle on about someone else's sin. Some of them were rolling their eyes.

Kip spotted the women, glanced at David, then shook his head. David used his body to block Caroline's view. He despised the fact that it was necessary for her to suffer through the consequences of his transgression so publicly.

David ushered his family quickly toward the church, hoping to avoid any other stares and whispers. At the entrance of the Cathedral, he was met by Father Flaherty.

"David, Mrs. O'Donovan, I was hoping that you would attend as usual. I'll escort you to your regular pew in front." He leaned close to David and whispered. "Your situation is all people are gossiping about. It's terrible." David's heart sank.

"But why is Father taking us?" she whispered to David.

"It seems people are talking about us, me, Will." She shook her head and followed Father Flaherty.

"Wouldn't it be better to stay in the back? Fewer people will notice us," she whispered.

"I agree, but Father thinks we ought to sit in our usual pew, Caroline. We need to trust him." She nodded.

He ushered them in and down the center aisle amidst whispers and stares. David felt hundreds of eyes piercing into him, striving to look at the fool who had been unfaithful to his wife. *Please let us reach the front soon.*

The priest stopped, genuflected, then motioned for them to enter the front pew to the right. Caroline and David both genuflected and ushered the children into the seat. Father leaned down to speak to David, "Let me know if you have any problems today, David."

"Thank you, Father."

David knelt and made the Sign of the Cross. He tried to concentrate on some short prayers but became distracted. He closed his eyes and offered up whatever humiliation he had to endure for Will, the rest of his family and for the dying Missy.

From the choir loft came beautiful Gregorian chants. He sat back, preparing to enjoy the soothing hymns.

"Stop it, Will," Kathleen said, as Will began to pull on the side of her dress. She finally smacked his hand away. "Ouch!" he yelled. John now began to whimper. *This is going from bad to worse.*

Fr. Flaherty and the acolytes processed up the aisle as the choir and congregation sang:

Holy, Holy, Holy Lord God Almighty
Early in the morning, our song shall rise to Thee.
Holy, Holy, Holy, merciful and mighty,
God in three persons, Blessed Trinity.

David wanted to sing loudly, but instead sang softly. He wished that he could tell all those people staring at him that he would rather die than ever do that again with anyone other than his wife. He wanted to tell them that he was a sinner, in need of God's grace, that he wasn't a bad person, just someone who had made a very bad choice.

Facing the altar, Father Flaherty made the sign of the cross and said, "In Nomine Patris, et Filii et Spiritus Sancti."

At Communion, David remained in his seat with the children while Caroline went forward to receive the Eucharist. When she returned, he walked ahead and knelt at the rail and received the Body of Christ. He blessed himself, then stood up and joined Caroline and the children in the pew. Immediately, he felt peaceful, calm and joyful. This was true food for his soul. With it, he now felt grace-filled and prepared to bear this difficult situation.

* * *

Caroline dreaded the end of Mass, as she wished that she could avoid speaking with anyone this week. She knew that people were talking about them, but somehow while she had been involved in the liturgy, it didn't seemed to matter.

She and David and the children made their way up the center aisle to the doors of the church and outside to the area just in front of the Cathedral.

"Mr. O'Donovan?" she heard a man say. Her husband turned his head and immediately recognized the tall, bearded man with a smile. Caroline held onto John's and Will's hands while Kathleen remained in front of her. As David and the man began to speak, Caroline was distracted by whispering closeby and she glanced up to see three women just turning away. She hated this whole situation, the muttering, the gossiping, the pointing of fingers. And at church, of all places. Caroline was grateful for Father Flaherty. He had been so kind.

It was bad enough that David had been unfaithful. But to have that behavior grabbed and sprinkled throughout most of Philadelphia seemed too much for her to bear.

Welling up within her was the beginning of resentment and immediately, Caroline pushed it away.

People now blocked Caroline's view of her husband and the man.

"Will, stop!" Kathleen said. Caroline looked down to see Will smacking the side of Kathleen's head. She cringed.

"Will, I told you there's no hitting." She reached down and grabbed Will's other hand. "Kathleen, hold John's hand for me, please. It's necessary for me to hold both of Will's hands to ensure that he doesn't. . ."

"Ouch!" Will yelled. From the corner of her eye, Caroline saw someone approaching them. Caroline held her breath.

"Do you need some assistance, Mrs. O'Donovan?" She glanced sympathetically toward Caroline.

"Mrs. Carver. Thank you. Good day."

"You look like you could use some help."

"Is it that obvious?"

The woman leaned down and spoke to Will.

"Hello. What is your name?"

He stepped back and shook his head.

"It's Will, Mrs. Carver," Caroline offered.

Caroline watched curiously as Mrs. Carver said, "You look so handsome today, Will." He shook his head and scowled at her.

Mrs. Carver leaned close to Caroline's ear and spoke quietly.

"Mrs. O'Donovan, I wanted to say that what you're doing is

admirable. This must be so difficult. It's as if no one has anything better to do than gossip."

Caroline nodded. "Yes, it has been hard."

Across the street, four women whispered and pointed with haughty disdain. Mrs. Carver frowned, then walked briskly toward the group. "Do you ladies not have anything more fruitful to accomplish than to relish in Mrs. O'Donovan's heartache?"

The women lowered their heads and hurried away.

"Thank you," Caroline whispered to Mrs. Carver.

"We're ready," she heard David say.

"David, you remember Mrs. Carver?"

"Oh, yes. How are you and Dr. Carver keeping?"

"Fine, Mr. O'Donovan. If there is anything my husband and I can do for you, please let us know."

"Yes, thank you, Mrs. Carver."

* * *

In the carriage on the way home, David held the sleeping John on his lap, his son's face on his chest. Will leaned against his arm, his small, troubled eyes also beginning to close. David's stomach growled, but that was the least of his worries.

He glanced at Kathleen, who was sitting in the seat across from them. She was quietly taking her gloves on and off again. Caroline was staring out the window. For the most part, she had been avoiding eye contact with him all morning, which he supposed was better than looking at him with disgust.

He greatly appreciated the comments from a client of his, a Mr. Stanford, who approached him after Mass. He told David, "If there's anything that my wife and I can do for you and your family, please let me know." David had thanked him for the offer, but more importantly, he wanted to tell him how grateful he was that he did not treat him as an outcast.

David studied his wife's face. This whole experience was so much worse because of what it was doing to her. He didn't care about being snubbed or talked about. And that sort of talk generally didn't bother Caroline. Elizabeth and Edward and other neighbors often advised them to treat Jane and Kip more like servants, but she didn't listen nor did she care.

However, David knew that this type of gossip – the talking and whispering about his unfaithfulness and illegitimate child –

caused her great anguish. *Please, Father, give her the grace to be able to withstand this.*

The knowledge of his infidelity was still fresh, but he was confident that it would fade and that Caroline would grow to love Will.

She must have felt his eyes on her because she turned her gaze from the window and made eye contact. Caroline said nothing, but her sad eyes illustrated that she was still in mourning, grieving for the happy, seemingly uncomplicated life they had built together. He wanted to promise her that he would do everything in his power to bring that life back, no matter what the cost, but he kept silent.

"Mama, why didn't Mary come and talk to me today after Mass?"

Now, Caroline's eyes asked him, "What do I tell her?"

"Well, Kat," David began, "some people are talking about us taking in Will and many people don't like that we've done that." It wasn't an outright lie, but he couldn't share the exact truth with her.

"But why?" she asked.

"Well. . ."

"Is it why Mama is crying a lot?"

David blinked his eyes. He watched Caroline for her reaction, which was to direct her gaze again toward the window.

"Yes, I suppose so, Kat."

"Mama?"

Caroline looked down at her daughter. "Yes, Kathleen?"

"Are you mad at Papa?"

"Kathleen, I. . ." Caroline's voice was cracking. David could see that his wife's eyes were beginning to water. She wiped them with her gloved fingers and continued. "Well, maybe I'm a little mad at Papa. But I promised God that I would love Papa no matter what." Caroline then kept her eyes fixed on David. Behind the sadness and the pain, in her expression he could see the beginnings of forgiveness. *Thank you, God.*

68

Just after Christmas, Caroline and Jane pulled their coats closer to their bodies as they stood together on the porch and watched the four children playing on the front lawn. Despite the cold air, the winter sun had melted the dusting of snow on the ground.

"Can't catch me, can't catch me," Will was saying, then running off as Kathleen, John and Isaac tried to reach him.

"Will is a fast runner," the servant commented.

"He certainly is."

"And the children are all having such fun."

"I like to treasure these moments, Jane. They don't happen often enough."

"Missy's boy is adjusting so well. He's been here more than two months now and he's hardly ever bad any more."

"I know he wasn't 'bad' before, but he certainly must have been hurting inside to behave in such a manner those first few weeks."

"I'm glad you and Mr. David didn't see fit to beat him, although I know Mr. David swatted his back end a few times."

"I wouldn't be inclined to hit anyone, Jane, least of all my children."

"Yeah, yeah," Kathleen said, as she finally caught up to Will and tapped him on the shoulder. "You're so fast, Will."

"I sure am."

"Now I'm going to run and you have to catch me, Will."

"I go too," little John said.

"Yes, John, you can try to catch me too."

"Did you know that Mr. David's trying to arrange a trip away for the two of you?"

"Yes. It's just that four children is a tremendous amount of work for you to handle and you being with child."

"Oh, you go on about that. I can handle ten children, if necessary. I think it's easier to watch a lot of children than just one because they have each other to play with."

"I suppose there's a certain measure of truth to that, Jane."

"Look, Ma'am, there's a carriage coming up the laneway."

Caroline watched a small buggy ride up to the front of the house. A short rotund man got out and approached the pair on the front lawn.

"I'm looking for Mr. or Mrs. O'Donovan."

"I'm Mrs. O'Donovan."

"I have a letter to deliver to you, Mrs. O'Donovan. It's from the Sacred Heart Convent. It's addressed to both you and Mr. O'Donovan."

"Yes, thank you. " Caroline took the envelope from the man. He tipped his hat, then got into the carriage. As he rode away, Caroline stared at the letter. "Missy's at the Sacred Heart Convent, Jane." She opened the envelope and quickly pulled out the paper.

December 28th, 1881

Mr. and Mrs. David O'Donovan
Germantown, Philadelphia, Pennsylvania

Dear Mr. and Mrs. O'Donovan:

We regret to inform you of the death of Melissa Callahan last night. Miss Callahan requested that we send this letter to you when she passed on as you had offered to handle funeral arrangements. Should we be of any further assistance, please do not hesitate to write or visit us at the Sacred Heart Convent in Philadelphia.

Sincerely Yours in Christ,

Sister Regina Joseph, O.P. Mother Superior
Sacred Heart Convent, Philadelphia

"David said that he would be home from the city by two o'clock." Caroline's voice cracked as she spoke.

"She didn't look well two weeks ago." Jane wiped her eyes with her handkerchief. "Will you tell Will, Miss Caroline?"

"I don't know. He's come so far in just a few months. I don't think he'll be able to handle his mother's death right now."

"Missy didn't have any kin left. Her parents have both passed and she didn't have any brothers or sisters."

Several hours later, Caroline waited in the foyer and watched for David. When she saw his carriage pulling up, she stepped onto the porch to wait for him. The sky was clouding over and the cold wind blew against her face. As he rode closer, she could see he was smiling at her.

He called to her from the buggy, "Couldn't stand to be away from me for a few hours?"

She regarded him with tear-filled eyes. She walked up to the carriage and held up the envelope.

"What's this?"

Caroline took out the letter and handed it to him.

As he read it, his expression became somber, then he lowered his head. "Rest in peace, Missy."

"Would it be possible for you to return to the city and handle the funeral arrangements, David?"

"Of course. Kip can take me in the larger carriage. Would you like to come and say goodbye?"

"I would've preferred to say my goodbyes before she died. Two weeks ago, when I visited her, she seemed so happy to hear that Will was doing better."

"It would be nice to have your company. And we'll be alone and uninterrupted for the hour or so it will take us to ride to the convent. It will give us a chance to pray and talk together."

"Very well."

69

"The children will be fine with me," Jane said. "And you'll only be gone this evening. You go and say your goodbyes to Missy and don't you worry. Hearty is what my Ma calls me!"

Caroline let out a small laugh. She had never known a woman who was so strong and normal while carrying than Jane had been, first with Isaac, and now with this unborn child. She admired her, almost envied her, and figured that she was just one of those robust women meant to bear many children.

Kip winked at Jane and said, "See you tonight."

She nodded.

Caroline hugged Kathleen, then John and Will. David assisted her into the carriage.

They spent the first five minutes or so in silence. Caroline offered up a few prayers for Missy's soul and together, they prayed the rosary for Missy. When they finished praying, Caroline noticed the small plaque above the door of the carriage. "That the Divine Infant will light the road before you every night and day."

"It's an Irish blessing, Caroline."

"It's beautiful."

"Yes, that is why I had the plaque made." He paused. "We will be taking this back road, Caroline. It's a faster way to get to Philadelphia, but almost no one uses the road so it's not as well maintained."

"Are we in that much of a rush, David?"

"No, but Kip and I have been taking this road to avoid the many carriages on the main road. And it takes much less time."

"Is this the road you took me on years ago to be with Selly?"

David shuddered. "Yes, it is." He paused. "That seems like a lifetime ago, doesn't it?"

"Indeed. It's too bad that the snow has melted already." Caroline glanced out the window of the carriage. "I hope that we get more snow soon."

All of a sudden, there was a screech, a piercing snap, the carriage rocked back, then began to roll over.

Caroline slowly opened her eyes. It appeared as if she was facing a wooded area of some kind, but it was dusk and it was becoming difficult to see. *Where am I?* She began to shiver, her teeth chattering. The soft ground was damp and her dress and coat seemed to be soaked right through. She attempted to sit up but a shooting pain in her shoulder forced her to lie back down.

She opened her mouth to call for David, but no words would come out. Finally, she managed to say her husband's name in as loud a voice as she could muster. She heard no response. She carefully, slowly pulled herself up, wincing as she tried to stand, then dropping back down again. Caroline lifted up her dress and gasped when she saw that her right leg was scraped from ankle to thigh. Other than that, she seemed to have no other injuries, apart from the pain in her shoulder.

She turned around, then let out a startled gasp when she saw their carriage on its side with no sign of the horses.

"David!"

"Miss Caroline?" she heard Kip's normally deep voice softly say.

"Kip, where are you?"

"I'm. . . here, Miss Caroline."

Caroline followed the direction of his voice and dragged herself to the other side of the carriage. The bottom half of Kip's body was lying beneath it. A pool of blood was drifting slowly from under his back and legs.

"Kip, you're bleeding!"

"Yes, Ma'am, I am."

"What happened?"

"I think an animal squealed and it must've scared the horses. The carriage tipped back and one of the wheels came off. I think the horses are long gone." Kip's deep voice seemed high-pitched.

"Let me help you." She took hold of his hands to pull him out from under the carriage.

"Ahhh!" he screamed as she yanked. "Please don't do that, Ma'am."

"But you're bleeding, Kip. I must get you out."

"Don't worry yourself about me. Mr. David's still in the

buggy, I heard him moaning a few minutes ago. Best you get him out first then perhaps. . ." he winced again. "Perhaps I can get out."

"Oh, Lord," she mumbled. Caroline grabbed a stray box and stepped on it. The carriage door had already been torn off. She peered inside. Darkness was closing in and Caroline could just make out where David was lying, unconscious, on the side – now floor – of the buggy.

"David!" she screamed. He began moaning. "David, please."

"Caroline," he whispered, "are you. . .hurt?"

"My leg is hurt, but otherwise, I'm fine. We've had an accident. The horses got spooked and it looks like one of the wheels came off. Kip is under the carriage and bleeding."

"My head hurts."

Caroline shuddered. *That's what Liam said just before he died.*

He lifted himself up. "I think I'll be able to get out of here."

Caroline reached her hand inside to assist David through the door, carefully trying to avoid added weight on Kip lying underneath.

David held his hand up, then fell back down. Kip moaned.

"I'm not sure I can lift myself out, Caroline. Kip, are you injured?" David hollered from inside the carriage.

"Yeah, Mr. David. It's hurting real bad. I feel like I'm gonna pass out."

"Hold on, Kip, I'm going to try again."

David tried to stand up, then his eyes started to close and he slumped back inside the carriage.

She gasped. Though she was now feeling an overpowering urge to retch, she called to him. "David, please." He was unresponsive. She crawled closer to Kip.

"Oh, Kip, what shall I do? You both need help. And I've scraped my leg."

"Not sure, Ma'am. We. . .passed a few cottages on the way, perhaps a mile or so back. You. . .think you can walk that far?"

"I don't have a choice. But I don't want to leave you and David. And you're both in the middle of the road."

"Not many people use this road. Don't worry none about that."

"But Kip. . ."

He weakly opened his eyes. "Miss Caroline, I don't think I'm gonna. . ." He tried to take a breath, his lip quivering, then managed to whisper. "Tell Jane I love her."

"Kip, you can tell her yourself. I'm going to get you. . ." His face, his whole body became limp, his eyes remained open, staring at the now darkening sky. "Kip, please, please don't. . ." She touched the side of his arm, now still, and she knew that he was gone.

She held her hand to her mouth. She began to cry, long, loud sobs.

"Caroline, don't. . .cry. I need you to be strong," she heard through her weeping.

"David!" she leaned her head inside the carriage door. "David, Kip's. . .dead."

He whispered, "You. . .need to get help."

"I know. Kip said there were a few cottages about a mile back."

"The horses? Where are. . ." he mumbled.

"They're gone. They must have gotten loose as a result of the accident."

"I wish we had brought Big Red. He would've returned." His eyes half open, he studied his wife. "Your leg's hurt, Caroline."

"Yes, I know."

"You can't crawl two miles."

"I'm going to endeavor to walk on it."

At that moment, Caroline heard whinnying. "I think I hear one of the horses, David. Perhaps I should go and find him."

"Ah, I know," he muttered, "your equestrian prowess will save the day."

"How can you be teasing me at a time like this?"

"I. . ." As he tried to sit more upright, he winced and Caroline, for the first time, saw dark fluid beneath his jacket.

"David, you're bleeding too," she said softly, her voice shaking.

"It's nothing, it's just. . ." He lifted up his jacket and she gasped when she saw a wound in his stomach. She started to sob.

"Caroline, don't. "

"David, please! Don't die! Our children need you! I need you!"

He nodded, then half-closed his eyes. "You must. . .get help."

"Yes, yes, I'm going. David, please hold on. Please," she pleaded with him.

He nodded and raised his arm. Caroline reached inside the carriage to squeeze his hand. She let go, then whispered, "I love you, David. Please, please don't leave me." Though he didn't respond, Caroline could see his chest rising and falling. "Please, Lord, keep him safe." All at once, a cold breeze whipped against her and she began to shiver. She reached into the carriage and pulled out a blanket.

She took off her drenched overcoat, then draped a blanket over her shoulders, her wet dress weighing her small body down.

She slowly straightened and immediately felt faint. She remained still, placing her hand on the overturned carriage and steadying herself for a moment. Her eyes were drawn to Kip's motionless body, still under the carriage, the dark wetness underneath him, his open eyes no longer able to see. Caroline's heart ached. She wished that she had another blanket to lay over Kip. *Jane is going to be heartbroken.* "Rest in peace, Kip, and may God have mercy on your soul." She bit down on her lip to stop from crying. She couldn't think about Kip right now. She must focus on getting help for David. Otherwise. . .well, she wouldn't think about the otherwise.

Caroline searched for the lantern and soon discovered it close to Kip's body, smashed and what was left of it, lying on its side. *Without any light, how shall I find my way?*

Caroline found that if she moved carefully and avoided putting excessive weight on her injured leg, it was bearable. Her shoulder was throbbing.

Perhaps I can find the horse on the way back to the nearest cottage. "Please, Lord, let David be all right. I will do anything." Then she muttered, "Thy will be done; give me thy grace to endure."

As Caroline limped along the road, she tried to stay to the right along the edge of the forest, although it was becoming difficult to see anything.

Hobbling along the side of the road, Caroline winced as she

scraped her injured leg on a few bushes jutting out from the forest. She took a deep breath and continued, her leg burning with every step. She fought the impulse to take shelter in the forest. Staying on the road with the edge of the trees as her guide seemed to be her only hope.

Caroline shivered inside her wet clothes and pulled the blanket closer to her body. Soon, she felt wetness on her head. Looking up, she saw that it was now beginning to snow. Within ten minutes the small white flakes filled the darkness around her. The wind now felt like hands holding her back. She leaned forward and pushed her body against the elements.

* * *

David roused as snow blew into the overturned carriage. He felt weak and dizzy. The wound in his stomach stung and he could feel sticky wetness all over his clothes. Strangely enough, he wasn't worried about dying. He was more concerned for Caroline. How would she handle it if he passed away? His heart ached as he recalled her pleading with him not to die.

He had no idea how long she had been gone, but in a blizzard of this sort, it would be nearly impossible for her to find her way. He asked his favorite saint, St. Jude, to help Caroline. "St. Jude, pray for Caroline, make it possible for her to find help." Then, remembering the plaque in the carriage, he recited the blessing, "That the Divine Infant will light the road before her. . .whatever it takes, God, please, please help her."

70

Her teeth chattering, her body trembling, her arms were wrapped tightly against the cold, Caroline moved ahead, slowly, painfully.

All of a sudden, she stumbled into the forest. The blanket dropped and she slammed hard on her injured leg. The intense burning pain caused Caroline to lose her breath, and for a moment, it seemed like she was going to lose consciousness. *I must keep going, no matter how much this hurts.*

With her hands, Caroline searched for the blanket and pulled it around her shoulders. She reached out and held onto the trunk of a tree and forced herself up. Her leg blazed. As she pushed herself up, she realized that, with the darkness, it was impossible to see the road.

Caroline kept her arms in front of her and she swung around desperately stretching out her arms like a blind person. For several frantic seconds, she waved, each time hitting a tree or branch and seemingly no closer to the road.

She remained still for a moment. A gust of cold air almost knocked her over and she began to shiver violently. Her teeth now chattered so much that she was sure they would break. The cold wind burned her ears. Although she still clung onto the wool blanket, she realized that it had now become wet.

I can't do this. I'm not going to be able to get help for David. She plopped down on the snow-covered ground and began to sob.

Caroline thought of her children and her will to live became strong. She would reach into the deepest recesses of her soul and her body, and strive with every fiber of her being to make it through this hopeless situation. *St. Jude, pray for me.* She slowly stood up.

Amidst the whiteout, she squinted and could see an object shimmering twenty feet in the distance. She pushed her way through the wind and snow, following the light as her guide, until she finally reached a small bell.

She came upon a clearing of some type, the soft reflection of the metal illuminating several feet in front of her. It was not only dark, the blowing snow made it impossible to see. Caroline put her hands out in front of her and, not feeling anything, continued to walk straight ahead.

Hopelessness again began to take root in her, and her quivering lips began to cry. She shook her head as if in answer and she pushed against the wind and bumped into a wooden post. A heavy woolen cloak hung from the top of a fence. She yanked it down.

Caroline dropped the wet blanket and gratefully wrapped herself in the over-sized garment. The coat was warm and Caroline welcomed the heat. She inched through the blinding snow and within a few minutes, bumped into a porch. "Thank God."

She reached out for the railing, then pulled herself up to the small porch. She banged frantically on the door until a man opened it. He was tall and broad-shouldered. Perhaps fifteen years older, he had short graying hair. His expression was one of concern.

"Come in, Miss, come in and sit by the fire."

"No, no." She was shivering and was finding it difficult to speak. "We. . . must. . .go to my husband. He may die."

"Just a moment while I get my coat."

"Thank you, Mr. . ."

"Mr. Ferguson, Jim Ferguson, Ma'am."

The man held up the lantern and escorted her to his large barn. "Give me a minute to hitch up the horses. The sleigh will be faster. You sit up front and hold the lantern, Ma'am."

Caroline got in and took the light from him. After hitching up the horses, he slipped in beside her. "I must take it slow."

"Yes, I understand."

"You said it was up the road apiece?"

"Yes, my husband said the road's not well-maintained and few people use it, but if someone comes along, they'll ride right into the carriage."

"No worry about that. Your husband was right that few people use the road. No one would be riding on it in this storm."

"My name is Mrs. Caroline O'Donovan. I found this coat on your fence back there."

Mr. Ferguson shrugged his shoulders. "Doesn't look familiar, Mrs. O'Donovan."

Caroline urged, "Please, sir, we must go quickly."

"Of course, Ma'am."

In the sleigh, she put the collar of the coat up and her hands in the pockets to keep warm. In the right pocket, she felt a small paper. She took it out and held it close to the lantern. It appeared to be a holy card with the picture of a man with a beard. The writing was barely legible, and she had no patience at that moment to care what it said. She slipped it back into the pocket.

Mr. Ferguson kept the horses at a brisk pace, but within minutes, the animal hesitated. The overturned wagon was covered by a generous dusting of snow.

"This is it. Thank you, sir."

Mr. Ferguson assisted Caroline down from the sleigh and the two of them stood next to the overturned carriage.

"I've returned, David," Caroline said, leaning into the carriage.

He roused enough to mumble, "Caroline?"

"Yes."

David moaned as Mr. Ferguson lifted him out of the carriage and onto his sleigh while Caroline followed behind.

"Let's put this blanket over him, Mrs. O'Donovan. It'll keep him somewhat dry. I'm sorry I don't have a roof on my sleigh."

"That's fine. Please hurry."

"What about your servant here?" Mr. Ferguson bent down and studied Kip's snow-covered form under the carriage.

"He's gone," she responded. "But we need to take him home for a proper burial."

"Mrs. O'Donovan, I'm going to need your assistance while I lift the carriage up, perhaps you can pull your servant's body out from under it. Do you think you can manage with your own injuries?""

Caroline cringed, then nodded. "Yes, I think so." Then to David, she whispered, "I need to leave you here in the sleigh."

He nodded.

She made her way to the carriage and crouched down at Kip's head. "What should I do?"

"When I lift the carriage, you pull him out from under it."

"Very well."

Caroline first brushed off the snow which had accumulated on Kip's body, then gripped onto the servant's arms. Her eyes began to water. She had known Kip for many years and had rarely touched him, other than when he occasionally offered his hand for assistance.

"I'm going to count, Mrs. O'Donovan, to three. On three, I'm going to raise the carriage and then you pull your servant out as quickly as is possible."

"Yes."

"One, two, three." Mr. Ferguson hoisted the carriage about six inches. Caroline pulled as hard as she could. She had never understood the term "dead weight" until now. She knew Kip wasn't a heavy man and yet it took all her effort to move him a little bit at a time.

"Mrs. O'Donovan, I'm going to have to put the carriage down. Can you manage?"

"Yes, I. . ." *Just a few more inches.* She dragged him just beyond the carriage. She breathed a sigh of relief and laid him down on the ground. "I did it!"

"Well done." He hurried to the sleigh, picked up a blanket and wrapped it around Kip.

Caroline pulled herself onto the seat of the sleigh and gently placed David's head onto her lap. As she held onto her husband, he began moaning, "Caroline?"

"Yes, I'm here. We were just getting Kip out from under the wagon."

"Is Kip. . .all right?"

"No, David, remember I told you that he passed away? We're taking his body back for burial."

David mumbled, "Damn."

The sleigh vibrated with a thump as Jim laid Kip's body over the horse. *Kip didn't deserve to die. How will I tell Jane?*

Mr. Ferguson got in and sat himself in the remaining small section of the front seat. "Sorry, Ma'am, for the tight quarters. I mean no disrespect."

"Not at all, Mr. Ferguson. I'm thankful you're able to help us."

He shook the reins and the sleigh moved forward. "I'm going

take your husband to the doctor. He's only about two miles away.

"Yes, please hurry."

Jim pulled in front of a small farmhouse, got out and knocked on the door. Immediately, an older, heavyset man answered it.

Caroline couldn't hear the conversation, but watched the older man pull on his coat. They approached the sleigh with a lantern.

"This is Dr. Hailey, Mrs. O'Donovan. He will take care of your husband."

"Yes, thank you," she replied. The two men lifted David from beside her and quickly took him into the house. She followed them inside.

They hurried to a small examining room. The men laid David on a table and took his coat off. In the light of the house, Caroline drew in a sharp breath when she saw that the side and back of David's shirt was covered in blood.

"Jim, grab my bag by the door, would you, please?"

"'Course, Doc."

"And would you also get me some water from the well and heat it on the cookstove?"

"Yes, sir."

"Mrs. O'Donovan, please. Come and stand beside your husband."

Caroline stood next to the table and picked up David's hand. He opened his eyes and winked at her. "I'm going to be all right, Caroline." Looking at her outer covering, he said, "Nice coat."

"It's been keeping me warm. I found it up the road."

"You found it?"

"Yes. Unfortunately, my dress was already quite wet."

"Mrs. O'Donovan, please feel free to remove your coat and sit by the fire. This will take but a few moments."

"Yes, thank you, Doctor."

The doctor took off David's shirt and examined the wound. "Looks pretty clean, not a lot of dirt in there. I'm just going to wash it out and sew it shut, Mr. O'Donovan. It's deep but not deep enough to damage any organs in this area of the stomach. You've lost a fair amount of blood."

"Doctor?" David asked.

"Yes, Mr. O'Donovan?"

"Would you please check my wife's leg?"

"Certainly. I'll attend to that after I sew this up."

After the doctor had cleaned and bandaged her wound, Caroline was tucking David into one of Doc Hailey's spare beds and kissing him goodbye. "I don't want to leave you."

"I'm fine, Caroline. You need to get back to the children. Perhaps Jim will take you."

"But what about Missy? I must make funeral arrangements for her."

"Mrs. O'Donovan, I would be happy to take you to the Sacred Heart Convent. I know where it is. My sister, God rest her soul, used to live there."

"But it's snowing, isn't it, Mr. Ferguson?"

"Yes, Ma'am, it is, but it's only a light snow now and with my sleigh, we could probably make it there in half an hour."

"Yes, very well."

"Mr. Ferguson, would you mind taking my wife home once you're finished there?"

"No, I would not mind at all, Mr. O'Donovan. I'd be happy to oblige in any way I can."

On the way to the convent, they continued at a brisk pace. The sleigh easily plowed through the snow, the frigid cold air stinging her face as they moved along. Thanks to the good doctor, she now had a woolen scarf which she pulled up and around her face. Soon they arrived at the convent. Caroline suddenly felt lightheaded.

At the door, a short middle-aged nun with thin wireframe glasses greeted her and Mr. Ferguson. "May I help you?" she asked, her voice sounding childlike despite her age.

"Yes, we're here to discuss the funeral arrangements for Missy."

"Are you Mr. and Mrs. O'Donovan?"

"I'm Mrs. O'Donovan. This is Mr. Ferguson." Caroline stopped, unsure of how to introduce him.

"I'm Mrs. O'Donovan's driver, Sister."

"Yes, of course. I'm Sister Helen Marie. Good evening to both of you. I wasn't sure if anyone would visit with the storm.

Come, right this way." The nun led them to a small room off the foyer. "May I take your coats?"

"I'd rather keep my coat on," Mr. Ferguson said, as he sat on one of the chairs in the office.

"Well, I suppose it would be all right if you took mine." Caroline handed the diminutive nun her large coat. The woman proceeded to hang it on a rack near the door. "My dress is still damp. My husband and I were in an accident on our way here."

"Oh, dear. How dreadful. Are you both unharmed?"

"My husband was injured and our servant died."

"I'm so sorry. God rest his soul." She paused.

"Mrs. O'Donovan, if you should like some dry clothing, our sisters have no need for clothing of the world so we have many dresses in our textile room. You might be able to find one that is your size, although it may be out of fashion."

"That would be kind of you. Perhaps I can do so after I've seen Missy."

"Yes, very well."

"We will send notice to the undertaker near our home to come and retrieve Missy tomorrow, Sister."

"That's fine."

"Mr. Ferguson, I'll return momentarily."

"Take your time, Mrs. O'Donovan."

The nun escorted her down a long corridor with Caroline limping the entire way. "I'm sorry, Mrs. O'Donovan. Are you able to walk?"

"Yes, I will be fine."

At the end of the hallway was a plain white door.

"Are you certain that you will be able to handle this, Mrs. O'Donovan? You have endured quite an ordeal yourself."

"Yes, yes, I shall be fine."

"Missy was a wonderful young woman. She told me that you and your husband have taken her child in as your own."

Caroline forced a smile but immediately felt awkward. She hoped that Missy hadn't shared with the good sister that David was the true father of Missy's son.

Sister Helen Marie opened the door. Immediately, Caroline was struck by the odor of death and, for a moment, she felt nauseated.

She followed the nun to a narrow bed at the far side of the room. It looked like Missy was sleeping and a white sheet was pulled up to her chin. At the site of her gaunt, gray face, Caroline stifled a gasp. Missy had lost more weight in the two weeks since she had last visited her. Now, she seemed like a skeleton with skin.

"I'll wait outside while you say your goodbyes."

"Yes, thank you."

"Take as much time as you would like, Mrs. O'Donovan."

The nun closed the door and Caroline let out a whimper. "Oh, Missy." She leaned close and brushed back a strand of her dark hair. Caroline touched the emaciated and cold skin on her forehead. The expression on her face was a peaceful one. Caroline made the Sign of the Cross. "May God have mercy on your soul." *Don't worry about Will. We'll take good care of him.*

After she was given a clean, dry dress, Caroline met the nun in the office. "Good evening," she said, as she went to the coat rack to retrieve her coat, which was nowhere to be seen.

"Mr. Ferguson, what has happened to the coat I was wearing?"

"Your coat, Mrs. O'Donovan?"

"Yes. It's not here," she said.

"I don't know. No one has been in here except for me and the good sister."

"Mrs. O'Donovan, I do remember hanging your coat on the rack," the nun said. "I'm not sure what happened to it."

"Well, it wasn't actually my coat. I found it near Mr. Ferguson's house."

On the floor below where the coat should have been was the holy card Caroline had discovered in the pocket of the coat earlier. She picked it up. It showed the face of an older man. Below the picture were the words, "St. Jude Thaddeus, pray for us." Caroline smiled and put the card in her skirt pocket.

"Like I told you, I don't have any close neighbors, so I don't know how the coat got there," Mr. Ferguson offered.

"Well, it doesn't matter, Mrs. O'Donovan. I shall be back with a coat for you to wear home."

"Thank you kindly."

Sitting on the sleigh on the way home, Caroline stifled a sob at the enormity of it all: Kip's passing, Missy's illness and death, their carriage accident. Her father had been right. Death was indeed a natural part of life. She would never like it, especially when it occurred so suddenly and so tragically. But she would have to accept it as part of life's inevitabilities.

"Are you all right, Mrs. O'Donovan?"

"Yes, yes, I'll be fine. Just overwhelmed with everything that's happened."

Amidst the sadness, Caroline found herself feeling hopeful.

Help me to say the right words to Jane.

Mr. Ferguson stopped the sleigh in front of the O'Donovan home and he assisted Caroline down. From the corner of her eye, she could see Jane rushing out the front door. The porch and lawn were now covered with several inches of snow. The sleigh remained still, the blanket covering Kip, his body laying over the horse.

"Miss Caroline, what happened? Where's Mr. David? Where is Kip? I was just. . ."

Caroline studied Jane's mid-section which was just beginning to swell with child. The servant stared at the covered bundle molded to the animal like a horseshoe. She finally made eye contact with her mistress, worry now stretched across her face.

"Miss Caroline? What. . ."

"We've had an accident."

"An accident?" Slowly, tentatively, she approached the horse. She lifted the blanket and gasped loudly.

"No, no!" Jane collapsed on the ground beside the horse and began to sob.

"I tried to help him, Jane, but the carriage had rolled on top of him. There wasn't anything we could do." Caroline paused. "I'm so very sorry." Caroline rubbed Jane's back in a gesture reminiscent of a time when Caroline was newly widowed.

"Before Kip died. . ."

Jane lifted her head and, for a moment, stopped crying. The servant's eyes were clouded with tears, the droplets making a thin path down her cheeks.

"Kip told me to tell you he loves you."

Jane's lip quivered then she began to sob again. After a minute or so, she stopped and straightened. She wiped her eyes with the back of her hand and brushed down her apron. "I put the children to bed. They're all asleep."

"Jane, if you want, I'll stay with you." The servant stared straight ahead, silent. She turned and faced Caroline and began to speak, her eyes glassy, but unfocused.

"No, Miss Caroline, I'm going to be fine. Perhaps Hallie can assist me with Kip's body."

"Jane, don't do that now."

"I need to see to Kip, get him ready for burial."

"I'll help you." Caroline's heart ached for Jane.

"No, Miss Caroline, you're limping and your leg is hurt. I'll call for Hallie."

"Perhaps Mr. Ferguson can help. Where did he go?"

"Mr. Ferguson?"

"Yes. He's the man who assisted me in bringing David to the doctor's house and brought me home." Caroline looked beyond the sleigh. Mr. Ferguson was leaning against the side of a small tree and smoking a cigarette.

"Mr. Ferguson?" Caroline called.

"Yes, Mrs. O'Donovan?"

"I wonder if you would mind helping Jane with Kip's body?"

"'Course, I will. And I'd be glad to help you over the next few days, Mrs. O'Donovan, if you need it."

"I would be most grateful if you were able to do so."

"I'll need to see to some things at home. I'll return tomorrow."

Hallie opened the front door. "Miss Caroline, you're finally . . ." Hallie stopped when she saw the group standing by the horse and Kip's body.

"Kip's. . .gone, Hallie," Caroline said.

"Oh, no." Immediately, Hallie's eye's widened and she blinked away the tears. She put her arm around Jane's shoulder.

Mr. Ferguson took Kip's body off the horse and brought him into the foyer of the house. The women followed him.

"You can put him right here on the floor," Jane said,without emotion.

"Perhaps Mr. Ferguson can move him to the couch in the parlor or on a table somewhere?" Caroline offered.

"No. I don't want to be messing up your furniture. The floor is easiest enough to clean up."

"I'm certain we can find a blanket to cover it, Jane."

"If it's acceptable to you, Ma'am, I'd prefer to leave him here for now, at least until I wash him up."

"Yes, very well."

Mr. Ferguson spoke up. "If these women don't need me, I'm going to return home to see to some chores, then I'll be back in the morning." He tipped his hat.

"Yes, thank you. I am most grateful for your assistance."

"You're welcome, Mrs. O'Donovan."

Caroline glanced at Jane. She was staring, eyes unfocused, straight ahead.

"Are you going to be all right, Jane?"

"Yes, Miss Caroline, I'll be just fine," she said so quietly, Caroline had to strain to hear her. "You go on to bed, Ma'am." But Caroline remained there, not wanting to leave her.

"I got to get him ready for the funeral, Miss Caroline."

"Jane, that can wait, you need to. . ."

"Miss Caroline, begging no disrespect, I need to prepare my husband for burial. Hallie can help me."

"Yes, yes, all right." And Caroline stepped away, nodded to Hallie and carefully walked up the staircase.

The next morning, Caroline woke early. She sat up and tried to pull her legs over the side of the bed, then she realized that her injured leg burned and ached. In fact, her whole body hurt, so she remained still for a short while.

It took a painfully long time for her to dress. She walked to the top of the staircase and looked down at the scene below. On the floor near the study, Kip's body lay dressed in his Sunday clothes. Hallie was sleeping on the bottom two steps of the staircase and Jane was sitting beside her husband.

"Jane."

Jane turned and looked up. "Miss Caroline."

"You haven't been to bed yet, have you?"

"No, Miss Caroline, I haven't. Can't say I'm tired."

Caroline quickly descended the steps, stepping beside Hallie, who was now sitting up. "Oh, Jane." They tenderly embraced and remained silent for several moments.

"Miss Caroline?"

"Yes?"

"I know Mr. David's going to be at the doctor's, and Mr. Ferguson won't be back till later today, so we'll have to bury him ourselves. I've already started digging a hole out by the edge of the forest. He used to go there and sit and pray. I know he'd like to be buried there."

"You've begun to dig a hole?" Caroline asked, incredulous.

"Yes, Ma'am. Hallie helped me. The ground's not yet frozen."

"Jane, I'm certain that it would be no problem to ask Mr. Ferguson to help you when he returns. And what about some sort of box to put him in?"

"Well, begging your pardon, Miss Caroline, but Kip isn't in his body anymore. It don't really matter what kind of box he's in . . ."

"Miss Caroline's right, Jane. Kip ought to be buried proper," Hallie offered, then walked toward her friend.

Jane turned and stared at her husband's body, now dressed in finery. For a few moments, all three women were silent.

"Would you mind reading something from your Ma's Bible, Miss Caroline? Me and Hallie will move him to the grave."

"Jane, please, Kip needs to be in a box or coffin. And in your condition, you shouldn't be lifting him. Can't you wait a day or so and I'll get a coffin delivered?"

"No, Ma'am. I'm stronger with child than most women without, and I need to get him buried. Once he's in the ground, I can start getting on with my life."

"Listen to me, Jane. I think you ought to consider waiting a while to do a service. I can send for the preacher and for your mother. You need to have your Ma with you right now. And what about Isaac?"

"I want to get this over with. I'll tell Ma later on today. As for Isaac, he's too young. I need to get this done, Ma'am."

"You need to listen to Miss Caroline. You're not thinking clearly right now," Hallie offered.

"No, I just need to. . ." Jane's lip began to quiver and she squeezed her moist eyes shut. She put her hand to her mouth to quiet her sobbing. "Kip is. . .gone."

Caroline pulled her servant to a sisterly embrace and allowed her to cry.

At the top of the steps, Kathleen squealed. "Mama, you're home!"

Jane pushed herself away and wiped her tears. Caroline rushed up the stairs, trying to shield her daughter from the scene below. "Yes." As she hugged Kathleen, her daughter was trying to steal a glance at Kip's body on the floor. "Why is Kip laying on the floor, Mama?"

"Kip passed away on the trip, Sweet, and they're getting him ready for burial."

"That's sad, Mama."

"Yes, Sweet, it's sad." She paused. "Would you stay upstairs in case John, Will or Isaac wake up?"

"'Course, Mama."

Caroline turned around to see Jane again kneeling beside her husband.

"Hallie," Caroline said, "take Jane upstairs. See if you can get her to rest."

Hallie put her hand on Jane's shoulder, "Come, Jane."

Jane shook her head.

Caroline crouched down in front of the grieving widow. "Jane, please do as I say. You need to rest." Jane's eyes, etched with pain, closed then opened.

"All right, Miss Caroline."

Later that day, the group gathered solemnly at the grave. Mr. Ferguson had built a plain wooden box for Kip and set up a simple cross and the fresh dirt was now almost dry. The preacher held a Bible in his hands. Patsie held onto Jane, who had a stoic, calm expression on her face. Isaac was in front of his mother, his eyes darting from the dirt grave to his mother's face.

Caroline stood between the preacher and Jane, with Kathleen, Will and John in front of her. Mr. Ferguson kept his distance behind all of them, his hat in his hands and his head bowed.

The preacher began:

The Lord is my shepherd; I shall not want. He maketh me to lie down in green pastures: He leadeth me beside the still waters. He restoreth my soul: He leadeth me in the paths of righteousness for His name's sake.

When he finished, Jane said,   "I best get some lunch on, Miss Caroline."

"No, Jane," Patsie offered. "I'll be knowin' Himself won't be mindin' it if I stay ta be helpin' ye fer a wee while. I'll be gettin' some lunch on and be watchin' Isaac. Ye need ta be gettin' yer body back ta bed before ye be collapsin'."

"Ma, I just need to. . ."

"Yes, Jane, think of your baby," Caroline spoke up.

"Ye be needin' some rest. And I'll not be takin' no for an answer, Daughter, even if I have to be puttin' ye in the bed meself."

Jane's eyes lowered. "All right, Ma." As they began walking back to the house, Jane stopped and turned toward Caroline. "Miss Caroline?"

"Yes, Jane?"

"The tables sure have turned on us, haven't they?"

"The tables?"

"Remember when Mr. Liam died?"

Caroline nodded. "Yes, Jane, I do."

That night, when the children were asleep, Caroline sat up in bed, unable to rest, her leg and shoulder throbbing. She couldn't erase Jane's sad expression from her mind, of the young grieving woman standing, chin held high, near her husband's grave. Her servant's demeanor was quite a contrast to her own in the day or so after Liam's death.

She stood up, wishing that she could forget death for the next few days, but with the planning and attending of Missy's funeral before the new year, Caroline would not likely have the opportunity.

Caroline knocked on Jane's bedroom door.

She heard no answer so she carefully opened it. Jane was not in bed nor in her room. She listened and could hear Isaac's even breathing.

Caroline crept through the hallway, then down the steps in search of her servant, listening for sounds of grief. Hearing no noise, she turned to make her way back up the steps when she heard creaking. From her position at the staircase, Caroline gasped as she saw the shadow of a figure standing at the doorway of the parlor. "Jane, you scared me half to death!"

"I'm sorry, Miss Caroline. I couldn't sleep." The servant was dressed in a nightgown and bed robe. Despite the loose clothing, Jane's growing stomach was noticeable. Caroline placed her hands on Jane's shoulders. They embraced in the darkened hallway.

"Miss Caroline?" Jane said, pulling away.

"Yes?"

"Talk to me."

"Pardon?"

"I need you to talk to me so I don't dwell on my Kip being gone. Talk to me about anything, about Mr. David, about. . ." Jane's head lowered.

"Very well. Come into the parlor." She led the grieving woman to the sofa and sat her down. Caroline shivered, then bent down in front of the hearth and threw another log into the flames. The fireplace cast a pool of golden light into the room. The clock in the hallway was chiming as Caroline took the chair beside Jane. They both sat quietly while the numerous chimes echoed through the house. Eight, nine, ten.

"Miss Caroline?"

"Yes?"

"I never got to give Kip a kiss goodbye.   The busyness of life just made it seem so unimportant. I thought we'd have years and years together."

"Jane."

"How did you get through those first days after Mr. Liam died?"

"I don't know. It's all a blur now. I just remember thinking that I would never be happy again."

Jane stifled a sob. "Tell me about your childhood, Miss Caroline. You never knew your Ma, did you?"

"No, I didn't. . ."

Then Caroline began to speak of her childhood, waiting, hoping that Jane would eventually want to rest.

71

Caroline adjusted the pillows while Mr. Ferguson assisted David onto his bed. David remained frustrated that he wasn't yet able to do simple activities by himself, but he was thankful that he was finally home.

"Thank you," David said. Caroline sat beside him. When Mr. Ferguson left the room, she commented, "I don't know what I would have done without him these past several days. With Kip gone, he's been a tremendous help."

"We owe him immense gratitude."

"Yes, we do."

There was a quiet knock at the door. Jane stood in the doorway with a tray. "Mr. David, I made you some consommé." She walked toward the bed.

"Thank you."

Jane placed it on the table beside his bed. "Is there anything else I can do for you, Mr. David?"

"No, that will be fine." Before the servant reached the door, David called to her.

"Yes, Mr. David?"

"I wanted to tell you how sorry I am about Kip. I wish I could have helped him."

"Don't you worry about that, Mr. David. Miss Caroline told me. There wasn't nothing you could do for my Kip."

"Well, he was a good man and I will miss him."

Jane's head lowered, then almost immediately, she lifted her chin. "Thank you for saying so, Mr. David." She left the room and closed the door behind her.

David laid his head back on the pillows behind him. Caroline reached for the bowl of consommé at the table. "Want to try some of this, David? It smells delicious."

As Caroline began to feed him, he stopped her. "I can probably do it myself. What I really want is to see the children."

"I didn't want them jumping on you so I asked Hallie to take them outside."

"I understand, but I would like to see them now."

"Of course." Caroline leaned in to kiss his forehead and whispered, "I've missed you. I'm so glad you're home."

"I am as well," he replied, as she left the room. Within minutes, pounding on the steps and in the hallway told him that his children were coming to welcome him home.

"Papa, you're home!" Kathleen ran to his bedside with Will following behind and Caroline and Hallie trailing as they held John's hand.

"How are you, Kat?"

"Oh, I'm fine, Papa. Mama said we couldn't hug you yet, but that we could say hello."

"That's right."

"Where'd ya get hurt?" asked Will.

"Right here, son." He lifted his shirt up to show him the bandage that now covered a large area of his stomach.

"You got lots of hair on your belly, Papa," said Will.

"Yes, Will, I do."

"You gotta big hurt?" said John, staring at David's stomach.

"Yes, John, it's a big hurt."

"Can I give your tummy a kiss and make it better, Papa?" Kathleen asked.

"Kat, I think you better give me a kiss right here, on the cheek," he said, pointing to his face. She carefully leaned in to kiss his face.

"Papa," she whispered.

"Yes, Kat?"

"Mama has been smiling all day because you were coming home. She missed you."

David glanced at Caroline. She was using her handkerchief to wipe the side of John's face and she was frowning as he was pulling his face away from her. She was a beautiful woman even when she scowled.

"Mr. David, Isaac wanted to see you too," said Jane from the door. Her son, Isaac, stood quietly by her side.

"Hello, Isaac. How are you? I'm sorry to hear about your Pa."

He nodded and moved behind Will and Kathleen. "You got hurt, Mr. David?"

"I did. Want to see the bandage?"

He nodded.

"It's big," said Will. "Wait'll ya see it."

David lifted his shirt up to show Isaac, and his three children again stared with wide eyes. It seemed ridiculous that the doctor had placed a large bandage on such a small, though deep, wound.

He looked past Caroline and the children to see Hallie standing at the foot of the bed. Without speaking, Hallie seemed to say, "Glad you're all right, Mr. David." As he put his shirt down, he could feel himself blushing.

"All right, time to go back downstairs, everyone! Let Mr. David get some rest." Jane took Isaac's and Will's hands and Hallie took John's hand with Kathleen close behind.

"Bye, Papa," Kathleen called from across the room.

"Bye, Kat. Come back and visit me later."

"Oh, I will, Papa. I will."

*　　*　　*

Caroline caught a glimpse of Hallie watching David. Was it relief that she saw in the servant's eyes? Certainly, everyone was grateful that David was recuperating well.

She watched Jane and Hallie take the children from the room.

"Time to change your bandage."

He took off his shirt and she carefully unwrapped the bandage. The wound appeared to be healing well, with no redness or swelling. She washed the area, then applied a clean bandage.

"In a few weeks, you'll be as good as new."

"A few weeks?"

"Yes, and we will be able to. . ." She tenderly caressed the area above the bandage on his stomach, then leaned down and placed a soft gentle kiss to his chest.

"A few weeks? No, Caroline, a few days. . ." he said, his eyes determined and his mouth upturned in a smile.

Epilogue

Caroline reached inside her bottom dresser drawer, lifted out Liam's cigar box and set it on her bed. How different her life was from the first time that she had received this. Her heart had been grieving so much back then that she could not fully appreciate anything or anyone in those early days: not Liam, not Kathleen and certainly not David. She couldn't even be thankful to God, the Author of life.

She had wanted a life with a perfect ending like most novels, an ending with a tidy, neat and happy conclusion. Instead, she had learned that life was about taking each moment, good and bad, and making the best of it. Most importantly, it was about trusting God, that His grace would be all she needed to endure.

She tenderly traced the letters, then opened the box. On top was the letter from Liam, his words written in David's hand, the piece of paper which not only changed her life, it took her on a journey of love, adventure and faith.

Nostalgically, Caroline picked up the envelope with Liam's opened wax seal and lifted out his letter, the back of it covered with mud stains. Her heart was heavy with emotion as she read some of his last words to her:

I want you to know that I love you very much and I want you to be happy. . .I have asked David to consent to enter into a marriage of convenience, a marriage in name only, you and David.

"Yes, Liam, I am happier than I have ever been."

"I'm glad," she heard, then could feel David as he hugged her from behind. Caroline, still clutching the letter, turned around and embraced him. After a few moments, she pulled away.

She again picked up Liam's last letter which had asked Caroline to consent to an In Name Only marriage, and held it in front of her husband.

"David, do you think he knew that it would end like this, with you and me?"

"I'm not sure." He laughed under his breath. "It wouldn't surprise me if he thought it might end like this."

Their newborn infant began to cry. David reached into the crib and picked up their child, a fair-haired son they named Patrick Andrew. The baby turned his head and opened his mouth.

"I think he's hungry, Caroline."

"Indeed," she said, taking the baby from him.

"I'm grateful to God that the birth went so well this time."

"Amen to that."

She sat on the edge of the bed and began to nurse.

David sat beside her and pressed a light kiss to her cheek. "Do you know how much I love you?"

She nodded.

Suddenly, Caroline felt tremendous gratitude to God for her life with David and their children. Years ago, when Liam died, she thought that her life was over. In reality, it had only just begun. Life had become a miraculous adventure.

Author's notes:

During the 19th century, it was accepted practice that couples would refrain from sexual intercourse during pregnancy. The understanding was that relations could be harmful to the developing child.

This, however, is not the modern day recommendation. Unless the wife is at risk for miscarriage, intercourse during pregnancy is now considered to be a safe way for married couples to enjoy intimacy.

In the 19th century, there were no reliable moral methods of avoiding pregnancy except for complete abstinence. Nowadays, couples may morally avoid pregnancy by using Natural Family Planning, a safe, healthy and effective method.

Acknowledgments:

I am indebted to many people. First of all, to Father Arthur Joseph for spiritual direction. To my husband, James Hrkach, who patiently spent hours discussing plot lines and character development with me.

Special thanks to Michelle Sinasac for helping me to write Patsie's lower class Irish accent.

Many thanks to the following people for their candid and honest feedback on various drafts of this novel: Alana Blunt, Christopher Blunt, Kathy Cassanto, James Hrkach, Sarah Loten, Jeanette MacDonald, Martha Jahn, Nancy Jahn, Laurie Power, Ginger Regan, Regina Rolph, Josie Scott, Michelle Sinasac, Jessica Smith, Sarah Smith, Ingrid Waclawik, Louise Waclawik, Lynne Zander.

Thank you to PM Dupuis for overall editing, Laura Brestovansky for copy-editing and to Sarah Loten, Cheryl Thompson, Ginger Regan, Louise Waclawik and Lynne Zander for proofreading. To the Arnprior and District Museum (Janet Carlile and Cathy Rodger) for the use of their Victorian bedroom (which was used in the cover photo) and for the authentic period clothing which they generously allowed our cover models to wear. To Our Lady of Perpetual Help Church in Braeside, Ontario for allowing us to use Church property to photograph the back cover photo. To Tom McCabe for answering questions regarding sacramental marriage.

To Brittany Robinson, for posing for the cover photo. Special thanks to my sons, Ben Hrkach and Tim Hrkach, for posing for the back cover photo.

Ellen Gable Hrkach
June, 2009

About the Author

Ellen Gable is a wife and mother to five sons. She was born in New Jersey, USA. She has been married to James Hrkach for 28 years and has called Canada her home that entire time.

Ellen has had articles published in various magazines in the United States and Canada as well as many websites. She and her husband create the "Family Life" cartoon in Family Foundations magazine.

For the last 26 years, they have been actively involved in Catholic apologetics, teaching Natural Family Planning, participating in Marriage Preparation and promoting chastity. Ellen also writes a monthly column for www.AmazingCatechists.com. called "Sexually Speaking."

In Name Only is Ellen's second novel. Her first, *Emily's Hope*, won an Honorable Mention Award for Religious Fiction in the 2006 Independent Publisher Book Awards.

For more information, check out the following websites:

www.innameonly.ca
www.fullquiverpublishing.com
Ellen's blog: Plot Line and Sinker at
http://ellengable.wordpress.com

Ellen would love to hear your feedback regarding her books. Please feel free to write her at:
feedback@fullquiverpublishing.com
To purchase more copies of this book, go to the Full Quiver website at **www.fullquiverpublishing.com** or write to us at:

Full Quiver Publishing
PO Box 244
Pakenham, Ontario K0A2X0 Canada
(613) 623-1029
info@fullquiverpublishing.com

CPSIA information can be obtained at www.ICGtesting.com
Printed in the USA
LVOW121330210513

334835LV00009B/23/P